PRAISE FOR MARILYN BAY WENTᴢ ᴀɴᴅ ᴘ ᴀᴀᴀᴀ ᴜᴀᴀᴀ

"Through a historical lens, Wentz acquaints readers
with Colorado Territory during the 1860s. With charm and
classical simplicity, she weaves a story of two young people,
Gray Wolf and Georgia, who merge their lives together despite
cultural and religious differences. Wentz reveals her intimate
knowledge of the Colorado landscape and historical events
during the years leading to the 1864 attack on Cheyenne
and Arapaho Indians encamped in southeastern Colorado
Territory. From a historical perspective, Wentz provides a
dimension of familiarity for understanding the bad blood and
broken treaties that politically existed during those years. Yet,
as a storyteller, she invites readers to take a close look at the
common spirit which binds all humanity. *Prairie Grace* brings
home the importance of living together in harmony through
mutual trust and respect."

> —DANA ECHOHAWK, Managing Director, Center for Colorado & The
> West at University of Colorado Denver

"*Prairie Grace*, written by Marilyn Bay Wentz, contains
well-researched and historically accurate material on the
relationship between the white and Native cultures. Amidst
the history there are accurate and informative horse training
segments that show how horses truly can be approached.
Overall I found it to be a highly entertaining and enjoyable
read, and I would recommend it to anyone. Marilyn Bay Wentz
managed to tug at our heartstrings with the cruelty of history
but still leave us feeling good about the God that we serve and
the world that He created."

> —KEN MCNABB, Ken McNabb Horsemanship, Greybull, Wyo.

"Reading *Prairie Grace* is an opportunity to learn about Colorado history during the Civil War in an entertaining way. The events and personalities of the Indian Wars, the Sand Creek Massacre and the politics of early Denver swirl around Georgia MacBaye, a ranch girl who aspires to become a doctor and falls in love with a young Cheyenne brave."

—BYRON STROM, great-great nephew of Silas Soule, one of the few U.S. Army heroes of the Sand Creek Massacre, Des Moines, Iowa

"Prairie Grace is wonderful! Honestly, I have never been a fan of historical fiction because accurate historical facts are not usually there. But in your work....... I love your writing because it includes <u>accurate</u> facts and places. I love that about every chapter. The storyline and the development and believability of the characters are outstanding!"

—CLIFF SMITH, 5th Grade (History) Teacher at Strasburg Elementary School and Curator of the Comanche Crossing Museum

"Prairie Grace by Marilyn Bay Wentz is a very well-documented book of historical fiction. I would recommend this read for any student of early eastern Colorado history, or related topics of Indian and homesteader's daily life. Actual events are recorded involving the fictional characters to entice readers to reach the remarkable ending!"

—JEANNE DIEDRICH, Kelver Public Library branch of Arapahoe (Colorado) Library District

"*Prairie Grace* is a quick read that keeps you looking for more. Wentz brought out the human trials, the heartache, the joy, the atrocities, and the hope that were prevalent among the different cultures of that era. There is a true depiction of the intercultural conflict among all people that has done so much to bring down and hinder all nations from flourishing. This story is easy to insert yourself into the scenes and imagine what part you would play if you were alive back then. I look forward to Wentz' next book."

—DICK GEHRING, Past President, Kansas Buffalo Association & Owner/Operator, Black Kettle Buffalo Ranch

"*Prairie Grace* is a fast moving, history driven, God centered read. Marilyn Wentz has woven a story of faith through true historical events in Colorado. While getting to know the real and fictional characters, we can picture their struggles. Wentz' description makes them come alive. I highly recommend *Prairie Grace* to anyone, male or female, 12 and up."

—PASTOR CHRIS AND KAREN JOHNSON, Journey Church, Strasburg, Colo.

Prairie Grace

by Marilyn Bay Wentz

© Copyright 2013 by Marilyn Bay Wentz

ISBN 9781938467820

Prairie Grace is a work of fiction. The characters are both actual and fictitious. With the exception of verified historical events and persons, all incidents, descriptions, dialogue and opinions expressed are the products of the author's imagination and are not to be construed as real.

Published by

köehlerbooks™

210 60th Street
Virginia Beach, VA 23451
212-574-7939
www.koehlerbooks.com

Publisher
John Köehler

Executive Editor
Joe Coccaro

Visit the author's website at
www.marilynbaywentz.com

Dedication

I didn't have to think too hard before deciding to dedicate my first novel to my mother, Mildred Nelson Bay. A lifelong writer herself, she is my grammar guru, encourager and proofreader.
I love you, Mom!

PRAIRIE GRACE

a novel

Marilyn Bay Wentz

VIRGINIA BEACH
CAPE CHARLES

Chapter 1

MacBaye Ranch, Bijou Basin,
Colorado Territory, Spring 1862

Georgia MacBaye didn't dislike gathering eggs or milking the family's Jersey cow, Blue Bell. It's just ... well ... there were so many more exciting things to do. She opened the milking stanchion and released the gentle cow. A basket of eggs in one hand and the bucket of milk in the other, Georgia left the barn for the house, its reddish-brown adobe blending in with the prairie. The second story appeared an extension of the imposing bluffs. Her father chose the site in the Bijou Basin because the big oak trees reminded him of South Carolina. He told Georgia he hoped it would make her mother feel less homesick. He also had practical reasons for building where he did. The bluffs to the west blocked the fierce winter blizzards, and the Bijou Creek, just out their backdoor, provided the MacBayes and their stock with water.

This morning, the rugged beauty was not what caught her eye. Snaking single file down the bluffs was a procession of Indian ponies. The pace of the horses and the absence of war paint told her the Indians meant no harm, but she couldn't be certain.

Georgia ran toward the house like a startled hare, milk splashing over the sides of the pail, eggs cracking. "Indians ... on the bluffs ... come look!"

"Ring the dinner bell, Georgia," her mother, Loraine, screamed, panic rising in her voice.

With the alarm sounded, Georgia's father and brothers, James and Henry, were in the house within minutes.

Georgia's father pulled down the new Henry repeating rifle from the rack above the parlor fireplace, his work-worn hands slamming the lever down to load a bullet into the chamber. The comfortable parlor with its embroidered doilies and fine furniture was at their backs, as Pa, James and Henry stood facing the front door. Georgia read anxiety, not panic, in her father's weathered face.

"Close the curtains, Loraine," Pa barked. Then he softened his tone. "I don't expect any trouble, but I prefer to be able to see them without them seeing us."

A few tense minutes later, the Indians pulled their ponies to a stop in front of the MacBaye house. Georgia, who had ignored her mother's edict to hide in the root cellar, parted the lace-trimmed gingham curtains that framed the kitchen window. She tossed back wavy auburn hair that had escaped her ponytail. For all she knew, the hair had never made it into the ponytail. She was unconcerned with such details. She wondered if the Indians, who had now made their way into the unfenced pathway at the south end of the main pasture, could see her freckled nose and hazel eyes pressed against the glass. Nevertheless, she just had to get a glimpse of them astride their powerful mounts. Most were adorned with feathers, beads, porcupine quills and snake rattles. Naked chests, a shade or two darker than the buckskin they wore, glistened with sweat. Was it nerves, exertion, the warm spring day, or a combination of all three that caused them to sweat? Their presence, their power, their passion—all of it was frightening, yet exhilarating. They were so close that Georgia could not only hear them talking in their strange tongue, but she could also smell the familiar melding of human and horse sweat combined with sagebrush ... and *What is that smell? Bear fat?* The settlers used crushed sagebrush to keep mosquitoes at bay, a trick they'd learned from the Indians. An application of rendered bear fat, she knew, was another Indian way to keep away insects.

Georgia watched as the leader, adorned in a full, flowing feather headdress, dismounted. She guessed him to be her father's age, in his mid-forties. One of the younger braves also dismounted. She studied the young brave as he lifted a bundle from his travois and hoisted it onto his shoulder. She guessed him to be about nineteen, the age of her older brother, James. This brave and the leader, a tall sinewy man with half a dozen jet-black braids flowing down his back, walked toward the MacBayes' front door, stopping about twenty feet away.

Georgia's father propped his rifle inside the door, stepped onto the porch and raised his arms, palms open, to make it clear he was unarmed.

"Lean Bear," Georgia heard the tall man say, patting his chest with his open hand. He paused as the young brave brought the bundle forward and deposited it with great care on the ground. A young Indian moaned and grimaced in pain amid the bundle of animals' skins.

"Lean Bear asks white medicine woman to make boy well. Good brave sick many days." Lean Bear's stilted English boomed with authority. "Indian medicine doesn't work. Many, many buffalo trample brave warrior." His voice broke and he swallowed hard before he continued: "Please make Gray Wolf well again."

White medicine woman? What is Lean Bear saying? Georgia wondered. Before her father could respond, Ma opened the front door and walked to his side. Georgia noted with amusement that even in this tense situation, her mother maintained her perfect Southern belle posture.

"He must have internal injuries," Georgia's mother said,

able to diagnose most any ailment. "Let's see if he has the fever."

Ma squatted down beside Gray Wolf, touching his forehead and bare chest with the back of her hand.

"He's burning up," she said. "We have to get the heat out of his body. He's very sick." She paused. "Let's get him into the house."

Georgia's mother gestured toward her family's home, and the young brave picked up Gray Wolf and carried him into the MacBaye ranch house. She led them to a room adjacent to the kitchen, pulled down the patchwork quilt and patted the feather mattress. The young brave understood and placed Gray Wolf on the bed with care. The brave who carried Gray Wolf into the house and Lean Bear stepped back as Ma took charge of her new patient. She pressed Gray Wolf's abdomen at dozens of different angles, eliciting gasps of pain.

Georgia's mother looked up at the concerned faces. "I think he has internal damage—could be the kidneys. I need to get some dandelion tea down him and make an herbal poultice to extract the fever," she said as she headed to the kitchen to prepare the remedies.

Pa let out a sigh of resignation as he ran a calloused hand through his auburn hair. Georgia knew he was thinking what she was. Her mother's medical knowledge was recognized by the white settlers in the area. Now, it seemed the Indians—at least these Indians—had also learned of her reputation as a healer.

Lean Bear and the young brave who had carried Gray Wolf into the house, watched and waited, as if eager to see what the white medicine woman would do. Ma moved in and out of the room, applying the poultices she created. Over the past few years, Ma had instructed Georgia which herb combinations to stuff into the cheesecloth pouches to reduce fever or to calm a queasy stomach or any other of dozens of maladies. Georgia's mother lifted her patient's head so that he could sip the nourishing dandelion tea. Georgia knew that in any other setting, her mother would have acted with much greater caution, but when it came to the healing arts, there was no one better or more certain of what to do than Loraine MacBaye. And now, Georgia, who at age fifteen had learned much of her mother's healing technique, worked alongside.

At midday, Ma sent Georgia to kill and dress a chicken. Georgia always hated killing a faithful layer when her producing days ended, but she didn't think twice about scooping up the cocky, young red rooster that got more aggressive each time she collected eggs. She broke his neck with a precise two-handed jerk so that he felt nothing when his head met with the axe. She took the dressed and plucked rooster into the kitchen, where they would boil the carcass for hours to make nourishing bone broth for Gray Wolf. Georgia chuckled to herself. *Ma believes the South American saying, "A good bone broth can even bring the dead back to life."*

Georgia glanced out at the cornfield and saw the faithful team of oxen. "Daddy, you left the team in the field," Georgia said. He darted out the door toward the field he had been plowing hours ago when she rang the dinner bell to alert the men that Indians were approaching.

Upon further observation, Georgia noticed the oxen stood heads down, having moved no more than fifty feet from where her father had left them that morning. She mused over the irony that her father had adopted the practice of Western plainsmen, who used oxen, rather than horses, for fieldwork. Georgia knew she had acquired her love of horses from him, but she knew that both of them would have to admit the patient, plodding oxen were the better choice for plowing and bringing in a crop. A pair of horses left alone for hours would have torn off their harness, ripped up the newly sown field and disappeared. She smiled as she watched her father lead the gentle, forgiving oxen pair off to be unhitched, watered and secured in the sturdy corrals he and her brothers had built when they first settled the place.

Only now did she notice the greening prairie grass and the ankle-high winter wheat that peeked out beneath the tufts of dirty snow from the late spring storm. An impending explosion of green grasses, dotted with yellow, red and purple wildflowers, would soon turn the winter barrenness into a landscape to nourish man and beast, refreshing body and soul. Her thoughts this morning had been on training the sassy little sorrel filly her father had bought from a neighbor. Instead, she had spent the day helping her mother heal an Indian brave.

As the sun sunk low on the horizon, Georgia saw Pa hurrying back to the house.

"They're gone, Thomas," Ma said.

"Who's gone?" Pa asked, still puffing as he entered the house.

"The Indians," her mother said. "Well, not all of them. They left Gray Wolf, of course. He's better but in no condition to travel."

"Did they say when they would be back?" he asked.

"No. I was going about my business, and I didn't even notice when they left," she said.

"Well, if that doesn't beat all," Pa said, laughing. "When we decided to move West, I worried about how to defend my family and my stock from Indians, but I never worried about inheriting one!"

※

Five days later, Gray Wolf emerged from his delirium. It seemed the poor boy had no memory of how he got to the MacBaye Ranch or why he was there. He lunged at the door in a feeble attempt to escape, but his weakened state and considerable pain made it easy for Pa to restrain him.

"Easy there, young feller," Thomas soothed. "Fetch him something to eat, so he knows we mean him no harm."

Georgia ran to the springhouse at the edge of the creek. She lifted the crock out of the cool water, removed the cork lid and poured creamy milk into a tin cup. She was grateful that Blue Bell had freshened a few weeks earlier when she gave birth to her second calf. There was enough milk for all of them to have their fill, and there was plenty of cream left over to make butter. Yes, butter—she got a slab of that as well. Returning to the house, she slathered the butter on a piece of bread fresh from the oven that morning.

Taking a breath and slowing her pace, so as not to frighten Gray Wolf and send him into another fit, she presented him with the cup of milk. He smelled it, turned the cup around in his hands and then tasted it by dipping a finger into the milk and putting it to his lips.

"Go on there and drink that rich Jersey milk. It'll do ya some good," Thomas said, smiling. "You may not be used to drinking milk, so take it easy, son."

Next, Georgia handed him the slab of bread slathered in butter. "Try this," she coaxed. Again, he smelled the food and touched it with his finger. Georgia nodded approval. He pulled off some bread crust and popped it in his mouth. A smile appeared at the corners of his lips. Soon, both the milk and the bread disappeared.

That night, Pa slept in Gray Wolf's room to ensure he didn't harm himself or them. The next day, the brave ate everything offered him without reservation. "Please" and "more" seemed the extent of his English vocabulary until the following evening when he seemed to be trying to piece together the circumstances that brought him to the MacBayes.

"Lean Bear?" Gray Wolf asked.

"Lean Bear brought you here to see the white medicine woman," Pa said, gesturing toward Ma. "She made you well."

Gray Wolf nodded and motioned toward the door. "I go."

"You are still not strong, Gray Wolf," Pa said. "We will help you get better."

"Trust us, Gray Wolf," Georgia added, smiling.

Gray Wolf lay back on his bed, nodding.

The next morning, Georgia decided Gray Wolf was strong enough to eat with them at the dining room table. She guided him to a chair and patted the seat. He sat, but when he seemed uncertain what to do, Georgia noticed that he looked to her for subtle signals. When she folded her hands in her lap, Gray Wolf did likewise. Out of the corner of her eye, Georgia saw him put his hands on either side of his soup bowl, as if preparing to raise it to his mouth to drink his soup. She hastened to pick up her spoon, fill it with soup and raise it to her lips. He imitated her.

Gray Wolf never again mentioned leaving the ranch to find Lean Bear.

※

Days turned into weeks. Gray Wolf had put on weight and muscle. He was strong and virile. The herbs and bone broths, along with the fall's hearty ranch diet of garden potatoes, carrots, beets, greens, wild plums, eggs, beef and game, had turned his body from one that looked like flesh stretched over bones to that of a robust young man. His skin was a creamy brown, the hue of stout coffee with plenty of cream. His hair hung just below his shoulders. Most of the Indians Georgia had seen had jet-black hair, but Gray Wolf's was more like coffee without cream. He was the same height as James and her father, "a good amount taller 'n average," as Pa had once described his height. Yet Gray Wolf was not as stout as the MacBaye men. He was muscled yet lithe, like a pronghorn antelope. Georgia imagined he could run almost as fast and long as a pronghorn.

Fall was a busy time, as Georgia's family worked from dawn to dusk to harvest, store and dry the food that would sustain them and their livestock over the winter. The MacBaye men cut hay, left it in the field to dry for several days, then used the wagon and oxen to haul it to the barn and hoist it into the loft. They picked ears of corn and laid them in the yard to dry. Later, Georgia and her mother would grind the corn between stones to make cornmeal for baking, leaving the remaining corn to feed to the chickens, horses and cows when the cold weather made it difficult for the animals to maintain their body weight.

The men cut, bundled and then threshed the wheat to separate the grain kernels from the stalk. The MacBayes put the largest, fully formed wheat kernels in the root cellar in burlap sacks. They would grind the kernels into flour to use for making bread and pancakes, as it was needed. The rest was their seed for the next crop. They would plant it in the fall. If there were excess sacks of wheat, the MacBayes would take them to sell on the annual supply trip to Denver. Nothing went to waste. Inferior wheat kernels became animal feed. The chaff, also called straw, became animal bedding for cold, wet times. Pa, James and Henry made the backbreaking work look easy, Georgia thought. Though the tasks were unfamiliar to Gray Wolf, he was a willing student and a hard worker.

Georgia would have preferred to work in the fields with her father and brothers, but tradition kept her closer to home. She helped her mother harvest potatoes, carrots, onions, beets and winter squash and stashed them in the root cellar. She did enjoy cutting, washing and drying the many herbs her mother cultivated for healing and for flavoring food. She hated to admit it, but she enjoyed helping her mom boil down wild berries and plums with honey to make jams and jellies. She teased her brothers and made them do things for her in exchange for tastes of the sweet fruity preserves.

Georgia included Gray Wolf in her practical jokes. That afternoon she stood at the stovetop stirring a delectable smelling sauce. Gray Wolf had just come into the house from helping do evening chores, and, like any hungry man, the cooking sauce drew him into the kitchen. He plunked down at the table a chunky but finely hewn piece of wood taken from a downed cottonwood at the creek the first winter they spent out West. Pa was a good carpenter, and he had insisted on fashioning a long table with benches on either side to seat the family and any guests they might have.

"Do you want some hot green chili sauce?" Georgia drawled, a mischievous gleam in her eye.

He nodded, and she scooped a ladleful into a bowl. He took his time, blowing to cool the stew, as he had learned to do at the MacBaye dinner table. A few seconds later, he put a big spoonful in his mouth and swallowed. Georgia could no longer contain herself. She spun around to look at Gray Wolf, who reddened, choked and coughed. Perhaps she shouldn't have done it, but it was the same joke the Mexicans who'd built the MacBayes' adobe ranch house had once played on her. She knew the sauce was eaten as a condiment, but to an innocent who thought it was a stew, there would be several minutes of extreme discomfort, as Gray Wolf demonstrated by fanning what must have felt like flames coming from his mouth.

"I understand why the Mexicans say this sauce keeps away sickness," her father said the first time he tried it. "If you eat it, your breath is so strong not even your horse will come near you."

Gray Wolf seemed shocked she had duped him until he saw her shoulders shake from her hidden laughter. Soon they both laughed. Georgia hoped, no, dreaded, no, hoped he would pay her back.

Not wanting the merriment to end, Gray Wolf looked for an opportunity to pay back Georgia for tricking him into eating the bowl of chili sauce. His opportunity came the next morning after breakfast. He saw her leave the house through the back door with the bucket she used to pick berries. He took apart a string of rattles made from rattlesnakes he killed that summer and attached the individual rattles to long straps of rawhide. Slipping out the back door after her, he stopped short of where she stood picking berries at the edge of the creek. He dropped to his belly and crawled unnoticed to within a couple of horse lengths of her. Then he eased the rattles toward her on their stiff rawhide straps. When all were in place, he began to wiggle the straps, mimicking the sounds rattlesnakes make as they prepare to strike. Georgia jerked, lost her footing and fell backward into the shallow creek.

As she turned to flee the contrived rattlesnake den, Gray Wolf saw that her entire backside from the waist down was caked with mud. He watched as she waded downstream, no doubt anxious to put distance between herself and the poisonous snakes. When she climbed up from the creek bed, Gray Wolf picked up Georgia's abandoned berry bucket and hurried to the house. While he waited for her, his eyes rested on the smooth finish and the handsome wood grain of the table and chairs. The furniture was much finer than the makeshift pieces he had seen at the trading posts the Cheyenne frequented. His thoughts were interrupted by Georgia trudging into the kitchen. No doubt, her soaking wet dress and waterlogged lace-up boots had altered her otherwise nimble and energetic gate. How long would it take before she noticed the bucket of berries she had dropped at the creek? His eyes crinkled in amusement. He had placed her bucket and a single rawhide string with a rattle at the end next to the wash bucket. Gray Wolf stood, moving behind her without a sound, the remaining rattles dangling from his neck.

Georgia spun around to face him, the fire of realization in her eyes. "I should be hoppin' mad at you for scaring me near to death and wrecking my new calico." She was spitting mad. Gray Wolf grinned at the trick, but had he gone too far? Was she so mad she wouldn't speak to him?

In her next breath, his fears were allayed. "But my daddy always says we gotta be willing to laugh at a joke on us as much as one we pull on someone else." She burst out laughing, and for the first time since the buffalo stampede brought him to death's door and to the MacBaye homestead, Gray Wolf laughed with abandon.

Chapter 2

Gray Wolf liked the MacBayes' fun-loving, yet hard-working life. He thought about his own family as he repaired the corral where the MacBayes kept their horses and cattle when they weren't out on the prairie pastures.

His biggest frustration was communicating. He knew some English, which was spoken by a few members of his tribe. But mostly, he relied on a combination of hand signals and broken phrases. The language struggles made him feel more like a child than a brave around the MacBayes. But he never felt humiliated by them. They were kind and patient, especially Georgia.

Gray Wolf looked up to see Georgia walking toward the corral. Her settler-style cotton dress hugged her trim waist and swished as the long legs it covered moved quickly toward him. "I brought you a cinnamon bun and some buttermilk if you need a break." She thrust a cup and a delicious smelling piece of bread toward him. "You look deep in thought. Do you miss your home?"

Gray Wolf wanted to impress Georgia, so he described a

time when he was a young boy and his parents were still alive, a time when life among the Cheyenne had been good. "We hunted buffalo always. Herds big," he said, holding his arms outward. "We killed many and had much to eat, hides for trade. After hunts, we race horses, eat until ...," he poked his stomach, "hurts."

"What happened?" Georgia was watching him with rapt attention.

"Whites come. They are more than the buffalo. They live Cheyenne hunting ground. Buffalo, deer, all leave." Gray Wolf realized his hands clenched into fists. He feared he would scare Georgia, but he couldn't relax.

"I didn't think about that, I mean that we pushed out the game." She shifted, uncomfortable, anxious to change the subject, he thought. "What about your family? Do you miss them?

"Ma, Pa died. I have one sister."

"I'm sorry, Gray Wolf. I thought the man that brought you here, Lean Bear, was your father." Georgia's discomfort shifted to curiosity. Her eyes bore into his.

"No, Lean Bear my uncle, my mother's brother." Must he admit the truth to her? Her eyes would demand it, he knew. "Cheyenne custom: parents die, uncle take children into his tepee. Lean Bear's eldest wife treated us like stray dogs. She no want us in her tepee." He hated to admit this to himself, much less to Georgia. *What will she think of me? Will she see me as just a Cheyenne brave that no one wanted?* he thought.

"When I go back to Cheyenne, I prove I am brave warrior." He decided not to tell her that one of the ways he could prove himself or "count coup" was by killing a white man. "I get tepee, wives, horses. Many, many horses."

Georgia's eyes were wide. Had he told her something he shouldn't have? Had he given her reason to disrespect him? Surely, she could understand an orphan boy's rejection by his uncle's wife was not his fault. He hoped she would understand. He needed her to understand.

"Many wives you say. Guess that's the Indian way." Georgia looked dismayed, or was it disappointment he saw in her inquisitive face? Gray Wolf understood her dismay. The white man had only one wife. He knew this, because the religious men who came to the Cheyenne camps told them God would punish them for having more than one wife. Gray Wolf would explain to Georgia that it was their way of caring for widows more than a man's lust to have relations with many women, but as he thought about the English words to explain it, he looked up and saw her sprinting off toward the barn.

※

Gray Wolf enjoyed helping the MacBayes with the fall work, and felt like an accepted part of the family. However, he was not enthusiastic about the leather-bound black book Georgia's father, Thomas, read every night after supper.

"For by grace you have been saved by faith. It is the gift of God, not of works, lest any man should boast ..." Gray Wolf heard Thomas drone on. He sighed and then yawned, gestures he had learned from James and his younger brother, Henry. He hoped his signs of boredom would dissuade Thomas.

"So, according to the Scripture I just read, is there anything we can do to earn salvation?"

Had Thomas mistaken Gray Wolf's sighs and yawns for confusion? He meant no disrespect; he just had no use for the white man's god.

After a long pause, James spoke up: "It's right simple, I guess. All we gotta do is place our faith in Him, and He'll save us." Then, lowering his voice, "I know that applies to us, and the Negroes, but what about the savages, the ones who are stealin' from them white settlers?"

"Just 'cause a man's different from us, son, doesn't mean God don't love 'em and want 'em to be a part of His family. Ain't a one of us hasn't done something to displease Him, but He loves us and calls us to be His children just the same."

Gray Wolf scooted his chair closer to the table. "You say white god loves Indians?"

"Shor does, son." Thomas turned the pages of the book, running his finger down the page. "John 3:16 tells us that He loves all people and that anyone who believes in Him will have everlasting life. That means anyone who believes will live forever with God in Heaven."

"Black robes come to Cheyenne; tell them to become white if they want white god to love them." Gray Wolf's face twisted. He gritted his teeth. "Lies, they tell us lies, so we sign peace treaties, buy firewater."

Thomas slammed his fist on the table, sending eating utensils flying. "Shameful! It is downright shameful that so-called men of God would use religion to manipulate people." Pink came to his face. His voice softened. "What I'm trying to say is this is not the god we serve, Gray Wolf."

✳

A few nights later, Thomas read the story of Jesus's crucifixion, raising a multitude of questions. Gray Wolf did not understand why Jesus had to die to save people or why he didn't fight against the ones who whipped, tortured and killed him. In his thinking, Jesus was a coward, not a brave warrior.

"God's ways are higher than our ways, son. As humans, we would have fought, but if Jesus had done that, He could not have completed God's work on earth. Submitting to ridicule and a torturous death makes Jesus the bravest warrior ever, don't you think?"

Gray Wolf had to think on that.

Several evenings later when Thomas read the Ten Commandments, Gray Wolf asked if the white man's Wise One Above would condemn killing when men fought their enemies in battle.

Thomas chuckled. "You ask difficult questions. I guess I'd have to ask what the battle is fixin' to accomplish." Thomas leaned forward, his fingers laced, cradling his chin. "If a man is fighting to protect an innocent like his home and family or to right a wrong, then, yes, it is right to kill another man in battle. However, killing another man because I am angry and hate him, or if I want to have what he has, then, no, I don't think God would want me to kill a man or be part of such a battle."

Gray Wolf thought about this. When the Cheyenne hunted buffalo or went after the Pawnee or Kiowa to get back women, children and horses stolen from them, the white man's Wise One Above said fighting was right. Men raiding other tribes or wagon trains to take their horses, weapons, women and children had seemed greedy to him, and he guessed the Wise One Above wasn't pleased with those things either.

"What would your god say when Cheyenne kill white settlers because they killed and chased away buffalo, deer, and antelope, and the Indians freeze or starve to death?" Gray Wolf asked.

Thomas's eyes shot up. "Really? Your people starve to death because the settlers have chased away game? Isn't there plenty for all of us, Gray Wolf?"

"Some years good. Some years bad. Warriors must travel many days to find deer and buffalo. Sometimes find none. People very hungry. Old ones, children die."

Thomas scratched his chin. "I guess I hadn't thought about there not being enough game for us all. Our government is working on a peace agreement."

He had heard the Cheyenne chiefs talk about the many government agents who made promises they never kept. "Indian agents take food and blankets the Great Father in Washington sends to Indians," Gray Wolf said.

Again, Thomas's eyes shot up. "Are you sure 'bout that, Gray Wolf?"

"Very sure. Lean Bear, other chiefs traded many buffalo and antelope hides for coffee, sugar, food in cans. They know this is the food they should have for signing peace treaty, but Indian agent asks us pay for it."

A year ago, Gray Wolf, like most Cheyenne, thought all whites were like the corrupt government agents who came to their camps to persuade the Indians to sign yet another meaningless treaty, but Thomas was different. *Why didn't the Great Father in Washington send Thomas to make peace with the Indians?*

As the winter cold set in, the MacBayes stayed indoors when they weren't feeding animals, chopping wood or hunting.

Georgia saw Gray Wolf's discomfort sitting indoors. "What do the Cheyenne do in the winter when it is too cold to be outside?"

"Cheyenne braves hunt every day."

"Don't you store food?"

He supposed Georgia had never seen a Cheyenne camp. Her question was sincere. "We live in tepees and move often. Our squaws dry buffalo and pound it with berries, but we eat this only when there is no game or we are moving or on long hunting trips." A squaw's babies would have to be crying from hunger before she would break into the stash of dried meat. Gray Wolf doubted this ever happened to settlers' babies. They seemed to have plenty of food since staying in one place allowed them to preserve and store their excess for leaner times.

Thomas and Henry spent hours looking at books. James was more restless. Both he and Gray Wolf looked for tasks to occupy them. When they got out the array of hunting rifles and knives and prepared to clean them for the second time in a single week, Thomas cleared his throat, "Boys, you're gonna clean the metal plum off them weapons if ya keep polishing 'em like that. If you're looking for something to do, pull the hides outta the barn and start scraping 'em."

Later that morning, Thomas, James, Gray Wolf and Henry brought a flat of cattle, deer and antelope hides into the house to salt and scrape, a process that removed pieces of fat and hair from the hide, stopping spoilage and decomposition. Next, they boiled the brain of a deer killed the previous day and applied the mixture to the hide. After repeating this process a second time, the men softened the hides by rolling them over polished wood pieces. Finally, they set the hides near the fire to dry them. Now, a skilled leather worker could make it into clothing, boots, tack and other items needed by settlers and Indians alike. It was a process with which Gray Wolf was well acquainted. Among the Cheyenne, the women did most of the tanning, although Gray Wolf often helped his sister tan hides in winter. Thomas gave each of the boys their pick of a hide and told them they could use it for anything they liked. James began fashioning his hide into a scabbard for his rifle. He accepted Gray Wolf's demonstration of cutting and lacing the edges for a tighter and more attractive finish, yet he all but ignored what he learned and finished the scabbard with his crude lacing.

Gray Wolf decided he would wait until Christmas morning to reveal what he made, for he had been told that Christmas was a special day, with feasting and gift giving. He also knew Christmas had to do with "the book."

Georgia and Loraine had been busy in the kitchen, and now unfamiliar, yet enticing odors wafted from the kitchen into the parlor. When Gray Wolf entered the kitchen, hoping for a taste of the cooking food, he was shooed out by Georgia. "Don't think you'll get a taste from me, Gray Wolf, though I know the pumpkin pies and anise cookies are mighty tempting."

Christmas morning dawned cold and clear. After the animals were fed, the MacBaye family sat down to a breakfast of ham and fried potatoes. Loraine's special cinnamon rolls were added to the regular breakfast fare.

When breakfast was finished and the table cleared, Thomas got out "the book." There was nothing unusual about this, but then he said, "Today we will read the Christmas story." Gray Wolf liked the story of the woman Mary who had a son without a human father—that sounded much like a Cheyenne story. He was less impressed when Thomas explained that this baby grew up to be the man Jesus, who refused to fight against his captors.

"Because Jesus was the greatest gift ever given, we celebrate by giving each other gifts," Thomas said.

This was Gray Wolf's cue. He went to his bed and pulled out the Cheyenne-style winter boots he had made for Thomas with the hide. "These are for you." He handed the boots to Thomas.

Thomas's face beamed with pleasure as he examined the boots. "They're beautiful, Gray Wolf," Thomas said, running his hand over the soft leather and the deer-fur lining. "The stitching is perfect; no snow will get in there."

Gray Wolf responded to the praise: "Cheyenne warrior wear in deep snow, feet warm and can still run fast."

"Well, if that isn't something! Very, very fine work, Gray Wolf. Thank you!"

※

Winter trudged on, so Gray Wolf accepted Loraine's invitation for him to join Georgia in her school lessons. James and Henry were finished, as Loraine called it, with their book learnin'. At first the symbols Loraine said were the alphabet looked confusing, but he learned the sounds of each symbol and could say first one, then many of the words on a page. Loraine's face lit up when he said the words. She looked pleased, even surprised.

Several weeks later, Loraine told Gray Wolf and Georgia that they were going to study American history. She started with the discovery of America.

"How can you say Christopher Columbus discovered America when my people have always been here?" he asked.

"I see your point," Loraine said. "I guess you could say it is white man's history, and I'm not about to try to rewrite that!" She laughed. Gray Wolf didn't understand what was so funny.

She then told her two students about President Abraham Lincoln issuing a preliminary Emancipation Proclamation on September 22, 1862. "My aunt who lives in Philadelphia wrote me about the proclamation and the fighting. The Southern states are enraged with President Lincoln imposing this on them. It is all-out war in the eastern part of the United States," Loraine told them.

Abraham Lincoln's campaign for the presidency as an anti-slavery candidate, and his Emancipation Proclamation, fascinated Gray Wolf. Loraine tried to explain the plight of the slaves, but Gray Wolf didn't understand why the "black white men," as the Indians called them, didn't send their chiefs to free the slaves from their captors.

"There are no chiefs to fight for the black people," Loraine said, "so white people must fight for them."

"Do the white people like Abraham Lincoln?" he asked.

"Yes, a lot of people like Mr. Lincoln," she said, but Gray Wolf noticed that she hadn't said she liked him.

"I like Chief Lincoln," he said. "He is a brave fighter for his black white men."

"Yes, he is," she said.

※

Several days later, Loraine told Gray Wolf that since he liked Abraham Lincoln so much, she was going to teach Georgia and him about Frederick Douglass.

"Who is Frederick Douglass?" Georgia wanted to know.

"Is he like Chief Lincoln?" Gray Wolf asked.

Loraine shifted in her chair, her gaze intense yet focused on neither Gray Wolf nor Georgia. "Frederick Douglass is the reason we came west to settle in Colorado Territory. I would not have budged from my tranquil, comfortable life at Spring Grove if I hadn't heard him speak with such eloquence on the evils of slavery and how it crushed the soul of the slave and the slave owner alike."

Georgia, who had been dawdling with her schoolbook and slate, snapped to attention. "Ma, you always said Pa's being a Scotsman made it impossible for him to stay put at Spring Grove. I remember when Pa went to Washington for business and came home just before Christmas that year. He told us about the free land out West. Just like that, we imagined ourselves rounding up cattle on a ranch out West!"

"That's right," Loraine said. "On his trip to Washington that year, your pa learned about some new legislation that the U.S. government was considering to encourage Americans to settle the Western Frontier by giving them large plots of land. The law was called the Homestead Act."

Gray Wolf was confused with all the new words, but even more so, he was confused about how the Great White Father, or the government as the whites called him, could give away land to the white man when the earth couldn't be owned by any man. *How can a man own something he can't carry with him?*

Loraine continued: "Once he learned about the pending Homestead Act, he would never have been happy with plantation life. Your Pa was restless. On an established plantation, such as Spring Grove, there is little left to build or achieve. Your great-great grandparents on your Pa's side immigrated to the American Colonies from the Scottish Highlands a century ago. Many Scots had to relocate to the American Colonies because they came out on the losing side of battles with England or had plotted to free Scotland from British control. The MacBaye clan, however, being the independent, adventuresome type, decided to begin anew in the New World where they could work hard, own land, and build wealth without having to worry about landlords or increasing rents."

"Were your people Scots as well, Ma?" Georgia asked.

"No, my dear. I'm English. It seems plantation life suited my people. We were satisfied with hosting teas and balls, listening to fine music and sleeping on a soft bed." Loraine chuckled. "I was raised on a Southern plantation, but as I grew older and saw the slaves doing forced, backbreaking work to earn their owners a privileged life, I began to question the morality of one man owning another. Your Pa was more pragmatic. His view was a reflection of the obvious, that slave labor was the only thing that made plantations profitable.

"Pardon me, Gray Wolf, for not answering your question,"

Loraine went on. "Frederick Douglass was a slave who learned to read, write and reason. He's like 'Chief' Lincoln in that he wants to do away with slavery of the Negroes."

"Where does the Negro come from?" Gray Wolf asked.

"Well, many generations ago, they lived in Africa until they were captured and taken to North America. They have been slaves ever since."

"Is Africa far from North America?" Gray Wolf asked.

"Very, very far," Loraine said.

Gray Wolf thought about when he was a child and the Pawnees had battled with the Cheyenne. The Pawnees carried away horses and children, including his mother and him. The Cheyenne captives were forced to work at the Pawnee camp until the Cheyenne braves attacked and reclaimed them. He wondered why the black white warriors had not fought to take back their people. Now he understood. They were too far away.

"Is Frederick Douglass a great chief who fights for the black white men?"

"I guess you could say that, Gray Wolf. Mr. Douglass is fighting for them, but not in the way you imagine. He uses words and intellect to reason against slavery, so that the white people will free the slaves and change the laws so they can never again be slaves of the white man."

"How does he fight with words?" Gray Wolf asked.

"I heard Frederick Douglass speak when I was in Philadelphia visiting my aunt. I had been raised to believe the Negroes were an inferior race, that they were not capable of learning and debating, but hearing him changed my thinking. I remember one thing he said: 'Where justice is denied, where poverty is enforced, where ignorance prevails, and where any one class is made to feel that society is an organized conspiracy to oppress, rob and degrade them, neither persons nor property will be safe.' "

Loraine paused. Gray Wolf hoped she would continue, and she did. "Mr. Douglass spoke with such passion and conviction, as he recounted his white owner teaching him to read. She later regretted teaching him because it made her realize that he and his fellow Negroes were human beings. From then on, I knew he was right and that slavery was as bad for whites as it is for the Negroes.

"Up to that time, I had justified being a slave owner because I knew that at Spring Grove we treated our slaves well and punished them justly when they did things that were against our rules. I realized that the purpose of most of the rules was to keep slaves from becoming independent and thinking for themselves. I know now why there was a law in South Carolina against teaching Negroes to read. An educated slave was a dangerous slave. That address by Mr. Douglass changed everything for me. I knew I could no longer own another human being."

"What did you do, Ma?" Georgia asked.

"That's another long story that will have to wait for another time. You both need to get back to your schoolwork."

Chapter 3

MacBaye Ranch, Spring 1863

Georgia's birthday in May was celebrated with a cake and homemade gifts. She opened a dress of finely woven brown calico with blue and yellow flowers trimmed in cotton lace from her mother, a bedside table from her father and Henry, a functional but very homemade-looking set of saddle bags from James, and a pair of leather boots from Gray Wolf. The dress was befitting a lady yet not ostentatious. She knew her mother would have preferred to see her in a silk ball gown over the simple cotton dress. She was most intrigued with the boots. Like the pair he had made for her father for Christmas, Gray Wolf had displayed superior craftsmanship in his fashioning of the sturdy but feminine boots. The best part came when she pulled them onto her feet. A perfect fit, like being barefoot. They were lightweight, yet the rabbit-fur lining was warm and soothing.

"Thank you so much," she squealed. "You've made my sixteenth birthday extra special."

Later that evening, as Georgia passed her parents' bedroom

on the way to her own, she heard them arguing.

"Gray Wolf is a part of our family now, Loraine, and I want him to go with us to Denver," Thomas said. "I don't much fancy leaving him home to fend for himself. The seeds will be in the ground, the cattle on pasture, and the cow dried up. There's nothing for him to do all day. He might as well come with us. He might enjoy it, and we could use his help moving the steers and helping us load up the supplies we buy."

"Why subject him to such stares and ridicule?" Ma said. "I just don't see the point of it ... it's not like he's aching to go to the theater ... or to church. As far as help goes, James and Henry can do the herding and loading of supplies."

"I'm surprised at you, Loraine. You, who made the freeing of every last slave at Spring Grove the condition for moving West, are objecting to having an Indian boy go with us on a trip to Denver? You, who loves the South and plantation life yet named emancipation of our slaves as the price to pay for me to homestead this ranch, refuse to treat a boy who is not unlike our own son with some dignity?"

Georgia could tell from his voice that her father was angry, perhaps more angry than she'd ever heard him. "Is it really Gray Wolf that you're concerned about, Loraine, or are you worried about the stares that will be directed your way? You lectured me about the evils of slavery, yet you are unwilling to walk down the street with an Indian and be seen by people you don't even know?"

"And his presence might endanger us," she sputtered, grasping for any excuse to leave Gray Wolf at the ranch.

"I can't believe you would say that after all the times he has been so protective toward you and Georgia. I would trust Gray Wolf as much as James or Henry to defend you two."

There was silence. Then, Georgia heard her mother contritely respond, "You're right, Thomas. It's my pride. Gray Wolf has never given me any reason to doubt his intentions. I guess it's wrong of me to want justice for those not as fortunate as me without being willing to treat them like fellow human beings."

✳

The following day, the MacBayes and Gray Wolf would join neighboring settlers traveling to Denver in April. The first couple of years, Pa and James had made the trip to Denver by themselves or with other ranchers to buy food and household supplies. This year would be different. It had been a good year at the ranch. The cattle herd had grown large, and the ranchers said that beef prices in Denver were high. After saving back enough for the family and any neighbors that might fall on tough times, Pa told them he had decided to take the extra steers, fat from grazing the prairie and eating the MacBayes' corn, and sell them.

"I'll need you boys to help herd them," he said to James, Henry and Gray Wolf. "We'll also take some extra sacks of grain and the tanned hides we don't need. It will be a nice trip for all of us, and we'll be back home in a week or so."

Georgia stiffened when her father said he needed the boys to herd the steers. Her father would gladly have included her as a herder, but her mother thought it was unladylike. Nonetheless, she was excited about the adventure, the time they would spend with the other settlers' children, the thrill of sleeping in a different place each night. There was no doubt she had inherited her father's Scottish wanderlust. She thought to herself that Pa must love her Ma to have stayed as long as he had at Spring Grove.

Georgia could see that James and Henry were eager for the trip as well. She expected that James was already picturing the new rifle he had been talking about buying. Henry, a more "refined" boy, as their mother would say, was probably more interested in the sights and sounds of the city and would bear the trip to get him back to civilization.

She was glad her parents had decided to take Gray Wolf. "We'll have a grand time. You'll see." He nodded and smiled.

The next few weeks at the ranch were a flurry of activity. Once the wheat and corn were sown, preparations for the trip began. Pa had motivated them. "It's a lot more work takin' six people to Denver for a week than it's been when one or two have gone." He impressed on all of them the commercial importance of the trip. "We need to take care to pack our goods with care. Denver folks will pay well for good quality cattle, grain and hides. We'll need the money we get from these things to buy coffee, sugar, dried beans and whatnot."

Georgia wondered if the "whatnot" included a saddle for her. She also liked the peppermint sticks at the Mercantile. She heard Ma tell Pa that they needed to buy cloth to make dresses for the two of them and shirts and trousers for the men. They all needed new shoes. Georgia would have been happy wearing trousers and work shirts like her father and brothers, at least while she was working with the horses and doing chores outside, where no one would gawk at her attire.

"It is unseemly for a young lady to be seen in men's clothes," Ma had protested. "At your age, you should be attired in dresses that go all the way to the ground and cover your arms. Proper young ladies should wear petticoats and gloves and carry a parasol to protect their skin."

The thought of any plains woman, young or old, wearing fancy gloves and carrying a parasol, was laughable. *The only gloves I'll ever wear will be durable leather ones, and I won't lose any sleep if my skin turns the color of my leather gloves,* Georgia thought.

Pa organized the outdoor work to prepare for the trip. "James, shell the corn we harvested and dried in the fall and bag it. Henry and I will round up the cattle and corral them. Gray Wolf, I want you to bring the hides we cured from the barn loft and check for spoilage. Clean them up and wrap them skin-side down." Georgia knew that the instructions given Gray Wolf were unnecessary. He was as skilled or more so than Pa in preparing hides.

Georgia and Ma washed clothes and prepared food for the journey. Georgia fetched potatoes, carrots and onions from the root cellar. She brushed off the dirt and stuffed them into leather pouches. Her mother baked bread for the beginning of the trip. Crackers, which would stay good for months, would be a mainstay for the second part of the trip.

The afternoon before the MacBayes were to join the other settlers from the area for the trip to Denver, the men loaded the hides and grain onto the wagon. It was the same wagon the MacBayes used to come West. Pa, who had removed the canvas covering once they had settled, placed it back on the wagon.

The men helped Georgia and Ma load the food, bedrolls and clean clothes. Ma would sit on the front seat and Pa would drive the wagon. Georgia envisioned her mother sitting there in a dress plumped up with petticoats, wearing matching cloth gloves and that ridiculous parasol of hers.

The next morning, the MacBayes were up before dawn. Gray Wolf and Georgia brought the team out, and Pa hitched the horses to the wagon. James and Henry saddled their horses and herded the steers they intended to sell into the corral. When all was prepared, Georgia saw Pa enter the house and come back out a few minutes later with Ma on his arm. She was dressed in a new, brown- and yellow-flowered calico—no petticoats or gloves. Instead of a parasol, she wore a medium brimmed straw hat. Georgia was relieved. At least in appearance, Ma would fit in with all the other women settlers.

Pa looked pleased with the transformation in his wife's attire, smiling as he helped her onto the seat at the front of the wagon. "What a stylish and beautiful plains woman you've become m'dear."

Georgia envied her brothers and Gray Wolf. They would ride horses to Denver, herding the steers. Gray Wolf sat proudly astride the sorrel filly she had worked with since last summer. She was glad he would ride the swift, sensitive young horse. He had watched her train the filly, learning to use the same light touch she did to get a horse to obey her cues. His wide grin and appreciative nod gave her a warm glow inside. She found a spot to sit in the packed wagon. What ridiculous ideas her mother had! "Proper young ladies must be appropriately attired and travel seated in a wagon. It is not proper for them to ride a horse astride," Ma had reiterated when Pa suggested Georgia ride the filly on the trip to Denver City.

Unlike Georgia, who once out of Ma's presence would roll her eyes and mimic her mother's ideas of what a "proper young lady" should be and do, Pa took a more rational and respectful approach. "Loraine, Georgia is not a Southern belle. She must be able to ride. It is not a shameful thing. To the contrary, Georgia is quite admired for her abilities in training horses."

In the end, Pa and Ma reached a compromise: Georgia would ride in the wagon to Denver City and ride horseback on the return trip, with Henry, James and Gray Wolf taking their turn riding in or driving the wagon.

Chapter 4

The three-day trip to Denver passed without incident, for which Gray Wolf had heard the adults express gratitude. The teenage boys, on the other hand, ached for adventure. Throughout the trip, Gray Wolf heard them brag about how they would defend their belongings and families from Indian attacks, bandits, charging buffalo, and every other conceivable peril. He smiled in amusement at how similar they were to Cheyenne boys.

There had been only one threat to the travelers' safety, and it had come on the first evening of the trip. A young girl named Marie Baker was sent to fetch water from the stream to prepare the evening meal. Her terrified screams brought the men and older boys running. Marie had stepped into a rattlesnake den and was unable to retreat. Most of the rattlers were slithering through the grass to get away, but several of them turned toward Marie, coiling their long bodies, sounding their trademark warning.

Thomas, James and Gray Wolf were the first to reach the

perimeter of the snake den. Thomas spoke to Marie to calm her.

"The most important thing you can do right now is to be quiet and not move a muscle, not a single muscle, do you understand, sweetheart?" he soothed.

Meanwhile, James and Gray Wolf used a lariat to draw the snakes' attention away from Marie. When the rattlesnakes were beyond striking distance from the young girl, James drew his pistol and Gray Wolf his rawhide whip, and they began to eliminate the threat. James, Gray Wolf and the younger boys cut the rattles off the dead snakes, ostensibly to assure Marie the snakes no longer were a threat—but they had ulterior motives. A few days later when the rattles had dried, the boys had a new way to play pranks on their mothers and to terrify the girls.

Gray Wolf felt fortunate that the settlers had not run into any of the late spring storms that were capable of dumping a foot of wet snow across the plains. It had been a carefree trip, and by tomorrow evening, he understood, they would reach their destination. He remembered hearing Lean Bear and the other chiefs talk about the great white camp at the base of the mountains. He was anxious to see it.

Because springtime brought abundant prairie grasses, all of the travelers opted to use their teams of horses to pull their wagons, rather than the dependable and hardy but slower oxen. While living with the MacBayes, Gray Wolf had learned that the oxen were entirely practical for farm work. But he and Thomas loved the horses. As Thomas pointed out, horses pulled a wagon with style, and, unlike the oxen, they could unhitch and ride them once they reached Denver.

The afternoon shadows were growing longer now, so the wagons stopped at the next clearing to set up camp. James and Henry unloaded bedrolls and cooking utensils. Loraine sent Georgia to the creek for water. Thomas and Gray Wolf unhitched the horses and led them downstream from where the settlers were filling their buckets with water for drinking and cooking. This way, the horses could drink as they willed, without concern for muddying the settlers' drinking supply. When the horses finished, the men led them up onto the creek bank. Thomas took out the brush and hoof pick he carried in his antelope skin pouch and began to brush one of the horses. Gray Wolf took the other brush and imitated Thomas. The horses were losing their winter coats, so the shed fur was everywhere. The transformation was quite remarkable. The team had left the ranch as fuzzy fur balls and now had shiny coats, which revealed their muscular frames. Next, Thomas lifted one leg at a time and cleaned all the dirt and manure from each hoof.

Gray Wolf was fascinated with the process and the simple tools used to groom the horses. Thomas taught him early on to perform these tasks with care and expertise. The Cheyenne were known for their horsemanship skills, but until he came to the MacBayes, grooming a horse and picking its hooves were new to him.

In the months Gray Wolf had lived with the MacBayes, he knew that caring for the horses was of utmost importance to Thomas, although he knew plenty of white men who did not care for their horses. Thomas loved his horses, and he took pride, sometimes too much pride, according to Loraine, in their training and appearance. But, as Thomas explained, there were practical reasons to see that the horses were groomed and fit.

"Neglecting a horse's grooming can lead to an itchy hide." Thomas would rather take the time to stimulate the hide and remove dead hair and skin than to let the horse knock down fences and other things, scratching itself. "The most important tool is the hoof pick," he told Gray Wolf. "This little tool used every day has prevented plenty a horse from becoming lame. Alotta folks think a trim and shoeing every few months is all they gotta do for their horses, but it ain't so."

Gray Wolf marveled at the improved appearance of Thomas's team. The horses went to the stream shaggy and caked with dried sweat. They returned to camp with gleaming coats. The horses walked beside Thomas and Gray Wolf like a fawn beside its mother. The men led them to the grazing area near camp and released them to eat. Many of the others had to drag, pull or whip their horses to get them where they wanted them.

Horses had forged the connection between Thomas and Gray Wolf, who soon learned how much Thomas loved his horses, and he admired the care Thomas gave them. The Cheyenne loved their large herds of painted ponies and swift racing steeds, but Gray Wolf could see that Thomas and his horses had a special bond. He didn't have to rope them or chase after them. They came to him willingly.

Gray Wolf loved Thomas's easy manner and his willingness to spend time showing the Indian brave new things. He remembered once when the two of them were outside building a fence for a new pasture when Georgia ran out calling to her father, "Pa, the day is too beautiful for work. Let's go riding. We need to check the cattle grazing yonder before the snow comes, don't we? I'll saddle the horses. Won't you please come? He can come too," she said, pointing at Gray Wolf.

He had first resented the intrusion of Georgia into the newfound bond he felt with Thomas, but he soon found that she was much too fun and daring to resist. Georgia used every excuse she could muster—real or contrived—to get Thomas and Gray Wolf to go riding with her. "Ma needs us to check on the Johnsons," she said one time. The next time, she cajoled them to ride to the top of the bluff to see if the herd of antelope still grazed on the other side. "Game could become scarce, and we'd better keep track of the herd movements."

The next time the men saw Georgia approach with the horse bridles in hand, Thomas winked at Gray Wolf. "My Georgia's a woman but still has the heart and energy of a child." A moment later, he raised his eyebrows as he listened to his daughter's impassioned plea to join her for a ride along the creek.

"I promised your Ma I'd get her chicken house started today, but I 'spect Gray Wolf here would be willing to ride out with you." Georgia turned on him like cornered prey, and he knew his fate was sealed. He didn't mind riding with her. He and Thomas had to feign otherwise, but Gray Wolf had become more and more fond of their rides together. He was captivated by her enthusiasm and wild pursuits.

They trotted their ponies atop the bluffs and raced them along the fields where there was no danger of slipping or falling into prairie dog holes. He always let her think he was doing her the favor of riding with her, but if he was honest with himself he would have to admit that he loved riding and being with Georgia.

Gray Wolf also was intrigued by Georgia's ability and horse training methods. The Cheyenne were excellent riders. They had the ability to mount any horse—broke or otherwise—and muscle it into submission. Georgia's methods were very different. It took her more time to train a colt, but she could do so without breaking its spirit. Only men and very strong boys or women could handle a Cheyenne horse by themselves. The horses Georgia and her father trained seemed yielded and willing, never switching their tails or pinning back their ears, not offering to buck, rear or lunge forward out of control.

A Cheyenne warrior's horsemanship was second in importance only to his bravery in battle, so it pricked Gray Wolf's pride for him to acknowledge, even if only to himself, that he could learn from this white squaw. He watched her work a young horse by first pushing it away from her and then seeming to ignore it, which made the horse pursue her. She took lots of time to introduce a young horse to the saddle and bridle as well as to any other objects that might frighten it. Instead of seeing how fast the horse could run when she first mounted it, she tested how it would stop and turn. She loved to run fast, but that came later when Georgia felt certain she had control over a horse.

The horses weren't the only thing he liked about the MacBaye Ranch. He liked the soft bed and staying in one place. The Cheyenne moved often, usually because they had to follow game or flee their enemies. It seemed in recent years they often moved to hide from the white soldiers. Gray Wolf also liked feeling that he belonged to a family. Since he and his older sister were orphaned as children when their parents caught the white man's disease, Lean Bear, his mother's brother, had cared for him. When the buffalo were plentiful, all was well, but Gray Wolf couldn't help feeling the resentment of Lean Bear's squaw when she had to share scarce supplies with him.

He enjoyed the generosity and laughter of the MacBaye household, but most of all, he liked Georgia. She was tough and tenacious, yet beautiful and feminine. She could do most anything, and her resourcefulness never ceased to amaze him. She had worked tirelessly alongside Loraine to pull him from near death back to strength and robust health. Most of all, she made him laugh.

He knew Lean Bear had risked much to bring him to Loraine MacBaye a year ago, so he believed his uncle cared for him. He also knew the buffalo were fewer and fewer. Had Lean Bear intended to leave him forever with the white man? Had Lean Bear's squaw nagged him until he agreed to abandon Gray Wolf to the whites, or had Lean Bear feared that the young brave might starve to death or be killed if he remained with the Cheyenne? He wished he knew, for already he had begun to think like the settlers.

Thomas taught him how to raise crops and cattle. He liked the way the whites prepared and stored food to keep them nourished all winter. He liked learning to read, and he had to admit that he even liked "the book." Deep in his soul, Gray Wolf, like all Indians, knew there was a Wise One Above. Thomas told him that people didn't have to appease the Wise One Above through rituals or by cutting their bodies. Rather, they could come boldly before Him and make their requests known to Him. Thomas said the Wise One Above had sent His Son to the people to save Indians and whites alike and that anyone who thought he could do enough good things to earn heaven was arrogant.

Indeed, if all white men were like Thomas MacBaye, Gray Wolf imagined himself becoming one of them. But all white men were not like Thomas.

✷

As the sun set on the third day of the trip, the MacBayes' traveling train of twelve wagons drew within view of Denver City. Thomas had explained to the family that the city was first established as St. Charles, a settlement that had sprung up nearly overnight when gold was discovered in Cherry Creek. While the Cheyenne counted wealth in horses, Thomas had explained that the prospect of finding gold and becoming rich lured all types of men and even a few women to Denver and its surrounding mining fields. Men wanted for crimes back East and those fleeing their homes for other reasons joined upstanding citizens in a frenzied search for gold. The frenzied prospectors sought the glistening nuggets, hoping to become rich and famous, Thomas had tried to explain. For some, it wasn't even wealth they sought, but the anticipated thrill of discovering something rare and valuable. Whatever their motivation, whatever it was from which they had fled, they worked tirelessly, many losing their health or even their lives to peril, illness and exhaustion.

Gray Wolf had heard Lean Bear and the other elders talk about what to do with the infestation of whites. Lean Bear had urged the elders not to worry, reminding them how they had traded with the whites for guns, ammunition, blankets, coffee, flour and sugar. He reminded them that many of the white men had taken Indian wives and had treated Indians with honor. The Cheyenne opposing the whites, mostly young braves eager to prove themselves in war, argued that they were driving away the buffalo and other game. They wanted to fight the whites, rather than talk peace with them. Gray Wolf couldn't disagree that the treaties the Cheyenne chiefs had been persuaded to sign benefitted the whites much more than the Indians. Each peace agreement further reduced Cheyenne hunting grounds and rarely delivered the promised supplies to compensate them for the loss.

"Why these men want gold?" Gray Wolf asked Thomas, seeing little value in a shiny rock that could neither be eaten nor used to fashion weapons.

"I find the frenzied search for gold that consumes such men

odd. But then again," Thomas said, "who am I to think critically of them when I have felt and followed a similar drive to go west and become a rancher."

Gray Wolf could see that it was fortunate for the gold prospectors that Thomas and men like him worked the land and hunted game, for without the farmers and ranchers, the prospectors would have starved.

Chapter 5

Georgia knew it had been a good year at the ranch. They had twice as many cattle to market, and even though they kept back more wheat and corn than before, they still had twenty-five additional bushels of wheat and a wagonful of corn to sell. Her mother hadn't been crazy about giving up her sleeping spot in the wagon to the grain, but Pa had joked that he would make up for having his Southern belle sleep on the ground for nearly a week by buying her all the calicos and knitting yarn she wanted. He told Georgia he might even find a porcelain tea set like the one she had left behind in South Carolina.

Many of the young adults and children—with the exception of James, Henry, Georgia, and one other family—had not seen a city before. Compared to Charleston, Philadelphia, or even St. Louis, Denver was little more than a big watering hole, but it was the center of commerce and a considerable change in scenery for the plains dwellers. The skyline included a few grander homes and storefronts, including a bank and a church, but most of the structures were hastily and shoddily constructed shanties, which housed gold prospectors. It wasn't always the case that gold seekers could not afford better homes, rather, Pa said they didn't want to take the time away from prospecting that it would take to build better dwellings.

Denver sat in a shallow valley, nestled at the foot of the towering Rocky Mountains. As the travelers approached the city, they could see the majestic, snow-capped Rockies enveloping the small hamlet, the way a mother hugs a brood of children. Beyond was the clear, bright-blue sky.

The travelers had set up camp on the edge of the city. They pulled their wagons into a protective circle, a formation all of them had learned as they traveled by wagon train to their homes on the plains. The adults had to exercise considerable effort to focus their children's efforts on setting up camp. The children begged to go into the city, anxious to see this exciting world.

Following a supper of beef, beans, cornbread and dried fruit, all warmed up over a campfire from their noon meal, the MacBayes and Gray Wolf unrolled their bedrolls on the ground next to their wagon, as they had done every night of the journey.

In the middle of the night, the MacBayes awoke when Marie Baker's father, who had clearly spent the last several hours at one of Denver's many saloons, barged in. "Hazel, where's my supper. I need my supper and libation now, woman," shouted the drunk, stumbling into the camp circle as he bumped into Gray Wolf, who was just waking up.

"Hazel, get my gun. There's a stinkin' redskin heathen here. He's likely to kill and scalp us all by mornin'."

"Quiet, Charlie," begged Hazel in a low but urgent voice. "He's with the MacBayes, remember? No threat to any of us."

"If yur not gonna get my gun so I can shoot him, I'll git it m'self."

Charlie reached into the front of his wagon, which was next to the MacBayes' wagon, and pulled out his rifle, swinging it around into Gray Wolf's chest. His action was so abrupt and aggressive that it caught all of them by surprise. Pa and James sprang to their feet and moved around behind the gun-wielding drunk. Like most drunks, Charlie was unable to focus on more than one thing at a time, making it possible for Pa and James to apprehend Charlie and grab his rifle without incident. He soon forgot about "the Injun," as Hazel hustled him off to sleep. As a precaution, Pa put Charlie's rifle as well as a pistol he found in his neighbor's wagon, safely under the seat of the MacBaye wagon.

Georgia had heard that Charlie liked his liquor, but even so, it did not account for his sudden turn of violence toward Gray Wolf. Pa told them he suspected Charlie had gotten more than liquor at the saloons he patronized.

"I hope tonight's incident isn't a foretaste of things to come," Pa mumbled as they settled back onto their bedrolls.

※

Despite the disruption in the middle of the night, most of the group was up early, making breakfast and preparing to go into the city to conduct business. At the insistence of her mother, Georgia put on a clean dress after running a wet cloth over her face, neck and arms. Ma combed and plaited her long, wavy auburn hair into a single braid. Georgia knew that if she didn't find some excuse to leave, her mother would continue until she looked as silly as a courting grouse. She would pin Georgia's hair to the back of her head in a tight bun with delicate combs. Next she would make sure Georgia's fingernails were cleaned, filed and polished with her little pumice rock. She might even try to paint Georgia's eyes with her kohl pencils. No, Georgia wouldn't have it. Clean and neat she could do, but painted and prissy, that was taking it just too far.

"Now that's lovely," purred Ma as she accentuated Georgia's already rosy cheeks with her rouge. "You're such a lovely young lady, just a touch of kohl, and—"

At that moment, Gray Wolf returned from the creek bank where the horses were tethered. He had cut his hair. It hung just above the shoulders in the length of the settler men. He was dressed in work pants and a cream-colored shirt Georgia recognized as her father's. He wore his own deerskin boots and the porcupine quill and turkey feather decorated buckskin jacket, which hung on him like it belonged to a much older brother when he first arrived at the MacBaye Ranch. The jacket displayed his broad shoulders and powerful chest in a way that made her blush. His skin was no darker than the settlers who had spent hours in the sun, working the land or cowboying. The only feature that set him apart was the prominent bone structure of his face and fierce handsomeness.

Georgia's musings were interrupted when Gray Wolf shouted, "Sorrel has small cut on foot."

Georgia rejoiced at having a legitimate reason to flee her mother's rouge and kohl. She grabbed her pouch of herbs and wraps and hurried to the creek bank. Her sorrel filly had managed to cut itself across the right back fetlock. It looked like another horse had kicked her. The cut was superficial, but it needed attention. She added crushed apple tree leaves and aloe to beef tallow to make an antibiotic rub. The filly, who first tried to move away from Georgia's treatment, eventually relaxed, allowing her to slather the herbal rub over the wound.

"Georgia good medicine woman. Like mother," Gray Wolf said proudly as Georgia reorganized her pouch.

She smiled at him, enjoying his admiration. Later she would chide herself. Gray Wolf was practically a brother to her. She felt chagrined for the not-so-occasional fluttering in her chest every time he paid attention to her, yet not wishing to disrupt the feeling, Georgia helped Gray Wolf groom the sorrel filly. Then she handed him the bridle, and he slid the bit into the filly's mouth and tied the leather throat latch to keep the bridle in place. Next she handed him the saddle blanket, followed by the saddle. She knew using a saddle was an adjustment for him; he preferred to ride bareback, as most Indians were accustomed to doing.

Later, Georgia watched as Gray Wolf and her brothers

herded the cattle into the army corrals. From there they would go to the army commissary to negotiate prices for their cattle, grain and tanned hides. Georgia admired her father's shrewd business acumen. He also would check with the general store and several brokers to see where the best price and terms were likely to be had. Then he would drive a hard bargain for the fruits of their labor. It was a skill he had learned and perfected as a plantation owner before coming West.

And so the day went. Georgia had great interest in commerce, yet another trait that perplexed her mother. It was Georgia, rather than one or both of her brothers, who accompanied her father as he went from the U.S. Army commissary to the general store to two other places of business to bargain for a good price for his grain and hides. Despite his ability to hold a poker face when bargaining, Georgia could tell that the prices quoted were higher than he expected. He nearly took the officer's offer, telling him he liked the price quote but wished to check around before making a decision. It was a good thing he did, because the officer's bid was barely more than half the final price Pa settled on.

"It doesn't look like buying you that new saddle will be any problem at all, little girl." Pa was almost giddy as the last merchant counted out his payment in coins and bills. "Whadid I tell ya, but we'd do well this year," Pa continued, as he and Georgia made their way to where the boys and Georgia's mom waited. "The miners must be so crazed lookin' for gold that they don't have time for growing food. The prices for just about everything near' doubled."

As Pa doled out three gold pieces to each of the boys and Georgia, he said, "Ya'll have worked hard along with your Ma and me, and we already decided that you'd each have a share."

Georgia noticed that James scowled when her father gave Gray Wolf his handful of coins. "Don't be feelin' like them coins are gonna burn a hole in your pockets, now. Spend wisely."

She knew James would be off to find a new rifle. Henry was more likely to buy books and drawing supplies. It was clear looking at the perplexed expression on his face that Gray Wolf had no idea what to do with his coins. She motioned him to follow her, as she and her parents walked toward the business district of the city.

"Oh, Thomas, look. See the sign? There, across the street, it's a doctor's clinic," Ma said, excited about her find. "I'd like to stop and see if the good Dr. Williams indicated on the sign that he might sell me some herbs I can't get out on the plains."

Georgia accompanied her mother into the clinic, while Gray Wolf and Pa waited for them on the street outside the building. Dr. Herald Williams seemed happy to sell Ma white willow bark, a pain reliever, chamomile for digestion problems and dried cranberries from back East to stave off scurvy during the winter months when vegetables and fruit were scarce. He also suggested Ma keep laudanum on hand. He said it was a strong medicine for pain relief.

Less than twenty minutes later, Georgia and her mother left the clinic with their purchases and joined the men. From there, they walked several blocks to the commercial district of the city. They had their pick of several general mercantile establishments. They chose a large, freshly painted store with a broad wooden porch front. When they opened the door, a bell attached to the hinge signaled to the owner he had customers.

Ma asked the mercantile operator for everything on her supply list: white sugar, coffee, yarn, knitting needles, yards and yards of calico, lace, new shoes or boots for each of them, a new cast-iron skillet, thread, needles, buttons and snaps. Pa bought ammunition and other supplies while urging his wife to buy the china tea set she had been eyeing. Georgia observed with amusement that they were more excited than a couple of kids on Christmas Eve.

"Can't help but noticin' the accent, folks," the shopkeeper said as he wrapped their purchases. "I'm guessing you're mighty glad you got out of the South when you did."

"We're happy to have settled in Colorado Territory," Ma drawled, still focused on her shopping.

"I reckon the South with its plantations and all isn't too keen on President Lincoln's emancipation of the Negro slaves. They say it's their right to own slaves, and ain't no Northerners goin' tell 'em otherwise. South Carolina was the first to announce they wud be sucedin' from the Union, and soon afterwards the other Southern states joined 'em."

"Are the Rebel forces still prevailing?" Pa asked, joining the conversation.

"Seems that way for the most part," the shopkeeper said, assembling the MacBayes' long list of supplies.

"I can't really support the Rebel cause, but it's a little difficult to know our former friends and neighbors are at war with the rest of the country." Pa fingered several boxes of ammunition and added two of them to the MacBayes' growing mound of supplies. "At least out West we're away from the mess."

"Not entirely. They're calling for boys to join up from all over the North so as they can force them Rebs into submission. Even been rumors they be calling our boys out here to fight."

"Will James and Henry have to fight, or you, Daddy?" Georgia asked.

"Don't you worry now, young lady. Ain't likely yur kinfolk'll be asked ta join up. Besides, we're soon to be at war with them Injuns," the shopkeeper snorted, and then turned red in the face when he saw Gray Wolf standing with the MacBayes.

"What kinda Indian trouble you talkin' about?" Pa asked.

"Them Injuns showing up everywhere, on the wagon trail paths, on ranches, at the back steps of homes just outside the city."

"Has anyone been injured?"

"No, not yet. Right now they's just asking for food and all, but just give 'em time, and they'll be raping women and murdering settlers."

"Don't ya think that's a pretty big jump from begging food to murdering? I do know a lot of them Indians are hungry. The buffalo herds they depended on before whites came west have dwindled to almost nothing, and the game is over hunted as well." Pa glanced at Gray Wolf, as if to say he was the authority on the statement.

"Things are changin' and everyone just has ta get used ta it. Why, I expect the Fightin' Parson won't take kindly to Indians scaring our women and children," the shopkeeper said, looking up from his tablet where he added the prices of the MacBayes' purchases.

"Who's that you say?" Pa said, leaning on the counter as Ma continued to accumulate supplies.

"The Fightin' Parson they call him. Haven't you heard about Colonel John Chivington?" The mercantile owner didn't wait for a response. "He and his men protected us all from them blasted Southern rebels at Glorieta Pass down in New Mexico. Some Texans was coming our way, fightin' for the South they was, and Chivington found their supply trains and blew 'em all up good. For his good soldiering, he's been named Commander of Colorado Territory."

"Guess I hadn't heard that."

"Yessiree, happened just about a month ago now. Chivington came riding into Denver City, pledging to take on our Injun troubles."

Georgia left to join Gray Wolf, who had spotted hunting knives in one of the glass display cases. As she asked the shopkeeper to show him the selection of knives, she noticed poorly veiled disgust, or was it fear, on the shopkeeper's face. "Come on, Gray Wolf, let's see what is in the shop across the street."

The two walked to a smaller general store where they found a similar selection of hunting knives and asked to see them. The lady minding the store called her husband out to wait on them. He shifted from foot to foot, looking at Gray Wolf's fringed jacket instead of his face when he spoke. Moving at a turtle's pace, he brought out the tray of knives from behind the glass display case.

"My brother is a paying customer." Georgia hated the rudeness and distrust they demonstrated by their reluctance to wait on Gray Wolf.

"I have no doubt." The shopkeeper's eyes raked over Gray Wolf. "I sure would hate to have my knife used to kill and scalp one of our settlers."

Georgia wasn't sure if Gray Wolf understood the conversation until he spoke to the shopkeeper. "No. Only hunting and skinning animals. We go." The last part was directed at Georgia.

Rather than stew over the injustice, Georgia entered a livery and asked for a recommendation of a quality saddler. They were directed to a shop several blocks away, into a section of town that was more recently—and more hastily—built. Georgia found that the store carried a nice variety of quality tack. About an hour later she left, with Gray Wolf carrying a saddle that would be all her own. She had asked the friendly saddle maker for a recommendation for a more accommodating mercantile, explaining that Gray Wolf wanted to buy a hunting knife. The owner of the mercantile was, as promised by the saddle maker, glad to sell to an Indian. Gray Wolf purchased a knife and some fur-lined leather gloves.

As they walked toward the older part of town where the MacBayes had left their team and wagon, Georgia noticed people were staring at them, not just at Gray Wolf but at both of them.

"What's a pretty little thing like yourself doing with a heathen redskin?" a man with a half-emptied whiskey bottle slurred, stumbling toward her. She saw others nod in agreement.

"He's my brother," Georgia spat back.

"Once a redskin, always a redskin," shouted a woman. "Besides, he stinks like the animal he is."

"We've been traveling for a week now, can't bathe proper, ma'am. Besides we're ranchers, not uppity city folk."

Georgia was about to launch into her survival-on-the-plains speech and how everyone had to work together and learn from each other when Gray Wolf put his hand on the back of her arm and turned her away from the crowd. "Not safe here," he said.

As they walked back toward the wagon, crossing through the more established area of town, the stares and rude comments continued. Georgia breathed a sigh of relief when they turned the corner where the wagon was tethered. She was further relieved to see that her father, mother, James and Henry were there, waiting for them.

The conversation was lively and enthusiastic as the MacBayes returned to their campsite. All except Georgia and Gray Wolf chatted, reveling in the family's economic prosperity and the new goods they purchased. The aggressive cruelty toward Gray Wolf and Georgia's loyalty endeared them to one another even more, but it also brought into question their status as a family.

"White people hate me, hate Cheyenne," Gray Wolf said to her later that evening when they were alone.

"Some white people hate Indians, but they're … ignorant. Not all white people are like them, Gray Wolf," Georgia said. But she couldn't get the hatred and danger she felt directed at Gray Wolf, and by association, at her, off her mind.

Chapter 6

Early the next morning the plains families packed their wagons and left Denver. As soon as the wagons and horses were back on the prairie, Gray Wolf felt his tension eased, but the experience had seeded a permanent ambivalence toward whites. Georgia also carried the experience deep within her. She was seething.

The new saddle was a perfect fit for Georgia's filly. The fresh oil job accentuated the intricate tooled design of the leather, making it glisten in the sun. Had Georgia not been so preoccupied with the hostility she and Gray Wolf had just experienced, she would have breathed in the earthy smell of the leather and felt the comfort of the slightly padded seat. Instead of reveling in the expanse of ever greening prairie, Georgia thought about what had happened the previous afternoon as she and Gray Wolf shopped.

It was no surprise that the long days of riding and the trauma that resulted from the filly cutting its fetlock were taking a toll on the young horse. They had fallen behind the other riders.

Gray Wolf seemed uninterested in waiting for her, so she pulled her mount back slower still until she was alongside her family's wagon.

"Can I ride in the wagon with you and Pa? I need to rest the filly. It's a long trip for her, being as young as she is and all."

"Sure, honey, your father and I would love your company. Jump on up," Loraine said, boosting her daughter onto the wagon seat. Georgia was already taller and heavier than her mother, but she thought Loraine still saw her as the little girl with pigtails that ran beside the wagon when the MacBayes first made their way out West. "You've changed so much since we left South Carolina," her mother drawled, more to herself than to Georgia.

"Like your Pa you were made for this country. You are strong and adventuresome. You would have been a horrible Southern belle," Ma chuckled.

Georgia didn't know if it was a compliment or condemnation. She had always felt compelled to hide from her mother her desires to explore the outdoors, ride horses and hunt game. Otherwise, her mother chided her for "unladylike" behavior. How could she, the tomboy, ever please her mother?

"Until a few years ago, I envisioned you as a young woman, strolling the massive grounds of Spring Grove, entertaining guests in our ballroom, but instead you live in an adobe ranch house with almost no social life outside our family. I always saw you wearing elegant ball gowns and graduating from a lady's finishing school. Instead, you wear dresses made from calico, work hard with your hands and are schooled at my kitchen table."

Georgia remembered Spring Grove. It was a place and a lifestyle far back in her past and one to which she couldn't imagine returning. Though the MacBaye children had been delighted to learn they would be settling out West, the decision had been abrupt and unexplained. She hesitated to bring it up, as though the discussion might make her parents change their minds about moving West, but Georgia's curiosity got the best of her.

"Ma, why didn't Old Jeb and his family come out to the West with us? I miss him sometimes."

"Do you remember when we studied the writings of Frederick Douglass this winter? When you were a little girl, I read his writing as well as his and other's arguments against slavery, and your father and I decided to sell the plantation, free the slaves and move West."

"You mean Old Jeb was our slave?" The realization hit her hard.

"Why, yes, Georgia. All plantations are run by slaves."

"Rosie, Charles, Jeremiah ... they were all slaves? We owned them?"

"That's right, Georgia. I ... I couldn't be a slave owner, and your father, well, he had always wanted to homestead, so we struck a deal of sorts."

Pa joined the conversation. "When Ma demanded we sell out and free our slaves, I thought it was a preposterous proposal, as rash and foolish as the Biblical account of Esau selling his birthright to Jacob for a bowl of stew. As it turned out, we willingly gave up what we would have lost by now anyway. And we're out of harm's way. Ma's a clever woman, Georgia!"

"What happened to all our ... ah ...," she stumbled, the word being thick and distasteful for her to say, "slaves?"

"We freed them, Georgia. It was the right thing to do. Their lives will not be easy, but they are free."

"Where did they go? Do they still work at Spring Grove?"

"We don't rightly know," Pa said. "The man who bought Spring Grove said he would give any that wanted to work for him a job, but I don't think he would treat them very well. The neighboring plantation owners probably wouldn't want to hire any of them, either."

"Why don't you know what happened to the slaves, Pa, and why wouldn't our neighbors hire them?

"We knew that once the neighbors learned we had freed all our slaves, neighboring plantation owners would be angry with us and might try to keep us from doing what we had decided, so we gave all seventy-three of our slaves their freedmen papers the morning we boarded the train to come West. Even our families refuse to write us for what we did."

"But, why, Pa? We did the right thing, didn't we?

"For those who wanted to keep slavery the law of the land, what we did was unconscionable. Our decision no doubt made it even more difficult for our neighbors to keep their slaves under submission. We knew it was like starting a fire in our pasture that was bound to spread to our neighbors' fields. We regret causing problems, but your mother was so determined ... and now I know, she was right."

Georgia felt shocked and a little embarrassed that her parents had been slave owners. Old Jeb had been so kind to her. He taught her to work with horses. He told her to honor her parents. She felt stunned.

Ma squeezed her shoulder. "Don't hate me."

"I couldn't hate you, Ma. I'm so glad you did the right thing. I could never have been happy at Spring Grove."

"Plantation life would have stifled you, as it did your father. He always loved your enthusiasm and skill as an agriculturist. I loved his involvement in your life, so I grudgingly permitted you to wear boy's overalls and spend most of your free time in the fields or at the horse barn. From the time you were young, your father told me it was you, my daughter, who had a sense of how to get animals to move where you wanted them. You spent hours down at the livery, observing and learning all you could from the stable boys and Old Jeb. You know, at first, the Negroes felt very uncomfortable with your presence in the horse barn, but they soon responded to your genuine desire to learn and help with the horses."

Now Georgia understood why the everything-needs-to-be-so-proper mother of hers had ended up in Colorado Territory. "Ma, you gave up so much to settle here."

"If you count riches and things, you are right, my dear," Loraine said. "But I wouldn't trade Spring Grove and all its trappings for the joy I see in my husband and children. You, Pa, James were made for this country. Henry is the only one I could imagine enjoying plantation life."

Her sense of pride that her parents had freed their slaves was overwhelmed by the guilt she felt from being a member of a slave-owning family. Maybe guilt wasn't the right word, because one should not feel guilt if he had not committed a wrong. As far as she knew, the settlers agreed that slavery in America should be abolished. What would they think if they knew her parents had owned slaves? What would Gray Wolf think of them if he knew they had owned slaves? Shame washed over her. It was a good thing Gray Wolf had ridden on ahead. Then another thought, a horrifying one, occurred to her: *If Gray Wolf lived in South Carolina, would a plantation owner have made him a slave?*

✳

The settlers were in high spirits as they traveled toward their homes on the Eastern Plains, but Gray Wolf continued to feel troubled. It wasn't anything they did to put him ill at ease. They invited him to join them in hunting rabbits and the plentiful pronghorn antelope. The last afternoon of the trip, the settlers decided to set up camp early near some springs, so that the young people could enjoy a swim. Gray Wolf waded through the cool water, but felt none of the camaraderie he had previously experienced.

He expected rambunctious, daring Georgia to be running through the edges of the springs by now, diving into the water, and splashing him and the others, but she stood by herself at the edge of the water. He still wasn't sure what had changed, only that he felt an impenetrable gulf between himself and the settlers, between himself and the MacBayes, and most disturbingly, between himself and Georgia. It all had to do with Denver City. How he wished they had never gone there.

Gray Wolf continued to feel like an outsider peering into a

stranger's campfire, seeking the warmth of the fire yet not daring to come close enough to enjoy it. If the overwhelming sense of not belonging was an enemy, he didn't know how to fight it.

At nightfall, the MacBayes and Gray Wolf devoured a supper of beef stew and Loraine's cornbread baked to a perfect golden hue. Because they made camp at midday, the dried beef, potatoes and carrots, seasoned with prairie sage and onions, had cooked all afternoon. Even with the heavy stew filling his belly and the night crisp and quiet, sleep eluded Gray Wolf.

※

The settlers broke camp the next morning, knowing it was their last day on the trail. By noon, most of the wagons, including that of the MacBayes, had split off to head for their respective ranches. Gray Wolf noticed that Georgia rode her sorrel filly.

"Let's go home by way of the bluffs. It's a beautiful view," Georgia implored her father. He agreed, although it meant a strenuous climb up the back side of the bluffs, rather than circling around them. Gray Wolf hoped spunky Georgia was back, but she made no effort to bring him into her conversation. He hoped she would challenge him to some death-defying feat, as she was wont to do, but she did not. She continued to trot the filly alongside the wagon.

Cresting the ridge of bluffs, the entire MacBaye Ranch was in sight, but that was not all that was visible. Gray Wolf knew immediately the identity of the visitors. He also knew why they had come. As they neared the ranch, he could see that Lean Bear rode his best horse and was decked out in full regalia. No doubt, he wanted to impress the MacBayes. He knew his uncle wouldn't want the white medicine woman to think he was an ordinary Cheyenne warrior. He was a chief.

"Pa, are those the same Indians that brought Gray Wolf to our doorstep?" Georgia asked. "I wonder why ...," she said, trailing off as realization sunk in.

Since leaving Denver City, Gray Wolf had decided that he

must return to the Cheyenne. He didn't belong in the white man's world. He thought about how he would secure a horse. He certainly wouldn't take one from the MacBayes or anyone else without asking, and he thought it unseemly to ask them to give him one. A horse was no longer a problem. Lean Bear had brought several extra mounts.

The MacBayes and Gray Wolf picked up their pace and soon were in the yard of the ranch house. Gray Wolf greeted his uncle, not with a handshake or an affectionate hug he had learned from the MacBayes, but with a respectful salute.

"I am glad to find you well," his uncle said in Cheyenne. "I knew you would live."

"I am very well, thanks to the healer," said Gray Wolf, the Cheyenne words rolling off his tongue like butter from the springhouse. The stoic, restrained emotion all Cheyenne exercised when talking with an elder, even a close relative, now seemed strange to him. He would miss the warmness of the MacBayes. He wanted to ask Lean Bear why he had not come sooner, but that would have been disrespectful.

Lean Bear turned to Thomas and Loraine and spoke English. "You, very good medicine woman. I bring gifts to thank you healing Gray Wolf."

He directed the men accompanying him to give Loraine a beautiful, tanned buffalo hide. On her father, Lean Bear bestowed a fine bow and three arrows, perfectly balanced and adorned with turkey feathers.

Thomas ran his hand over the strong but flexible willow wood. The bow was carved, sanded and decorated with care. "We cherish your gifts. The Cheyenne are fine craftsmen."

Gray Wolf knew his uncle's understanding of English was limited, so he turned to him and spoke in Cheyenne. Lean Bear's face showed he was pleased with the praise Thomas spoke.

"We would like you to join us for supper. Won't be much seeing as how we've been gone for over a week, but we'd be obliged if you'd eat with us."

Gray Wolf translated Thomas's invitation, and Lean Bear

responded in Cheyenne. Gray Wolf turned to Thomas. "Lean Bear is grateful for your invitation, but wants to return to Cheyenne camp while still light. He thanks you much for keeping me ... as your own son. I told him you treat me like a son." Gray Wolf swallowed hard.

Lean Bear spoke again to Gray Wolf. This time he did not translate his uncle's words. "I get my things. We leave soon. Lean Bear is in a hurry."

Loraine followed Gray Wolf to the house and into his sleeping area. "The fur is yours to take. You may want to use it to carry your belongings. I'm going to get you some of that mint tea you like so much, and you can take a little jar of the berry preserves to share with your family." Her voice quivered and fell off.

Returning to the yard, he said his goodbyes to James and Henry. Thomas grasped him around the shoulders with his right arm. "We'll miss ya terrible. Now, you can't leave without sayin' goodbye to Georgia. She's in the barn."

Georgia was sitting on the three-legged stool she used when she milked Blue Bell, but the cow was dry and out on pasture. Strong, brave Georgia seemed so alone sitting there in the milking stall. He squatted on the ground beside her, and finally, she looked at him through tear-brimmed red eyes. "Why do you have to leave, Gray Wolf?"

"Georgia, we knew this day would come. I wish we'd had more time, but—"

"I want you to take the sorrel filly. She's a fine horse and nearly trained."

"The filly is yours, Georgia. You love her. You teach me to train. I can do this with my uncle's horses, with my horses."

Georgia nodded and then flung her arms around his neck. "You must come back."

Already he felt his heart strings pulling him back. He must go before he could not pull himself away from her. "Goodbye, Georgia. You're a good friend, a good sister."

Chapter 7

Georgia ran to the hitching post where the filly stood patiently, unsaddled but with the bridle still in place. She mounted and kicked the young horse into an all-out run. When they reached the top of the bluffs, both were panting hard, the filly because she had run uphill for more than a mile, Georgia because her body convulsed from sobbing. The shame she felt since learning that her family had owned slaves had caused her to distance herself from Gray Wolf, but she didn't want him to leave.

I didn't even get a chance to tell him we're not like that anymore. She took a deep breath in a vain attempt to halt the trembling. Squeezing her eyes shut, she leaned forward over the young horse's crest and mane. She loved the sweet "horse" smell, unrivaled by any other, but the sensation distracted her only for a second.

It was dusk and the warmth of the spring day was gone. She heard a coyote howl, then a series of yipping from multiple coyotes, signaling they had been successful in bagging a rabbit or prairie dog. She shuddered. It was the way of life on the prairie, but she always pitied the terrified animal hunted down by the coyotes. Her ma would have had her hide if she'd known Georgia was far from the house by herself, but she wasn't ready to go back. She nudged her mount at the girth on one side and moved the reins in her left hand to the opposite side, signaling the filly to turn. She then squeezed with her lower legs, directing her mount to move forward down the bluff. Once the duo reached the creek, instead of crossing and returning to the ranch house, she used the same gentle, almost imperceptible cues to direct the filly to walk south along the creek.

She wanted to scream, to cry out to God, to ask him why He had allowed Gray Wolf to leave them. In that moment, she remembered Old Jeb's words at an earlier sorrow. She had been just five or six years old when her old dog, Patch, died.

"Little missy, you jus' go 'head now and ask the Heavn'ly Father why he's a taking dat der dog from you. He's a big god. He can take you screamin' out to 'im. You gotta know how very much He still cares 'bout you, little one."

Just as the words calmed her then, they brought peace now. That wasn't all. An idea she had for several years popped into her head, as though it was the title of one of Ma's schoolbooks. She thought it strange the idea of going to medical school had come as such a strong yearning during this time of angst. The desire to learn more about modern medicine, to help those in need, had been in her mind and heart for as long as she could remember, but tonight it was all she could think about.

Her sorrow at losing Gray Wolf wasn't gone, but it was accompanied by confident assurance of what she needed to do next.

She shivered. The cold spring night had chilled her to the bone. What had she been thinking to leave without even donning a coat? Before she had time to chide herself anymore, she saw a light and realized that the filly—without any direction from Georgia—had carried her home.

"Good girl, Cheyenne," she said, patting and praising the

filly. *Cheyenne.* That's what she would call the sorrel filly. It was a fitting tribute to Gray Wolf and his proud tribe.

At the barn, Georgia dismounted and brushed the sweat off Cheyenne. She checked to make sure the filly hadn't picked up any stones in her feet on the trek to and from the bluffs and back along the creek. She slipped the bridle over the horse's ears and turned her into the corral. She would let her out to graze in the morning.

As she turned to go to the house, she saw one of the oil lamps the MacBayes used to light their way at night coming toward her.

"Georgia! You're home. We were worried. Where were you all this time?" Pa shouted his relief at her return.

"I'm sorry, Pa. I didn't mean to worry you. I just ... well ... I was so upset about Gray Wolf leaving that I had to be alone to think."

"I was caught off-guard too, Georgia. I'd begun to think of him as a third son, but it wasn't really logical to think he wouldn't rejoin his people eventually. He seemed content to live here with us, but he seemed just as happy to leave. I don't get it. I never took Gray Wolf to be the type to let others make his decisions for him."

"Me either, Pa," Georgia said. Her teeth chattered from the cold.

"Good lands, child, you don't even have a coat. Git yurself in that house before ya freeze to death."

"Yes, Pa."

How long had she been gone? The rest of the family had eaten and cleaned up. Ma warmed up some beans and cornbread for her to eat.

"Ma, I know what I want to do," she said as she downed the last of the beans.

"What do you mean, Georgia?"

"I want to study medicine. You've taught me all the herbal remedies, to set broken bones, and how to diagnose and treat so many maladies, but I want to know more about modern medicine. I've read about antibiotics, surgeries and anesthesia. I want to learn how to use these to help people."

"I thought you ran that horse up the bluff like a crazy woman because you were bothered with Gray Wolf leaving, but it was about medical school?"

"No, well, I mean, yes, I ran off because I was upset about him leaving us. Then I got to thinkin' what Old Jeb told me when Patch died, how God cares about me and is in control of it and all, and then the next thought I had was how very badly I want to attend medical school. It's not so strange, you know. I've talked before about it."

"Yes, Georgia, you have, but you were younger. I figured it was no more than a whim. It seems more of a certainty now. Am I right?"

"You are, Ma."

Ma considered her daughter and confessed: "Before I met your Pa, I had aspirations of becoming a doctor. My father's friend, Dr. Samuel Dickson, had a practice back in South Carolina. I loved to visit his office. Even if I had succeeded in convincing my parents to let me pursue my dream, medical schools didn't admit women, but things are different now. It's been over ten years since Elizabeth Blackwell earned her medical degree from Geneva College in New York City."

"Really, Ma, a woman doctor?"

"Oh, yes, Georgia, since Dr. Blackwell broke that ground, several women have earned degrees in medicine."

"I want to learn more, but New York is very far away."

"Case Western Reserve University in Cleveland has a fine medical school. It admits women now, but you would need more university study before you could apply to attend."

Georgia sighed. "Cleveland is more than halfway to New York. I want to stay out West."

Ma appeared deep in thought, then a half-smile formed on her face the way it did when she thought of something clever to say. "Do you remember Dr. Williams, the doctor in Denver City whose office we visited just last week? He had a small school for students, and he let them work alongside him just the way you learned from me."

"I do remember, Ma. Maybe we can write him. I'll get my quill and parchment."

※

Two months later, Mr. Johnson stopped in to the MacBaye Ranch on his way back from Limon with an envelope for Georgia. It had the return address of Dr. Harold Williams, Denver, Colorado Territory. She ripped it open with chastisement from her mother to take care lest she tear the letter. She read it out loud.

June 30th, 1863

Dear Miss MacBaye,

I do remember your mother and you. She wanted to prevent her family from developing scurvy. Your mother was wise to purchase the herbs and dried cranberries. She is well advanced in her understanding of human health, and I am pleased to hear that you are following in her footsteps. The rural areas of this territory are much in need of this advanced medical ability.

Although your request to join our school gave me pause, as I have never received such a request from a young lady, I believe you are passionate about the study of medicine. Furthermore, after meeting you this spring and reading your letter, I am confident that you possess a basic medical knowledge and the desire to learn, both of which are vital for success. I am, thus, pleased to invite you to study here at my clinic. Your tuition, room and board will be ten dollars per month, a steep amount, perhaps, but you will easily make ten dollars each month administering medical treatment to patients under my tutelage, following the first two months of book study. If this is acceptable to you, you will want to travel to Denver later this summer, so that you will be ready to start your studies in the fall. Classes begin the 15th of September.

Sincerely,
Dr. Harold Williams

Georgia whooped. "I've been accepted," she said, waving the letter in the air and twirling her mother around in a circle as if on a dance floor.

✖

On the appointed day in late August, Georgia rose before dawn. Ma prepared the normal breakfast of eggs and fried potatoes, but Georgia was too excited to eat a single bite. She kissed her mother and brothers goodbye. Her father would ride with her to a stagecoach and wagon train stop called Limon. She remembered that they had stopped there on their trip west. It was the point where the MacBayes and several other families left the wagon train and traveled south and west to find land for their homesteads.

Pa assured Ma that at the Limon stop he would be able to find a wagon train on its way to Denver. He would make arrangements with the wagon train boss to see that she was safely delivered to Dr. Williams's school.

Earlier in the summer, Pa and Ma had asked around for neighbors who might be traveling from the Bijou Basin to Denver in late August. Allowing Georgia to travel by herself to Denver was out of the question. Lone travelers were much more likely to be robbed, kidnapped or killed by outlaws. And rumors held that Indian attacks had increased as well. Try as they might, it seemed no one from the Bijou Basin planned to travel to Denver in August. Pa had been ready to cancel the trip, suggesting that Georgia write Dr. Williams to ask for a year's extension on the invitation to attend his school, when she convinced him they could make the trip to Limon together and then look for traveling companions.

Georgia and Pa left early, riding hard to the northeast toward Limon. Though armed with rifles and riding strong, swift mounts, they felt urgency in their travel. They stopped only to water their horses. Even headstrong Georgia, with her throw-caution-to-the-wind approach, felt relief when they crested a hill and spotted the modest stop less than a mile away. It was a good thing they had arrived. Less than thirty minutes of daylight remained.

Unlike so many settlers who would have run their horses hard and dismounted in relief once the settlement was in sight, Georgia and Pa immediately slowed their horses to a walk to give them an opportunity to cool down before retiring them for the night. At the wagon train and stagecoach stop, they first saw to the welfare of their horses, then went to inquire about food and lodging for themselves.

"You betcha, we got a good kitchen and plenty of sleepin' rooms," a wiry little man with glasses and poor posture told Pa. His pregnant wife was busy working in the kitchen. "That'll be fifty cents a night for each of you."

Pa didn't even protest the exorbitant rates. Either he was too tired, or he wanted to stay in the operator's good graces. Georgia wasn't sure.

"When's the next wagon train expected through here?" Pa asked.

"You want a wagon train headed east or west?"

"I didn't figure any wagon trains would be headed east, given the push to move west these days."

"Frontier life don't suit everyone, ya know. Ain't a lot going east, but every now and again we git a wagon train o' folks going back to where they started."

"We need a wagon train going west. My daughter, here, needs to be in Denver by September 15th to start medical school."

"Medical school, you say? Whatever does a girl need with studyin' medicine?"

"Well, sir, should you find yourself hit by an Indian arrow or should that wife of yours need help when the young'un is comin', I spec you'd be glad to get any sort of help, whether it be from a male doctor or a woman with the same trainin'," Pa said to the wiry little man.

He didn't reply to Pa's question, instead he busied himself at the counter, which looked as disheveled as he did. "Ain't no regular schedule for wagon trains. I won't see one for weeks, and then there'll be several in as many days. I can tell ya there will be a stagecoach along tomorrow afternoon. It'll stop for the night and then head out early the next morning."

"A stagecoach, you say?"

"Yes, sir, in here every Monday, Wednesday and Friday, like clockwork. Fast too. You'll be ta Denver in two days."

"Two days! You don't say. That's as fast as a man on horseback."

"That's just what the stagecoach aims to do, as fast as a man on horseback but with all the luxury of coach travel. They use the best horses and drivers. Mighty fine way to travel, if ya ask me."

"And what's the fare from here to Denver?"

"Pa," Georgia whispered, "I don't want to travel by stagecoach. I can't take Cheyenne if I do."

Ignoring her, the stagecoach stop operator wiped a sweaty hand over his greased back, graying hair, and turned toward Pa. "Fifteen dollars."

"Fifteen dollars? I'm not wantin' to buy the stagecoach, just purchase passage to Denver. That's less than ninety miles from here."

"Yes, sir, stage travel is first class."

Pa whistled. "I think we'll wait and see if a wagon train comes through."

A week later, no wagon train had come through the Limon station. When the next stagecoach arrived, Pa explained his dilemma to the driver. The following morning, before dawn, the stagecoach departed the Limon station with Georgia seated in coach, Cheyenne tied just outside her window, and Pa fifteen dollars poorer.

✳

The driver pushed the team of horses pulling the stagecoach hard. Georgia was glad when they stopped for a midday break. She felt no need of a break, but she knew the four-horse team needed one. After much too short a break, the driver hitched up the team, boarded his passengers, and, again, they were on their way toward Denver. The driver, a small man in his thirties with a drooping mustache and hard lines in his face, pushed the horses even harder than before. Georgia had run horses fast across a prairie, but it was much harder for horses yoked together to pick their way and avoid obstacles that could injure them, and the stagecoach was a much heavier load, even for a team of four horses.

Georgia pitied the horses, but she also knew their travel would be in jeopardy if the driver didn't rest his team. They pulled into a station, just as the sun was setting. Georgia rubbed down Cheyenne and staked her out to graze, next to the exhausted stagecoach team.

The next morning when the passengers began to board, Georgia was flabbergasted that the driver had hitched the same team to the coach. She also saw that one of the horses was holding up a leg, clearly not wanting to put any weight on it.

"You can't be planning to use these same horses again today, sir," she said.

"Now, little miss, you leave the choice of horses up to the men. The stagecoach company paid good money for these horses, with the guarantee we could take them all the way to Denver."

"I'm sure you can take them all the way to Denver, but not without a couple days of rest and nourishment. And the blue roan mare won't make it halfway there without someone to attend to her foot."

"She's fine. They're all just fine. Now, you jus git on in and quit worrying your pretty little head."

"Your arrogance will get us all killed!" Georgia shouted.

She climbed up into the coach to get her bag. "I'll not ride with an outfit that treats its horses and passengers with such carelessness," she said, jumping down from the coach, her bag in tow. Georgia tied her bag to Cheyenne's saddle with several adept tugs. She was glad the new saddle had long, thick leather thongs for saddle strings.

"Now, see here, missy, you can't be a ridin' all the way to Denver City by yourself. Ain't safe. And 'sides, your pa didn't raise you—" the driver tried to reason with her.

Georgia cut him off mid-sentence. "My pa raised me to have good sense, mister. We'll get along jus' fine." Hoping that was true, Georgia spun Cheyenne around and kicked her toward Denver.

Chapter 8

Fort Laramie Treaty Indian Hunting Grounds,
September 1863

Lean Bear's arrival at the MacBaye Ranch had been no surprise. The only thing that surprised Gray Wolf was that he had not come sooner. The evening they left, Lean Bear told Gray Wolf the reason for his delay. "I and other Cheyenne chiefs were honored to the big house of the Great White Father."

"You saw the Great White Father, Uncle?" Gray Wolf knew his uncle was an important man among the Cheyenne, but that he had met with the Great White Father ... now that was something indeed.

"I saw him and his wife. I was honored to be the one chosen to speak first, but I was so nervous I could hardly remember what I wanted to say to him. Once I found my tongue, I told him that the Cheyenne and Arapaho wanted peace with the whites. I told him we would teach our young people to live in peace with the white man. He thanked us for coming and said he also wanted his children to live in peace with us."

"What were the people there like, Uncle?" Gray Wolf asked, the Cheyenne words rolling off his tongue, as sweet and smooth as honey. He wondered if they had looked at his uncle and the other chiefs with contempt as the whites in Denver City had looked upon him.

"I've never seen such enormous encampments. Washington, D.C., where the Great White Father lives, is much larger than even the Ogallala powwows in the Black Hills." Lean Bear swooshed his right hand from the left side of his waist in a sweeping motion to the right side of his body, emphasizing the near infinite size of the city. "I realize now, we must make peace with the whites. There are so many of them. They will never stop coming. It is important that you understand this, Gray Wolf. If we don't make peace with the whites, the Cheyenne will be no more."

"Yes, Uncle." Gray Wolf believed it was possible. "The healer's family showed me that we can live together in peace."

"Look, Gray Wolf, the Great White Father gave me this," Lean Bear said, holding up a shiny medallion. Gray Wolf could see that there was a design on it. "And he gave me this," he said, handing a paper to Gray Wolf.

Gray Wolf looked at the words on the page. He didn't understand all of them, but many he did. "It says you have met President Abraham Lincoln and that you have pledged to live peacefully with the settlers. There are some other words, I don't understand ... Uncle, did you really meet with Mr. Lincoln?"

"The Great White Father *is* Mr. Lincoln. Do you know this man, Gray Wolf?"

"The healer taught me about him. He is a good man. He wants the white black man to be free."

※

Try as he might to forget Georgia, Gray Wolf could not. He loved her. There, he admitted it. *I love her*. Though he had only left the MacBaye Ranch a few days ago, he longed for the twinkle in Georgia's green-flecked-brown eyes that made him feel like he could see into her soul.

It wasn't until he left with Lean Bear and returned to his band's village life that he felt the depths of his loss. He welcomed reconnecting with his fellow Cheyenne, and he loved hearing the drumbeat and chants as he fell asleep at night, but his heart ached for Georgia. When he heard the haunting trill of a flute, he wished it was he playing a flute to woo her.

He determined he would not let his inner turmoil spoil the day or its purpose. He was leading one of three hunting parties dispatched the previous week from Lean Bear's camp. While the women harvested berries and roots from the creek beds, the hunters scouted game. He smiled, again thinking of Georgia. If she were Cheyenne, she would have picked her share of berries, mounted a fine horse, and joined the men hunting. She may have already brought down a deer by now.

Gray Wolf's mind turned to practical matters. The meat supply was much lower than it should be as they approached winter. The days were getting shorter and cooler. The leaves fell from the cottonwoods that grew on the banks of the creek. A sheet of orange and gold cracked as the horses walked over the brittle leaves. In past years, the Cheyenne killed dozens of buffalo. The buffalo robes kept them warm during the cold winters. They used the bones to fashion eating utensils and household tools. Sinew became sewing thread. Buffalo bladders made fine water and soup containers or toy balls for the young boys. They traded excess robes for ammunition, sugar, coffee, flour, and other needs and wants.

The Cheyenne were adept at smoking and drying buffalo meat and other game. They ground some of the dried meat with berries to make pemmican, which would sustain the braves on hunting trips or the entire band when it was on the move.

The hunters had started their search for game to the south near Fort Lyon where Lean Bear's band was camped, but when days of search yielded nothing, the hunting parties moved north and west. The prairie was dry now. The lush, emerald green grasses of early summer were brown. Lean Bear and some of the other Cheyenne chiefs had joined Black Kettle in signing the Fort Wise treaty. They thought it would bring them peace with the white man. Only after the ink was dry on the treaty did they learn that it greatly contracted their hunting grounds from that of the Fort Laramie Treaty brokered a decade earlier. Gray Wolf thought his uncle would understand the hunting party's need to go beyond, well beyond, the treaty boundaries.

Despite intense dancing and imploring the Wise One Above, Gray Wolf's hunting party still had not spotted a single buffalo. Instead, they had turned their search to the creek draws to look for deer that sought water and shade from the intense midday sun. The horses' breathing grew heavier as they had to labor to carry their riders through the deep sand of the now waterless creek bed. Ever-present prairie breezes were cool, reminding them that winter cold and barrenness were on the way.

Pronghorn antelope were a distant third choice for the hunters. They were more difficult to kill than deer and their carcasses smaller than either buffalo or deer. But it mattered not. They too were absent today. It seemed the prairie was devoid of all living things. Not even a rabbit ran across the hunters' path.

As he had become accustomed to doing when he lived with the MacBayes, Gray Wolf began to ask the Wise One Above for direction. Almost before the silent words for guidance were off his lips, he felt an overwhelming urge to turn away from the creek, out into the open ground. They would find no deer on the open prairie, especially in the heat of the day. The other braves followed Gray Wolf as he galloped his mount westward.

Cresting a hill, they came upon a fancy wagon pulled by four horses. Gray Wolf remembered the settlers calling this type of wagon a stagecoach. The passengers would sit in seats with a cover over them. A team of four horses pulled the stagecoaches he saw in Denver, but only one horse, a blue roan with an injured leg, stood beside this stagecoach. The cut harness indicated someone had stolen the other horses. He assumed the blue roan was left behind because of the leg injury. As Gray Wolf and his

braves drew near, they could see that the stagecoach passengers
had been murdered, mutilated and robbed.

"The work of the Dog Soldiers," Gray Wolf spat out in
disgust. Dog Soldiers was one of five Cheyenne warrior societies.
His Uncle Lean Bear was a chief in this society, and his uncle's
brother, Bull Bear, was as well. These soldiers were the
Cheyenne's fiercest fighters, known for battle success against
great odds. However, in recent years, some of them had become
cruel, raiding and stealing, not for the benefit of their people but
for personal enrichment and fame. Conflict between the elders,
who wanted to make peace with the whites, and the young Dog
Soldiers, who pledged to drive them off the land, was escalating.

The sight of the mutilated stagecoach passengers infuriated
Gray Wolf. "Our people need food for winter and these renegades
spend their time killing settlers and stealing horses. They have
no common sense or they wouldn't anger the settlers. What
happens if the whites become so angry they won't trade buffalo
robes for guns, ammunition and food?"

"What buffalo robes?" one of the braves asked, expressing
the hunting party's collective frustration.

Seeing the trail of dust beyond the stagecoach, Gray Wolf
and the other braves kicked their ponies into a gallop.

He would catch up to the renegades and teach them a lesson,
he thought, fuming. He understood their anger at not being
able to find the hordes of buffalo that just a decade earlier had
roamed the plains, but he did not understand their need for
violence, especially violence taken out on the innocent.

He recalled the argument when his Uncle Lean Bear had
joined Black Kettle in an effort to convince Dog Soldiers to cease
their random violence against the whites.

"There's no honor in killing women and babies," Black Kettle
had reasoned.

"You're wrong," the young brave had shouted at his elder.
"There is always honor in defending our home, our ways and
our buffalo herds!"

The horses were lathered and beginning to slow from

galloping when one of Gray Wolf's braves pointed to a spec in the road ahead. As Gray Wolf rode closer, his heart jumped into his throat. It was Georgia's sorrel filly. Gray Wolf's braves pulled their horses to a stop. The dog soldier leader—Gray Wolf thought his name was Soaring Falcon—let out a war cry as if he were charging a fierce enemy, rather than pursuing a solo rider. Soaring Falcon's crude language, directed at Gray Wolf, invited the arriving braves to join the fun.

Soaring Falcon had knocked Georgia to the ground, and true to form, she was spitting mad. She was probably terrified as well, but with Georgia, it was hard to tell the difference. It was clear to see the Dog Soldiers admired her courage, but that didn't stop them from taunting her from the safety of their horses. Gray Wolf could see that Georgia had her right hand on her rifle. He hoped she had the sense not to use it.

The taunting braves were amused that a girl carried a rifle. If only they knew what an accurate shot she was, they would have kept their distance. Gray Wolf had ridden close enough to intervene when Georgia lunged at Soaring Falcon's horse and flapped her skirt at it aggressively. He had seen her do this while training a young horse to establish herself as the horse's leader and to desensitize it. Soaring Falcon's horse had no such training. It reared and spooked, depositing the brave on the ground at her feet as it skirted sideways and ran off. Before he hit the ground, Georgia had the rifle pointed at Soaring Falcon's head, just beyond his reach. Her finger was on the trigger, ready to fire, and Gray Wolf had no doubt she would have done just that had her tormentor-turned-captive attempted to escape.

Gray Wolf had no choice but to intervene. "Don't shoot, Georgia."

"Don't intend to iffin' this guy'll git up on his horse and ride off," she said without taking her eye off Soaring Falcon and as if Gray Wolf's intervention was expected and normal.

Gray Wolf translated Georgia's threat for the benefit of Soaring Falcon but made her words his own suggestion. He knew that her words would ignite the dog soldier's anger. A Cheyenne brave, especially a dog soldier bent on eradicating his hunting grounds of all whites, would never back down from a woman's challenge. Gray Wolf feared Soaring Falcon would live up to his reputation of being short-tempered. Georgia stood ramrod straight, her rifle trained on the defiant dog soldier. Gray Wolf knew Georgia could put a bullet through the dog soldier's heart in an instant. He also knew that if she did, his companions would overtake her, and when they did, there would be no mercy. He prayed Soaring Falcon would listen to him. "This squaw is the daughter of a healer, my friend," Gray Wolf said. He neglected to provide further details about their relationship. He didn't want the vengeful dog soldier to humiliate her or even kill her, just to get back at him.

Gray Wolf nearly collapsed with relief when Georgia withdrew her rifle. Soaring Falcon pulled himself up with as much dignity as he could muster, spat on the ground, and then swung up on the back of a flashy paint horse behind one of his companions. Gray Wolf, though he trembled with relief from the averted tragedy, thought to wish them well as they searched for the spooked horse, but he thought it better not to push his luck. Georgia must have recognized the amusement that crept into his eyes. He saw the twinkle in her eyes as she turned to mount her filly. She was as tough as they came. He had been frightened for her, for both of them. Had the confrontation escalated, he would have fought for her. He was a skillful warrior, but he, they, were sorely outnumbered by the Dog Soldiers.

Gray Wolf told his hunting party that it would be bad medicine for them to neglect to escort the healer's daughter to her destination. He knew they would think nothing of him doing so. All of them knew he had spent more than twelve moons in the home of a healer, learning their ways and their tongue.

"Why are you riding by yourself, Georgia? You put yourself in danger."

"I'm on my way to medical school in Denver, Gray Wolf. I want to study to learn even more than my mother."

Gray Wolf couldn't tell if she was angry with him or just

guarded, but it was not a warm reunion. Was Georgia really so oblivious to the danger in which she had placed herself, he wondered. "You are courageous but not stupid. Why do you travel alone?"

"I was on a stagecoach, but the driver mistreated the horses so much that I feared we would never arrive in Denver. I took the filly and decided to ride myself. They should be along shortly, unless ..."

Georgia looked alarmed. "I knew it. The driver pushed them too hard, and the stagecoach is stranded behind us. We have to go back, Gray Wolf."

Gray Wolf had to tell her the stagecoach passengers were dead. "The Dog Soldiers were wearing new scalps."

Georgia's face dawned with understanding. "Dead? They're all dead?" Gulping hard, she turned her head away.

"We came upon the stagecoach. The passengers had all been killed with Indian arrows and lances." He left out that they had been mutilated. "We rode this way to find them and got here just in time. Who knows what they would have done to you."

"You knew those men were murderers and you just let them ride away? How could you let them go?

"I wanted to get them away from you, Georgia. They would have hurt you ... or worse."

"They have to pay for murdering those stagecoach passengers."

"In their thinking, they are defending their hunting grounds, their homes."

"It was cold-blooded murder."

"For the Dog Soldiers, all whites are alike. They want to kill every one of them. They believe that not killing settlers is the same as condemning their own people to death. For them, killing whites is ... what do you call it? Self-defense."

"I will report them when I get to Denver, Gray Wolf. It must be done."

"If you do that, all Cheyenne, no, all Indians, will be under attack. Is that fair? The whites are just as bad about putting the crimes of a few Indians on all Indians as the Dog Soldiers are at doing the same with whites."

The shadows grew longer. They were nearing the start of what was an ever-expanding Denver City. He wanted to haul his pony to a stop and make time stand still.

"It's why you left, isn't it, Gray Wolf?" Georgia said, now pensive. "You were a good man, but the people in Denver made you feel like a murderer."

"Something like that, Georgia." He wanted to tell her how much he missed her, but what good would it do? "You and I know not all people are like the bad ones. We have to make our people understand, Georgia."

"I know … but I still miss you."

He had to change the subject. "Study well, Georgia. You are already a great healer. Learn much. I leave you here."

With that, he turned his pony and sped back to where the other braves waited.

"It sure didn't take you long to get to know the healer's daughter, Gray Wolf," Long Nose teased. "I thought you might just keep walking with her, right into the city."

If the truth be known, Gray Wolf had thought about doing just that, but painful memories from his previous visit to the city reminded him of the gulf between his world and the white world. More importantly, he recalled the gulf between Georgia and himself. Though the sun was setting, calling daylight to a close, he refused to set aside his memories of the day, his memories of Georgia.

Aware they were well beyond Fort Wise treaty boundaries, the braves rode from dusk well into the night to put distance between themselves and the city. They veered south of the trail where they had found the stagecoach and later Georgia. Once satisfied they were well away from any settlements or thoroughfares, Gray Wolf sought a creek bed to make camp.

With the party's braves taking turns keeping watch, Gray Wolf had no worry for his or their safety, yet his miraculous meeting with Georgia brought back memories of his year with the MacBayes. Had he not arrived when he did, he knew the Dog Soldiers would have raped or even killed her. He remembered the strong urging he felt after asking the Wise One Above to guide him to game. He was grateful they had found Georgia, even though it had been the game they sought. Once again, he asked the Wise One Above to guide him to the herds of deer and buffalo.

✸

The hunting party rose at dawn and readied the horses to return home. Once mounted, each man dug into his last day's supply of pemmican.

"Not only will we not be bringing meat back, we have eaten all the reserves sent by our women," said Moonwalker, a young brave who had just taken a wife. "We hoped to have a baby, but now ... maybe it's better not."

"The Wise One Above is punishing us," Long Nose said.

"The Wise One Above doesn't punish us. All difficulties are meant to bring us closer to him," Gray Wolf blurted out before realizing it was what Thomas told him about God, the Father.

"I've never heard the elders say that, Gray Wolf. Are you now a medicine man?" Moonwalker mocked.

"I'm no medicine man, Moonwalker, but we will find buffalo." He was sure of it.

✸

At midday, the braves felt and heard the delicious sound of buffalo pounding the earth. Better yet, they were very close to Lean Bear's camp. Moving in the direction of the pounding hooves, Gray Wolf saw the largest herd of buffalo witnessed in several years. The braves' whipping and yipping stirred the ponies into a frenzy. Only Gray Wolf's mount was calm, yet when he asked his horse to run into the herd, it was the first to reach the stampeding buffalo. Eight braves brought down fifteen adult buffalo that afternoon.

Moonwalker rode his pony to the camp to tell his young bride the good news and to ask those in camp to come to the hunting site with horses and travois to transport the buffalo carcasses. Had the hunting party found buffalo farther out, they would have had to skin and dress them all by themselves. It would have taken multiple trips to get the carcasses back to camp.

People from all teepees worked until it was dark to skin and dress the buffalo carcasses. They would begin scraping the hides, cleaning off bones and cutting up the meat in the morning but tonight would be a celebration. Fifteen buffalo, along with rabbits and the occasional deer, could sustain Lean Bear's clan until spring.

"I see your hunt was a success, Gray Wolf," Lean Bear greeted his nephew with pride.

"The Wise One Above was merciful to us. We have enough meat for the winter, but not so many robes that our men will be tempted to trade them for whiskey."

During the feasting and dancing, the women chanted praises of the successful warriors. The other two hunting parties had returned empty-handed. Gray Wolf responded with acknowledgment of the braves in his hunting party, but when the women sang adulations, singling him out, he felt awkward. He sang the praises of his fellow hunters and hoped to remind all of them that successful hunts were not always within their own control.

Gray Wolf had hoped the success of the hunt and the respect of his peers would enable him to remove his foot, once and for all, from the white world, but it did not. The immediate worries over food were gone, and for the first time, Lean Bear's wife was happy to welcome him back into the family circle.

Because Gray Wolf had proven himself as a warrior, his uncle gave him a tepee to share with his sister, Meadow Lark. Even still, he could not find contentment among the Cheyenne.

Chapter 9

Georgia made it to Denver City safely, a thirty-mile trek alone once she had left Gray Wolf and the hunting party. She noticed that the city had grown since her visit only a few months ago. Additional shanties, small and poorly constructed, edged the city, daring passersby to enter.

The shanties, for the most part, appeared vacant. Based on early conversations with her father, Georgia assumed most of the residents were working their claims. Gold fever had hit hard. Denver had its commercial districts and nice homes, but most of the growth was in the form of temporary housing and businesses that catered to miners. At least that was the case on the outskirts of the city. She flinched when an intoxicated man stumbled toward her, mumbling incoherently. He smelled like he hadn't bathed all summer. Georgia cued Cheyenne to sidestep the trouble and hastened their pace. It was not like Georgia didn't care, but she had little patience for folks whose actions or inaction caused them troubles. Soon she passed through the shanties to the better established part of the city.

Georgia looked for an open shop where she could ask directions to Dr. Williams's school. She saw a livery, nestled between a saloon and a blacksmith's shop. Reining in Cheyenne, she tied the filly's lead rope to the hitching post and went inside. The familiar smells of hay and straw comforted her. The whinny of a horse answered by its paddock partner eased the tension that had been building in Georgia since she entered the city.

"Sir, can you tell me where I might find the practice of Dr. Harold Williams?" she asked a man her father's age who sat at a desk just inside the door. His skin was leathered, no doubt from many hours in the saddle. He looked fit and commanding. She assumed he was the livery owner. "I visited his clinic 'bout a year ago with my ma. Guess I came from a different direction. Nothing looks familiar, so I was hopin' you might point me in the right direction."

"Dr. Williams's office and school is two blocks west and one south of here, ma'am." The man pushed back from the desk and stood. "It's not surprising you can't find yur way. Denver's growing so fast, sometimes I get lost. Who's needin' a doctor?

Georgia debated whether or not to tell him the reason she sought the doctor. Expecting another reprimand about the inferiority of women doctors, yet not wanting to fib, she replied, "No one is ailing, sir. I am one of his new students. I've come from out east, the Bijou Basin region."

"I see," the man said, looking a bit surprised, yet not showing the distain for her admission that the stagecoach stop operator had. "That's a fine lookin' sorrel filly you got there with you. You needin' to board her for the night, ma'am?"

Georgia had given no thought to where she would keep Cheyenne. "I'm supposin' Dr. Williams has a carriage house."

"I know for a fact he does not. His horse and carriage board right here."

"Oh, I see," she gulped. "How much would a month of board set me back?"

"Well, iffin' you was willing to muck out your own stall and groom this filly yurself, I could let ya keep her here for five dollars a month, that's assumin' she's not difficult or bothersome to the other horses."

It was an expense she had not anticipated. Five dollars was half again as much as her fees to attend Dr. Williams's medical school. She considered for only the briefest moment the possibility of letting the livery rent out the filly but decided it best to level with the fellow. "Being a rancher's daughter and all, I hadn't really thought about the added expenses for my horse. At home, she grazes out in the open. I have no problem agreein' to the cleaning and grooming, but even five dollars is too much for me."

"Well, do you want to sell her then? A fine horse like that with any training at all would fetch a hundred dollars, maybe more," the livery owner said. She could see he was trying to be helpful.

"Oh, no, I would never sell Cheyenne. She's a fine-bred filly. I don't mean to brag, but, well, I trained her myself, and she'll do anything I ask of her. You shoulda seen how she stood her ground just this afternoon when a bunch of renegade Indians knocked me off her back. Most horses woulda run off scared to death, but not Cheyenne. She'll be loyal to a rider who has earned her trust."

At this, the livery owner raised his eyebrows, indicating he didn't entirely believe her. What was it he didn't believe, she wondered. That she trained Cheyenne herself, that the filly didn't run away during the attack or that she was attacked by Indians? She also knew she couldn't continue this conversation or she would end up telling the man about the murdered stagecoach passengers. She winced at the thought of what happened to them, but she knew Gray Wolf's admonition not to tell about the murders was prudent.

She decided to try another approach. "What if I were to come every morning 'cept on Sundays and muck out all your stalls and brush your horses on an alternating schedule? I can train young colts too. Could we call it even?"

The livery owner smiled. "Young lady, I can see you are a determined one. If your ability is half of what you say it is, I'd be pleased ta have you work here. It seems more men pour into this city with every newspaper article announcing another strike of gold nuggets. I'll admit having a young lady do livery work is unconventional, but I like you a lot. We've got us a deal." He thrust forward his right hand to seal the agreement.

"Georgia MacBaye, sir," Georgia said, grasping his hand in a firm shake. "You won't be disappointed, ah, Mister—?"

"Fletcher, ma'am, the name's Edwin Fletcher."

Mr. Fletcher led Georgia to the stall for Cheyenne. He showed her where to get hay, straw and water for the filly, as well as where to find the pitchfork and bucket to clean the stalls. Georgia loosened the saddles' strings to untie her bag from the saddle. Then she undid the back and then the front cinch of her saddle. She removed the saddle and blanket, pulled up the latigo and cinch and set the saddle on the ground, gullet down, as her father had instructed her. She removed the brush from her saddlebag, and went to work cleaning the filly's coat. She finished by picking debris out of Cheyenne's hooves with her metal hoof pick.

Mr. Fletcher whistled. "You do know your way around a horse. When you're finished, you can put your saddle away on a rack in the tack room."

Georgia followed him, placing her saddle, blanket, bridle, halter, lead rope and other pieces of tack on the rack he indicated. Removing her gun and saddlebags, she returned to the stall to make sure Cheyenne was settled and to retrieve her bag of personal belongings and books.

"I don't expect a lady will be needin' a rifle in Denver City, miss," Mr. Fletcher said.

"It's not for use in Denver City, but for the travel to and from," she said, noting that the muscles in his face seemed to relax.

"Miss MacBaye, I'm going to send one of my boys with you to help carry your things. You have a lot to carry, and the sun's nearly set." When Georgia began to protest, Mr. Fletcher held up his hand, indicating he insisted she comply. "I sure would hate to have some passerby get the town all riled up about a lady toting a gun down the streets of Denver City." His smile reminded Georgia of her father when he reprimanded her for something she should not have done but was proud she'd had the determination to do. Shoving her hair up into a hat to get away with entering the Bijou Basin's young men's shooting contest and then winning it before being disqualified when the organizers learned she was a girl, came to mind.

Georgia and Mr. Fletcher's stablehand arrived at Dr. Williams's doorstep just after the sun sunk below the mountain peaks.

"Good evening, Miss MacBaye. Dr. Williams has been expecting you," the lady who answered the door said as she directed the stableboy to take Georgia's bag and other belongings to the second floor bedroom. She looked to be about ten years older than Georgia, but maybe she looked older because her dark, braided hair was twisted up into a stylish bun. She had olive skin and the slightest accent, similar to the Mexicans who had built the MacBayes' adobe house, Georgia thought.

Georgia gawked at the elegant, tall-ceilinged rooms and the winding staircase. "It's beautiful," she said more to herself than to the young woman who had opened the door.

"Dr. and Mrs. Williams thought it best you board here in their home, you being the only young lady in the class. I hope you will be comfortable here, miss. You can call me Miss Lucy. I'm the doctor's housekeeper, and I help Mrs. Williams with the cooking." Georgia liked Lucy's broad smile and the way she made her feel at home in Dr. Williams's grand house. She thought that Lucy was someone she could trust.

Climbing the stairs, Georgia thought about the sharp contrast between this house and the shanties on the edge of the city. The wood was oiled and polished, the brass shone and the tile floor looked clean enough to eat off. The windows were trimmed with smart lace curtains, allowing the last vestiges of the day's light to flood the house with crimson and gold. Georgia unpacked her few belongings. From Mr. Fletcher's comments, she surmised that city folk didn't fancy a lady carrying a gun, although she doubted few men in Denver City would leave home without the protection of a rifle or at least a pistol. Reluctantly, she tucked the scabbard and rifle under her bed. She dipped one of the embroidered linen handkerchiefs her ma had given her into the water in the basin, dabbing and scrubbing until she had removed most of the dirt and sweat from her face. Miss Lucy instructed her to freshen up and then come down for supper. She supposed that might also include changing into one of the gowns her mother had packed for her.

When Georgia returned to the kitchen thirty minutes later, Lucy informed her that she and the other medical students would be joining them. Seeing the china and silver, she had to admit her mother was right to insist she bring the fussy gown.

Miss Lucy directed her to the parlor and introduced her to three young men she assumed to be her new classmates.

Georgia felt she would die from embarrassment when Bostonian Gregory Allerton punctuated his greeting by pulling her hand to his lips and kissing it. Thankfully, Jonathan VanDerKemp and Edward Williams limited their greetings to a "Pleased to meet you, miss" and "How do you do?" Georgia hoped she did not look as embarrassed as she felt.

"My uncle, Dr. Williams that is, told me one of our classmates would be a young lady," Mr. Williams said and waited for Georgia to respond. *What does he expect me to say? Was that an insult? Should I defend myself?* she wondered.

All the young men's eyes were on her, waiting for her response. "I understand it's a first for the school," Georgia said, intentionally not answering their unspoken questions. "Mr. Williams, why did you decide to study medicine?" she asked, sweet as pie.

"Me? Why did I decide to study medicine?" He looked like the question had caught him off-guard. "Well, I guess, because, well … everyone in my family studies medicine."

Georgia had not meant to embarrass him. She wanted the question to turn the conversation. At that moment, Dr. and Mrs. Williams arrived home, and introductions began anew. Georgia was relieved to see that Mr. Allerton greeted Mrs. Williams in the same manner that mortified her. Mrs. Williams, on the other hand, was impervious to the kiss on her hand.

"Shall we?" Dr. Williams said, gesturing for them to move into the dining room. "Our housekeeper and Mrs. Williams have prepared a wonderful supper for us." Georgia had forgotten how hungry she was. It had been over a week since she had eaten anything but stagecoach stop fare or dried meat and other cold foods. Lucy's meal of ham, scalloped potatoes and pickled red beets tasted heavenly. It was served on china that was cream colored with a delicate blue and yellow floral design. On each piece of silverware was an engraved "W". Georgia breathed a sigh of relief that she had paid attention when her mother insisted on reviewing formal dining etiquette with her before she left the ranch.

"I couldn't help but hear my nephew answering a question about his reason for studying medicine," said Dr. Williams. "I'd very much like to hear from the rest of you on this topic." He paused, and Georgia looked up to see him looking at her. "Miss MacBaye, why don't you start?"

"My mother is called on often out on the Eastern Plains if folks have a medical question or illness. She has read a lot and worked alongside a doctor back in South Carolina, where she grew up. She also knows a lot about using herbs, both cultivated and those growing in the wild, for medicinal purposes. I have learned much from her, but I really need to understand more by studying modern medicine. I want to say, sir, I'm much obliged to you for accepting me into your school."

"We are honored to have you, Miss MacBaye," Dr. Williams said. "And you, Mr. VanDerKemp, why are you studying medicine?"

"My father and grandfather are both doctors. I guess I never thought to be anything else," Mr. VanDerKemp said.

Mr. Allerton did not wait to be asked. "The Allertons, as well, have been physicians for multiple generations. In fact, our lineage goes back to some of the first Americans." Georgia thought that interesting, but it was anything but when Mr. Allerton launched into a fifteen-minute monologue outlining generation by generation his lineage back to the Mayflower. "So, you can see, my family has been in this country for nearly two hundred and fifty years. Some find it strange that I would risk life and limb to sojourn in this savage Western Frontier, but I admit to finding Boston a bit stifling, even, dare I say, boring. I do beg of you not to utter a word of this to my family, lest they disown me," he alone laughed at his own joke.

"What of the Indians?" asked Mr. VanDerKemp, another Easterner, who had fortunately spared his fellow guests the details of his ancestry. "Do they fascinate you or terrify you?"

"A bit of both, I confess. I wonder if we might see one of the creatures whilst we practice medicine with Dr. Williams. What do you think, sir? Are there Indians roundabout Denver City?" Mr. Allerton asked, turning toward Dr. Williams.

"Unless there is some treaty to be negotiated between our officials and the Indian chiefs, the only place in Denver City that you might see an Indian is at the U.S. Army trading post. The Indians there are mostly misfits, alcoholics, the insane, that sort of thing. The only way you'd ever have opportunity to treat an Indian is out on the plains, and I wouldn't recommend you venture out there on your own."

"Uncle Herald, don't you recall this spring when a young Indian brave came into town with a wagon train of settlers?" Edward joined the discussion. "They said he went about town buying supplies like all the others."

Georgia snapped to attention at the mention of Gray Wolf's visit to Denver City in April. What would they think of her if they learned she was the one accompanying Gray Wolf? What if they knew he had lived in their home?

"I don't expect that to happen again, Edward," Dr. Williams said. "Indian hostilities are increasing. Most every day we hear of some atrocity or another. Even the peaceful Indians are keeping their distance now that Governor Evans has authorized Colonel John Chivington to shoot any and all Indians his troops come across."

Georgia gasped. "They can't do that!"

"Can't do what, miss?" Mr. Allerton said.

"Shoot any and all Indians. That's as ludicrous as Governor Evans issuing an order to shoot all Irishmen or anyone with Dutch heritage," she said, amused that the second nationality mentioned caught the attention of Mr. VanDerKemp. "Just like any ethnic group, there are some bad apples amongst the Indians, but most of them are just minding their own business, working to feed their families. Don't the authorities know the problems it'll cause if folks start shooting any Indian they see?"

"Governor Evans is just trying to protect the citizens, Miss MacBaye. Why, Indian attacks on travelers and settlements have nearly shut down westward expansion to Colorado. Something must be done. What would you have the governor do, Georgia?" Dr. Williams asked.

"Believe me, Dr. Williams, I know there are some hostile Indians, but most are not that way. I also know that the Indians are struggling to feed themselves. The once plentiful buffalo have been hunted to the point that few are left. The Indians depend on the buffalo for food, clothing, shelter. Everything, really. Most of the hostilities you mention are because of the lack of game."

"The government has tried over and over to negotiate treaties with them, but they don't seem to want to abide by them," Mr. VanDerKemp said. "Just yesterday I read in the newspaper that Governor Evans earlier this month traveled all the way to Kansas to meet with Cheyenne Chiefs Black Kettle and White Antelope, and they didn't bother to show. Some business about the Cheyenne Dog Soldiers preventing them to talk peace with the governor."

"It's not the Indians who don't abide by the treaties," Georgia snapped. "The U.S. government has yet to keep a single one of them. Treaty makers promise the Indians provisions, which never come, so they go out to hunt on ground granted them by one treaty or another, which has been disallowed by a later treaty. It's no wonder the Indians don't trust us. Even still, Black Kettle, Lean Bear, War Bonnet and the other Cheyenne and Arapaho chiefs are doing all they can to keep the peace," she said with far more passion than she had intended.

"How do you know this, Georgia?" Dr. Williams asked.

Georgia paused, thinking how to answer his question. She wanted them to know she spoke the truth, but she was afraid for Gray Wolf, for the Cheyenne, even for herself, if she admitted too much. "Out on the Eastern Plains, we know the Indians. We've learned how to live side by side. Governor Evans and Colonel Chivington are making judgments about people and situations they know little about."

Georgia hoped she wouldn't be kicked out of school before the first day of class. Silence extended, the only sound that of silverware clinking against fine china.

"There's at least one man in the U.S. Army that agrees with you, Miss MacBaye," Mr. VanDerKemp said, then adding, as he winked at her, "Silas Soule is a man of reason, not to speak of him being a fellow Dutchman."

"Who is Silas Soule?" Georgia asked.

"Silas, now Captain Silas Soule, is from my hometown of Bath, Maine. His father was a rebel-rousing sort of abolitionist, so the family moved to Kansas to join the Jayhawkers in fighting off the boys from Missouri who'd have the South secede in order to keep the Negroes enslaved." VanDerKemp continued, "He is no religious man, but he believes in what our Constitution says, that 'all men are created equal.' He's a man of reason and fairness. Rumor is he will be dispatched to Fort Lyon out on the Eastern Plains to negotiate with the Indians. I know if anyone can work out the differences between them and us, it'll be good ole Soule."

"Governor Evans is a good man too. I went to medical school with him at Clermont Academy. Maybe he does need to spend some time with the settlers, so we don't go doing something we shouldn't." Dr. Williams looked deep in thought.

The guests had long ago finished their coffee and cherry cobbler topped with whipped cream. "Class will commence at the clinic tomorrow morning at eight sharp," Dr. Williams said. They bid each other good night.

※

Indeed, class commenced at exactly eight the following morning. Dr. Williams drew in his students, and Georgia liked his methodical approach to teaching. She found herself enthralled with the study of bacteria and Louis Pasteur's germ theory of disease and later with the instruction on anesthesia and surgery. Georgia knew the answers to most of Dr. Williams's questions and was often the first called upon. If her answer was wrong, she amused both her teacher and fellow students with her energy and enthusiasm as she tried to explain her erroneous conclusion.

Georgia worked hard at everything. She stayed up late to study the many books in Dr. Williams's library and rose early to go to the livery to fulfill her contract with Mr. Fletcher.

Cheyenne was restless and beginning to look unfit. She almost spoke with Mr. Fletcher about renting her out but changed her mind, remembering the stagecoach driver and how he had driven his team to the detriment of all. She decided she would take a break from her studies on Saturday and take Cheyenne out for a ride.

When she told Dr. Williams of her plans, he insisted she have one of her fellow students accompany her.

Before she could protest, Mr. VanDerKemp spoke, "I would be glad to ride along with you. A break from our studies is a splendid idea."

Thirty minutes later, Georgia and Jonathan VanDerKemp headed out the door to the livery. Mr. Fletcher charged her colleague fifty cents to rent a mount for the afternoon. Georgia was amused at Mr. VanDerKemp's insistence on rising up and down in the saddle as his bay gelding trotted down the main thoroughfare toward the eastern edge of the city. She was certain the posting trot favored by easterners would exhaust him by the end of the day. Posting in the Western saddle with its longer stirrups made the practice look awkward.

Cheyenne was frisky, which could be expected, having been cooped up in a stall for days on end, but she minded her manners. Georgia knew that if she even thought about galloping off, Cheyenne would sense the imperceptible cue. So Georgia was careful to sit deep in the saddle to limit the filly to a brisk trot.

The classmates passed the U.S. Army post and entered open country. Georgia asked Cheyenne for a lope and Mr. VanDerKemp followed. He bounced so much in his saddle that she feared he might fall. He seemed relieved when she slowed Cheyenne to a walk.

"I take it you've had a lot of riding lessons, Miss MacBaye?" he questioned, still struggling to gain his composure.

"No lessons, just a lot of hours in the saddle. Settler kids start riding no sooner than they've started ta walk." To be accurate she should have said that boy settler kids start riding very young, but there was no need to make her classmate think she was any odder than he already did.

"I see."

After a few minutes of silence, he again attempted to engage her in conversation. "Is it true Indians cut off a lock of scalp when they kill an enemy?"

"I've known that to be the case, but some say the Indians learned to scalp an enemy from the whites."

"You don't say?" Mr. VanDerKemp was astonished. "Why would we teach them to do that?"

"It was a way of proving how many of the enemy they killed. Some whites paid Indians by the scalp for killing their enemies."

That suspended polite conversation. It wasn't Georgia's intent that the grisly fact end the discussion, but she didn't mind the silence.

They rode along the creek, Cherry Creek the Denverites called it, dropping down into the sandy bottom. Georgia knew the loose footing was good for rebuilding Cheyenne's muscle. She also knew walking through the deep sand would quickly tire the horses, reducing the chance of one of the horses spooking and dumping her, or more likely Mr. VanDerKemp, on the ground. She reveled in the joy of being on horseback in open country. The smell of rich earth and decaying plants reminded her of riding in the creek behind the MacBaye Ranch. Cherry Creek was dry this time of year, full of leaves, a blanket of gold, green, brown and orange that crackled under the horses' hooves.

Georgia picked up the pace to dissuade her classmate from attempting to make further conversation. She didn't mean to be unkind, but his questions made her laugh. Other than medicine, she could not think of a single thing she might discuss with him. They rounded a bend, spooking a flock of turkeys. Georgia's first thought was regret for not having brought her rifle. A fat fall turkey would make a mighty fine Sunday dinner. She had tucked the pistol into the top of her right boot but knew she couldn't kill a turkey cleanly with a pistol.

Her thoughts were interrupted by Mr. VanDerKemp's shriek. Georgia looked up in time to see him hit the ground as his mount spooked and then reared on its hind legs.

"Are you hurt?" Georgia rushed to where the horse had deposited him.

"Just some bruises. Good thing I landed on soft ground or our medical treatment skills would have been called into use."

Georgia was relieved he maintained his sense of humor. She could not really blame her classmate. He knew little of the bay gelding he rode, and like most horses it had not been trained to trust its rider when something spooked it. She gave the gelding a few minutes to calm down and then went after the horse. When the horse started to run from her and Cheyenne, she chased the gelding and then turned and walked away. The third time she charged the gelding and then walked away, the gelding followed her, head down and sedate. She snatched up the gelding's reins and led him to Mr. VanDerKemp, who now stood, brushing the sand and leaves from his coat.

"I do thank you, Miss MacBaye, although I have to confess I've never seen anyone catch a horse quite like that. I figured either I'd be walking back to the livery or maybe you'd have pity on me and let me ride behind you."

His riding behind her had crossed her mind, doubling her efforts to secure the loose horse. "No need for that, sir. The trick with a loose horse is to make it known right away that your mount is the lead horse. Once that's established, any horse will follow you just as it would follow the lead horse in a wild herd."

Perhaps Georgia had judged her classmate too harshly. Arrogance, that's what it was that had caused her to despise him. Jonathan VanDerKemp was, after all, paying to ride a horse from which he was dumped, merely as a favor to her. And, he continued to be in good spirits despite the considerable damage to both his ego and his backside. She whispered a prayer for forgiveness and determined to be more charitable.

Georgia was a horse's length from Jonathan when a rifle exploded, the shell hitting the sand of the creek bed, just feet away, around the bend. The horses jumped and pulled away, but Georgia was able to contain both her mount and the bay gelding.

"Indians," Jonathan shouted, scrambling to his feet, his bumps and bruises forgotten for the moment. "Quick, let's take cover behind those bushes."

"Naw, it isn't Indians. Just someone huntin' turkeys."

As if on cue, a man on a tall gray horse charged around the corner. He pulled his mount to a sliding stop in the sand. "Pardon me, ma'am, sir, I didn't know I was sharing the hunting with anyone. I expect my bullet came mighty close to you two there."

"Yes, sir. We, well ... I thought it was some hostiles. Gave us a start. I'm Jonathan VanDerKemp and this is my classmate Miss Georgia MacBaye. Miss MacBaye needed to exercise her horse, and I came along for the ride. A bit more excitement than

I anticipated, I must admit."

"Isaac Van Wormer," the man said, his horse prancing with nervousness. Georgia guessed Mr. Van Wormer to be about fifteen years her senior. He had a commanding presence about him. "Classmates, you say? What school do you attend?"

"We're medical students, studying with Dr. Harold Williams."

"Oh, yes, Doc Williams. Has a fine reputation. Personally, I try to stay away from needin' to see a doc, but if I ever did, Dr. Williams would be my first choice. Come to think of it, I'm glad this hunting expedition of mine didn't turn into a need to search out the good doctor. Sorry to have scared you young folks."

"Any luck with bagging a turkey?" Georgia asked. "There sure was a lot of 'em."

"No luck. I'm getting tired of beef. I was hoping to supplement it with fowl."

Jonathan remounted the gelding. "Nothing wrong with a nice slab of roast beef, Mr. Van Wormer."

"True enough, but being a cattle rancher and all, there is never an end to my beef supply."

The words cattle and ranch aroused Georgia's curiosity. "Where is your ranch Mr. Van Wormer?"

"Just about twenty miles south and a bit east of here."

"So you headed home yet today?" she asked, noting the setting sun.

"Oh, no, I live in Denver. My foreman, Nathan Hungate, runs the ranch and lives on the place. Lately, the biggest challenge has been keeping the Indians away from the cattle herds. They're making off with one here, two or three there. Pretty soon, they'll all be gone and there'll be no calves to fatten and sell."

Georgia thought about home and wondered if they'd lost any cattle to Indian raiders. "Is losing cattle to Indians a new thing?"

"I suppose we've lost a few here and there. It's hard to tell when we come up short what has happened. Could be wolves, death from natural causes or rustlin', but lately, we've seen Indians chasing off the animals. We've gone after them, that is my ranch hands have, but never been able to bring back the stolen cattle."

"Mr. Van Wormer, it's been very nice to make your acquaintance, but it's about time Georgia and I get back to the city."

"Indeed it is. Do you mind if I ride back with you? It's not every day I run into a fellow Dutchman."

The trio followed the dry streambed northwest for a mile and then headed straight west to the center of the city. At Sherman Street, they turned north. Two blocks in, Mr. Van Wormer jerked his gray horse to a stop. It was a large, two-story house with a wide porch. Not an ordinary homesteader, Georgia thought.

"Eleven South Sherman Street. I'll be saying good night here."

Five minutes later, they arrived at the livery. As Georgia groomed and fed Cheyenne and completed her other barn chores, she noticed that Jonathan, as he had instructed her to call him, moved with discomfort. He didn't seem to blame her for the fall, but she doubted he would offer to accompany her a second time.

Chapter 10

Lean Bear's Camp in Southeastern Colorado,
November 1863

Game was scarce now that the weather had turned cold, making Gray Wolf all the more thankful for September's successful buffalo hunt. The families in Lean Bear's camp had eaten all the fresh buffalo they wanted for several weeks. The rest of the meat was dried into jerky and pemmican. The dried buffalo, along with winter hunting and the roots and berries the women found, would keep them fed all winter. Earlier in the season, they had traded buffalo hides for dried squashes by the southern tribes who stayed in one place long enough to plant, harvest and dry a crop. It was not an excessive amount of food, but it was enough. He again thanked the Wise One Above for helping the braves find and kill the buffalo two moons earlier.

Once all bits of meat were scraped from the hides, they would salt them. Later, they would tan the hides to make the skins pliable, then the women would fashion the hides into clothing, boots and moccasins. The buffalo robes were not so many that they would be able to take them to the trading posts to exchange for salt, coffee, sugar, flour, beads and trinkets.

The food and trinkets were fine, but excess robes had been a curse to the bands that traded them for whiskey. The chiefs warned their people against whiskey, declaring it a curse the white man cast on the Indians. Lean Bear told them it was a curse they didn't have to accept. Lean Bear's band rejected the addictive drink, but Gray Wolf had heard stories of entire bands trading hundreds of buffalo robes for a few kegs. Not only had the braves squandered their hard work in hunting and dressing the animals, the women, who worked many hours to prepare the robes, were rewarded with several weeks of the braves' drunkenness. Braves who let whiskey consume them didn't hunt, and they didn't protect their villages. Drunken men railed at and even beat their wives and children, activity unheard of in a sober village. Gray Wolf had heard tales of Indian women and children hiding out in creek beds for days, even weeks, because they feared what the braves might do to them. If they were unable to find roots and berries, they went hungry. There was no one to protect them. The Pawnee carried off squaws of one band hiding from their drunken husbands and fathers. The men were too drunk to know when it occurred, and then too hung over to care that their women were forever lost to them.

Gray Wolf was very thankful that the Wise One Above had provided just enough meat to see them through, but not enough to make men lazy.

The hour was early, but Gray Wolf had gone out to inspect and work with the horses. His eyes immediately went to the jet-black stallion that he hoped to make his new hunting pony. The colt had a flowing mane and tail. The white star on its forehead and three half-stockings made the black beauty distinctive. Before Lean Bear left to join the other chiefs in council, he told Gray Wolf he could have the pick of his herd. Gray Wolf chose the stallion because he liked his intelligence and curiosity. Gray Wolf knew he could train the stallion to be a dependable mount. And because the stallion was young, he would be strong and healthy for many years to come.

It no longer pricked his pride to admit that he had learned a great deal about training horses and judging a horse's disposition from Georgia. Thinking about it and using her methods helped him remember her, to feel close to her. It gave him pleasure to use what he had learned from her, although he would never admit that to the others. Georgia's methods expended more time on the front end of the training, but resulted in a more dependable and thoroughly trained horse. Hadn't he been reminded of this when Georgia was able to spook Soaring Falcon's horse, leaving the foolish dog soldier on the ground, disarmed?

Gray Wolf was one of the few young braves who trained a horse in seclusion. The others made a joke of muscling their way onto a new mount and riding as it bucked and ran in panic. Most of the braves were more interested in impressing the young women than they were in training a good mount.

Gray Wolf had put in all the groundwork with the young stallion. Nearly a moon ago, he mounted the young horse for the first time, pleased to find that his work had paid off. The horse neither bucked nor reared nor bolted. It trusted Gray Wolf and quietly moved forward, taking the gaits he asked of it.

This morning, Gray Wolf had decided to take the stallion out for a long ride to the southwest of the camp. The cool air caused the stallion to respond with abundant energy. *Just let 'em move out nice and easy and expend all that energy themselves,* he remembered Georgia telling him when he was tempted to hold a frisky horse with a tight rein.

As Gray Wolf and the black stallion crested a hill, Gray Wolf saw a line of Indians in the distance, moving in his direction. *Cheyenne.* Very soon, he could see it was Lean Bear and the braves who had accompanied him to the council of chiefs.

"Uncle Lean Bear, how honored I am to be the first to welcome you back," Gray Wolf shouted as his horse came to a stop. He knew the honored speech was expected, although after living with the MacBayes, it seemed strange to him that relatives would converse with such formality.

"I'm glad to see you are well, Gray Wolf. Is this the young stallion you pledged to me you would train? You've done very well, Nephew."

"Yes, Uncle, he's a beauty. He'll be a fine hunting horse."

They rode in silence back to the camp. Gray Wolf thought his uncle looked tired, his shoulders slumped, his eyes dull. For the first time, he thought he looked old, not regal and strong, as he always had. Once the horses were attended, Lean Bear motioned for him to enter his uncle's tepee.

Gray Wolf warmed himself at the fire in Lean Bear's tepee, waiting for him to speak.

"Sit, Gray Wolf. I have much to say to you. News from the council is troubling."

"What troubles you, Uncle?"

"There is grave disagreement among us. The elders, especially those of us who visited with the Great White Father during the time when eyes hurt from bright snow, want peace. We know the whites are too many to hold back. We must live in peace with them, even if it means we are no longer hunters and warriors. I have seen visions of our people returning to the ways they lived before the horse, putting seeds in the ground and living from grains and vegetables, not from hunting buffalo."

"But the Cheyenne have always hunted buffalo and never lived by putting seeds in the ground. That is the way of the whites."

"Many, many years ago, we were farmers. We stayed in one place and watched our crops grow. Then, the Cheyenne came to the great, open plains and started to hunt buffalo. When the horse came, we tamed it to help us hunt even more buffalo, but it has not always been so."

"Will the young braves quit hunting buffalo and live from the seeds they put in the ground?" Gray Wolf asked.

"That is the disagreement. The young men do not want to leave our way of life. I understand this. But they must know that things will change, and the Cheyenne cannot survive if they do not change. As we sat and smoked the peace pipe, I saw things I have never seen. Young men shouted at their elders. They defied them. They refused to listen. Sadly, the worst are my society, the Dog Soldiers. They still insist on killing all whites, good or evil, male or female, adult or child."

Gray Wolf remembered the massacred stagecoach passengers. He remembered the close call with Georgia. "The Dog Soldiers seem bent on shedding blood, even of the innocent. Why?"

"Dog Soldiers have always been courageous warriors. When there is an impossible task, the Cheyenne call on them."

Gray Wolf knew it saddened Lean Bear that he had never joined the Dog Soldiers. Until the successful hunt several moons ago, he believed his uncle didn't view him as a man, as a brave. He had not discussed his dislike of the Dog Soldiers with Lean Bear until now. "I know it would have pleased you, Uncle, had I pledged to be a dog soldier, but I don't want anything to do with their cruel and bloodthirsty ways. They're hot-headed, not open to listen, to reason. You've always taught me to walk in humility and to honor others. I can't be one of them!"

"The dog soldier society was once a very honorable one, always courageous but honorable. Their attitudes changed once the whites came to the plains. The Dog Soldiers, like all of us, are afraid of losing their homes, their families, their way of life. I don't like what they are doing, but I can understand it."

"Uncle, do you disrespect me for not becoming a dog soldier?"

"Gray Wolf is a fine warrior. He has proven himself as a hunter. He lived courageously with the whites, learning their ways and their tongue. He is kind and strong."

Lean Bear had stopped short of saying he was proud of Gray Wolf, but it was the closest his uncle had ever come to expressing pride in his nephew. Gray Wolf did not know how to respond, and even if he had, the huge lump in his throat prevented it. "Will we have war with the whites, Uncle?"

"I fear once good weather returns, the Dog Soldiers and others may increase their attacks on settlers. The elders argued with them for many days, but they will not listen. They think they can push the settlers off our hunting grounds, but they are very wrong. The result will be bad for all Indians."

※

A week later, Moonwalker and Gray Wolf went downstream from camp to look for game. As he had become accustomed to doing, Gray Wolf asked the Wise One Above to guide them to the game. The warriors dismounted and tied their horses to a fallen tree trunk to walk into the thick brush to look for rabbits. They had to crawl on hands and knees to get under the brush, and when they emerged on the other side, a young mule deer buck stood not fifty feet from them. Gray Wolf raised his loaded bow, and in a single swift motion sent an arrow straight into the heart of the buck. It dropped where it stood.

"A perfect shot," Moonwalker said, slapping him on the back. "We don't have to chase down our supper, and the meat will be perfect because you dropped him where he stood."

"We can string him up there and be back to camp by midday. Your squaw will be glad to cook you some venison stew tonight. What with those roots and herbs she has from earlier, it will be a real feast for a couple still honeymooning," Gray Wolf teased his friend.

The men got to work cleaning the deer and removing the hide. Nothing would be wasted. Even the bladder was saved to make a sporting ball for the young boys.

Moonwalker was skilled at dressing a deer. A few quick cuts, and it was gutted. The heat from the fresh carcass turned the air into a mist when it hit the cool air. Gray Wolf hung the edible organ meats on branches to dry and separated sinews used for fashioning hunting bows and piecing together buffalo robes for tepees. The sticky, rapidly cooling blood soaked into the sand.

"My wife will be happy," Moonwalker said, gesturing at the deer carcass. "She hoped we would get some sugar and flour from the fort. She's rather fond of cooking with the white man's food."

"There were not enough buffalo robes to trade for white man's food or his whiskey—not such a bad thing." Gray Wolf used the hunting knife he purchased in Denver to remove the hide without tearing it. "Whiskey makes some Indians crazy."

"Not as crazy as broken promises," Moonwalker said, spitting on the ground. "The whites have yet to abide by the terms of any treaty they've made with the Cheyenne, yet our chiefs keep smoking the pipe with them. It's going to get really ugly when braves and their wives and children begin starving to death, while the promised provisions sit stacked in Agent Colley's possession. He was supposed to give us the provisions in exchange for our leaving the settlers alone and only hunting down here around the Sand Creek."

Gray Wolf had heard rumors about Agent Samuel Colley and his men selling Indians provisions that would have gone to them as terms of the treaties their chiefs signed. "So it's true that conniving coyote is selling food that should rightly be ours?"

"It's true. Everyone says the same thing. Whites are nothing but a bunch of lying thieves."

"Not all whites are liars. The healer that saved my life, the one my uncle took me to see, she and her family would share their last meal with me. I know they would."

"As long as Mr. Colley and white men like him are in charge of the distribution of provisions, there won't ever be peace between the whites and the Cheyenne."

"If everything they say he does is true, Colley's an evil man, but it is unfair to assume all whites are evil because Colley and his friends are. Don't you agree, Moonwalker?" Not waiting for a reply, Gray Wolf continued, "Maybe not getting provisions is a blessing in disguise. Just think, if your tepee was full of flour, sugar, coffee, and cans of white man's food, would you be out here with me today hunting?"

"Food a man didn't work for makes him lazy, I agree, Gray Wolf. But taking away the ability of man to work and hunt to feed his family gives a man no choice but to look for food from the forts."

"Let's hope we are far enough from the Indian Agency and the white forts to stay away from trouble when it comes. And let's pray we'll continue to be able to find game." Gray Wolf cleaned his knife and stowed it in a leather pouch.

They had skinned and dressed the deer and were loading the carcass, hide and offal onto the black stallion. The animal looked wary but stood still while Gray Wolf secured the wrapped deer carcass around his horse's girth.

"I can't believe your stallion let you load it up. Most horses, especially the young ones, spook when a carcass comes anywhere near them," Moonwalker said, holding tightly to the headstall on his own mount, attempting to keep it from bolting.

"I had a good teacher," Gray Wolf mumbled, swinging up on the back of the stallion behind the deer carcass.

Chapter 11

Denver City, January 1864

Georgia and her fellow medical students finished their classroom study and were in the practical stage of their training. Dr. Williams gave his students time to take vital signs, examine their patients and reach a diagnosis, yet he was quick to interject when a teaching moment was at hand or his students' inexperience in any way compromised the care of a patient. They treated patients with knife wounds, those shot in duels, miners with lung conditions, and even the occasional wealthy, inactive patient with gout.

Dr. Williams referred patients, mostly children in the early stages of scurvy or rickets, to Georgia. Both were diseases her mother had guarded the family against by ensuring they ate a diet with adequate fruits and vegetables. Georgia would instruct the parents of these children to prevent scurvy by ensuring they ate more fruits and vegetables, and when they could acquire it, cod liver oil. Most could afford canned tomatoes or dried berries in the winter and then had a wider variety of produce from which to choose in the summer and fall. Rickets also was easily remedied with two to three glasses of fresh cow or goat's milk every day. She felt badly for the children suffering rickets. They would not reach their full height and some suffered bone and muscle pain. Although the addition of milk into their diets would prevent further damage to growing bones, once the leg bones had softened, there was bound to be some bowing in the legs. "Cowboys and cowgirls" she called the little ones suffering from this condition.

Georgia noted that Dr. Williams seemed to refer patients to individual students based on their expected medical practices. She diagnosed and treated nutritional maladies, learned how to set bones, remove bullets and suture cuts. He asked her, more than the others, to assist with surgeries. She knew how to measure chloroform, administer it, and test to ensure that the patient felt nothing before making an incision to remove a foreign object. Dr. Williams said Georgia was better at stitching up an incision than he. *Must be from all the sewing I did or stitching up cuts on horses and cattle at the ranch*, she thought.

Jonathan and Mr. Allerton treated the wealthier clientele, alcoholics, those with gout and those with mental instability. Dr. Williams was preparing them for private practice on the East Coast, near their homes, Georgia surmised. She thought she had the three of them pegged correctly. She wasn't sure exactly what type of patients he referred to his nephew, perhaps a little of everything or was it what was left over? She got the feeling her classmate Mr. Williams was attending medical school out of obligation, more than a commitment to the profession.

Denver had suffered a series of blizzards before and after Christmas, keeping everyone close to hearth and home. Dr. Williams's household, which included his four students, ate a fat tom turkey that Georgia had shot in the creek bed. This fact, at Georgia's request, was not announced. It was a secret between her and Dr. Williams, who understood her desire to fit in, or at least appear to fit in with the genteel Denver society.

Lucy's resourcefulness and the Williams's very adequate larder had provided them with a delightful array of traditional and not-so-traditional foods over the Christmas season. On Christmas Eve, Lucy served tamales, some made with pork and others with almonds and dried cherries. She said her mother had taught her to make the tamales and that no Christmas Eve would be complete without them. On Christmas Day, they dined on roast turkey, mashed potatoes, yams, dried fruit pudding, sweet and savory pies and other sweets.

Georgia had hoped she would receive news from home at Christmas, but the weather prevented the delivery of mail from the Eastern Plains. By mid-January, however, she had a nice, long letter from her mother, updating her on everything at the MacBaye Ranch. There was some interesting news as well:

... It probably won't surprise you to learn that James has joined the Colorado First Cavalry. He's always been a man who loved his firearms and seems happy with a wandering life, at least for now. He and his unit are assigned to search out hostile Indians. I do hope that what he learned about Indians while Gray Wolf was here with us will enable him and his fellow Cavalry men to be discerning, rather than killing every Indian they come across.

The letter contained more news about the ranch, including the increase in stock numbers and her father's planting plans for the coming spring. She was certain her father had told her mother to include these details, as they were not facts her mother knew. Her pulse quickened as she read the next paragraph:

We were surprised in December when a knock came on our door, and it was Gray Wolf! He brought with him a freshly dressed turkey. No doubt he remembered our tradition of eating turkey at Christmas. He stayed with us for three days, enjoying beans and cornbread, and we enjoyed the dried, smoked buffalo he brought with him. I was sure to send him home with some jams and dried vegetables. He said he was grateful that his band was successful in securing food for the winter but that many of the Cheyenne were not as fortunate. Many of them are hungry already and begging for food at the forts. He said the Indians were promised food in exchange for remaining peaceful but that the food never came. I feel sad for him and his people, but I don't know what we can do to help. At least he seemed well.

The letter went on about which settlers had moved into the Bijou Basin, who was marrying whom, and so on. Georgia wanted to know more about Gray Wolf's visit. A few sentences were not enough. Did he ask about her? Did he tell them he had rescued her on her journey to Denver? She hoped he didn't tell them about the murdered stagecoach driver and passengers. That might cause her father to ride straight to Denver to bring her back home, despite it being the middle of January. How she wanted to know where he was and what he was doing.

Georgia reread the letter. When she finished, she decided to go to the livery to do her stable duties, but while she was still changing into her work skirt and shirtwaist, she was interrupted by a knock at her door.

"A letter for you, Miss Georgia. The postman just delivered it."

What a nice surprise. Her mother had received her letter and responded, Georgia thought. Two letters in one day! "Thank you, Lucy." As soon as the letter was in hand, she knew it was not from her mother. The stationery was ivory linen with "Miss Georgia MacBaye" written in bold script across the envelope. It looked like an invitation. She opened the envelope and pulled out the card on matching ivory linen.

You are cordially invited to a Dinner Party at the Denver residence of Mr. Isaac Van Wormer, Eleven South Sherman Street, on the 21st of January 1864.

Van Wormer. *Wasn't he the man Jonathan and I met in*

the fall when we were out for a ride? Why in the world would I be invited to a dinner party? Wouldn't Ma be proud? Once again, she was glad her mother had sent her off with several formal gowns. Stopping by the school on her way to the livery, she learned that Jonathan too had received an invitation. They would go together, he suggested. *How bad can a dinner party at the house of a man who hunts turkeys be*, Georgia reasoned.

※

Eleven South Sherman Street was lit up inside and out with candles and lanterns. Dr. Williams had offered to have Georgia and Jonathan delivered to the house in his own carriage, but they convinced him they could easily walk the half-mile. As they neared the house, Georgia began to have second thoughts about the wisdom in that decision. Her feet would have felt fine for the duration of the walk in cold weather had she been able to wear her boots, but the occasion dictated she wear more delicate and far less comfortable formal slippers. Another "necessity" her mother insisted she bring and for which she was grudgingly thankful, even more so as she realized the grandeur of the event.

Mr. Van Wormer greeted them. "Georgia, why who would have ever thought the fine horsewoman I met near Cherry Creek was such a charming young lady. And Jonathan, I see you have fully recovered from your fall. Please come in and warm yourselves by my fire."

Georgia felt like the proverbial fish out of water. Jonathan seemed nervous, but not overwhelmed. She suspected he was far more accustomed to such parties than she was.

"How do you do, Miss ...?"

"MacBaye, sir. I'm Georgia MacBaye."

"Pleased to meet you, Miss MacBaye. Major Edward Wynkoop at your service. Allow me to present my wife, Mrs. Louisa Wynkoop."

"Major Wynkoop, aren't you the commander at Fort Weld?"

"One and the same."

"My brother has just joined the Colorado First Cavalry. I wonder if you might know James MacBaye."

"I've met him. He is a recent recruit from the Eastern Plains, no?"

"That's right, sir. We come from a ranch in the Bijou Basin. I have been here studying medicine since September and just learned from my mother's letter that my brother has joined the Colorado First."

"Studying medicine, you say, with Dr. Williams?"

"Yes, sir."

"I'm very glad to see a woman in the profession. You know, there are times a woman doctor can be better at the profession than a man. Now, you won't tell good ole Doc Williams I said that, will you?"

"Oh, no, sir." He was the first man she'd ever heard praise women doctors, and he wasn't just making conversation. He really believed there was a place for women in medicine.

"What made you want to become a doctor, Miss MacBaye?" Mrs. Wynkoop asked.

"My mother is good with administering healing herbs and other remedies. She also knows a lot about nutrition. People come to her all the time, seeking advice about their health, and she knows simple ways to heal people and help them be strong again. Of course, she says it is not her that heals, but the Lord above who is the true healer."

"Ah, so true. My grandfather was a physician, and I thought he knew everything there was to know about the human body. Once he told me that with each year he studied and practiced medicine, he realized how little he really knew and how amazing the body is."

"My mother taught me a lot, but I also wanted to study modern medicine. Both she and my father want me to learn as much as I can."

"And have you had a lot of experience treating patients?"

"Oh, yes, ma'am. Dr. Williams made us do bookwork first, and now we are treating patients. Of course, it's easy with all the tools, medicines and everything available to us. Once I return home, I 'spect I'll have to rely more on my wits and what I can use herb-wise to treat patients. I do hope to bring some medical instruments and a supply of the common medicines back home with me after my schooling is finished. I also want to learn more from the Indians. They don't suffer scurvy or rickets, some of the conditions that are common to so many settlers."

"You don't say ... how do you know this?" Major Wynkoop, who had been listening to his wife and Georgia talk, re-entered the discussion.

Georgia considered how to answer. She could talk about her experience with the Cheyenne minus Gray Wolf, but felt this man was a straight shooter, not one she wanted to shortchange by not being fully honest. "There are a lot of Indians, Cheyenne and Arapaho, mostly, that move through the Bijou Basin. Cheyenne Chief Lean Bear brought his nephew to our ranch after he'd been injured and asked my mother's help. His nephew lived with us for a year. We learned a lot from each other."

Mrs. Wynkoop gasped. "An Indian living in your home. Were you frightened?"

"Ma'am, I think he was much more frightened of us, at first anyway, than we were of him. He taught my father and brothers new techniques for tanning hides, and he made wonderful boots. He showed us how to dry meat and blend it with dried berries. I'm convinced the pemmican they make, which is a staple for the Cheyenne over the winter, is a good part of the reason they don't get scurvy or rickets."

"I'll have to make a note of that," the major said.

Georgia continued, pleased with the reaction: "He was very interested in learning farming, and he liked his studies."

"Studies, you mean he learned to read, write and work figures?" she asked, astonished.

"My ma said he was a better student than me. He learned to read and write basic English in just a few months. I think he already knew how ta do figures. Seemed that way when we spoke. He would make marks on wood or paper for his calculations."

Mr. Van Wormer called his guests to attention. Georgia counted sixteen.

"Thank you all for coming this evening. I had planned to have this dinner party Christmas week, but Mother Nature prevented it. January is a mite cold for going out in the evening, so I appreciate your accepting my invitation. Some of you know each other, but so as no one is slighted, let me do the honors of introducing each of you."

He turned to his right and said, "I'm sure all of you know our decorated Colonel John Chivington and Mrs. Chivington."

Is this the man who led the effort that cut off the supply trains of the Confederate Army in northern New Mexico? The one Governor Evans had called on to drive out the Indians? Georgia studied his face but found no compassion, no mercy in his eyes.

"Mr. and Mrs. William Byers, founder of our esteemed newspaper, the *Rocky Mountain News*. To his right are Captain Silas Soule and his lovely fiancée, Miss Hersa Coberly. And these two young people right here could save your lives someday— Miss Georgia MacBaye and Jonathan VanDerKemp. I met these two medical students this fall when I was turkey hunting on Cherry Creek. Miss MacBaye hails from the Eastern Plains, Bijou Basin, not far from one of my own cattle ranches, and Mr. VanDerKemp, well, we Dutchmen have to stick together," he said, winking in good humor.

Georgia felt heat rising to her cheeks. She feared she would blush with the attention turned on them.

"Now let's see if we can do my housekeeper's roast beef some justice. She spent all afternoon roasting it just right for us," Mr. Van Wormer said, gesturing for his guests to move into the dining room.

Georgia was pleased that the Wynkoops were seated to her right. To her left sat Jonathan, with Captain Soule and his fiancée. Colonel Chivington was asked to say grace. Georgia had read that he earned his nickname the Fighting Parson because of his strong abolitionist views while serving as a minister in a pro-slavery state. He had insisted that "by the grace of God and these two revolvers" he would preach his convictions to the less-than-receptive congregation. Despite the man's conviction that slavery was wrong, a view she completely endorsed, she felt an instant dislike of him. He ended his otherwise routine prayer with, "And guide us in your service as we route out the hostiles that infest this land. Amen."

Mr. Van Wormer invited his guests to help themselves to the steaming dishes the housekeeper had placed on the table. The smell of slow cooked beef and roasted vegetables overtook Georgia's nervousness. She tried to eat in the slow, dignified manner that her mother insisted was appropriate for a "proper young lady." Her mother's admonition also came with instructions on which eating utensils to use at which times. With two forks to her left and an additional spoon at the top of her plate, she was grateful for her mother's etiquette lesson.

The beef and vegetables were roasted to perfection with onions, garlic and rosemary. She enjoyed her host's dinner immensely and was eager to accept seconds when the plates were passed around a second time.

"Pardon me, miss, but you have quite an appetite," Colonel Chivington boomed from across the table.

Georgia turned pink in the face when she realized he was addressing her. Swallowing the last bite of roast beef, she responded, "Pardon me, I'm a rancher's daughter and haven't tasted a good piece of beef like this since I left home." She hoped the explanation would suffice and the conversation would move elsewhere. If not, she feared she would blurt out what she was thinking. *I've tried my best to be a proper lady. My mother has worked hard to make me so, but I fear I've failed ... and I don't really care.*

"No worries. I rather like to see a young lady eat like she enjoys it, rather than making it a duty."

Georgia was grateful for his understanding, but disliked his manner. He addressed her with exaggerated simplicity. Did he think her witless?

"Yes, sir," she mumbled, struggling to gain composure.

"Where is your father's ranch?"

"It's a homestead in the Bijou Basin." Georgia immediately regretted admitting they were homesteaders to the arrogant man.

"Ah, and have you lost property to the hostiles?"

She wasn't about to mention Gray Wolf, but neither was she going to let him demean the Cheyenne. "To the contrary, sir, we've found the Indians rather helpful."

"How so?" The colonel looked confounded.

"We've learned how to tan hides, make pemmican, that sort of thing," Georgia said. "If it weren't for the Mexicans who built our house and showed us what to plant in the arid ground and the Indians who showed us where to hunt, I doubt we would have made it through our first year. I suppose the Indians are like any race. There are good and bad among them."

"Some friendlies. Isn't that something," Chivington said as though searching for a way to bring the subject back under his control.

"What do you say, Miss MacBaye, to the developing Army position that the only good Indian is a dead Indian?" Captain Soule intervened.

Georgia hated being the center of the conversation, but she hated backing down even more. "I would say it is a very foolish position and one that will get even more people killed."

"What do you mean it will get more people killed?" Miss Coberly asked. "If the Indians are eliminated, they won't be able to cause problems."

Georgia recognized the question for what it was: repeated rhetoric, rather than hatred. She kept her anger in check. "I would appeal to you from both a practical and a moral point of view. I do think it is possible for Indians and whites to live together. On the second point, how can we call ourselves Christians if we aim to eliminate an entire race—man, woman and child?"

"So, Miss MacBaye, you'd have us just turn a blind eye to these red devils stealing from, killing and capturing white settlers? That doesn't seem very Christian either, and I should know what I'm talking about," Colonel Chivington boomed, showing his impatience that a mere girl would disagree with him.

"I would not stand by and let that happen, but I also would not punish someone who had not been proven to have done wrong. I guess that would be like executing everyone seated at this table if one of us left tonight and committed a crime on his or her way home. Just 'cause we ate together and are all white wouldn't mean all of us are bad because one is."

After an extended silence, Captain Soule said, "It's hard to argue with you there, Miss MacBaye. Perhaps the presence of more soldiers will discourage those bent on destruction."

"That's exactly why I've been petitionin' the higher-ups to send us more troops or to let us raise our own Colorado regiment of volunteers!" the colonel said, pounding his fist on the table so hard that the silverware bounced.

Georgia jumped inwardly but refused to be cowed by the power display of Colonel Chivington. She addressed Captain Soule. "That would help, but I think the real problem for a lot of the Indians is that they are hungry. Their hunting grounds have been greatly reduced by treaties, and the white settlement has pushed out the buffalo."

"The government is virtually feeding them as it is," Captain Soule said.

Mr. Van Wormer entered the fray: "From what I've been hearing, there is dissension because the Indians were promised provisions for leaving their hunting grounds for the settlers to use, yet the Indian agents often make them pay for what should legally be theirs."

"That's not right," Mrs. Wynkoop said.

"No, it's not right, but neither is preventing a man from providing for his family," Captain Soule said.

"Well now that we're agreed on that, let's enjoy some pie for dessert," Mr. Van Wormer said, effectively diffusing the tension and setting the stage to move the guests on to a more amicable conversation.

Shortly after the guests were served their pie and coffee, Colonel Chivington and the Wynkoops thanked Mr. Van Wormer for his hospitality and rose to leave. The other guests soon did the same. Captain Soule and Hersa Coberly volunteered to take Jonathan and Georgia back to Dr. Williams's home. Georgia thought to protest, but remembered how badly her feet hurt from the formal slippers, and it was much colder out now than when they had arrived.

Later, as Georgia lay in bed recounting the conversation, she wondered why she seemed to create tension in any conversation she joined. She argued with the shopkeeper when Gray Wolf had wanted to buy the hunting knife. She had managed to offend her fellow medical school students the first night she was in Denver. And tonight she had turned Mr. Van Wormer's gathering upside down, managing to offend most of the guests. She supposed that was the price of speaking her mind. Her mother, again, was right. Georgia would not have made a good Southern belle.

Chapter 12

Lean Bear's Camp, Southeastern Colorado, February 1864

G ray Wolf heard hooves pounding and looked to the southwest where he saw visitors riding into camp. No sooner had they dismounted than the wind began to howl, confirming arrival of the winter storm. Daylight was quickly disappearing as dark clouds descended from the northwest. Camp elders had predicted the storm by looking at the sky earlier that day, which made the arrival of visitors even more unexpected. Their business must be urgent to travel at sunset with the impending storm, reasoned Gray Wolf.

Lean Bear warmly greeted the regal old chief and the warriors who had traveled with him. "We are honored the great Chief Black Kettle would visit our humble camp. Come, let us smoke the pipe and hear what has brought you to us with such urgency." He motioned for Gray Wolf to join them.

Lean Bear's band traveled often and had no meeting lodge, so he invited Black Kettle's entourage to enter the tepee of his first wife, who scurried about preparing food. She shouted at Lean Bear's other wives to help her. The three women hastened to combine their pots of boiling meat and vegetables, adding dried meat and water so there was enough for the visitors. Gray Wolf hoped, for their sakes, that no one noticed that the soup was thinner. When everyone finished eating, the women served them coffee. Lean Bear's wives must have stored away the coffee for a special occasion such as this, thought Gray Wolf, because he had not had coffee for months. It tasted good, though a bit sweeter than he preferred.

"Many of our people are hungry," Black Kettle, the old chief, said. "They do not have meat in their cooking pots, and I fear they will die of starvation or disease if they cannot eat nourishing meat and marrow." He paused, and tears welled up in his eyes. His voice was unsteady when he again spoke. "They cannot hunt the buffalo to feed themselves and provide clothing for their families. If we live by what we promised when we smoked the peace pipe with the white man, our young and elders will die. Even those who have enough to eat are growing bitter. I fear they will wage war against the whites when the geese return and the buffalo calves are red."

"This too has been bothersome to me," Lean Bear said, placing a closed fist over his heart. "I understand the young warriors' desire to fight the whites and to recapture our hunting grounds. I too wish we could return to the days when the buffalo herds could not be counted, and the creek beds were full of deer. But the whites have plowed the ground and brought in their cattle to eat the grass the buffalo once ate."

"Many will die if we fight against the whites," Black Kettle said, shaking his head in defeat. "Maybe the Cheyenne will be no more."

"The young warriors do not understand that they may kill some of them, but more will come, and their soldiers will come and kill our women and children," Lean Bear said. "I have been to the home of the Great White Father. I have seen how many whites there are. They will never stop. We must make peace with them." Lean Bear packed tobacco in his ceremonial pipe and leaned over the fire in the center of the tepee to light it. He presented it to his guest of honor.

"We are in agreement, then, my brother." Black Kettle smoked the pipe and passed it to a brave seated next to him. "I come to you on this windy, cold night to ask if you and your nephew will join us to ask that food be given to our people. If you are in agreement, once the storm passes, we will travel to White Antelope's camp to ask him to join us to go to ask this of Agent Colley."

"Stay here in my tepee until the storm has passed, and we will do as you ask. Now, go with Gray Wolf to unload your ponies and take them to the creek bed before the storm blinds us."

✳

Three days later, Chiefs Black Kettle, Lean Bear, White Antelope and some of the other Cheyenne chiefs who were in agreement that peace needed to be discussed, had gathered and were riding east to Fort Larned in what the whites called Kansas Territory to meet with Indian Agent Samuel Colley.

Gray Wolf knew most of the warriors that had come to Lean Bear's camp with Black Kettle. He had raced horses or hunted with them at one time or another when the Cheyenne bands gathered for powwows. One warrior, a man whose Cheyenne name was Beaver, was unfamiliar. He looked to be Gray Wolf's age and spoke perfect Cheyenne, but there was something that was different about him. As the young warriors staked out the horses for the night, Gray Wolf's curiosity got the best of him.

"I see you take great care with your horse," Gray Wolf said to Beaver.

"My father bought him for me. He's fast. A great hunting pony."

Gray Wolf did not disagree, but how could he ask him what he really wanted to know? He decided a more direct approach was the only way to get the answer he sought. "What is your name? I hear the braves call you Beaver and also George. Who gave you your name and what does it mean?"

"My father, William Bent, gave me my English name. He is a white trader and rancher. My mother is Owl Woman, daughter of Cheyenne Chief Yellow Wolf." He stopped, as though he wished to say more but thought better of it.

"White names don't have any special meaning," Gray Wolf said, hoping to prompt Beaver to continue. "It's not like Indian names. Parents just choose names of relatives or a name they like when their children are born."

"You are right." Beaver said.

"Should I call you George?"

"I prefer Beaver when among my mother's people. Does it bother you that I am half-white?" he asked, defensive.

Gray Wolf hadn't meant to offend the brave. "Not in the least," he said. "I'm curious, that's all."

"You're not white, but you speak the white tongue with ease. Why?"

Continuing in English, Gray Wolf related the story of his uncle taking him to Loraine for healing and how living with the MacBayes for a year had given him great insight into their way of life. "I can't admit this to anyone else," he said, lowering his voice, "but there are things about the white way of life that I really miss."

"Oh, yeah, like what?"

"Well, I like the warm ranch house, the soft bed, cornbread and beans, staying in one place, and ..." No, he wouldn't tell Beaver about Georgia. He could barely admit to himself how much he missed her.

"And what?" Beaver stood looking at him with amusement. "Is it a girl?"

"How did you know?"

"Just a guess." Beaver turned serious. "Forget it, Gray Wolf, or your children will end up like me."

"What do you mean, like you? Why do you say it's bad to be like you?"

"You know how torn you feel, like you have one foot in the white world and one in the Indian world?"

"Yes, it is exactly how I feel. How did you know?"

"I know because it is how I feel every day of my life." Beaver looked thoughtful. "You can feel that way, but you can leave it behind, because your parents are Cheyenne. The only thing pulling you both ways is what's inside. On the outside, no one knows. No one wonders if you're on the Cheyenne side or the white side."

"Is that how you feel? Like you can't be completely in one world or the other?" Gray Wolf was hungry to talk with this brave who understood him.

Beaver shrugged, as if to say it didn't matter. But it did matter. Gray Wolf could see that. When he and Beaver rejoined the others, they switched back to speaking Cheyenne.

※

It was a typical early March morning when the delegation came into view of Fort Larned. The bright sun was beginning to thaw the muddy ground, making travel slower and messy. If there was one thing that was important to a Cheyenne chief and his braves it was to present oneself to strangers in a way that impressed the host. The men braided their horses' manes and tails with beads and feathers. Each man wore his best and most colorful attire. Gray Wolf had learned that this habit of decking oneself out to the hilt was what scared whites. They associated the bright paint and feathers with a war party. It was easy to understand the confusion, now that Gray Wolf thought about it. War parties attired themselves much the same but added paint to their faces and their horses' hides. It was a subtle distinction. Gray Wolf had tried to convince his fellow Cheyenne that their arrival would be less alarming to the fort occupants if they were to skip the finery. They ignored him.

The fort's watchtower must have spotted them, because while they were some distance away, a line of soldiers rode out to meet them. Gray Wolf and the other Cheyenne braves continued their easy lope toward them. Just as the whites had trouble discerning the intentions of Indians, so the Indians could not gauge the intention of the soldiers.

When there was a wide river's width between them, both lines pulled their horses to a stop. Black Kettle raised his lance, and Gray Wolf saw that a white swatch of fabric was attached to it. The chief waved the lance and walked forward with several of his braves, including Beaver, flanking him. The rest of the Cheyenne waited where they stood.

Gray Wolf was too far away to hear what they said, but he could see that Black Kettle talked first. Then Beaver talked, translating, he surmised. When the soldier talked, Beaver translated his words for Black Kettle. Shortly, Black Kettle waved his lance, signaling them to follow him to the fort.

When they were at the fort, the doors opened and the soldiers entered. The doors closed, leaving the Cheyenne delegation waiting outside. In typical fashion, a gathering of destitute Indians had populated the land around the fort. Lean Bear told him about these desperate souls, guessing what brought them to beg for food and alcohol from the forts. Today, he saw Cheyenne, Arapaho, and even a few Sioux, all having long since lost their dignity and desire to hunt for food. Most wore dirty, torn buckskin clothing and reeked of alcohol. There were those who talked to themselves and shrieked randomly. He wondered what came first. Was it poverty that led to insanity or alcoholism that led to poverty? Most were men, but he noticed some women looked the most destitute. All seemed to have a baby on their hips. No doubt any food they acquired went to feed their babies. He was saddened to think of the service these women must provide to the soldiers or other Indians in order to survive. *Where are their husbands or brothers?* he wondered. Most likely they had been killed, either hunting or while raiding some settler's ranch.

The shadows were long when the door of the fort opened and Agent Samuel Colley emerged to greet them. "You're still here.

I figured you might have tired waiting for me and left by now."

Black Kettle spoke, and Beaver translated. "We have a matter of great importance to discuss with you and have traveled two days to come here."

"Oh, alright, then, come on in, but this will have to be quick. I have plans for this evening, and you need to be out of here by then."

Four of the braves stayed with the horses, and the others, fifteen in total, entered the fort.

Agent Colley haphazardly gestured toward a table in the courtyard of the fort, displacing soldiers who had been playing cards. "We'll sit over there, but you'd better make this quick."

Beaver didn't translate Colley's words, but his lack of respect for the chiefs was obvious. Even an Indian who was starving would have offered visitors food and drink, and speaking before the peace pipe was passed was unthinkable.

When they were seated, Colley made no attempt to hide his irritation. "I've no provisions for you. I see you've come with nothing to trade, so I can't help you. You need to go back home and get food wherever it is that you get it. Can't you see we have too many Indians here already?"

Beaver continued to translate for Black Kettle: "We didn't come to ask for food for ourselves. We came to talk of peace. Because many of our people, as you have said, are hungry, we fear they will soon fight the settlers because they are angry and because they must feed their families."

"You look at me like it is my fault they are hungry. You see for yourselves how the Indians hang around the fort, begging for food instead of planting fields to grow their own food."

"Putting seed into the ground is unknown to my people," Black Kettle responded through Beaver. "Many, many years ago, we did this, but now we hunt the buffalo, and we cannot hunt the buffalo because they have left, and your Great White Father wants all Indians to stay in small areas where they cannot hunt buffalo or deer. Only rabbits and prairie birds live here, and they are too little food for us."

Lean Bear spoke this time, and Gray Wolf said his words in English. "We come to you to ask your help because we will not be able to stop our young warriors' wrath when they have no food. We fear they will kill settlers and burn their houses. We want you to tell Governor Evans that we want peace." Then Gray Wolf added what Lean Bear had not spoken. "And we want you to give our people the food they were promised."

Agent Colley's face turned white. "Your people can have any food they pay for." He pounded his fist on the table. "And don't expect any sympathy from Governor Evans. It was you chiefs, after all, who stood him up last fall. He hasn't forgotten that."

Gray Wolf translated the words. Lean Bear, Black Kettle and White Antelope spoke angrily amongst themselves.

"The white man will not keep his word," White Antelope said, rising to leave.

Before Gray Wolf could translate, Beaver turned to Colley. "Your words anger our chiefs. They wanted to meet with your chief during the time of the winter moon, but the Dog Soldiers prevented them from coming. The people are listening to the Dog Soldiers now because they are hungry and cannot hunt. Our chiefs have come to see you to ask you to help, so that white settlers are not killed. Will you be responsible for these deaths?"

Colley stomped off, yelling at his men to bring food for the "damned Injuns."

Neither Beaver nor Gray Wolf translated. The chiefs stood to leave as a wagon of sugar, flour, coffee and canned food was shoved at them with the admonition of the solider: "Get your food and leave."

Two of the braves picked up the tongue of the wagon and wheeled it out of the fort, dropping it for the vagrants to raid.

"Foolish man." Black Kettle shook his head, disappointed in the outcome of their visit with Agent Colley.

The Cheyenne returned to their waiting ponies and rode off at a gallop. They would reach White Antelope's camp in the middle of the night and sleep there.

Chapter 13

Denver City, April 1864

*D*enver City Vulnerable to Indian Attacks, Colonel *Chivington Requests Funds to Raise Volunteer Regiment*. The *Rocky Mountain News* lead story was the talk of the town. Shopkeepers, except those selling arms, despaired of the impact on sales. People scared of Indian attacks weren't buying clothing and household goods. They stayed home with their rifles at their sides. The following day's news seemed to confirm the threat. *Cheyenne Warriors Steal Government Cattle*. The story outlined the theft near the Sand Creek Reservation. Colonel John Chivington was addressing the situation by sending Lieutenant George Eayre and fifty-four troops from the Colorado First Cavalry to hunt down the thieves.

How would Lieutenant Eayre know who the thieves were? Georgia wondered. Besides, they were probably starving to death. Anyone who knew anything about Indians knew they preferred to eat buffalo and would eat beef only as a last resort. She thought about Gray Wolf and hoped he wasn't starving. He was a good hunter. She believed, hoped, he would be able to find game.

Georgia felt guilty that her first thoughts after reading the newspaper articles had been for Gray Wolf, rather than for her brother James. Since receiving her mother's letter in January, she had inquired of soldiers and officers she met, asking of his whereabouts. A month ago, she treated a young Cavalry man for a minor knife wound. He claimed he acquired it while sparring with hostile Indians. She knew he was lying. The depth and direction of the cut indicated it came from clumsy whittling or misplacing his knife in its case before mounting a horse. She despised such false boasting, but decided not to embarrass the man. Instead, she asked him if he knew James. Not only did the soldier know James, he offered to take her to the Camp Weld barracks the following day. She thought it odd that James had not found her. Nonetheless, she accepted the soldier's offer.

It had not been a joyful reunion. She recalled part of their conversation: "Someone's gotta rid Colorado Territory of these thievin', murderin' Injuns. Why not me?" Boasting, James had looked around to see who might have heard him.

Georgia thought how joining the Cavalry had changed her brother, and not for the better. "We're all much obliged to the Cavalry's protection from the Southern Rebels and the Indians who are up to no good, but—"

"All the Injuns are up to no good, Georgia, and it's the Cavalry's job to eliminate 'em."

"All of them? James, you can't be serious. Think about Gray Wolf. He lived with us for a year, and—"

"Now, Georgia, we can't be sentimental. That sort of thinking will get us all killed."

"Callousness will get you killed faster." Georgia couldn't believe what she was hearing. Had joining the Cavalry changed him so, or was this the real James? She knew he was never close to Gray Wolf. Not as her father and she had been. But she never thought James had hated him like he seemed to now.

The explosive conversation had cooled somewhat, and they

parted with civility, yet long afterward, she had questioned what had changed James. She hadn't seen him since.

※

A week later, the headline of the *Rocky Mountain News* lead story read: *Indian Depredations Escalate, No One is Safe!* The article outlined two incidents. North of Denver, Indians destroyed newly erected telegraph lines, stole livestock and drove settlers from their homes. At Fremont Orchard, an all-out fight had broken out between the Cheyenne Dog Soldiers and Cavalry troops, leaving two soldiers killed and two wounded. Georgia hoped James had not been among them. The article concluded, *It appears it will be a long, hot summer for our settlers and soldiers, as they fight off Indian attacks.*

In an attempt to get her mind off the danger engulfing Denver, Georgia decided to do her chores at the livery. With Indian attacks on her mind, she decided to take the pistol she had hidden under her mattress. She checked the lock, and tucked it inside her right boot. It wasn't the most comfortable to walk with the pistol there, but her eight months in Denver City had taught her that city folk didn't take kindly to women carrying firearms. She suspected more carried them than she knew, but they sure didn't make it known. She supposed it was her rural upbringing and her father's unconventional thinking that a woman should always be prepared to defend herself that made her feel naked without a gun at her side. Even in Denver, she carried a knife with a folding blade in a leather case on the inside of her skirt waistband. She had never had to use it to defend herself, although it had come in handy several times at the clinic to lance a festering wound or cut off a pant leg.

She completed the cleaning that paid Cheyenne's board and started to groom the filly when she heard a ruckus. Stepping into the livery aisle, she saw a horse crash backward into a stall divider. A man was pursuing it with a bullwhip, and when the frightened creature continued to rear and lunge, the man cursed and cracked the whip again. He hadn't struck the horse, but his intention to intimidate it was clear. When the man saw her, he shouted at her to get away from the "crazed" horse.

"Put that whip down, NOW!" she screamed.

"I'll do no such thing. This gelding done dumped me outside the mercantile, and I had to walk all the way back."

He pulled the bullwhip back to send another pop at the frightened horse when Mr. Fletcher entered the livery.

"Your blasted horse needs to learn a lesson." He snapped the whip again. Wood splintered as the cornered gelding reared and fell backward through another set of stall dividers.

Georgia had never seen Mr. Fletcher angry before, and she made a mental note never to do anything to make him angry. He ran at the man, knocking him to the hard livery ground with a thud. As was the case with most bullies, the man was a coward who could not win in a fair fight. Mr. Fletcher quickly subdued the man, tying his arms behind his back and shouting for one of his employees to go for the sheriff.

While the scuffle ensued, Georgia had managed to calm the gelding enough to grab its reins. She wanted control of the horse so it wouldn't run over the two men fighting on the livery floor. As soon as she had the reins in one hand, she began to stroke the gelding on the neck and at the withers to calm it.

When Mr. Fletcher returned to the barn after handing off the disruptive client to the sheriff, Georgia was working the gelding in a small, controlled circle. She knew it was unrealistic to ask the frightened animal to stand still. She had learned that the best thing to do when a horse was frightened was to give it confidence that the handler, in this case her, had things under control. Now the gelding willingly moved its feet as directed.

Mr. Fletcher watched for several minutes, then spoke. "You sure do have a way with horses, Georgia. I thought you were bragging that first day I met you, but I can see you were straight with me."

"A horse is real uncomfortable without a herd leader to protect 'im. I guess they kinda see a human in this role if we are willing to do what they think a herd leader should do. Making a horse move the way you want 'im to lets 'im think you are the leader and that you will protect 'im. Least that's what someone taught me."

"Interesting approach you have."

"It works, and I'm not near as apt to get hurt in the process." She let the gelding stand and stroked his neck. He licked his lips as he dropped his head in submission to her.

"That lip lickin's a sign he is relaxed. I think he's a good horse and could be a dependable one if we could make 'im quit spookin' at everything. If yu'd like, I can ride 'im through the streets and let you know what I think he's thinkin'."

"If you're up to it. I got a report that the idiot I sent off with the sheriff was yanking hard on the reins, spurring him, and whipping him with that blasted bullwhip. Guess he got fed up with it and dumped him in front of the mercantile. I suppose he was pretty embarrassed, but it's no reason to take it out on the horse."

Georgia had already noticed the telltale signs of harsh handling. The gelding had bloody punctures on his sides from over-spurring, and his mouth was very sensitive to any movement of the bit. She moved the bridle, slipping it over the gelding's ears with great care. From her own tack, she brought out a bosal, a Spanish-style head piece with no bit. She fitted the contraption around the gelding's nose and slipped it over his ears. "There you go, buddy. There's nothing here to hurt that sore mouth of yours. Nothing wrong with a bit and spurs if used well, but they sure can be cruel if a rider is of a mind to make 'em so." She spoke more to the gelding than to Fletcher.

Because she was used to it and the gelding and Cheyenne appeared to have similar body conformations, she put Cheyenne's blanket and saddle on the gelding. She made sure the cinch was tight enough to hold the saddle in place, yet loose enough to give the gelding room to breathe. She circled the gelding several times more, as she had done before changing tack. When she felt it was ready to mount safely, she stepped up into the stirrup and swung over his back. He stood, calm as an old plow horse. She used one rein at a time to pull the gelding's head, first to the right and then to the left.

"These are my breaks," she said again, more to herself and the gelding than to Fletcher. "I just want to make sure that if you decide to run off, buck or rear on me, I can shut it off real quick by pulling you into a circle. You're a little stiff, but that's to be expected considering you've not been worked this way."

She urged the gelding forward with a gentle squeeze of her feet on his sides, taking care not to squeeze where the man had injured the horse with spurs. As she left the barn, she heard Mr. Fletcher say, "Darnedest thing I ever saw, but seems to work. You're one rider I won't be worrying about."

Georgia held the gelding to a walk. She wanted to see what he was going to do before asking for a faster pace, because the faster the horse went, the harder it would be to stop it if something went wrong. She traveled along Sherman Street until she ran into Cherry Creek. The creek had always reminded her of the Bijou Creek behind the MacBaye Ranch. Instead of bluffs to the west of the street, the great Rocky Mountains with their snowy caps rose into the cloudless, brilliant blue sky. She could not ride in the creek bed, as she had in the fall when she and Jonathan met Mr. Van Wormer. The heavy winter snows had melted, and while it was no raging river, a couple of feet of water gurgled down the creek. Residents had built dams of rock and wood to make it easier to draw water. She noticed that there were more houses around the creek, many of them very close to the water. Land that had been outside the city when she arrived in Denver last fall was now considered part of the city. Most of the structures were hastily built cabins, but there were several rows of multi-story homes and apartments of better construction.

The gelding had given Georgia no problem. He responded, almost intuitively, to her cues. She was contemplating the unfortunate situation of livery horses forced to be the mount of whoever hired them when she saw a familiar couple coming her way. It was Mr. and Mrs. Edward Wynkoop. She had seen them several times at church since meeting them at Mr. Van Wormer's dinner party, and they were always friendly.

"Good afternoon, Miss MacBaye. I see Dr. Williams gave you a day off from the clinic." The major was his jovial self. "I'm glad to see you enjoyin' the fine weather."

"We had an, ah, incident at the livery, and I volunteered to take this gelding out to calm him down," Georgia said, dismounting.

"Oh, Ed, I just adore the adventuresome spirit of this young lady," Mrs. Wynkoop said. "Don't you wish you could recruit young ladies like Georgia?" She laughed, but Georgia knew she meant it as a compliment.

"Indeed, I do, Mrs. Wynkoop." His expression sobered. "Have you told Georgia about where his majesty, Colonel Chivington, is sending me?"

"You're leaving Camp Weld, sir?" Georgia asked.

"I've been assigned to Fort Lyon, formerly Fort Wise, in Southeastern Colorado."

Georgia gasped. "According to the newspaper, there aren't enough troops to protect Denver City. Why would Chivington send you away?"

"They say they are concerned about Confederates infiltrating Colorado Territory by way of the Arkansas River Valley, but I have my doubts it is a serious threat. This new assignment is being trumped up to be some big honor, but I think they have other motives." He lowered his voice as though he was letting Georgia in on some big secret. "I think Chivington and Evans are chomping at the bit to go to war with the Indians and they don't want someone like me getting in their way. I keep pushing for peace talks with the Indian chiefs."

"So, Mrs. Wynkoop will become a plains woman—not exactly where I pictured you, ma'am."

"Oh, no, Georgia, the children and I will stay in Denver City." She winced. "It's too far, and according to my husband, too dangerous for women and children."

"Dangerous, why is that?"

"You read the papers, my dear. Haven't you heard about all the depredations?"

Major Wynkoop added, "I'm sure it is only a few trouble-makers, but we're hearing that the Cheyenne, Arapaho, even the Sioux will be joining forces this summer to wage war on the settlers."

Georgia couldn't believe what she was hearing. Less than a year ago, Gray Wolf lived in their house. Lean Bear had come in peace to take him away. "I guess I'd thought the papers to exaggerate the danger. Do you really think there will be war between the settlers and Indians?"

"It's possible. I want to be in a place to do everything I can to stop this. Chivington and Evans may think they are getting me out of their way, but they are putting me closer to the Indians, so that I can talk with them."

"My husband will be requesting Captain Silas Soule join him as second in command at Fort Lyon." She smiled at her husband. "It gives me some comfort to know Silas will be there with you."

"When do you leave Denver City?" Georgia asked.

"Next month."

"Then I'll have a chance to say goodbye before you leave."

"Yes, you will. We'll be at church Sunday," Mrs. Wynkoop volunteered.

"I'll see you Sunday." Georgia turned to mount the gelding.

"One more thing," Major Wynkoop said, stopping her. "I almost forgot to tell you that I will be requesting your brother James accompany me to Fort Lyon. While I'm not sure he's as feisty as you, he's a solid horseman and an excellent shot. His experience with Indians and the Eastern Plains will be invaluable to me."

From the last conversation she had with her brother, Georgia doubted he shared the major's view on the impending Indian war, but she hoped being handpicked for the Fort Lyon assignment would make James rethink his point of view.

Chapter 14

Smoky Hill River, Western Kansas/Eastern Colorado,
May 16, 1864

The chiefs' unsuccessful visit with Agent Colley added kindling to the growing fire of distrust and anger against the whites. They collectively scoffed at the Fort Wise Treaty that restricted their movement and hunting grounds while giving nothing in return. Black Kettle, White Antelope and Lean Bear still talked of peace with the whites, trying their best to describe to them the vast resources and number of whites that would move west in coming years.

"Why do you tell us this? That we might be scared into slinking away like the coyote when he sees he is outnumbered?" asked Star, a dog soldier, who was loyal to Lean Bear but frank in his distrust of the whites and their treaties.

Not all Dog Soldiers were as respectful. Gray Wolf saw braves yelling at their elders, something that a decade earlier would have resulted in the offender's expulsion from the tribe. The young braves in the dog soldier and other societies spoke defection and encouraged their fellow society members to openly defy their elders. His people were losing their soul. Moral decay was evident everywhere.

The disrespect of elders and dissension among the Cheyenne worsened as news reached their camp that white soldiers had killed several dozen and wounded many more Northern Cheyenne camped on the North Platte River. War cries reached a fevered pitch the day the Dog Soldiers rode into camp with tales of soldiers burning and looting their unoccupied camps.

Despite the tension between elders and young braves, and despite the fear and uncertainty that escalated with every bad report, the routines of the season continued. If nothing else, the Cheyenne were a people of tradition, and their traditions were driven by the seasons.

As they had done each spring, the time when the buffalo calves are red, the individual Cheyenne bands had gathered together to hunt and celebrate, ushering in the season of green grass for the herds and a more abundant food supply. Camped together in the Smoky Hills, the gathering could last for weeks or even months. Braves went out from the camp in hunting parties when the weather was good, and if they returned successful, all the Cheyenne joined in feasting and dancing. It was also a time young people met and matches were made.

Meadow Lark, raised a traditional Cheyenne woman, waited to be wooed by a brave of her liking. Two years older than Gray Wolf, she told him she hoped this year she would find a husband and move into her own tepee. The past three summers she had waited for first one young brave, then another to send an emissary to her tepee to ask Lean Bear's permission to marry her. Each year she waited in vain, as braves sought young women with whom they shared a blanket, a practice that only those of low-moral standing condoned. Now, though it had become common practice, Meadow Lark told him she would not share a blanket with a brave, even if it meant she would remain in her brother's tepee.

Gray Wolf thought to find her a husband himself, but she

would be mortified if she learned he had made the arrangement. He liked her company, but he understood her desire to marry, to have her own man and to raise children.

This morning as he contemplated Meadow Lark and what would become of the Cheyenne, he saw a cloud of dust to the east. Jumping on the young black stallion, he rode out to see who was approaching the camp.

Dog Soldiers were whooping and hollering as they drove cattle toward the camp. Their booty included a settler's wagon heaped with cans of food, clothing, buckets and all sorts of things settlers used in their homes and fields. The cattle were running hard toward the tepee village. The braves in their ignorance must have assumed the cattle would turn before they got to the village. While at the MacBayes' ranch, Gray Wolf learned that cattle did not behave like buffalo. Cattle stampede through things—not around. They would run plumb through the village, mowing down people and tepees in their path.

Gray Wolf ran his mount at breakneck speed toward the cattle, hazing them with the blanket he had worn to stave off the chill of the morning. The braves chasing the cattle were angry, but there was no time to explain his actions, and explain he would, if he didn't choke them first.

The hazing worked. Just before reaching the tepees furthest to the east, the cattle turned sharply to the south, skirting the village.

"Is the great Lean Bear's nephew so high and mighty that he'd send the white man's cattle back to them?!" shouted a hot-headed brave not older than sixteen.

Gray Wolf was angry and the adrenaline was still driving him. "You fools! Raiding whites will bring retaliation on us, and you nearly let cattle stampede your own village. What other foolishness have you done today?"

The brave was enraged by the reprimand. "You are a weak coward. You criticize us for providing for our people."

"What you provide is destruction."

The braves continued their triumphant entry into the village, soaking up the admiration of the villagers.

Later, Gray Wolf saw them distribute the white womens' fancy dresses, work clothing, dolls, toys, canned food and other things they had pillaged from settlers.

Gray Wolf knew it was only a matter of time before soldiers or their Indian scouts saw the Cheyenne showing off their booty, giving them cause to launch a counterattack. Lean Bear agreed with Gray Wolf that the Dog Soldiers' raid of the white wagon train or ranch put all Indians in grave danger.

A warrior on watch spotted a cloud of dust far to the west and returned to tell the chiefs that soldiers were on their way.

The warriors prepared their ponies and themselves for warfare. Lean Bear and Black Kettle agreed that a united front was important. They also knew they had to keep the soldiers far from the village. Even if they managed to hide the clothing and household goods from the troops, they were bound to hear the cattle lowing or see them grazing in the meadow with the Indian pony herds. They would know the Cheyenne had pillaged and stolen cattle, and they wouldn't care that it was the action of a few foolish teenagers.

Over a hundred warriors rode west to meet the soldiers. Black Kettle called a halt and instructed them to wait until they could see the intentions of the Army troops. While they waited, the young, inexperienced braves bragged about how many soldiers they would kill and how the women would sing of their bravery for years to come.

The young braves were itching for a fight even before they had assessed the enemy. The longer they waited, the more certain Gray Wolf was that they would charge the troops with reckless disregard for their safety or the safety of their fellow warriors.

As the troops came into view, Lean Bear must have seen the howitzers. "They bring big fire guns."

Gray Wolf saw his uncle and Black Kettle talking.

Lean Bear rode to the center of the line of Cheyenne warriors and shouted, "They will kill us if we charge. The soldiers' big guns can kill many at one time. I have visited the Great White Father in his house. I have a letter that says I am peaceful, and I wear the medal of peace around my neck. Stay here. I go to meet the soldiers."

Lean Bear and Star kicked their ponies into a hard run toward the approaching troops. Gray Wolf felt relieved. The soldiers would know, because only two rode toward them that the Indians meant no harm. And if there was any doubt, Lean Bear waved a white flag on his lance.

A gunshot shattered the hopeful calm. Gray Wolf's first thought was that one of the foolish braves had shot at the troops, until he realized that the shot came from farther away, from the line of soldiers. Lean Bear was on the ground. There was another shot, and Gray Wolf saw Star slump and fall from his horse. Three more shots. The soldiers turned and ran back in the directions from which they came.

Black Kettle shouted at the warriors not to pursue them. "Retrieve our dead, but go no further." Most complied.

Our dead ... Gray Wolf felt numb. His uncle, so alive, so wise, so strong, was dead. Black Kettle's orders not to pursue rang in his ears. The troops were nearly within rifle range, but he would not shoot his uncle's murderers with a rifle. He would put a Cheyenne arrow through them. As he reached back for an arrow from his quiver, a lightning bolt cracked, seeming to break the sky in two. Seconds later, rain, very, very heavy rain fell, darkening the sky and creating a wall between him and the soldiers. "No," the Wise One Above seemed to say.

He reined his stallion to the north in pursuit of Lean Bear's murderers. The animal was drenched in white foamy sweat. Gray Wolf was soaked from the rain, but he could feel the hot, salty dampness of the stallion beneath him. The dark cloud of rage began to lift, clear-headed reason taking its place. He slowed the stallion to a trot, then to a walk.

"Why did you let them shoot Lean Bear?" Gray Wolf was angry with the Wise One Above. "He was a good leader, a seeker of peace."

Thomas's words came to him: *We should not blame God for the evil done by men.* The logic of the statement made sense at the time. They had been discussing thievery in the Bijou Basin. Livestock belonging to the MacBayes' neighbors had been driven off and the house ransacked while the family was at church.

Questions were many, but answers did not come. Gray Wolf continued to ride northwest—why, he did not know. Long after sunset he came to a grassy gully with a spring. He dismounted, dropping to his belly to drink in the cool, fresh water.

The stallion drank and rested, then returned to drink some more. "You took very good care of me today, even when I couldn't care for myself, but I didn't treat you very well, boy. I'm sorry," he said, patting the stallion's neck. "You were as fast as lightning and as strong as thunder, yet wiser than me. Your strong heart kept us both safe. I will call you Wise Heart."

Exhaustion engulfed Gray Wolf. He slept, waking twice as he dreamed of gunshots and Lean Bear and Star falling from their horses. When he woke, the sun was already high in the sky. Wise Heart was enjoying the rest as he munched on the lush, green grass. Gray Wolf had failed twice to hit a rabbit with an arrow. The gully was a good place to sleep and drink, but he needed to move onward.

Riding west, Gray Wolf came upon a valley with familiar bluffs that cradled the MacBaye Ranch. Was it so unexpected that the Wise One Above would lead him to them, to Thomas, when he had so many unanswered questions?

It was late in the day, and Thomas appeared to be finished with his fieldwork. He was leading the oxen back to the barn when Gray Wolf rode into the ranch house yard, yelling a greeting.

Thomas ran from the barn to meet him. "How good to see you. You look very tired."

Gray Wolf slid off Wise Heart, nearly falling as he did. "Bad thing happened. Lean Bear is dead, killed by soldiers."

"When? Where?"

Thomas called for Henry and Loraine. Henry took Wise

Heart to the corral. Gray Wolf knew he would brush down the stallion and give him food and water. Loraine embraced Gray Wolf. "You look exhausted. Come in. Let me get you some food."

At the dinner table, Gray Wolf told the story of Lean Bear going to Washington, D.C., to meet President Lincoln, his insistence on making peace with the settlers, and how he had been shot without provocation the day before yesterday.

When he finished, Thomas was nodding his head in disgust, his hands rubbing his forehead. "What kind of idiots are they putting in charge of our troops?"

Loraine's eyes were moist with tears. "I'm so sorry. Your uncle was a fine and merciful man—a man of his word. It is a loss to your people, but a loss to the effort to bring peace between the whites and the Indians as well."

"I believe the Wise One Above brought me here to ask for your advice, as I—," he broke off, choking back a sob, "no longer have an elder to consult."

Thomas smiled at him. "You are wise to seek counsel, Gray Wolf. For when the heart is aching, the mind's reasoning is not always at its best. How can we help you?"

"I want to keep pushing the Cheyenne to seek peace, but how can I when we can't trust the whites ... well, most whites. Remember when you told me that there are times to make peace and times to fight? I don't know which one this is." He sighed. "With Lean Bear's death, I have the responsibility of feeding his family, as well as my sister."

"A wise man once said that to the degree that we are able, we should live at peace with all men. I think that is very good advice for you now. You shouldn't stir up trouble, but neither can you let your enemies kill or hurt you or your people."

Gray Wolf thought about this. "I was so angry with the young braves who find joy in killing and looting the innocent. They are wrong, but now I understand their anger. They feel they must do something. The problem is not that they desire to protect what is theirs, it's how they are trying to do it that is wrong."

"Your people need your wisdom, Gray Wolf," Loraine said.

"You will show them strength through compassion and bravery in your patience. Ask the Wise One Above what you should do, and He will be faithful to show you."

Gray Wolf sighed. Again, Thomas and Loraine's counsel was wise. He rose to leave.

"Oh, no, you're not leaving tonight. You need a few nights of sleep to be clear headed when you return to your people." She rose from the table. "I'll prepare your bed and a nice bath. You'll feel better in the morning. I know you will." Loraine smiled as she touched his shoulder. "Just a few minutes, and I'll have everything ready for you."

Loraine was right. He did feel better after a good night of rest. He knew what he needed to do. After savoring the hearty ranch breakfast, Gray Wolf bade the MacBayes farewell, mounted Wise Heart and turned the stallion east toward his people.

His still grieved over the murder of his uncle, but the clarity of what he needed to do made it tolerable. He rode east, stopping in the grassy gully to eat his midday meal. He smiled when he opened the leather saddlebags Thomas insisted he take. They were stuffed with his favorite foods. He would eat the cornbread first, saving the salted pork, dried apples and berry preserves for another time. The other bag contained a bag of dried pinto beans. He would show Meadow Lark how to soak and cook the beans with the salted pork.

It was the first time since Lean Bear was killed that he had thought about his sister. She was probably worried sick about him. Black Kettle certainly told her that he had chased after the troops that killed Lean Bear. She was no doubt mourning his death, or at least, she would assume him captured. He couldn't wait to see her and show her he was well. He also thought of Lean Bear's three wives, now widows. Lean Bear had only three children between the three wives. His only son was a baby. Gray Wolf didn't know whether he could feed them, but he would try.

Hadn't the Wise One Above guided him to the buffalo herd and helped him find game when other braves returned to the camp empty-handed?

He had left the MacBaye Ranch at dawn, but even riding at a good clip, he knew he would have to spend the night on the open prairie. He didn't want to ride at night or push Wise Heart as he had the day Lean Bear died. Sand Creek was a good sleeping place. The banks of the dry riverbed provided protection, and he knew the site. In past years, the Cheyenne had made Sand Creek their spring gathering spot. It would be an easy ride from Sand Creek to the Smoky Hill River where the Cheyenne were staying.

Gray Wolf rode into camp. Meadow Lark greeted him. "We thought you dead. What happened, brother? Come, you must tell me."

Gray Wolf recounted his anger and the way it had driven him to charge, unthinking, after the dozens of soldiers, the miraculous intervention of the rain, and his travel back to the MacBaye Ranch. "I know the Wise One Above is real and that he hears when we call out to him. He saved me. He did, Meadow Lark."

"You are not even a chief, Gray Wolf. Why would the Wise One Above listen to you?"

"He listens to everyone, sister, not because we are great or wise or even good. He just wants to. I know it is true."

Meadow Lark changed the subject. "Gray Wolf, you have returned in time for the Ceremony to Renew the Sacred Arrows. It starts tomorrow. Already the young braves are doing the sun dance, looking up into the sun to gain strength to please the gods. They say this year's ceremony is more important than ever. All must come with sincerity if we are to have success in pushing back the whites."

"And what does Black Kettle say of this?" Gray Wolf felt his angst rising. It was no longer anger he felt, only sadness that the young braves would waste their lives thinking they could push the whites off their land.

"The same thing. He wants us to make peace with the whites,

but no one is listening to him anymore," she said, not expressing her opinion about it.

"Has Lean Bear been honored?" Gray Wolf knew the Cheyenne dead were usually cremated the same day they died, but sometimes a chief would be laid out longer, giving everyone time to pay their respects.

"The same day he died."

"His third wife has already gone back to her father's tepee, and his second wife has shared the blanket with a subchief that swooped in the moment Lean Bear was killed. Only his first wife seems to mourn him. Who knows, by the end of the week, I might have been married myself, had you not returned," she said with a sarcastic snort.

Was one, even a great chief like his uncle, forgotten with such ease? Was there no worth in his life? Gray Wolf was disturbed by the disrespect demonstrated toward Lean Bear.

"Lean Bear is gone, Gray Wolf. His wives cannot live without his provision. You cannot blame them for finding new tepees." Meadow Lark was practical, but practicality was not what he needed at this moment.

"I don't blame them, sister. I, I ... just want life to mean more."

Chapter 15

Denver, May 25, 1864

Georgia woke with a start. The sun was bright and high in the sky. The clock in her room told her it was nearing 9 a.m., an hour by which she should have completed her barn chores, eaten breakfast and been at work in the clinic. She bolted out of bed and had her work dress and one boot on before she remembered why she had slept so late. Now she remembered the previous few days. Georgia and her three classmates worked from dawn to midnight or later for five days straight, napping in the clinic when they could. She remembered insisting her fellow students get some sleep and that they all work in shifts. Dr. Williams found Georgia dozing in the clinic between attending to the floor full of patients. No one had returned to relieve her, and the lack of companionship made it even harder to stay awake.

Heavy rains combined with melting high-country snow had sent a twenty-foot torrent down Cherry Creek late at night six days earlier. What was little more than a gurgling stream

grew into a raging river. The torrent swept away homes and
businesses. Camp Weld soldiers had sounded the alarm just
before midnight, allowing many who might have otherwise
perished to escape with their lives. Many residents, still wearing
their night clothes, had sought help at the clinic for broken
bones, gashes requiring stitching and other traumas.

Once Dr. Williams was aware of the flooding and the need
for medical services, he organized his students to serve those
who came to them as well as a search team for those who were
unable to get to the clinic. Georgia and Jonathan had gone to the
livery to hitch Cheyenne to Mr. Fletcher's wagon, but they got no
more than a hundred yards into the muddy, flooded streets when
the wagon wheels mired in the mud. Georgia regretted having
to leave the wagon in the street, but Mr. Fletcher assured them
there were greater concerns at hand. Returning to the clinic,
they rigged a gurney to fit between two horses. Cinch rings on
the horses' saddles held the gurney handles. It wasn't ideal. If
they needed to carry someone on the gurney, the riders had no
use of the stirrup on the gurney side. Like all other provisions
for dealing with the flood, it was a makeshift solution.

Mr. Fletcher had offered Jonathan and Georgia the choice of
his horses. Georgia first thought to take a steady pony that was
accustomed to pulling a wagon and would not be likely to spook
at carrying the gurney, but she changed her mind in favor of the
bay gelding. She had worked with him, and he had become, if
not perfect, dependable and predictable. He was larger, stronger
and had much longer legs than the pony; she knew what to
expect from him. Jonathan, because of his previous experience
with the gelding, had questioned her choice, but in the end, he
acquiesced.

The closer they got to the creek, the higher the water. Several
hundred feet from the creek, the water swirled around the bellies
of the pony and gelding. The horses' strength and steadiness
were crucial to the safety of those they rescued.

"With so many people on the street, it is difficult to decide
who needs medical help and who is simply in need of food, a

dry bed or someone to console them." Jonathan rubbed the back of his neck and scanned the throngs of people scrambling to leave the flood plain. "There, look, Georgia. She needs our help."Jonathan pointed to a woman with an unconscious child in her arms and another child hanging onto her wet, tattered skirt.

"Ma'am, over here. Let us take you and your young'uns to the clinic," Georgia shouted to get the young mother's attention.

Jonathan dismounted the bay gelding to help the young mother put her children on the gurney while Georgia held the horses. Once loaded, Georgia and Jonathan turned their horses toward the clinic, taking care to keep the gurney with the two children in it steady. The young woman walked beside them, wading through the flood.

Georgia and Jonathan delivered the young woman and her two children to the clinic and returned to the flood plain. They searched out and delivered people in need of medical help to the clinic all day, throughout the night and all the next day—more than thirty-six hours with not more than a wink or two of sleep. They were soaked from head to toe. Georgia's boots were full of slimy mud. Funny she hadn't noticed it before.

All told, Jonathan and Georgia had brought forty-three people to the clinic. Because space was limited, most patients were treated and discharged. Those with high fevers, ongoing nausea or severe fractures stayed. Georgia and her classmates cleaned and bandaged wounds with alcohol and applied a herbal mixture of elderberry, garlic, rosemary and thyme that Georgia had previously proposed to Dr. Williams. "My ma's concoction; seems to speed healing," she'd said.

The office of the *Rocky Mountain News*, built on stilts over Cherry Creek itself, completely washed away. Without an office or a printing press, the *Rocky Mountain News* was unable to print. In its absence, Georgia realized how much she had come to depend on the daily newspaper. The competing newspaper, *The Denver Commonwealth*, was gleeful that its competition had been swept away in the flood.

The Denver Commonwealth announced several days afterward that the flood had claimed the lives of nineteen Denver residents. "The death toll would have been higher, more than likely much higher," the paper noted, "had it not been for Dr. Williams and his fine group of young medical students, including a young lady! The students not only treated patients at the clinic, they went about the city, sorting through the wreckage to find anyone in need of medical care."

Adrenaline had driven Dr. Williams and the four students, as well as some volunteers assisting them, until they could continue no longer. With the need for emergency medical services declining, Dr. Williams had scheduled them on rotating shifts. Sitting on her bed, the dress pulled over her head and one boot on, Georgia realized she was not due at the clinic until noon. There was time to do her barn chores and eat an early lunch, which Lucy would be glad to provide.

Pulling on her second boot, she realized she had not cleaned stalls or fed Cheyenne since the day Jonathan and she had gone out to find people wounded by the flood. Ten minutes later, she entered the livery to find the horses fed and watered and their stalls cleaned.

"Glad to see you've joined the land of the living again," Mr. Fletcher's voice boomed.

Startled, she turned toward him. "You fed them. You did all my chores."

"What else would you expect a mere livery owner to do when his temporary stablehand is out saving Denver?"

"I was worried about the horses," Georgia said, smiling at him, "and about what you would think of me for not holding up my end of our agreement."

"You were pretty busy with more important things since that flood came roaring down Cherry Creek, and you've more than held up your end of the deal, Georgia. I even got my nice bay gelding trained. You know, I was thinking to sell that horse. He'd dumped more than one customer. Now he's one of my most dependable mounts."

"You're not angry with me then?" She noted with relief that the wagon they had left stranded in the street was back in its place, cleaned and polished.

"Heck no, little lady. I'm just glad you didn't get hurt yourself in all that water. You know the Indians warned us this could happen."

"They did?"

"Yes, ma'am, they did. I wasn't here then, but the old-timers say that when the first settlers came to build homes in Denver City, the friendly Cheyenne and Arapaho told them the creek would flood every now and again. At first, the settlers laughed off the idea that the tiny stream, which dries up to nothing, would ever flood. Then the Indians pointed to debris from a previous flood, still high up in them cottonwood trees along the creek. The settlers didn't waste any time moving away from the banks where they first thought to build, but all that was forgotten when wave after wave of settlers rushed to build their homes. I'm sure the folks who built on Cherry Creek were thinking it convenient to draw their water so close to their homes. Turned out to be a bad decision, a really bad decision." Mr. Fletcher pursed his lips and shook his head.

"You're sure right about that." Georgia nodded and turned to leave. She thought about her parents' adobe ranch house a hundred feet from the creek. She couldn't recall the exact conversation, but she knew Pa had consulted with the Mexicans and the Indians who knew the area to make sure the house was beyond the flood plain.

With all her barn chores finished for the day, Georgia hardly knew what to do with herself. She returned to the house, where Lucy greeted her.

"My goodness, girl, where you been?"

"I have barn chores every morning. Completely forgot about 'em during the flood. Mr. Fletcher did 'em for me."

"You went off without eating a thing. That's not like you. You come on in and eat some of this chicken salad and rye dinner rolls. The rolls are fresh out of the oven."

"Tastes heavenly, Lucy. Thank you." Georgia did not remember eating throughout the last five days. Surely, she had. "It's early, but I'm going over to the clinic to see if they need help."

Most of the patients were gone. A young man who'd had the bad fortune of having an appendicitis attack the night of the flood and had required surgery, was still recuperating. A young girl with a badly fractured leg and her mother took up another bed. The most troubling was a patient with gangrene in his foot. Dr. Williams was treating him and believed he could rid him of the gangrene, but he was not yet out of the woods.

Jonathan was in the last hour of his shift but seemed in no hurry to leave. He gave her the status for each of the patients, and when he finished, he began to repeat himself, adding more details, most of them unnecessary and unhelpful. "As I said, that fellow with the gangrene has to have his bandages changed every few hours. The herbal rub seems to be helping."

"Thank you, Jonathan. I think I can handle it from here. If you want to leave early, I don't mind at all." Georgia wondered what was keeping him at the clinic.

He turned and stepped in her direction. She thought he stood closer than he ought. "There's something I've been wanting to ask you. Sort of a request, I guess you could say." He stopped.

"What is it, Jonathan? What do you need from me?" Georgia thought it strange her very talkative classmate was now reticent.

"Oh, um, I'll just say it. I'd like to court you."

"Court me? Whatever for?"

"The reason most couples court, to get to know each other, so they can marry."

"Marry?" Georgia said it as if she had never heard of the word. Jonathan's words dumbfounded her. She mumbled something about not thinking about marriage until she was much older.

"We have a common interest in medicine, and we seem to work well together. I thought you might be interested. I plan to return to Maine when I finish my training. I'll set up a practice there. You could assist me until," he blushed, "we have children, of course."

Maine, children—was this man she appreciated as a classmate on the verge of proposing marriage? How had she encouraged him? She had never thought of marriage and him in the same sentence. The truth be told, she had not given much thought at all to marriage.

Georgia was unsure how to end the awkwardness. "It's a kind offer, but not one I can consider at this time." She wanted to be kind but firm. Instead, she thought it sounded more like her father telling a horse breeder he did not want to buy a particular horse.

Jonathan left with no further conversation, for which Georgia was grateful.

All through her shift, Georgia's mind reeled with Jonathan's offer to court her or marry her. There were worse things than marrying Jonathan, she thought. She had lived in the East as a child. Would it be the end of the world to move across the country? Yet she knew the sedate, routine life of a doctor's wife in civilized Maine would bore her to death. Her mother was so right when she said Georgia was made for this country. She really could not imagine trading her self-sufficient ranching life on the wide open plains for a clapboard two-story house where every day was safe and predictable.

She chuckled to herself as she envisioned the reaction of the gentle people in Jonathan's hometown when they learned that he had wed a gunslinging wife that passed her time training horses and hunting. No, Jonathan deserved a wife that could host proper dinner parties and who enjoyed afternoon teas with the church ladies auxiliary. He was kind and gentle and entirely patient with everyone. He had many qualities a lady would find attractive. Maybe that was the problem. She was more a frontierswoman than a lady. Any man who wanted to win her would have to accept, no, embrace her, as she was.

And then there was love. Shouldn't a gal love a man before agreeing to marry him? Certainly, people married for practical reasons, but didn't they expect love to grow? If not, what would keep the marriage together once the practical reasons for marrying no longer existed? She had affection for Jonathan, but she did not love him and she could not see herself ever loving him, no matter how practical it might be. When she thought of love, not affection, but that heart-pounding-out-of-your-chest feeling, there was only one face that came to mind.

Chapter 16

Southern Cheyenne Spring Encampment,
East of Fort Lyon, early June 1864

A war party that had been gone for three days returned with horses, mules, clothing and other items Gray Wolf recognized as belongings of settlers. This was not a party of teenage boys trying to prove their manhood by stealing livestock. Revered warrior Roman Nose and two chiefs, Two Face, and Big Thunder, rode with the war party. Gray Wolf saw with dread that the warriors proudly displayed scalps, long hair, short hair, red, blond and brown locks of hair. A child's rag doll, women's dresses, and hair combs like those Gray Wolf knew settler women to wear, were among the spoils. It wasn't soldiers the war party had fought. For a moment, panic rose in Gray Wolf as he thought of Georgia, Thomas, Loraine, James and Henry. Then he remembered that the warriors rode in from the east. The MacBaye Ranch was to the west of the campsite.

The celebration of the war party's success was short-lived. Before sundown, young boys tending the pony herd sent a message that Indians were walking toward the camp from the north. Gray Wolf joined Roman Nose and other braves that rode out to meet them. Thirty-five braves, squaws and children walked toward Gray Wolf and the others. The Indians' heads drooped and feet dragged. Some wore torn clothes and had gashes and bruises on their faces and arms.

Gray Wolf looked at Roman Nose. He did not know the man well. He was bigger, taller and faster than any other Indian. His stature, along with his chiseled features and hawklike nose made it easy to believe the reputation he had among the Cheyenne as a fearless warrior. There was no doubt that he recognized the people that walked toward them.

"All gone," said a brave who looked to be about thirty summers. "The soldiers ... they came. They burned our tepees and scattered our horses. There were fifty or sixty of them. They killed many and violated our women. Only we have escaped with our lives."

"My squaw and my son?" Roman Nose's gaze was both pleading and angry.

The brave shook his head, his eyes hollow.

"You betrayed me. You pledged to keep them safe while I was gone. I should drive this lance through your heart."

The brave dropped to his knees. He shook, feral sobs convulsing his body.

Gray Wolf feared Roman Nose might follow through on his threat. He stepped between the two. The distraction seemed to be enough to restore Roman Nose to his senses. With a piercing, extended cry, Roman Nose dug his feet into the sides of his pony and bolted north. Gray Wolf recognized the blinding grief and put Wise Heart into a gallop after him. He wasn't sure why he followed. Maybe he wished someone had done it for him when Lean Bear was killed. He also worried that Roman Nose might turn his lance on himself.

By sundown Roman Nose's horse slowed, and Gray Wolf pulled Wise Heart up beside him. Roman Nose seemed neither surprised nor appreciative Gray Wolf rode with him. Slowing their pace, they rode until after dark when they arrived at the campsite where the soldiers had attacked.

The moon was a mere sliver in the sky. Gray Wolf hoped Roman Nose would listen to reason. "Let's sleep here tonight, and at sunup we'll look for them."

"No, I must find them tonight. Maybe they still live."

Was it reasonable to think anyone was alive, or had reason left the warrior? Gray Wolf didn't know, but he dutifully went throughout the camp, checking for a pulse anytime he stumbled upon a corpse. Even in the dark, he could see that most of the bodies had been mutilated. The pathetic brave's claim that the women were violated was true. The smell of death clawed at his nostrils. By tomorrow, the smell would be unbearable.

Roman Nose's piercing cry told Gray Wolf he had found his squaw, and she was not alive. He walked in the direction of the cry, taking care to step over or around bodies. Roman Nose cradled a woman's body in his arms. He had pulled her into the open where he could see her face. Gray Wolf was close enough to see that she was naked. Her breasts and hands were cut off. Revulsion overtook him, and he wretched. Gray Wolf squatted on the ground, his hands over his face. His face felt hot and tight.

"I will kill them. I will kill them. I will mutilate them like they have violated you." Roman Nose stood, his wife's bloody corpse limp in his arms.

Gray Wolf sat. *What kind of evil man could butcher another human being like this?* Out of the corner of his eye, he saw something move. His first thought was that it was a scurrying rabbit or a coyote creeping up to take advantage of the carnage.

"Have you no respect for the dead?" He was angry to think that a scavenger was slinking in to carry off a body. He shot up, his hunting knife in hand, and in one quick movement tossed the tepee skin up and backward. There, crouching at his feet, was a child. In the darkness, he could not see if it was a boy or a girl, but the size told him the child could be no more than four or five summers.

"Don't be afraid, my child. We are here to help you. Come,

here, let me lift you up." Immediately, Gray Wolf's anger melted.

Slowly, the child, which he could now see was a boy, rose to his feet, but he did not look up at Gray Wolf. "What is your name little warrior?" The desire to protect the child overwhelmed him.

The boy still did not speak. He lifted his head just enough to peek at Gray Wolf. His body had no wounds that Gray Wolf could see.

Roman Nose no longer wailed. "Son, is that you?"

The boy's head shot up, and he ran to his father, who scooped him up in his arms and held him tightly. Gray Wolf exhaled. As he inhaled, the stench of death flooded his senses.

Roman Nose led them to a protected area outside the camp, where they stayed the night. Exhausted from the trauma, the boy was still sleeping when Gray Wolf woke. Bloodied, limbless corpses had dominated his dreams. He sat up with a start when he heard movement in the direction of the camp. With relief, he saw that it was Roman Nose, building scaffolding for the dead.

Gray Wolf decided it best to wake the boy and tell him to wait there until he or his father returned to retrieve him, rather than to have him wake on his own and fear he had again been abandoned. "Stay here and rest. Your father and I will come for you when we have dealt with the dead." The boy nodded. He had not yet spoken.

The men labored all morning, building burial scaffolds and retrieving belongings from Roman Nose's tepee. Gray Wolf turned his head to give his companion privacy as he once again held his wife, caressing her hair and face. Her face was cut so badly, Gray Wolf wondered how Roman Nose even recognized her. Oddly, he felt a twinge of jealousy toward Roman Nose, jealousy that he could love this woman with such passion and depth. There was only one woman he imagined loving this way, and she was beyond his reach. She lived in the world that had attacked this village.

It was obvious from the location in which Roman Nose found his wife's body that she had defended her young son. She had forfeited her life to save him. Roman Nose carried her body to the scaffolding and gently lifted her up onto it. "I can't let my son see her like this," he spat out.

Gray Wolf collected twigs and tumbleweeds caught in the brush to kindle a fire and complete the burial process before the boy came looking for his mother. It would be wrong to let coyotes or other predators devour or carry off the bodies of the dead. Walking through the devastated village, Gray Wolf kicked at a U.S. Army hat. When he did, his toe hit something hard. It was a pistol. He pulled back his leg to kick it as he had the hat but changed his mind and tucked it and a clip of ammunition into a pouch on his belt. Next, he wrapped the things from Roman Nose's tepee into buffalo robes and tied the big bundles with rawhide strips he found outside another tepee. He found several lariats that would come in handy in rigging up two travois to carry the buffalo robes.

While Roman Nose ignited and fed the fire under the scaffolds, Gray Wolf left to prepare the horses to return to where his band camped. He had tethered them the night before when they entered the camp and hobbled them in the morning so they could graze. He wasn't surprised to find the two stallions play fighting. He had rigged up a travois, a sort of wagon with poles but no wheels, for each horse to pull, but Roman Nose's horse would have nothing to do with it. It spooked and reared each time Gray Wolf brought the travois near. In contrast, Wise Heart stood still, looking bored as Gray Wolf secured the poles of the travois with rawhide. Next, he ran the lariat loosely around the stallion's neck, tying each side of the lariat rope to the travois poles. With Roman Nose's horse refusing to carry the other travois, Gray Wolf abandoned it, pulling its contents onto the travois hitched to Wise Heart.

Gray Wolf didn't respond to Roman Nose's sneer. "Turning your horse into a squaw pony, are you?"

The return trip was much slower.

"Where will your band go?"

"I have no band. My kinsmen let the soldiers butcher my woman. They left my son to die."

"Where will you set up your tepee? Where will your son live?"

"I have no need of a tepee. I will pursue the white man until there are no more of them. I'll not spare the women or the babies."

"What honor is there in killing defenseless children. Surely, you can't—"

"You speak truth, Gray Wolf. What honor is there in killing the defenseless? That is the question I have for the whites."

"The whites are many, Roman Nose. My uncle told me about their encampments, so much bigger than anything we can imagine." Gray Wolf decided to try appealing to Roman Nose's obvious affection for his son. "You have to think of your son. If you are no more, what will become of him?"

"I have to think what my son will think of his father if I do not avenge the cowardly and horrendous murder of his mother." Roman Nose looked down, almost with fondness, at his son. He was sleeping, cradled between his father's thighs atop the horse's withers. "I will leave the boy with you and Meadow Lark. If we succeed in eliminating the whites, I can come for him. You will keep him safe and teach him the ways of a warrior. If I am killed and the Cheyenne must become as whites, you will teach him to live in this new world."

✺

When Roman Nose left his son with Gray Wolf and Meadow Lark, the poor child had remained mute, refusing to eat or drink. On the third day, he woke in a rage, breaking bowls and cooking tools, screaming and crying. He was inconsolable. Gray Wolf had gone to look for Roman Nose, only to be told that he had left with yet another raiding party. Finally, Roman Nose's son had fallen, exhausted with grief, into Meadow Lark's lap, sobbing. After that, he was a different child—obedient, yet conversant and helpful. Gray Wolf had taken him out to see the horses. The boy enjoyed watching Gray Wolf start training a young horse.

Just when it seemed they would be able to be a family,

Roman Nose showed up at their tepee. He smelled of sweat and blood. Scalps, white scalps, hung all about him. He burst into the tepee without being invited, something no Indian in his right mind would do.

Gray Wolf was outside the tepee, skinning a pronghorn buck when Roman Nose approached. He followed the crazed brave inside the tepee, where Meadow Lark sewed hides and the boy played. "You dishonor us by not waiting for an invitation into our tepee. Please, sit." He motioned to a buffalo robe by the fire where the noon meal was simmering.

"I come to speak with Meadow Lark." Roman Nose waited. "Alone."

Gray Wolf looked at Meadow Lark. She tipped her head, and he stepped back outside. If Roman Nose continued his rant, Gray Wolf would intervene.

"I want you to be my squaw, to be mother to the boy." Gray Wolf heard the erratic pitch in Roman Nose's voice as he paced.

Had Roman Nose followed Cheyenne tradition and come to ask her to be his wife, Meadow Lark may have entertained the request. Had Roman Nose followed tradition, he would have asked Gray Wolf, for it was considered far too forward for a man to make his intentions known directly to his beloved. That way, if she did not share his affections, she would not be embarrassed to have to admit it. Roman Nose was highly decorated for his battle and hunting accomplishments and a good provider. Gray Wolf had never heard of him or his band being seekers of whiskey. All the young women thought him handsome, a desirable husband.

"I'm flattered, Roman Nose, that you would consider me, but I am a traditional woman."

"I need a traditional squaw to raise my son and tend my fire."

This made Meadow Lark angry. Gray Wolf could tell from her voice that Roman Nose had pushed too far. "I won't marry a man who thinks of me as a new horse. I'm not a horse, and I won't be your pack mule either."

Gray Wolf heard a crash. Roman Nose had responded by knocking over the simmering pot. Gray Wolf ran into the tepee, and, catching Roman Nose by surprise, he shoved him outside. Roman Nose stumbled, fell to the ground, rolled and popped to his feet facing Gray Wolf. He clutched a knife. Gray Wolf was strong and agile, but he wasn't ready to test himself against Roman Nose. He also knew he had to get Roman Nose away from Meadow Lark and the boy. He might be able to outrun his opponent, but if not, he would have a knife in his spine. The pronghorn carcass that hung from a lariat reminded him that the other lariat was within reach. Thanks to the MacBaye cattle ranching days, he was able to gather up the rope and quickly throw a loop over Roman Nose's head as he charged him. He had intended to let the rope drop down over Roman Nose's waist, but because he was moving, the rope tightened around his neck, making it easy for Gray Wolf to wrap the other end of the rope around the pole supporting the pronghorn carcass. When Roman Nose came toward him, he tightened the rope around the pole, keeping it tight enough that the brave couldn't escape.

Perhaps the noose scared him or maybe the growing crowd that had no doubt heard his ranting brought some sense into his head, but whatever the cause, Roman Nose signaled surrender by raising his hands in the air. Not wanting to humiliate him further, Gray Wolf loosened the lariat and slipped it over his head. Without another word, Roman Nose scurried away like a frightened hare.

A week later, Roman Nose was married to one of the adoring young girls, and Meadow Lark had to surrender the boy to his new child-wife.

Chapter 17

Denver, June 14, 1864

D r. Williams had become a sort of local celebrity for his advice on personal and public health following the flood. *The Denver Commonwealth* regularly printed his medical advice columns. He even shared some of Georgia's herbal remedies for the folks of Denver, always careful to credit his "fine young lady medical student Georgia MacBaye." A female medical student, a doctor some even called her, was an oddity.

Patients' attitudes toward her varied. Some were glad to be treated by a woman and said so. Others would have nothing to do with a woman providing a medical diagnosis and treatment. The worst patients, however, were the old men who leered at her. As always, Dr. Williams was quick to sort through the motivation and character of his patients and to assign them to the student who would give them the best care. Georgia was relieved he had no patience for inappropriate behavior from anyone.

Most patients could be seen during normal office hours,

allowing Georgia and her fellow students to settle back into their pre-flood routine. Georgia did her barn chores and worked Mr. Fletcher's bay gelding. It seemed to her that every time the livery rented out the gelding, he returned with injuries, or his bad habits resurfaced. Mr. Fletcher was glad to have Georgia work out the kinks and would have gladly given her additional horses to train, had she the time. Not only did he give her free hay, oats and stall rental for Cheyenne, he dropped a few extra coins into her grooming box most every time she worked the bay. "Much obliged for what you're doing here, Georgia," he'd say if she caught him in his generosity.

Georgia had worked an early shift at the clinic. She completed her livery chores but decided to return to her room since the day was rainy. She found her mother's letter, received the previous week, on her dresser. She reread it most every day but never grew tired of reading news from home:

13th May, 1864
Bijou Basin, Colorado Territory

My Dear Georgia,

I am writing to tell you why our annual trip to Denver City has been delayed. The heavy snows and spring rains have made travel difficult to impossible. Furthermore, your father and Henry have spent far more time preparing and planting the fields than in years past. No sooner did they prepare the ground than a spring torrent washed away the soil. They again plowed with the oxen and were successful in planting, but no more than three days later, another heavy rain washed away the seed. They have used twice the seed to plant the crop this year, and it is not yet up. This is the other reason for delaying our trip. We do not yet know how much corn and wheat we will be able to sell, should we have to use more of our supplies to plant seed a third time. Should the worst happen, we will have enough to feed ourselves, but will not have much to trade.

I have already started to ration my sugar and coffee should we be unable to make the trip or should we not have the money to buy them.

My garden is faring only somewhat better. It, too, required replanting. My fear now is that the seeds will rot in the ground. I have to confess, my dear daughter, that this country is wearing on me. I find myself longing for Spring Grove, for the green of the fields and forests in South Carolina. I am sure that in my recollection it is far more spectacular and our ranch far more unpleasant than is really the case, but I find myself often longing for it. The reality is that my homeland is likely war-torn. From what we read in the few newspapers we are able to acquire, much of this war is being fought on Southern land. I think often of my family and wonder how they are faring whilst the battles rage. I wish I knew how Old Jeb and the others have managed as free men and women. I know it must be hard for them, but I think they will survive.

There is another piece of news I hesitate to share with you, but I know I must. Henry has decided to go East to study. As you know, he had considered returning to South Carolina, but with no end in sight for this War Between the States, he has decided to study in Philadelphia. I have relatives there that he will stay with, and there are several universities from which he can choose. Fortunately, we put the money aside for him to study before the current hardship. When there is a break in the weather, your father will deliver him to the Limon stagecoach station, as he did you last fall. From there, he will catch whatever mode of transportation he is able to travel east. A year ago, few were traveling east. Now, with the sharp increase in Indian depredations, more settlers are returning to their original homes in the East.

Our neighbors are not immune to the rising panic that Indians will overtake us all. Do you remember the Johnsons who settled just south of our ranch? Mrs. Johnson is expecting a fourth child anytime now. Once the baby is born and strong enough to travel, they will go East, planning to arrive in St.

Louis before the cold weather sets in. Your father has agreed to buy their land and stock, although with the imminent crop failure, I do not know that he or any other rancher will have the money to do so.

James continues to enjoy the Cavalry. He writes us when he is able. He said he is serving in a unit with a Captain Silas Soule, second in command at Fort Lyon. He writes that he will find you should he have the occasion to travel to Denver with his Cavalry duties.

Gray Wolf was here overnight last month. He brought us the sad news that soldiers had just shot his uncle. You remember Lean Bear? He was the tall, regal man with the flowing feather bonnet who brought Gray Wolf to us when he was so sick and then arrived last spring to take him back to his home. This is the one who was killed. Gray Wolf said that Lean Bear had been to Washington and had met with President Abraham Lincoln. Can you believe that? He rode out to tell the soldiers he was a peaceful Indian, and before he could speak, they shot him off his horse. Gray Wolf was distraught, of course. We pray he will not overreact to the injustice, but if he were to do so, it would be understandable. We are in a position to see that there is heartbreak and misunderstanding on both the white and the Indian sides.

Henry regrets that he will be unable to see you before he leaves for Philadelphia, but you are in Denver to the west, and he must travel east. We trust you are well and enjoying your training. Your father and I will come to Denver City when we are able.

With Love,
Mother

Georgia folded the letter with care and placed it back on the dresser. It was not the last time she would read her mother's words. Just a year ago, everything had looked so hopeful for the MacBayes. What a difference a year could make, she sighed, whispering a prayer for better weather and for her mother. She also prayed for protection for Henry.

The quiet was interrupted by an urgent knock at her door. "Miss Georgia, you're wanted at the clinic," Lucy beckoned.

Georgia was rarely called to the clinic. She hoped nothing was wrong. At the clinic, the first person she saw was Jonathan. "Someone to see you. Two soldiers are waiting for you in the receiving area," he said.

"See there, Teddy, I told you my baby sister was a doc." James swept his hat toward her and tipped his head forward. "How are you? I'm sorry I should have visited you sooner, but I was not ... ah ... very agreeable the last time we met."

"Good to see you, James," Georgia said, extending her arms and giving her brother a hug. "You still with the First Colorado Cavalry?" Georgia was glad to see her brother, but cautious.

"Yes, ma'am. I've worked my way up to specialist in Captain Soule's division."

"Captain Soule, you say?"

"Yes, a right fine soldier. Wouldn't ask us ta do anything he wouldn't do his self."

"I met him in January at a dinner party. Seemed a reasonable man." Georgia directed her gaze at James's companion.

"I brought my fellow soldier, Teddy here, to see if ya might be able to stich 'im up. He decided ta go out drinkin' last night and got into a fight at one a them saloons."

Of course, her brother had not come just to see her. He needed a favor. "Let me see what is ailing you, Teddy." He uncovered his right arm to reveal a deep gash. "Nothing a few stitches and some ointment won't heal. Had your attacker's knife struck a little way one way or the other, it could have cut an artery. If you were drunk, you would have bled to death." Teddy's eyes widened.

Georgia went to the medicine cabinet and put a few drops of clove oil on a cloth. She had to be judicious in her use of medicines. The Indian attacks had brought supply routes to a virtual standstill. Who knew how long it would be before they could replenish their supply of medicines. After cleaning the cut so she could see the skin that needed suturing, she used the clove oil to deaden the skin around the gash. She told Teddy to look at James while she used an S needle and clean horsehair to close the wound. She then applied the herbal concoction that the clinic now used regularly and wrapped Teddy's arm with a clean bandage.

"It is really important that you take off the bandage and wash the wound every day. Then you can pour a little alcohol over it, let it dry and wrap it back up in a clean bandage." The instructions were not something she had learned from Dr. Williams. It was something her ma always did.

"Every day?"

"Yes, every day." She winked at him. "Cleanliness is next to godliness, and, if the wound gets red, more swollen than it is now or painful, I might need to lance it, and that's not much fun. So do what I tell you, and it'll heal up real nice."

"Yes, ma'am, I'll do as you say. Thank you."

Georgia turned to James. "Would you care to have dinner at Dr. Williams's house tonight? I'm sure he wouldn't mind."

James thought for a minute. "I'd like that. Let me see Teddy back to the barracks first. What time should I be there?"

"Six o'clock. It's right next door."

✳

Lucy was glad to set an extra plate, and Dr. Williams said he would be delighted to have James join them for dinner.

At precisely six o'clock, James knocked on Dr. Williams's door. Georgia led him to the dining room to introduce him to Dr. and Mrs. Williams.

"So, James, I suppose you are part of the Cavalry that is defending Denver." Dr. Williams had a way of making anyone feel at home.

"Actually, sir, I'm stationed at Fort Lyon, over two hundred miles southeast of Denver. With the high incidence of Indian attacks on freighters, contingents of the Colorado First Cavalry have been escorting freight wagons and travelers across the plains. We arrive in Denver, rest a day or two, and then head back to Fort Lyon with supplies."

"Do the Indian attacks scare you?"

"It's my job to defend folks. Besides, it's a lot better than sitting around at the fort guarding the herds or doing nothing."

"Do you think Denver City is at risk of being attacked by Indians?"

"No, sir, I don't. Most of the Indian incidents are stolen stock, horses, food, things like that. Once in a while, a settler gets brave and shoots an Indian, and then the settler's life is in jeopardy. Don't get me wrong, I'm not saying they should be allowed to steal and pillage, but outside of a few of the ones who are mean just to be mean, they rarely are violent toward the settlers."

Georgia wondered what had changed James's tone. The last time she spoke with him he was ready to kill any Indian that moved. Perhaps Captain Soule had brought reason to her brother. Maybe her father's reason, and his prayers, had changed him. Whatever motivated the change, she was glad. Glad for her brother and glad that the Cavalry had men with reasoned thinking.

Shortly after they finished dessert and coffee, James thanked Mr. And Mrs. Williams for their hospitality and bid them farewell. "It will be an early morning. We head back to Fort Lyon at six in the morning. I'd better turn in."

Georgia escorted James to the door. "I'm so glad you looked me up, even if it cost me some doctorin' to see you."

"Teddy's young, so I'm hoping he learned his lesson, but I sure do thank ya, sis."

"Do you ever think about Gray Wolf? Have you ever seen him?" There. She'd asked.

"No, I haven't seen 'im, but I find m'self looking at the faces of each brave I meet that fits his general description. I was angry when he lived with us and took so much of everyone's time and attention. Looking back, it was a good thing. His living with us helped me see Indians like I do whites, as individuals. Just like us, some are good, some are bad, some are lazy, and some are ambitious and hardworking. Gray Wolf is an honorable man. I wish I could see him again. I hope he hasn't been killed in the skirmishes."

Killed. It had not occurred to Georgia that Gray Wolf was dead. "Funny when I hear the stories of warfare and fighting, I always feel badly about the whites who are killed or injured. I never once though about Gray Wolf being killed."

James tried to reassure her. "I don't think you have to be worried about Gray Wolf participating in any of these raids. It's just not like him."

"I hope you see him ..." Not wanting to appear too eager, she added, "sometime."

"I told Captain Soule all about Gray Wolf, and he has pledged to let me know if anyone runs across him."

"If you see him, tell him ... I miss him." Georgia hated admitting this to anyone. It just slipped from her lips.

"Sure thing, sis," James said as though it would be a routine thing to tell Gray Wolf that Georgia missed him. "Good night. I love you."

"Good night. I love you too. I'll pray for your safety, James." Georgia was flabbergasted. James had never said he loved her.

⚹

The next morning, Georgia read in *The Denver Commonwealth:*

On Saturday night [June 11] two Indians stampeded 49 mules belonging to Daniels & Brown, about thirteen miles from this city, on the 'cut-off,' while the teamsters, four in number, were preparing supper. Two of the men pursued the Indians some thirteen miles, until they came in sight of about 120 head of ponies, horses and mules, when they judiciously returned to the wagons, as the Indian camp was evidently near... On

Saturday afternoon, the buildings of the ranch of Mr. Van Wormer, of this city, on Living Creek, thirty miles southeast of Denver, were burned down by Indians, as were the buildings of the next ranch. Mr. Hungate and family, who occupied Mr. Van Wormer's ranch, were barbarously murdered by the Indians. The bodies of Mrs. Hungate and two children were found near the house. They had been scalped and their throats cut. A later report brings news of the discovery of Mr. Hungate's body, about a mile from the same place. Moccasins, arrows, and other Indian signs were found in the vicinity. The bodies of these will be brought to the city this afternoon, and will, at the ringing of the Seminary bell, be placed where our citizens can all see them.

Georgia gasped. *Women and children murdered? Who would do that?* James had been wrong. Her thoughts then went to her parents. The MacBaye Ranch was more remote than Mr. Van Wormer's ranch, where the Hungate family was murdered. Her father had built a strong house, easily defended, and the adobe would not catch fire, but all the assurances she could conjure did not keep her from worrying about them.

Chapter 18

East of the Bijou Basin, mid-June 1864

The large encampment of Cheyenne had split off into smaller bands, as it was accustomed to doing during the summer to make it easier for them to follow game and hunt in smaller groups. Gray Wolf's band was camped east of the MacBayes, but he did not visit them. Although his band had kept busy hunting deer, pronghorn antelope and buffalo when they could be found, he was careful not to go near the MacBaye Ranch. Cheyenne voices in favor of attacking settlers grew daily, and Gray Wolf wanted to protect the MacBayes.

Gray Wolf felt guidance more than ever from the Wise One Above. He had become a dispute solver among his band and called often on the Wise One for wisdom in settling disputes.

Meadow Lark was glad to bring Indians with disagreements into their tepee to seek Gray Wolf's advice. "Brother, Little Elk believes his son-in-law has stolen two of his best ponies. He wants to ask you what he should do."

"Tell him to come in." Gray Wolf supposed Little Elk was less interested in talking about what he should do than he was in having Gray Wolf reprimand his son-in-law. Little Elk entered the tepee. Gray Wolf thought it strange that a man of forty-five summers would seek the advice of someone half his age. "Please sit." Gray Wolf gestured to a buffalo robe at his right.

After Little Elk gulped down half the sugared coffee Meadow Lark served him, he spoke. "Running Creek has dishonored me. He claims two of the young horses from my herd are his."

"These two horses, are they war horses or squaw's horses?" It was a common dispute. Gray Wolf prayed the Wise One Above would give him answers.

"They are young. They are fine war horses. I don't know how Running Creek thinks I don't notice he has taken them."

"Does Little Elk go to war or hunt using these horses?" Gray Wolf knew the answer, but he had to ask the question.

"My days of war are long over. Any hunting I do is on foot. I can no longer sit on a horse."

The irony seemed to escape Little Elk. Gray Wolf understood that horses were a man's strength and wealth. He also knew that whether the horses belonged to Little Elk or his son-in-law, as patriarch, all were considered Little Elk's property.

"Does your son-in-law honor his wife, your daughter, and does he keep your pot full of meat?"

Little Elk didn't seem to know what this had to do with anything. "Yes. This is not my complaint."

"Here is my suggestion. You go to Running Creek and tell him that you underpaid the dowry for your daughter when you gave her to him in marriage. Tell him you realize a woman of such great beauty and talent would bring a greater dowry, so you wish to give him the two fine war horses." Little Elk looked puzzled. Gray Wolf continued. "Since you have said yourself you do not need these horses, you might as well give them to him. This way you will turn dishonor to honor. He and the others will see you as generous and your daughter of great value."

Little Elk's brows furrowed in thought, then he let out a

great laugh. "I understand. It is good advice. You are wise for only twenty-two summers."

It was tempting to take the credit, but reliance on the Wise One Above had taught Gray Wolf humility. "I prayed to the Wise One Above for wisdom. He is the only one who is worthy of our thanks and praise."

"You speak truth, Gray Wolf." Little Elk stood and left.

⚜

That afternoon, Gray Wolf heard the earth rumble. Hoping a great herd of buffalo approached, he, Moonwalker and some of the other braves mounted their ponies. Their hopes swelled as the dust bellowed upward, growing larger. They split into two columns, one group prepared to flank each side of the stampeding buffalo herd. If the buffalo continued toward them, they would turn and run alongside the herd, killing animals on the outside and pushing the stampeding herd away from camp. If their presence spooked the buffalo enough to turn them in a different direction, the braves would pursue them from behind. The braves all were familiar with the hunting strategy.

The cloud of dust continued toward them. As it cleared, the hunters were disappointed to see that what they thought was a large buffalo herd was more than two hundred head of cattle, horses and mules herded by two dozen Cheyenne and Arapaho braves.

The braves driving the livestock backed off when they saw Gray Wolf's group. The panting animals slowed. Motioning and shouting for Gray Wolf and the others to join them, they pulled back yet more, slowing their ponies to a brisk walk.

Gray Wolf recognized some of the braves but knew none of their names. "From where do you come with so many animals?"

A brave that was larger and looked taller seemed to appoint himself leader of the group. "The chiefs sent us back with the livestock. We gathered them near Denver City. Cattle don't taste as good as buffalo or deer, but they are sure easier to find and kill." The brave laughed at his own joke.

Gathered. Gray Wolf contemplated this word. In the Cheyenne language, the nuance was used to mean taking something no one else wanted. Stealing the branded horses, mules and cattle was hardly "gathering." Once again, his first thoughts were the Cheyenne pilfering, how it was wrong and how it would endanger all of them. He would have used the word "steal," but that would have been too rude.

"Where did you 'gather' them?" The word felt like gravel in his mouth.

"From the settlers' larger ranches." The brave said it with incredulity, as if that were the only way to bring in food and horses. "There were some smaller ranches on the way back, but we didn't bother with them. Too much work for just a few animals."

Gray Wolf was relieved with this news. The big ranches were easier to steal from, less likely to fight the threat. They were tended by hired hands. The settlers would be more inclined to fight for the sparse possessions that sustained them. Still, he was irritated at the pillaging. "Do you see the marks on the hips of this stock?"

The brave looked at the animals. No doubt he had not noticed the brands. "Yeah, so what?

"Each rancher has his own personalized brand. The soldiers will know immediately the owner of each animal."

"Why does that matter?" The brave shifted his eyes with realization, yet he was not willing to admit the folly. "They'll be hanging slabs of meat before any soldier thinks to look for them."

"And the horses and mules?"

The brave swallowed hard. "It wasn't my decision. The chiefs told us where to go and what to take."

Of course, blame it on someone else. Only in this case, the brave was probably right. "Which chiefs?"

"Two Face, Big Thunder. Roman Nose was there too."

"Where are they now?"

Gray Wolf thought he saw a flash of emotion. Was it resentment or regret in the brave's eyes? "They went to punish the settler who killed one of our braves."

Gray Wolf's heart jumped. "What happened?"

"A ranch hand shot at us when we were rounding up some of these animals. He killed one man, wounded another. The chiefs said they must avenge the killing. It wouldn't be right to let the killer get away with it."

"Did you see the man?" Gray Wolf's fear rose.

"Not well, but he had a woman and two babies."

"Babies? Who will feed the woman and babies when the man is killed?"

"Oh, no, they will kill them all."

Gray Wolf shook his head. He was ashamed the Cheyenne had come to a place where they could kill babies without remorse. He knew the victims were not the MacBayes ... this time. He wanted desperately to ride to them, to make sure they were well and to warn them of the danger. Thomas was wise and paid attention to what happened around the ranch, but he would have no warning if the Cheyenne decided to take his stock. Gray Wolf knew Thomas would not stand by and watch everything he worked for be stolen or destroyed by these braves.

Gray Wolf's intervention halted the celebratory mood only for a moment. Soon the thieves, along with most of the braves from Gray Wolf's village, returned to herding the animals to the site of the next Cheyenne tribal rendezvous. The Cheyenne would be eating beef, rather than buffalo or deer, and riding new horses when they celebrated the Renewal of the Sacred Arrows during the summer solstice.

Moonwalker had become as morose as Gray Wolf about the Cheyenne's thieving ways. It could ultimately spell their doom. The two returned to the village by way of the creek. They came upon a herd of deer in search of water. Gray Wolf's arrow was straight and true, felling a young buck where he stood. The village was close, and so was darkness. They carried the slain buck between them on a thick willow branch. Moonwalker's wife and Meadow Lark were glad for the fresh meat, and they helped the men skin and dress the carcass. There was too much meat for the four of them to eat before it spoiled. In past years, they would have dried the venison for winter storage, but this year, even during summertime, there were Cheyenne families without enough food, so they shared the deer with them by leaving a chunk of wrapped meat outside their tepees. Giving it to them directly would have shamed the family in need. The next morning, the women set about packing the tepees while the men gathered and prepared the horses to move out. By mid-morning, they would be on the trail to join other Cheyenne bands in the annual four-day Renewal of the Sacred Arrows ceremony.

The special man arrows and bison arrows were said to have been handed down from many generations before them when the Cheyenne occupied the land to the north, the Dakotas. They were entrusted to an honored elder, the arrow keeper. As with all ceremonies, there would be feasting, dancing and chanting.

"Why are women not permitted to participate in the Renewal of the Sacred Arrows? Why must we be confined to our tepees until it is finished?"

Meadow Lark's question caught Gray Wolf off-guard. "It is a ceremony where the men seek power for hunting and battle from the gods."

"The sun dance is also an appeasement to the gods, but women dance in the celebration, along with the men, no?"

"I don't know why women can't be part of the ceremony to renew the Sacred Arrows," he admitted.

Later that day, Gray Wolf still thought about Meadow Lark's question. If Lean Bear were alive, he would ask him. Lean Bear had explained to him the old beliefs that the universe was split into seven levels. Spirits existed in nature, which is the reason the Cheyenne worshipped plants, trees and animals. Even the animals they killed for food were honored as spirits of the gods. They also believed modern problems, like the disappearance of the buffalo, happened because the Cheyenne had lost favor with the universe.

Gray Wolf shared this with Meadow Lark, a practical thinker, who responded, "Then what is the point of trying? If we've lost the favor of the universe, we might as well follow the buffalo off the jumps we chase them over."

"I don't think it's quite all that bad, sister." He laughed, but his uneasiness was not erased. Was the time of the Cheyenne coming to an end? Was the universe now favoring the whites? It seemed that way. Or was the god of the whites a more powerful god than the Wise One Above? He had so many questions. He wished he could talk with Thomas. He valued Thomas's counsel above all others, even Lean Bear. Thomas's god didn't seem to favor one man over another or one people over another. Each man made his own choices and was judged. He remembered that even in judgment, Thomas's god was compassionate. Hadn't this god sent his son to die for people on the earth— all people? When Gray Wolf first heard the story, he thought Thomas's god to be weak. Then another thought came to him: What if Thomas's god is the Wise One Above and his son is the One on the Earth? Too many questions. Gray Wolf hoped this year's Renewal of the Sacred Arrows ceremony would answer his many questions.

Four days later, the Renewal of the Sacred Arrows ended and Gray Wolf had more questions, not fewer. He sought out Cheyenne elders known for their religious knowledge. Starting with Meadow Lark's question and ending with how the Cheyenne would gain back the favor of the universe, no one could answer. The elders also told him it was wrong to ask too many questions. Gray Wolf decided that he must visit Thomas.

He rose before sunrise the day after the ceremony ended. The Cheyenne would continue their celebrations for at least another five days. Meadow Lark would be safe. He had told only her and Moonwalker that he would be gone. "If anyone asks, tell them I'm not well and have gone to seek healing," he told them.

He wanted no one to follow him to the MacBayes, putting them or their neighbors in jeopardy of attack or pillaging.

Wise Heart stood just outside the tepee. Gray Wolf rose and slipped out of the tepee, extending a handful of corn and wheat kernels to the stallion. It was a practice he had developed to keep his horse nearby and easy to catch. When Wise Heart finished his treat, Gray Wolf slipped on the horse's bridle and mounted without a sound. Most of the Cheyenne would be sound asleep from successive late nights of dancing and feasting. He hoped anyone who heard Wise Heart's hooves would assume it was a loose horse or an ambitious warrior going out for an early hunt. As soon as he was out of the encampment, he urged Wise Heart into a ground-covering lope, traveling away from the rising sun. He could see the bluffs that stood behind the MacBaye Ranch. The rising sun bathed them with light, erasing all shadows of the night. Dew-covered prairie grasses and delicate flowers of gold, purple and red seemed to beckon him westward. The screech of the occasional hawk and constant scolding of prairie dogs as he moved past their holes were the only sounds of the morning.

He slowed Wise Heart to a trot and then a walk, giving him time to cool down before the ride ended. Thomas was leaving the barn, a pail full of milk in hand, when Gray Wolf rode into the ranch yard.

"I see Georgia has not returned from Denver," Gray Wolf called to him, nodding at the pail of milk. It had always been her chore. Already, he felt his burden lifting.

Thomas looked up, his face changing from alarm to delight, "Gray Wolf, you caught me by surprise. You know with all the Indian attacks lately, we're all a little wary of anyone riding into the place."

Gray Wolf wondered if Thomas did not think of him as an Indian. "I've heard about the attacks." He hoped Thomas didn't ask how he knew about them. He wouldn't lie to Thomas, but he felt powerless that he was unable to stop the attacks and pillaging. "I'm back to ask you more questions."

"Come on in, son. I believe Loraine is fixing breakfast. She still hasn't got used to Henry being gone, so I know she'll have extra."

"Henry's gone?" Gray Wolf feared the worse.

"Yep, caught a stagecoach going back East earlier this month. He wants to go to university. To study."

Gray Wolf let out the breath he had been holding. "Study? Like Georgia and I did with Loraine?"

"Something like that. Only this is a special school way back in Philadelphia. You know, Henry always tolerated ranching, but he didn't love it, not like me ... or Georgia love it."

Gray Wolf slid off Wise Heart. "Should I put my horse in the corral?"

Thomas studied the stallion. "He's a beauty alright. Wish I had a mare to breed him to, but the only two females I have are, uh, otherwise disposed." Thomas circled Wise Heart, stroking his sleek coat. "Georgia has her filly in Denver, and Loraine's mare is heavy with foal." He thought for a minute, then said, "I don't want the horses getting into any sort of scuffle that might injure one of them. Leave the stallion in the stall next to Blue Bell. When I turn the horses out on pasture later, you can put your boy in the corral."

He had to warn Thomas. "Your horses are some of the best. Any brave would spot them as easy as they would a stampeding buffalo herd. You are in danger of losing them if you let them go far from the barn."

"I've thought about that, son, but I can't keep them in the barn or corral all the time. They'd be awful hungry and cranky."

"Can you put a fence to the back of the house? That way anyone trying to run them off would have to come through the yard, past the house."

Thomas's lighthearted manner turned serious. "That's a good thought. Are you trying to tell me the Cheyenne are planning to attack us?"

"Who knows what some of these braves might do." Gray Wolf didn't want to make excuses for the Cheyenne, but he wanted to explain. "Food is short, and the provisions promised by the Indian agent for abandoning old hunting grounds have not come through. Some are out for revenge."

"Revenge? For what?" Thomas cocked his head to the side and looked at Gray Wolf.

"Last month I went with a brave whose village had been massacred by soldiers. Roman Nose found his wife there, dead. She had been violated and butchered. He is angry and vows to kill all the whites he can. He doesn't care if they are willing to share the land with them, as you are. He vows, and this is a dishonor for me to say, to kill women and children, along with the men." He hadn't meant to say the name of the warrior.

"You must be mistaken, Gray Wolf. Soldiers wouldn't do such a thing."

"I am sure it was soldiers. Indians always use arrows along with rifles, and there were no arrows. We found soldiers' hats, belts, lariats. Even a pistol with 'U.S. Army' engraved on it. Remember, Loraine taught me to read." Gray Wolf hoped the comment would lighten the conversation. The bloodshed and thievery were not what he came to discuss. Well, maybe it was part of the confusion he felt.

Thomas ran his hand through his hair, nodding in disbelief. Gray Wolf understood how he felt. It was difficult to understand how anyone could do such a thing to another people. This wasn't warfare. It was murder—massacre.

They walked to the adobe house, entering as Loraine yelled to her husband, "What kept you so long! Breakfast's getting cold."

"Gray Wolf's here. Told him you'd have made enough for him to join us. Says he has some questions for us."

Loraine came running, her arms open to embrace Gray Wolf. "What a wonderful surprise. Yes, please sit down. It's the same as always—eggs, salt pork, beans. No potatoes. We had to use our eating potatoes to replant the garden."

The men pushed back from their empty plates, and Loraine took the dishes to the sink to wash. Gray Wolf crossed his arms and leaned forward on the table. "Do gods favor some people over others?" And, for Meadow Lark, he asked, "Does God prefer men over women?"

"I'm no expert on my faith, and I know nothing about what the Cheyenne believe." Thomas paused, his hands folded in front of his chin. "You remember the book we read when you lived here after your accident?" Gray Wolf nodded. Thomas rested his chin on his folded hands. "We believe this is God's letter to us. It gives us some history, tells us what the punishment for sin is and tells us how we can escape it. I see nowhere that God favors one people group over another or one individual over another. He did use the Hebrew people to bring salvation to the world, but that is not at the exclusion of anyone else. It says very specifically that God does not favor one race over another, men over women or even the rich over the poor."

"Does your god punish people or forgive them?"

"We've all done wrong. I think deep in our hearts, everyone knows that." Gray Wolf nodded agreement. Thomas drew a deep breath. "Our punishment is death, but we can escape eternal death, death of our souls, if we allow Jesus's blood to cover us."

Why did the conversation always come back to this Jesus, the one who refused to punish his attackers? Gray Wolf wondered.

"Do the Cheyenne have any customs or traditions where a man might give his life to save his family or a good friend?"

"Sometimes a very brave dog solider will stake himself to the ground on the battlefield. His valiant fighting and the distraction can allow the other braves to go around and attack the enemy from behind. I guess you could say he gave his life to save another."

"Well, now, imagine this same dog soldier doing this, not for his people, but for people who hate him, people who will never thank his family or acknowledge what he did to save them."

"That wouldn't happen." Gray Wolf thought dying for someone who didn't appreciate it was ridiculous.

"You're right, it is completely against human nature for a man to give his life for someone who despises him, but that is what Jesus did." Thomas paused. "So to answer your question, yes, he does judge people, and we often have to pay on this earth for bad things we have done. But he has made a way for each of us to escape the eternal punishment that is due us."

Gray Wolf admired this Jesus, but it was difficult to believe a god would behave this way. The Cheyenne respected bravery, but Jesus didn't seem very brave.

"The Cheyenne believe in the Wise One Above and the One Who Inhabits the Earth. There are also many other spirits, and they are in plants and animals, even the animals we kill for food. Who is more powerful, the Cheyenne god or yours?"

"It's good to respect God's creation, but we shouldn't worship what God has made, rather than worshipping God himself. Could it be that the Wise One Above is the same as the white man's God, the One Who Inhabits the Earth is Jesus, and the Cheyenne sense of spirits is what we call the Holy Spirit? I don't know, Gray Wolf. Ask the Wise One Above to reveal truth to you."

Truth. That was what he sought. Hadn't Little Elk just last week told him he spoke truth? He had asked the Wise One Above for wisdom, for truth. A weight of uncertainty began to lift. "I will think ... and pray."

"Good." This time Loraine spoke. "I've never known God to ignore someone who seeks Him."

Gray Wolf was glad he had come, but he wasn't ready to leave. "Do you want some help with that corral at the back of the house?"

"Sounds like a right fine idea, Gray Wolf. I'd appreciate your help."

Gray Wolf and Thomas had nearly finished the corral when they saw a rider galloping toward the ranch house. Gray Wolf could see it was a settler riding with urgency.

A boy of about thirteen summers pulled his horse to a stop. He looked at Gray Wolf with distrust, and Gray Wolf thought he remembered the boy as one of the Johnsons, one of the MacBayes' neighbors.

Addressing Thomas, still out of breath, he shouted, "It's my ma! The baby's coming. She sent me for Mrs. MacBaye."

Chapter 19

Denver, late June 1864

Today, as with every Sunday since the news of the Hungate murders, churchgoers talked of nothing but the Indian threat. The display of the mutilated bodies of Nathan Hungate, his wife and their two young daughters had achieved the goal of flaming the fires of revenge in the Denver citizenry. Georgia felt her room confining and hot. Beads of perspiration formed on her face and neck and ran down her face and back. She used one of the fancy kerchiefs Ma sent to wipe off the perspiration. She remembered her mother saying that Colorado summers were a lot easier to take than those in South Carolina. She couldn't remember. She had been a child when they came West. All she knew was the hot, breezeless day was stifling.

To take her mind off her fears and the confining heat, she got out parchment and ink and wrote a letter to her ma and pa. She finished the letter and read it one last time while she waited for the ink to dry.

22nd June 1864

Dear Mother & Father,

I hope that you are well. I pray that the replanted crops are thriving. Have you heard from Henry? When is he expected to arrive in Philadelphia?

We hear much about the Indian depredations here in Denver. I hope you are well and that our stock and crops are protected. If the truth be told, I cannot imagine Papa letting anyone threaten his property!

It is very hot in Denver. I miss the breezes that come off the bluffs on hot summer days. I long for the time when I can again be at our ranch, sleep in my featherbed, and, yes, I even miss milking Blue Bell. It need not be said, but most of all, I miss you both.

At least I was able to see James. He brought a fellow Cavalry soldier who had injured himself in a bar fight to Dr. Williams's clinic for care, and I stitched up the fellow. You would be pleased to know, Mother, that Dr. Williams is grateful to you for the herbal mixture. We use it often to help fight bacteria. It is cheap and readily available. This is of particular importance now that the Indian Wars have stopped many of the needed medicines from arriving in Denver. James is well. The Cavalry suits him. I was glad to hear that his attitude toward Indians has changed much since our last conversation. He even said he hopes to see Gray Wolf again.

I do not wish to appear unseemly proud of my accomplishments in Dr. Williams's school, rather, in order to show my gratitude to both of you for allowing me to come here and for paying my school fees, I enclose two clippings from the local newspaper that mention my contributions to medicine in this city. Dr. Williams tells me I have learned much. He has done his best to prepare me to return to the plains to assist you, Mother, in providing medical services for our neighbors.

I miss you very much and look forward to your visit this summer to Denver City.

Your Loving Daughter,
Georgia

Satisfied, she folded the letter, made an envelope to fit it and addressed the envelope. She tucked the letter into her pocket and hurried to the livery to saddle Cheyenne. Teddy, now well-healed and duly chagrined from his bar fight injury, had stopped at the clinic Friday morning to thank her for the "stitchin'." He told her he would pass by the Bijou Basin on his return to Fort Lyon and would be "right pleased" to deliver the letter for her.

The ride to Fort Weld was short and uneventful, appreciated in today's sweltering heat yet contrary to Georgia's adventuresome tendency. Teddy tucked the letter into his Cavalry-issue saddlebags, again assuring her he would deliver it the next afternoon.

※

The warm weather brought Denverites, cooped up in their homes throughout the snowy winter and wet spring, out into the parks and shops. Georgia had little knowledge of the city social scene, but she thought there were fewer public festivities than the previous fall when she took up residence in Denver City. Instead, folks talked of little more than the Indian attacks and what the Army and Governor Evans were doing to stop them. Even the War Between the States took backstage to gossip and supposition about Colorado's Indian Wars. More Indian attacks had occurred in Kansas and Nebraska than in Colorado. Certainly, there had been no attacks on Denver, but from the discussions of the citizenry, one would assume it was only a matter of days before the Indians would overrun the city. Dr. Williams's dinner table was no exception.

"One of my patients told me—of course I cannot name said

patient—that Colonel Chivington has given up on making peace with the Indians." Mr. Allerton paused for effect. "Apparently, some fellow named William Bent parlayed with Indian Chief Black Kettle to try to make peace, but Chivington says he's had it with the Indians. Says he has orders from General Curtis to attack all Indians regardless of whether or not they say they're peaceful. Won't stop until they're all eliminated."

Georgia could not contain herself. "If Denver feels threatened now, it'll get a whole lot hotter if the Army goes about attacking any Indian they come across. Truth is, only a small number of Indians are hostile."

"You're probably right about that, Georgia." Dr. Williams shifted in his seat. "Problem is, how do you know which one is hostile and which one is not?"

Dr. Williams's nephew joined the debate. "I for one favor Governor Evans and Colonel Chivington's efforts to raise a volunteer militia to fight the Indians to protect us."

"Without funding from the government, that will not happen." Dr. Williams set down the coffee he sipped. "And with government coffers already strained by the War Between the States—"

"Are we not citizens of this country, deserving protection like Americans who live in the East?" Mr. Allerton's head was lifted high and he gestured large. Georgia tried to hide her amusement. The stuffy Easterner, so proud of his New England roots, was incensed at being ignored. The settlers were used to it.

Lucy's cherry pie, hot out of the oven, redirected their attention. Passionate opinions made for good discourse but yielded no solutions. The merits of the cherry pie, on the other hand, had them all in agreement.

❋

The following day, Georgia read in the newspaper that Governor Evans had devised a plan to separate friendly Indians from hostile ones. His proclamation, addressed to the "Friendly Indians of the Plains," directed peaceful Indians to stay "in the vicinity" of Army forts throughout Colorado Territory. Here, the governor promised, "friendly Indians will be protected, given annuities and allowed to hunt buffalo and wild game."

Georgia laughed out loud. Did the governor think the Indians had their own newspaper? How would he tell them about his latest proclamation? She could imagine the reaction of the Indians. Gray Wolf told the MacBayes the Cheyenne received promises for annuities many times, yet the promises seldom materialized. And how would the whites discern "good" Indians from "bad." She could hardly see how soldiers with orders from Colonel Chivington to kill Indians on sight would protect them. And did Governor Evans really think buffalo and game would pour into the vicinity of the forts, as if obeying a summons? The whites or the Indians or both were in big trouble with Evans and Chivington in charge!

※

Two days later, Georgia answered the door to find James on the step.

"Come in, come in. It's good to see you." Georgia thought he looked bad—really bad. Red, puffy eyes made James look older than he was.

"I ... I come with bad news, Georgia. The worse news. Mother has died."

"Dead?" Georgia stepped back into the parlor, reaching to the back of a settee to steady herself. "Indians?" she asked almost in a whisper as James followed her inside.

"No. Nothin' like that. She went to attend Mrs. Johnson. Her baby was on the way." James clutched the stair railing just outside the parlor. Georgia feared he might fall.

"Come, James. Let's sit." Georgia waved Lucy away, her cheer shattered with one look at their faces.

James bit his lower lip, fighting tears. "The gentle mare Ma always took was heavy with foal, so Pa sent her off with a new horse hitched to the wagon. When she didn't come home by the next afternoon, Pa went lookin' for 'er. The Johnsons told Pa she'd left them the previous morning after delivering a healthy baby girl." A sob escaped him. "He returned by way of the bluffs and found the wagon overturned. Both she and the horse were dead. Looked like Ma had taken the shortcut that morning and they'd fallen from atop the bluffs. Guess the only good is she looked to have died on impact. Didn't suffer none." Georgia was glad James looked away. The pain in his face was too difficult to bear.

She sat stunned. Then the tears came, sobs of deepest grief. James held her. They sat without speaking. Lucy brought them coffee, saying nothing as she set two cups on the coffee table in front of them. Neither drank it.

When Dr. Williams returned from the clinic later in the day, he found them still seated in the parlor. Georgia's swollen, red eyes told him that something was wrong, very wrong. "My girl, what has happened?"

When she tried to talk, sobs made her hard to understand. "My ... ma, she's ... been killed."

She could not continue. James explained the tragedy to Dr. Williams, ending with, "Pa wants her to remain here to finish her schooling."

Georgia had regained her voice. "No, I must see Pa. I want to be at the ranch."

Dr. Williams agreed with her. "Georgia has learned much already, but she can come back anytime. I agree. She needs to be at home with her family now."

"You're right. I know my pa just wanted her to finish her schooling, but she'd never be able to focus on school." James pursed his lips and nodded his head. "If it suits you, sir, we'll leave in the morning. A Cavalry contingent is planning to escort me back to the Basin. Not safe for a lone ride, now with the Indian attacks, you know. Georgia can ride with us."

Lucy helped Georgia pack her things. Her eyes widened as

Georgia pulled the rifle from under the bed.

"I can see that I won't have to worry about your personal safety, Miss Georgia." Lucy attempted to lighten the sorrowful mood. "If we're done here, I'll go on down to the kitchen and fix up some food for you and your brother to eat on the trail."

Georgia wished she could tell Lucy how much she appreciated her help today and for the ten months she had lived at the house. "Thank you ..." Sobs again choked her ability to speak.

Lucy hugged her tightly, rubbing her back like a mother. "Sweetheart, I'm so sorry. You're a fine woman, and Dr. Williams says you're the best student he's ever had. Life is just hard sometimes. I know it's hard to believe, but the sorrow will ease with time."

"How do you know?" Georgia blurted out through sobs.

"I lost my own ma when I was about your age. My ma and pa both died of consumption the same year. That's when I decided to leave New Mexico and move to Denver. I still think about them all the time, but it's fond memories more than the terrible pain like you're feelin' right now."

All Georgia could do was nod. Lucy patted her back and smoothed back her hair. "I'll tell James you're packed."

Lucy stood to leave. "Lucy, thank you. Thank you for everything." Georgia hoped the simple words conveyed her depth of gratitude to the woman. Lucy nodded and smiled.

Dr. Williams told Georgia's classmates about her mother, so she didn't have to explain the details when they came to give their condolences and bid her farewell. Lucy prepared a light, early supper. Georgia couldn't say what it was. She would have preferred to go to bed without supper, but she knew she would need strength for the journey home.

Early the next morning, James and Georgia carried their things downstairs. Bless their hearts, Dr. Williams and Lucy had risen before the sun was up to tell them goodbye. They hurried off to the livery to saddle their horses. Most of Georgia's things fit in the large leather bags she tied behind the saddle. James put her remaining things behind his saddle, fastening the pack with long leather strings.

Mr. Fletcher was not yet up, so Georgia left word of her sudden departure with the stablehand on duty.

The ten-man Cavalry contingent, including Teddy, was ready to leave when Georgia and James reached Camp Weld. The mood was somber as they headed east, Denver still asleep behind them.

For the first time since she'd moved to Denver, Georgia was free on the open prairie. Kildeer birds ran on their spindly legs pretending they were injured. It was a tactic they used to draw predators away from their ground nests and young. Hawks soared close to the ground, searching for a breakfast rodent or snake.

They rode at a brisk trot, stopping midmorning at a ranch to water their horses and stretch their legs. The windmill worked, but the fence was in disrepair, and the door of the nearby ranch house flapped, opening and closing in the wind. Georgia wondered if it was the drought, the fear of an Indian attack or some other disaster that had chased away the settlers.

"Sarge, on account of the lady, I suppose we'll make camp tonight and then continue on to the Basin tomorrow morning?" Georgia welcomed the interruption to her thoughts. Eavesdropping was not polite, but she was not about to walk away.

"Can't rightly say. We're makin' real good time. It'll depend whether or not Miss Georgia will be able to keep up the pace."

Georgia snorted to herself. She had wondered why the men were moving along at such a leisurely pace. Now she knew they thought "the lady" could not keep up. She'd show them the kind of pace she could keep!

Georgia had kept Cheyenne in good shape with regular rides in the sandy ground of Cherry Creek. When the rest was over and all had mounted again, she eased the filly into a ground-covering lope. For the first time in nearly a year, she felt the thrill of riding the open prairie. The grasses were as lush and green as she had ever seen them. The flaming orange Indian paintbrush and bluebells, nestled among the sagebrush favored by the pronghorn antelope, presented a carpet of spring wonder. After getting used to the street odors of a developing city, the prairie smelled fresh and clean. Frightened rabbits bolted from their hiding places, racing across the path of the riders. Georgia felt exhilaration from the run across the festooned prairie, and she never tired from the feeling of a muscular, smooth-gaited horse as it carried her without effort across open ground.

The sergeant called for a halt to eat lunch and "rest the horses." From the looks of the men, it was they, not the horses, who needed a rest. She had to admit, the rest was good. Her appetite had returned and the food Lucy packed satisfied her hunger. She offered some to James, who grumbled something about not wanting to abandon his fellow soldiers. The soldiers gnawed on crackers and hardtack. The hard, chewy meat provided nourishment but lacked in appeal. It was different from the smoked beef and game the ranchers made in the fall. Now *that* would nourish the body and the senses.

"I had no idea you were such a horsewoman." The soldier who had talked to the sergeant about camping addressed Georgia. She wasn't sure how to respond, so she said nothing. "I 'spect we'll be arrivin' in the basin before sundown."

"I 'spect so," Georgia mumbled as she left to prepare Cheyenne to continue the journey.

With their destination well within reach, the Cavalry took the last leg of the trip at a trot. Several hours before sundown, they came to the Johnson place. Georgia felt no ill will toward the Johnsons, but seeing their place reminded her of her mother's death. Georgia's jaw clinched as James took the lead, directing them up and over the bluffs. It was a route she had taken many times, and it was safer by horseback than in a wagon. Even still, retracing her mother's ill-fated trip made her tense. She doubted the others knew it was where their mother had died.

As James crested the ridge of bluffs, he paused to look below. Georgia could not look. She gave Cheyenne her head and trusted the filly to see her home.

Georgia and James rode into the ranch yard. The Cavalry contingent would camp behind the house. When Georgia saw her father, she left Cheyenne at the hitching post and flew into his arms. She hoped she would be a comfort to him. Instead, sobs spilled over any words she attempted to speak.

He held her, without speaking, for a long time. Clasping both of her hands, Thomas stepped back.

"It is so good to see you, Georgia. I know it's selfish of me. You should have stayed in Denver, at the school, but I'm so glad you're here."

"Me too, Daddy. There's no way I coulda stayed knowin' what happened to Ma." Tears sprang to her eyes again.

James had taken care of their horses. "Pa, you'd be very proud of Georgia. Dr. Williams said she was his best student ever." He winked at Georgia.

"Is that right, now? My baby girl, the best medical student ever?"

Georgia could see that her father still had his easygoing manner, and there was no denying he loved his children, but a dull pain showed in his once laughing eyes. As sure as a kerosene lamp when its light is snuffed out, the light had gone out of Thomas's face.

The house looked unkempt. The stove had a coat of dust over it. *What has Pa been eating since Ma died?* Very little, it appeared. He looked thin, even unhealthy—not the hardy, fun-loving man who had taken her to the Limon stagecoach stop to travel to Denver less than a year ago. She set to work tidying the kitchen. She had to make a hot supper for them and the ten men in the Cavalry contingent. There was no time to soak and cook beans, but she found ingredients for cornbread, and there was a ham in the smokehouse. Though full of weeds, the garden yielded spring greens, which she cooked with the ham.

Her efforts were rewarded with accolades as the soldiers left the house early to turn in for the night. James slept in the house but would ride out with them in the morning. He had already taken two weeks off to bury their mother and help Thomas catch up on spring ranch work.

It would take Georgia days, if not weeks, to get the house and garden in order. She hadn't even seen the barn. There was probably a lot of work to do there too. *Just as well*, she thought. Not only were idle hands the devil's workshop, idle hands would increase the grief she and Thomas felt. Best to fill their days.

Georgia washed the supper dishes by lamplight. At least the kitchen would be clean. Weary, she climbed the stairs to her bedroom. She thought her father was asleep, but when she went to kiss him good night, she found he was not. He was lying on the bed, clothes and boots still on. The unkempt look of his bedroom and the wrinkled clothes told her it was not the first time he had slept in his clothes. She went to her own room, slipped on her nightdress and slid under the bedsheet. She had forgotten how cool evenings were on the prairie, even in summer. The sheet and light quilt felt good. Exhaustion overtook her, and she slept.

Chapter 20

Southeastern Colorado, July 17, 1864

G
ray Wolf rode Wise Heart to the crest of the hill. Looking eastward, he could see for miles. The heavy winter snows and drenching spring rains had given way to hot, dry weather, making it easy to see dust from herds of buffalo or travelers anywhere near the camp. Disappointed, he saw no sign of movement. Today was the sixth day Gray Wolf had ridden out to see if there was news from Fort Lyon—and it was the sixth day he had come back disappointed.

Gray Wolf had returned to the Cheyenne summer encampment from the MacBayes on the last day of the Renewal of the Sacred Arrows ceremony to find that Beaver had just ridden in from the south. The sweaty, matted hair of his horse told Gray Wolf that the half-Cheyenne, half-white brave had come with haste and specific purpose.

Beaver greeted him warmly. "My friend, I see that you are well." He spoke Cheyenne. "I have come about a matter of importance and urgency. I hope to meet Black Kettle and Bull Bear. Please join us tonight in the council lodge."

"Certainly, my friend." Gray Wolf moved toward Beaver, but he nodded and left in a hurry.

That night, Gray Wolf joined Beaver, Black Kettle, Bull Bear and the other chiefs. As the youngest there, he and Beaver were the last to smoke the pipe.

Gray Wolf could see that Beaver was nervous yet focused on his mission. He put down the pipe and spoke. "Chief Black Kettle, your feats as a warrior are many and your wisdom in leading your people is known by all." His words were the Cheyenne way of honoring an elder, a chief. "I appeal to your wisdom as I come in the spirit of my grandfather Chief Yellow Wolf, who also sought to make peace with the white man." His words were smooth and exact. "I, like you, fear for our people if we are unable to make peace with them."

After a long silence, Bull Bear spoke: "Tell me how I can make true peace with those who killed my brother, even as he held in his hand a letter from the Great White Father Lincoln that said Lean Bear was a peaceful Indian?"

More silence.

When no elder spoke, Beaver did. "It was a great wrong done your brother ... and all the Cheyenne."

Gray Wolf drew a breath, then said, "Lean Bear was a great chief. Not only was he a great warrior and a wise leader of his people, he, like Chief Black Kettle, saw that the Cheyenne must change if they are to survive. He told me many times that if we do not make peace with the whites, we will be no more. Days before he was shot by the soldiers, he told me we must consider a life of putting seeds in the ground and staying in one place, if that is what will bring us peace with the whites."

"Gray Wolf honors his uncle by continuing to speak Lean Bear's wisdom." Black Kettle stared at him, his eyes piercing the brave's innermost thoughts. Black Kettle turned to Beaver. "Why do you come to us? What would you have us do?"

"I must know if you are still intent on making peace?"

"We are," Black Kettle said without waiting for the others to speak.

Beaver nodded his agreement. "Then I will ride to Fort Lyon. I will speak directly with Colonel Chivington to ask for a peace council between you and him."

"Ride swiftly," Black Kettle urged.

Following the council, Gray Wolf felt hopeful. It was the first time in months that the Cheyenne had taken an initiative to make peace. He hoped the pillaging hadn't angered the whites, causing them to be unwilling to talk peace. He hoped it wasn't too late. But when Beaver didn't return right away, his confidence that peace could yet be brokered waned.

His fears were confirmed several days later when Beaver returned. "I fear we are in for war with the soldiers." Beaver looked exhausted and discouraged. "I tried to tell Colonel Chivington that attacking peaceful Indians will enrage the Dog Soldiers and others bent on war, causing even more bloodshed." Even his horse, which had been a source of considerable pride, looked exhausted and unkempt. "The fool said he is on the warpath and won't stop until he kills all Indians. He is quite unlike Wynkoop, the new commander of Fort Lyon. That is a man the Cheyenne can trust. His heart is true."

Commander, colonel—the titles meant little to Gray Wolf, but he knew the news was not good, which made the announcement delivered a few weeks later by a white messenger from the Indian Agent Colley more confusing. The chiefs and elders were called to council to receive the important announcement. Beaver and Gray Wolf were invited to join them.

Clearly under the influence of alcohol, the messenger, whose Indian tongue was poor, droned on with convoluted instructions that all "friendly Indians" were to gather somewhere, although where was unclear. After the man got distracted and then asked for whiskey, Beaver snatched the letter from his unsteady fingers, translating the letter for all of them:

COLORADO   SUPERINTENDENCY   INDIAN

AFFAIRS, Denver, June 27, 1864.

TO THE FRIENDLY INDIANS OF THE PLAINS:

Agents, interpreters and traders will inform the friendly Indians of the plains that some members of their tribes have gone to war with the white people. They steal stock and run it off, hoping to escape detection and punishment. In some instances they have attacked and killed soldiers and murdered peaceable citizens. For this the Great Father is angry and will certainly hunt them out and punish them, but he does not want to injure those who remain friendly to the whites. He desires to protect and take care of them. For this purpose I direct that all friendly Indians keep away from those who are at war, and go to places of safety. Friendly Arapahoes and Cheyennes belonging on the Arkansas River will go to Major Colley, U. S. Indian agent at Fort Lyon, who will give them provisions and show them a place of safety. Friendly Kiowas and Comanches will go to Fort Larned, where they will be cared for in the same way. Friendly Sioux will go to their agent at Fort Laramie for directions. Friendly Arapahoes and Cheyennes of the Upper Platte will go to Camp Collins on the Cache la Poudre, where they will be assigned a place of safety and provisions will be given them.

The object of this is to prevent friendly Indians from being killed through mistake. None but those who intend to be friendly with the whites must come to these places. The families of those who have gone to war with the whites must be kept away from among the friendly Indians. The war on hostile Indians will be continued until they are all effectually subdued.

JOHN EVANS,
Governor of Colorado and Superintendent of Indian Affairs

Black Kettle expressed the confusion they all felt. "Who do we believe, Evans or Chivington?"

"Governor Evans is a bigger chief than Colonel Chivington,"

Beaver offered.

"My band will go to Fort Lyon," Black Kettle said after considerable thought.

"We will join you," said White Antelope, a chief of over seventy summers.

Bull Bear was not satisfied. "How do we know we can trust them? I saw how they killed my brother when he went in peace to the soldiers."

Colley's drunk messenger stumbled out of the council meeting, heading toward his horse. Minutes later, the council, which had reached no conclusion on whether or not to heed Governor Evan's invitation to "friendly Indians," was interrupted by the return of a contingent of Dog Soldiers.

The return of marauding Dog Soldiers had become an almost everyday occurrence. They danced and boasted, gesturing suggestively at the young girls, who were fascinated by the spectacle. Instead of returning with game, as they should do during summer, they had fresh scalp locks. The loot was modest: worn clothing, a few cans of food.

Against his better judgment, Gray Wolf could not resist shouting to them. "I hope your women and children can be fed and clothed with those scalps!"

One of the Dog Soldiers spun around to face him. Gray Wolf recognized Soaring Falcon, the brave whose horse Georgia had spooked when she was en route to Denver City. The incident had left Soaring Falcon on the ground, Georgia's rifle pinning him there. The brave was eager for his long-awaited revenge. Soaring Falcon removed his knife from it sheath and sprung toward Gray Wolf, who grabbed his opponent's wrist just above where he held the knife. Gray Wolf thrust his arm down and behind him, forcing the brave to turn away. Further leverage and the knife fell out of his clenched hand. It had been a skilled and powerful move on Gray Wolf's part, but Soaring Falcon had not learned his lesson. He spun around, breaking Gray Wolf's hold on his wrist, but when he brought his foot up to kick his opponent, Gray Wolf grabbed his ankle and jerked upward. The brave found himself flat on the ground in front, gasping for air.

Abandoned by his fellow Dog Soldiers, he seethed with hatred. "You won't get away with this," he shouted through clenched teeth.

Gray Wolf turned and was walking away when Soaring Falcon yelled, "I bet your friends here don't know you're still in love with a white woman, with that healer's daughter, do they?!"

It was a hot summer day, but Gray Wolf froze in his tracks. The brave not only preyed on unknowing farmers and ranchers and their families, he wanted revenge for Georgia getting the better of him. Gray Wolf knew he had to diffuse the situation. In a gentler tone, he said, "Haven't seen her in a long time. She lives in Denver now."

"Maybe that's the truth, maybe it's not." Soaring Falcon stood, brushing the dust off his buckskin vest. Gray Wolf's reaction signaled that he had hit a sensitive spot. "No matter where the woman lives, the Dog Soldiers will be paying a visit to her mother."

Surely it was all bravado, Gray Wolf hoped. He would have no idea where the MacBayes lived.

"I guess you were so sick when Lean Bear took you there that you don't remember I rode with him." Soaring Falcon's shoulders were square now, his chin up, eyes defiant. "It was a nice place. Probably plenty of stock in the field and food and clothing in that nice house."

Gray Wolf hoped he would not faint. How could he have been so stupid to draw the brave's attention to Georgia and her family? The only deterrent he could think of was a gift, a very large gift. "If not for the healer, I would be dead. I owe much to this family—so much that I offer you five horses to stay away from them."

"Five horses, you say? So, you are so much in love with the healer's daughter that you would offer horses to protect her?" His tone taunted Gray Wolf. "Why would I want five of your horses when I can get more than that in a day's worth of raids?"

Gray Wolf could see that increasing his offer would only

diminish him in the eyes of this menacing brave. Without another word to Soaring Falcon, Gray Wolf returned to his tepee. He wanted no one but Meadow Lark to know his fear.

"I am sure it is nothing but an idle threat, Gray Wolf," Meadow Lark said as she put the pot of venison and wild greens and turnips in front of Gray Wolf.

"How can you say it is an idle threat? Most every day some hunting party returns with loot or scalps, not dressed game for cooking pots. You've seen it as much as I have, Meadow Lark!" Gray Wolf's nerves were calmed somewhat by the enticing stew that his sister poured into a gourd for him to drink.

Pouring stew for herself, she sat, contemplating his dilemma. "Speak with the brave's chief. Have him warn this hotheaded young brave not to harm the healer or her family or their livestock."

"Both your stew and your advice are good, sister."

That evening, Gray Wolf took his good friend Moonwalker with him to talk to Bull Bear about the threat to the MacBayes.

"The healer and her family cannot be harmed. It would be wrong to harm a healer, especially this healer." When Bull Bear didn't react, Gray Wolf added, "Lean Bear trusted her. Will you talk to Soaring Falcon's chief?"

"The problem, Gray Wolf, is that I don't know who his chief is, and, as you have seen, the young braves, especially the Dog Soldiers, are not listening to their elders these days," Bull Bear said.

Moonwalker intervened. "Please Chief Bull Bear, we would not have come to you if we didn't need your help. The problem will only escalate if Gray Wolf seeks out his chief. There is nothing else we can do."

"I will find out who has influence on these braves. Now, please go. This old chief needs his sleep."

Moonwalker and Gray Wolf left Bull Bear's tepee. Moonwalker was uneasy. "I do not want to disrespect Bull Bear, but I don't know if he will act. I think we must watch these Dog Soldiers to learn their next plans."

"What do you suggest?"

"I will go home to eat and sleep early. I will rise before dawn and pretend to prepare to hunt that I might see what they are doing and hear their plans. They do not know me, and I will be readying my hunting tools."

"It is a good plan, Moonwalker. Thank you. You are a dependable friend."

✳

It was still dark the next morning when Moonwalker shook Gray Wolf awake. "Wake up. The Dog Soldiers have left. They travel west this time, toward the Bijou Basin. The dog soldier who knows the healer is with them. We must ride after them."

Gray Wolf bolted from his buffalo robe. Still disoriented, he was glad he had laid out what he needed before he slept. Meadow Lark had prepared pemmican, a skin for water and a traveling robe for sleeping or cover in case of heavy rain or hail from an afternoon thunderstorm. With haste, he scooped up his rifle and ammunition, a bow and arrows and Wise Heart's bridle. His hunting knife was tied to his ankle.

Moonwalker and Gray Wolf were glad to find their horses grazing at the periphery of the herd. Once mounted, they pushed their horses into a gallop until they spotted the Dog Soldiers. It was still dark, but Gray Wolf knew it was the Dog Soldiers ahead of them. Not wanting to be seen, they slowed their horses to an easy trot. Moonwalker was right: The Dog Soldiers were headed toward the Bijou Basin. The sun had yet to peek over the eastern horizon behind them, but Gray Wolf could see the silhouetted braves veer north toward the pine forest. According to the elders, the pine forest was small in comparison to forests in the north, but to Gray Wolf and the other braves his age, it was all they knew. There were tall pine trees farther west, but this forest seemed to spring forth out of nowhere on the plains and surround the Bijou Basin. Lean Bear had told him that the rock below the ground stored water that nourished the pine trees. The pines provided welcome shade for riders in the summer and a wind break for those traveling during cold winter days, but today, Gray Wolf wished there was no pine forest to hide Soaring Falcon.

Gray Wolf and Moonwalker entered the pines where the Dog Soldiers had. They were much relieved to see the braves fanning out, a familiar hunting tactic. Maybe the threat was nothing more than a bluff, and it was game, not scalps, they were after.

They kept Soaring Falcon's party in their sight but did not approach them until midmorning when a shot was fired and shouts confirmed a deer was down. "Let's see if they need help," Gray Wolf said to Moonwalker as they trotted their ponies in the direction of the kill.

From a distance, Gray Wolf could see that a buck was down, not moving. He was always relieved when an animal died quickly. Not only was the meat tainted if a deer or antelope ran before collapsing, he hated seeing it suffer.

Gray Wolf shouted at the hunters while still far away in order not to startle them. "Do you need some help skinning and quartering the buck?!"

The hunters were not at all surprised to see Gray Wolf and Moonwalker. "Showing up just in time to take a share of the meat, are you?" said a brave Gray Wolf had seen in the camp this summer but did not know. He could not determine if the brave was joking or angry. "Sure, come on in and help. It's the hunting I prefer anyway."

With eight of them working, the carcass was skinned, quartered and wrapped for transport in no time. Gray Wolf and Moonwalker declined the offer to share the meat. It had not been their kill. As they finished, Moonwalker asked, "How did you know we were in the forest?"

"Soaring Falcon spotted you shortly after we left camp. Said your black horse is hard to miss," the brave said.

Gray Wolf's throat went dry, and he felt his heartbeat in his temples. "Where is Soaring Eagle?"

"He continued on north, something about better hunting in

the Bijou Basin. We thought it strange. Everyone knows deer stay in the trees, especially when it's hot."

Moonwalker and Gray Wolf sprinted to their tethered horses. Gray Wolf's war cry pierced the pine forest as the two galloped their horses north at neck-breaking speed.

Chapter 21

Bijou Basin, July 18, 1864

Since Georgia had returned to the Bijou Basin, hardly a day passed without someone seeking medical advice or treatment. Most came to the house, but for the most severe cases, she made house calls. Lars Olson, a rancher with whom her father sometimes traded cattle, came asking for Georgia's help with his wife's arthritis. Georgia told her to try some evening primrose oil and advised she eat more vegetables, warning that with arthritis there were no easy fixes. This seemed to open a floodgate of Swedish immigrants seeking her assistance. Late one afternoon, Mr. Karlson rode into the MacBaye Ranch. Between his great distress and broken English, she surmised an emergency and set out immediately, traveling several hours northeast of the Bijou Basin.

They arrived well after dark. Mr. Karlson's son, Alver, looked to be about six years old. He was pale, despite his sun-worn Swedish complexion. He lay face up on the floor, an ugly gash running from just below his hip to a few inches above his knee. Upon closer examination in the dim lamplight, Georgia saw that beyond the gash was a displaced femur bone. Alver had lost a lot of blood, but the bleeding had stopped. She had set bones and stitched cuts under the tutelage of Dr. Williams, but it was on a surgery table with good light. The Karlson home was a dugout in the side of a gully. The dwelling was as clean as it could be, but dirt and straw fell from the roof. A dugout was a common home for first-year homesteaders. The flickering kerosene lantern taunted Georgia's indecision. Was she afraid or prudent? Another look at the distressed yet hopeful faces, and her decision to set the bone was made. She used gestures to ask for hot water. While the water was heating, she prepared the chloroform. Remembering the formula to calculate how much to use based on the patient's estimated weight, she poured the minimum quantity on a cloth and an additional quantity on a second cloth. She dropped her scalpel, needle and horse hair suture string into the pot of boiling water. A few minutes later, she retrieved her surgery tools and placed them on a clean cloth. She washed her hands with her own lye soap, rolling up her sleeves past her elbows. She had learned much at Dr. Williams's school, but Ma's penchant for cleanliness added this extra layer of preparation. She wasn't superstitious, but she would take all the precautions she could. After all, Ma's patients seldom had high fevers or gangrene after she treated them.

Using words and demonstrating, she showed Mr. Karlson how to apply the chloroform and Alver's mother how to hold the lantern to give her the most light. The boy lost consciousness as expected when the cloth sprinkled with chloroform was placed over his nose. Georgia gestured for Mr. Karlson to take hold of his son's thigh. She pulled and twisted Alver's foot to put the femur into alignment, repeating the procedure several times without success. Sweat poured onto her face, and she was about to burst into tears when she remembered her mother's words: "Neither be lax nor proud of your doctoring. It is God and God alone who heals." Georgia whispered a quick prayer for guidance. It was then that she noticed a metal piece in the femur. It appeared small, but when she pushed on the metal, the end of a plowshare emerged from the back of Alver's thigh. No question what had caused the injury. The metal removed, Georgia was able to realign the femur. With her patient showing signs of regaining consciousness, she pointed at the second chloroformed cloth and gestured for Mr. Karlson to put it over his son's nose. She stitched together the inner tissues covering the bone and made a second set of stitches to pull the outer skin together, leaving just enough space to allow the wound to drain as it healed.

The Karlsons had insisted she sleep on the only bed in the dugout. By morning, Alver asked to eat. He seemed embarrassed when she cleaned and dressed his wound on the naked thigh. Both were signs he was on his way to recovery. She used hand gestures to tell Mr. and Mrs. Karlson she needed to return home. Mr. Karlson insisted on accompanying her.

Once out of the dugout, Georgia saw the barrenness of the place. There were no trees, not even a creek. The land beyond the dugout was flat as the bottom of a cast-iron frying pan. A hand dug well was the family's only source of water for themselves and their meager crops. Georgia could not imagine watering field crops with water pulled bucket by bucket from the little well. The MacBayes watered their crops and, if needed, the pasture by damming the creek until the water was high enough to force it into ditches. The network of ditches delivered water to the crop rows with a single shovel cut. The pasture, because it lay in the low area adjacent to the creek, needed water from the creek only in the driest times.

As they mounted their horses to leave, Mr. Karlson read her expression. "Ya, uts a leetle dirt house, but someday we build a big wud house. We buy cows and plant corn and wheat like ur fater."

Georgia nodded. The Karlsons would make it. She admired their determination. At least they had each other. The thought brought a lump to her throat. Her mother was gone. The trip to the Karlsons had distracted her from her sorrow but only for a while. She left Denver because she knew her father would need her and because she needed him. She thought being in the house would help mend her sorrow, the way her ma's adept stitching mended a big hole in a wool sock. Instead, being in the house seemed to multiply her sorrows. There were reminders of her mother everywhere. When Georgia worked in the garden, she remembered her mother telling her to plant the cabbage with wormwood to keep the worms from invading the cabbage. Marigolds kept bugs off the tomatoes. Planting beans and sweet corn near each other was good, she said, because what nutrient one took from the soil, the other returned. Each time Georgia made cornbread, she wished she had paid more attention to how her mother made it. Her cornbread always turned out flatter and tougher. Even the neighbors who called on Georgia for medical advice would say, "Now I remember, one time your mother said—" stopping when they remembered she was gone. Georgia found that even training horses provided little satisfaction these days.

One morning just a week after she arrived back at the ranch, Georgia's father had deposited her mother's diary and scrapbook on the kitchen table. "She would have wanted you to have these," he said.

The scrapbook had a family photo that was dated just before they left South Carolina. Georgia thought they all looked so stern and unattractive. Ma had told her posing for a photograph meant standing still for a long time so the photograph would not be blurry. Instead, it looked like they'd eaten the worst thing possible for dinner and were sick to their stomachs. She looked to be about five, Henry might have been eight and James ten or so. She found letters from people she didn't know. A woman who signed her name "Lucy" wrote, *Dear Loraine, Your departure from Spring Grove was a shock to everyone. I am told many of the neighbors are hopping angry on account of you and Thomas freeing all your slaves, but I think you are very brave. I only wish others had the courage to follow you.*

Later letters from this same Lucy indicated that Henry would be staying with her and her family. *This must be Ma's aunt.* She had married a Yankee and moved to Philadelphia. On the last pages of her mother's scrapbook were the newspaper clippings from the Denver paper referring to "Dr. Williams and his fine medical students, including one lady student by the name of Georgia MacBaye." Georgia had mailed the newspaper clippings with one of her letters. Her mother had pasted them into her scrapbook, with a note in her own handwriting below one of the clippings that read, "My beautiful daughter. I am so proud of you."

Hot tears had sprung into Georgia's eyes when she read Ma's writing. Even now, thinking about it made her cry. She was glad Mr. Karlson was riding a distance away from her, so he could not hear her sobs.

The memories of her mother were bittersweet, but it was her father that she worried about now. He was present in the body but it was as if his soul had already joined his wife. He completed his daily work with skill but no joy. Georgia and two of the neighbor boys had helped him cut the hay and wheat and bring it into the barn. The feed corn would not be ready until after the first freeze in late September or October, and swarms of grasshoppers had come in such numbers that she wondered how much corn would mature to be picked.

Georgia had started the seasonal work of gathering berries and making preserves. She had made several batches of pickles. The potatoes, carrots and beets were growing well with irrigation from the creek despite the slow start to the growing season. She picked and dried rosemary, mint, basil and chamomile as it ripened. They enjoyed greens with most meals now. Georgia had settled back into a settler routine, always ready for the interruption and willing to help any who came with a medical need.

Her father did not neglect his work, yet he planned no exciting ventures. The father Georgia remembered would have by now built some new contraption to make their lives better or their work lighter. One year he had built a chute to get the hay from the loft to the cattle feeders with minimal work and less wasted hay. In subsequent years, he had built the springhouse, a chicken coop and a patio in front of the adobe ranch house. He even built a fence around the garden to keep out the rabbits and the occasional loose cow. He didn't even tease Georgia anymore. He hardly spoke with her. She noticed that her father also spent a lot of time at Loraine's grave.

※

The terrain started to look familiar as Georgia continued her homeward trek. She shouted at Mr. Karlson to stop his horse. "I do thank you for bringing me back home, Mr. Karlson. Our place is just over that set of bluffs. You need to get on back and look after Alver."

Mr. Karlson took off his hat and pulled his horse closer to Cheyenne. "The Meesus and I ...we thank yu fur what yu did fur our son. Some day ... I make da money ta pay ya, Mees Georgia."

"You don't worry none about that, now, Mr. Karlson. Glad to have been of service. I hope we meet again."

Mr. Karlson pushed the hat back down on his head and with a wave, turned and headed back toward his home. He would reach home before dark.

Georgia let Cheyenne pick her way over the gullies and bluffs, still contemplating what she could do to help her father start living again. Thirty minutes later, the pair was cresting the last set of bluffs, the ones that cradled the MacBaye place. The view from the top of the bluff, looking down at the place, always gave her pleasure. She expected a similar satisfaction on this warm summer afternoon, but what she saw alarmed her.

The wheat stubble was black and the livestock was nowhere in sight. She rode down the bluff and across the creek as fast as she dared. The fence between the creek and the house was cut. The backdoor to the house swung in the breeze, attached to the door with a broken hinge. She did not dismount, in case the thieves were still there. Her rifle in her right hand, her senses intensified, she rode past the house toward the barn. In this moment, she saw him: an Indian on a horse. He had just turned in her direction. She raised her rifle at him, but her hand was trembling too much to fire. She took a quick breath to steady the shaking. The Indian walked toward her. Her finger was on the trigger.

"Georgia, stop!" The shout came from behind her. "Moonwalker is my friend."

Whirling around, Georgia saw Gray Wolf seated on the ground, her pa's head cradled on his lap.

Gray Wolf had come earlier to check on the MacBayes, certain Soaring Falcon and his accomplices had raided the ranch. When he arrived, he saw that they had set the wheat stubble on fire. It looked like they had tried to burn the house but without success. Adobe was packed earth, nothing combustible. Perhaps they had been too frustrated with failing to burn the house that they did not try to burn the barn.

The cattle and horses were gone. It looked like the men had rummaged through the house. At first Gray Wolf didn't see anyone, hoping above all else that Thomas and Loraine had been away from the ranch. Then Gray Wolf heard a pained call for help. His heart sunk. It was Thomas.

Gray Wolf then ran to the back side of the barn where Thomas was trying to pull himself up from the ground. He saw the arrows in Thomas's chest, but his scalp was intact. Odd, Gray Wolf had thought—Dog Soldiers always scalp their victims and very few survive it. At first glance, he thought the arrows might be removed. "Easy, Thomas, let me take a look." He knew it was not good. The arrows were deep.

Adrenaline and fear for Thomas had prevented Gray Wolf from collapsing in despair. Soaring Falcon had shot the arrows into Thomas, but Gray Wolf had not stopped him.

Thomas read Gray Wolf's face well. "It's not your fault, son. Remember when I told you we can't blame an entire people for the mistakes of one?"

Gray Wolf nodded. The lump in his throat was so big he couldn't speak. Then he saw it. A rifle leaning against the barn, well within Thomas's reach. "Why didn't you defend yourself, Thomas?"

"I could have shot him, with the rifle ... or my pistol." Thomas patted the second firearm at his hip. Gray Wolf had not noticed it before. "The man was so full of anger. He spoke the Cheyenne tongue, but I could see that hatred burned in him. He wasn't ready to meet his maker." Thomas looked into Gray Wolf's eyes as if pleading for him to understand his sacrifice. "I didn't let them take my scalp, though." He smiled faintly.

"You were willing ... to die for him, even though he hates you." It wasn't a question. Gray Wolf thought Thomas was the bravest man he had ever met.

Moonwalker, who had checked to ensure Soaring Falcon was gone, joined them behind the barn, interrupting Gray Wolf's thoughts. Moonwalker spoke in Cheyenne: "Is he badly wounded?"

Turning toward Moonwalker, his back to Thomas, Gray Wolf had said, "Yes, I fear his heart has been pierced with the top arrow. See the blood pooling on his chest?" Gray Wolf looked away so Moonwalker would not see his pain. "He will not be alive by sundown."

Moonwalker nodded. Pointing at the rifle, he asked, "Did the rifle misfire?"

Gray Wolf took a deep breath. "No, he felt compassion for Soaring Falcon. He died that his murderer might live."

Moments before Georgia arrived, Thomas had made a request of Gray Wolf.

"I'd always imagined myself living to a ripe-old age," Thomas said, "but this prairie is tough on a man and on his family. It took my Loraine." He pointed to the garden south of the house. "I'd be much obliged if you'd see to it that I'm buried beside her." Gray Wolf had wanted to ask what had happened to Loraine. He knew what had happened to Thomas. He had arrived too late. He might as well have shot the arrows into Thomas's chest himself. Thomas continued, "That's just a request. Not all that important. I know the Good Lord will carry my soul to be with Him regardless of where my body ends up." Rising up on his elbows, he had steeled himself against the pain. Grasping Gray Wolf's right forearm, a new emotion overcame him. "What I have to say next is the only thing that's really important." His eyes were moist. He smiled, sad but resolved. "It's Georgia. You must promise me you'll take care of her." Then halting but with great tenderness, "Love her."

Gray Wolf dropped his eyes. Had he not, he would have been unable to speak. He was honored that Thomas would entrust Georgia to him. How had Thomas known that Gray Wolf loved her?

"Yes, Thomas, I will guard her with my life. I will care for her ... I will love her." He had said it. He would, he already did, love her.

"Thank you, son," Thomas said, squeezing Gray Wolf's forearm with waning strength.

Georgia quickly dismounted from Cheyenne and ran to them. Two arrows with the telltale Cheyenne turkey feathers protruded from her pa's chest, one near his heart, the other lower and to one side.

Dropping to her knees beside him, she saw a pool of blood where the top arrow had penetrated. "Let's get him inside. I have my bag."

Thomas's speech was slow and slurred: "No, Georgia ... I've lost too much blood. Second arrow pieced my lung. I'm not suffering overly much ... Sit here ... with me ... daughter." He tried to extend his hand toward her. She grabbed it, leathered from long days in the hot sun and freezing snow, and held it tightly. His breathing was rough and uneven, confirming his own assessment that the arrow had gone into his lung.

Georgia had almost forgotten that Gray Wolf was there. His

eyes were trained on Pa. His tight mouth and haunted eyes told all.

Thomas's breathing became even more labored. He didn't move now, except to squeeze Georgia's hand. She was surprised when he spoke, although "home" and "Loraine" were the only words she understood. With his dying words, he wanted her to know he was at peace as he went to his eternal rest, went to be with his wife.

Sobs engulfed Georgia. She remembered Thomas as he had been before Loraine died—the laughing, energetic, teasing father who loved her and encouraged her to pursue her dreams of medical school. She mourned the father who had lost his wife and lost his will to live. She moved to cradle his now lifeless head, taking Gray Wolf's place. He must have slipped away to give her privacy. Rage then numbness replaced her tears.

It was dusk when Gray Wolf came for her. "Georgia, we must go into the house now."

She tried to stand, but her knees buckled underneath her. He carried her into the house and up the stairs.

From the window in her bedroom, Georgia could see Gray Wolf hoist her father's large body over his right shoulder and head to the house. She did not hear him until later when he brought her dried buffalo to eat. "It isn't much, but you need to eat. You need strength for the coming days." He was right. She chewed the meat dutifully, not tasting a thing.

Georgia's sleep was fitful at best. Rising before dawn, she went downstairs to find her pa's body on the floor in front of the fireplace. The murderous arrows had been sawn off. Gray Wolf was in the kitchen with Moonwalker. The men had no problem lighting a fire, but the eggs they put in the skillet had stuck and were burning. Georgia took over, ensuring they all had eggs and potatoes to fill their stomachs.

They ate in silence until Gray Wolf spoke. "I believe it is your custom to put the dead in the ground. I dug a deep hole beside the cross. Your father told me your mother's body was put there."

"Thank you, Gray Wolf." Georgia had not thought about the burial. She was glad Gray Wolf had. From the look of him, he had slept even less than she had last night.

"After we put his body in the hole and cover it, we need to leave. It is not safe for you to stay here. I want you to come with me."

Georgia nodded. She would decide later what she would do, where she would live, but for now, she could not think. She knew she could not bear being in this house alone.

After the breakfast dishes were washed, Georgia left for the gravesite. Gray Wolf and Moonwalker were gentle as they lowered her father's body into the very deep hole. Georgia knew she should say something, so she recited the 23rd Psalm. She could not bear to see the dirt fall on her pa, so she hurried back to the house. Wondering what one packed to live with the Cheyenne, she gathered sturdy clothing, blankets and her medical supplies. She noticed that Gray Wolf had already packed beans, preserves, cornmeal and flour. With the food filling one side of a pack, she was able to get all but two blankets into the other side.

Gray Wolf and Moonwalker returned to the house, and Moonwalker took the pack out to where the horses were corralled. Georgia noticed that the backdoor had been repaired and rehung. Gray Wolf closed both the back and front doors, making sure they were tight.

All the MacBayes' horses had been stolen by the thieves, so Moonwalker cinched the pack to Cheyenne, using the two blankets as a cushion between the saddle and the pack. Moonwalker and Gray Wolf unhitched their horses and swung up on their backs. Gray Wolf extended his hand to Georgia, who swung up behind him.

Chapter 22

Bijou Basin, July 19, 1864

Georgia seemed to melt into Gray Wolf as they rode together on Wise Heart. Her arms clung to his waist, his hair next to her cheek.

Georgia's filly followed along behind them, obedient as she carried the pack. Her herd was gone. A horse's nature made it seek the safety of the herd. Wise Heart and Moonwalker's horse became her new herd. It was one thing he did not have to worry about, but there were many things Gray Wolf *did* worry about. He was consumed with regret that he had ever spoken to Soaring Falcon, and then regret that he and Moonwalker had let the treacherous brave outsmart them. The "if onlys" were growing like a pebble pushed down a snowy hill in winter. If he didn't stop, they would overtake him. He had known Thomas well enough to know that the man would never have wanted Gray Wolf to take responsibility for the evil, revenge-seeking Soaring Falcon, but he was still racked with guilt.

Then there was Georgia. He had dreamed a hundred times of her by his side, her in his tepee, her knowing Cheyenne ways. But there was no joy in her being with him because she had little choice. He would protect her and provide for her. He had promised Thomas, but he would let her decide.

It was still well before midday, but the sun was beating down hard on the riders and their horses. Beads of sweat gathered on Gray Wolf's brow. He felt Georgia's moist forehead and cheeks on his shoulders. He felt her breath on his back. How he wished for both their sakes he could roll back time. Georgia had not asked what happened, who killed her father and burned the field or why he had not stopped it. Later, he would tell her that he had failed them. He could not tell her about Soaring Falcon. She would kill him or die trying. He would keep them apart.

"I must know where Soaring Falcon's camp is," Gray Wolf said to Moonwalker. "We cannot go where he camps. The woman and I will make temporary camp at the edge of the pine forest until you return with news of Soaring Falcon. Will you, my good friend, ride to the Cheyenne camp to seek this information and then return to us? Tell no one but Meadow Lark and your wife what has happened."

"I will do as you ask." Moonwalker must have been impatient with the slow pace, but he did not show it. "I leave you now." He whooped, causing his horse to jump, and was off at a gallop.

Just as the heat from the sun became unbearable, they reached the pine forest. The shade felt as delicious as if they had waded out into a swift moving creek. The pine fragrance welcomed them. The fallen pine needles provided a much needed cushion under the horses' hooves. Squirrels and rabbits scurried for cover as they passed.

Under the shade of the pines they continued their trek. Even with the slow pace, they would reach the designated campsite, the place where Moonwalker would return for them, well before sunset. Gray Wolf hoped that with Moonwalker gone, Georgia would talk. She did not. Gray Wolf longed to turn toward her, to gaze upon her face, to comfort her. Georgia sat behind him, not moving or speaking. Gray Wolf was ready for her to rail at him, to accuse him. It would have been better than the silence.

At midday, Gray Wolf handed Georgia several pieces of dried buffalo as they rode. She ate it, saying nothing. Several hours later, they reached an area dense with pine trees. A gully wound under a rock outcropping. They would make camp here. A set of sturdy trees flanked a small meadow. He could run a picket line between the trees to let the horses graze. It would be easy to start a fire without it being seen, and the outcropping would provide shelter from wind or rain. On cue, the sky began to rumble. Gray Wolf swung his leg over Wise Heart's neck and slid to the ground, his back to the horse. He turned to help Georgia dismount as she slid off, her back to him.

"Hold my horse while I get the pack off the filly and run the picket line." He handed her the rawhide reins.

The rain was coming down harder now, but the pack was covered. Everything they needed for the night—buffalo robes for sleeping, flint to start a fire, dried meat, water—were in a smaller pack around Wise Heart's girth. He loosed the rawhide that held the pack in place and motioned for Georgia to take it and move under the outcropping. Georgia had taken the buffalo robes out and laid them on the ground. He had hoped to hunt to get some fresh meat to roast for supper, but the rain made hunting and keeping a fire going nearly impossible.

Georgia sat on her robe, staring in his direction, but not seeing him. Again, he hoped she would speak. She did not. He handed her more dried buffalo and some berries he had picked from a bush near the picket line. Still staring in the same direction, she chewed the food. He wondered if she even knew she ate. When she finished, he handed her the skin of water. She drank until the skin that he had filled from the well at the MacBaye Ranch that morning was empty.

"I'm so sorry, Gray Wolf. I've left nothing for you," Georgia said. "It tasted so good … I wasn't thinking."

"You needed it." He hoped she had come back to him. "It's raining now. It'll be no problem to refill the skin."

She nodded but said nothing else.

The downpour ended as abruptly as it had come. He left the outcropping to look for a place to refill the skin. Finding a clear, fast-running creek, he took the horses to drink from it. After he had returned them to the picket line, he filled the skins at the creek.

When he returned, Georgia had slumped to her side, her back to him. He heard her attempt to stifle a sob. He could bear it no more. He moved close to her, and lying on his side behind her, he wrapped one arm around her shoulder. With the other, he cradled her head. It was as if the dam in a creek had been removed. Great body-rocking sobs sprung forth. Her body convulsed like braves engaging in the sun dance. As the sun disappeared from the horizon, Georgia's sobs subsided and were replaced with the deep breaths that told Gray Wolf she was sleeping. He held her through the night, not knowing if she needed him but knowing that he needed to hold her.

Gray Wolf woke at dawn, Georgia still cradled in his arms. He pulled away, hoping not to disturb her. He would shoot a rabbit and have it roasting by the time she woke.

Last evening's downpour had left a heavy dew and the earthy smell of soil moistened with rain. Birds called to each other as they hopped from tree to tree, energetic in their search for insects to feed themselves and their young. The rain had moistened the floor of pine needles, enabling Gray Wolf to move through the forest without a sound. He felt pulled farther into the pines. Fitting an arrow into his bow, he waited, crouching. Within seconds, a doe and her fawn crossed before him. He could not take a doe and leave her fawn to starve or be killed. Then, a small buck stepped into the clearing behind the doe and fawn. From his crouching position, he pulled back his arrow, aimed, and let it fly. Given time to aim, he drove the arrow right into the heart of the buck. It dropped without taking a step.

Gray Wolf ran back to the picket line to untie Wise Heart to help carry the deer. Back at the camp, he tied one end of a rope to the buck's back hooves and tossed the other end over the upper branch of a tree, tugging until the front legs of the animal were just off the ground. The blood drained and the organs removed, Gray Wolf began the tedious work of skinning. From the corner of his eye, he saw movement from the outcropping. Georgia came toward him, a skinning knife in hand. Removing a hide well took skill, especially on a young animal with a thinner hide. She moved her knife with competence, turning just so, applying enough pressure to remove the meat without tearing the hide.

"It is a fine hide, Georgia. It is yours. It will be soft and pliable after it is tanned."

Georgia nodded, her face expressionless. Gray Wolf was baffled and worried. Cheyenne women showed their grief with loud crying and shrill chants. Other than her sobs the previous night, her grief was not expressed. Had her soul left her? Would she ever be the same? He didn't know, and he had no idea how to help her. He worried how she would adjust to life with the Cheyenne. In her normal state she was not exactly traditional. Her favorite work was hunting, training horses and doctoring. Few Cheyenne women did this work. And then there was Soaring Falcon. If he saw Georgia, it would be trouble. Georgia did not yet know who killed Thomas, but she would eventually ask. He could not lie to her, but telling her the identity of her father's killer would be disastrous. Gray Wolf wanted Georgia, the real Georgia back, but he also was terrified to have the real Georgia back.

Gray Wolf started a fire, and Georgia cut off a slab of shoulder and impaled it on a tree branch to roast the venison. He wondered how long it would be before Moonwalker returned and whether they should leave the carcass hanging for future meals or try to smoke the meat for transport back to the Cheyenne camp. He decided they should smoke the meat. It would give them a job while they waited for Moonwalker. They fed the fire with moist leaves and dry, dead tree branches to create the heat and smoke needed to dry the remaining venison. Georgia cut off one of the hooves and cleaned it in the creek so that she could use it to scrape the hide clean. They would wrap the smoked meat in the hide to take it with them.

The fire burned all night. Early the next morning, they heard a rider approaching. Much to Gray Wolf's relief, it was Moonwalker. "I saw the smoke when I was far away. You're lucky there aren't Pawnee in the forest these days. How are you my friend?" He spoke Cheyenne because it was the only language he knew. "The woman, how is she? Does she grieve her father? It seemed she cares not that he is gone."

"No, Moonwalker, she loved her father much." Gray Wolf did not know why Georgia seemed not to mourn. "Maybe the whites mourn their dead in a way that is not ours or maybe the grief overwhelms her so she cannot cry."

Moonwalker shrugged, as if to say he had no opinion on the matter. "Soaring Falcon is not at the camp. The Dog Soldiers who hunted with him returned to our camp and went out again, but Soaring Falcon was never there. Perhaps he knows you will not tolerate his presence."

"Yes, that is good news. Here, my friend, have some deer for breakfast. Appreciate it, for as you said, we risked our lives to smoke it." Gray Wolf slapped Moonwalker on the back in a friendly manner before returning to the outcropping where Georgia waited.

He had to prepare her to enter the Cheyenne camp. The Georgia he knew would be well-received by the Cheyenne. She was friendly, outgoing, hardworking and brave—all traits esteemed by the Cheyenne. He worried that the fog that overcame her when her father was shot might be interpreted as sullen or uncooperative, or worse, that she might retaliate against all of them for what Soaring Falcon had done.

He entered the outcropping and found her sitting balled up in the fetal position, rocking side to side, half-moaning, half-crying. He squatted in front of her, grasping her shoulders in his hands. "Georgia, we must pack up to go to the Cheyenne camp." She did not respond. "We go to my people now, Georgia. You will share a tepee with my sister."

Gray Wolf had thought about the living arrangements. He

knew it would be difficult for Georgia to share a tepee with someone who spoke no English, but Meadow Lark was kind and patient. He would take his meals with them, but sleeping in the same tepee with a woman who was neither his wife nor a member of his family would harm Georgia's reputation and make her life with the Cheyenne more difficult. Already, he was worried about how the beautiful but headstrong Georgia would adjust. "Georgia, the women may try to strike or even spit at you when we arrive." Yes, it was a Cheyenne custom that would be very strange to her, Gray Wolf thought. Georgia had stopped crying. "Don't pay it any mind. It is their way. It doesn't mean they dislike you."

"I'll not embarrass you, Gray Wolf." Georgia stood and began packing the few things in the outcropping.

Chapter 23

As Georgia rode behind Gray Wolf toward the camp, she remembered a conversation with her father about discouraged settlers making the decision to abandon their homesteads and return to their homes in the East. It was unfathomable to her at the time.

Thomas had tried to explain it to Georgia. "Some folks just aren't made for frontier life, and some have encountered more disappointment than they can endure. You are strong, a frontierswoman through and through, but a day will come when discouragement threatens to overtake you. At times like these, look to the Good Lord, Georgia."

She had not understood faith, religion, talk about God and Jesus. It had been a way of life for her parents. Georgia knew she could turn toward this faith or away from it. The hole in her heart would not let her continue to be stuck in the middle. There would be no more doing the right things, saying the right things, to keep up appearances. She was at a crossroads.

They stopped at a spring for water and rest. Georgia marveled at the Cheyenne's ability to find water and shelter when all she saw was an expanse of browning prairie grasses dotted with yucca and the last of the summer wildflowers. She guessed Gray Wolf was taking it easy for her sake. He sat in the shade of the solitary tree. When she looked at him, he patted the ground next to him. Dropping beside him, she let out a sigh. A few feet away, a prairie dog popped its head out of its burrow and chattered, scolding them for daring to intrude on his prairie. How Georgia's father had hated the damage prairie dogs made. Eating off the roots of the prairie grass and other vegetation from below, each prairie dog was surrounded by bare ground. "Such a waste the blasted prairie dogs make. More 'an one horse has been lamed by stepping in them holes," Thomas had exclaimed.

With the memory came a lump in her throat. She was wrong to think she hid her sorrow from Gray Wolf. "Several times when I was struggling with things, your father told me to seek the Wise One Above."

Wasn't that the advice Old Jeb had given her? The last time she cried out to the Lord, He had given clear direction about attending medical school, but if she hadn't gone, maybe her ma, even her pa, would still be alive. *Lord, I don't even know how to talk to you, but I know you listen ... could ya just take away this terrible hurt or at least help me bear it? I've been bad about not talkin' to you regular like, but that's changin' now.*

Much like the last time she had poured out her heart about her sorrows, she felt an incredible peace. But she also knew there was more to this than a feeling. It was not a feeling or a religion. It was a relationship with her Heavenly Father. *Please, Lord, hold me, help me go on.*

They had ridden for several hours when Gray Wolf nudged Georgia and pointed over the horse's ears. Laid out across the horizon like a panorama model she saw in a museum once were tepees, maybe a hundred of them. She could see children running through the camp. A herd of horses grazed to the south. Most were paints and Appaloosa horses with a few bays, greys and sorrels mixed in. Georgia could see that the tepees were to the north of an embankment where a stream wound through the landscape.

When they were about half a mile from the camp, drums signaled the village of their arrival, sending throngs of women and children toward them. She hoped the shrill, high sound was a way of saying, "How do you do?" but it made her uneasy. When the welcoming party—at least she hoped that is what this was—reached them, Gray Wolf and Moonwalker greeted the women with gusto. What had Gray Wolf said? Had he explained that she was his white sister? Her time to guess what had transpired ended abruptly when one of the women grabbed her booted foot. Examining her boot for a second, she yanked downward, not to remove the boot for further inspection but to pull her off the horse. Gray Wolf spoke to the woman, and she stepped back.

"What are they doing, Gray Wolf?" Georgia tried not to show her panic. She noticed that Moonwalker had dismounted and was walking, his horse to one side, a young woman on the other side.

"They want you to walk with them," Gray Wolf said. "I told them you are in mourning, but they don't understand because Cheyenne women mourn like this," he gestured at a woman letting out a high shrill, "only louder." As if to punctuate his explanation, an older woman approached, tugging on Georgia's skirt.

I'll not embarrass you, Gray Wolf. Without great confidence, she flung her right leg over the horse's back and slid to the ground with as much grace as she could muster. As soon as she hit the ground, the women surrounded her, wailing and touching her face, her hair and her dress. She thought to touch them in the same way to deflect the attention from herself, but when she reached toward them, they grabbed her hands. No one struck her, but their faces looked angry, as if they were scolding her for some unknown trespass. The shrill wailing continued, but Georgia felt immense relief when the ring of women parted to allow a smiling woman to grasp her hand and lead her away from the "welcoming party."

The woman held firmly to Georgia's hand even when they were well past the throng. Georgia guessed her to be a few years her senior. Her skin was the color of coffee with cream stirred in to it and just as smooth. Her smile revealed straight, white teeth. Her broad face was punctuated with strong, high cheekbones, just like Gray Wolf's. She wore a deerskin dress decorated with quills, beads and small feathers. Dazzling. The leatherwork reminded her of the boots Gray Wolf made for her sixteenth birthday. There was no doubt. The woman leading her like she was an untrained horse was related to Gray Wolf. Relief flooded over Georgia.

The woman stopped in front of a tepee. Only now did she release Georgia's hand. Pulling back the hide flap that served as the tepee door, she spoke in Cheyenne, smiling. Georgia stepped into the tepee, and the woman followed her. The woman sat and patted the buffalo robe beside her. Georgia sat, and the woman smiled at her. She continued to speak. Georgia thought the words sounded kind. She was safe here. Looking around for the first time, she was surprised how large the tepee was. The open hole at the top of the tepee allowed the interior to be as light as any settler home with windows. The buffalo robes on which they sat were soft. The smell of tanned leather mingled with the earthy smells of moist earth and prairie grasses. The adrenaline that had propelled Georgia began to subside, the tension replaced with exhaustion.

Georgia had not noticed the woman leave. She returned with a dried gourd that was cut in two. It was filled with a steaming broth. Hand motions indicated Georgia should drink the liquid from the gourd. Looking into the broth, Georgia saw chunks of meat and turnips floating on the top. The broth filled her stomach, although it tasted bland without salt. When she finished, the woman motioned for her to eat wild strawberries placed on a platter carved from bone. The strawberries were delicious and prevented scurvy. Only Georgia or her mother would have thought about the nutritional qualities of the delicious fruit.

✳

Georgia woke, panic rising with the helplessness of not remembering where she was. A second later, reality flooded her memory. The woman who brought her to the tepee must have waited outside, for she came inside with more broth when she heard Georgia awaken. When she finished drinking the broth, Georgia turned toward the woman and said Gray Wolf's name in Cheyenne. It was one of two hundred or so words he had taught her over the year he lived at the MacBaye Ranch. The woman's eyes brightened. She nodded and left, returning with Gray Wolf a few minutes later.

"What do you think of my sister, Georgia?" Gray Wolf smiled at her. "She hopes you are feeling better. Her name is Meadow Lark." He then pronounced the name in Cheyenne, inviting her to repeat it.

Meadow Lark smiled and nodded. She had that same joyous and encouraging way that had made Georgia love Gray Wolf. "She will help you bathe in the creek and wash your clothes. She will give you dry clothes until yours are dry."

Funny, Georgia hadn't thought at all about bathing, but it was true she needed a good bath. She hadn't bathed or put on clean clothes since before she was called to attend little Alver.

Meadow Lark gathered clothing and some other items and motioned for Georgia to follow. They headed toward the embankment Georgia had noticed when they came into the camp the previous day. Meadow Lark pointed to what appeared to be the camp dump. Hand motions indicated it was that and the latrine. They climbed up the embankment and down the other side. The drought had dried the creek to little more than a trickle, but Meadow Lark knew where to find deeper pools for bathing and privacy.

Meadow Lark handed Georgia a skin sewed in a flask shape and motioned for her to put the liquid on her body. It smelled like animal fat scented with sage. The thick liquid felt soothing and did a surprising job of cleansing her skin. The water had

warmed slightly in the pools. She washed her hair and let
Meadow comb it out. Georgia pulled on the buckskin dress
Meadow Lark brought for her. By the time she was finished
dressing, Meadow Lark had washed Georgia's calico dress. Both
women sat on a rock and dried their feet in the summer air.
Meadow Lark slipped her moccasins back on and pulled out
another pair of beaded, soft leather moccasins for Georgia to
wear when they returned to camp.

※

In the days and weeks that followed, Meadow Lark was
patient, teaching Georgia to do daily work. She learned how to
cook on an open fire with the gourd and bone pots and utensils.
Most of the Cheyenne families had traded horses or hides for the
white man's flour, sugar, baking powder and coffee. Georgia used
the baking ingredients, along with eggs from birds or turkeys,
to make biscuits and pancakes. Meadow Lark and Gray Wolf
especially liked when she dropped the biscuit dough over boiling
buffalo stew to make dumplings. Georgia also made beans from
the stockpile they brought with them from the ranch and added
cornmeal—from corn obtained through trade with other tribes—
to the flour, game tallow and eggs to make an acceptable cornbread.

Georgia's fame as a cook spread. Soon the women from
neighboring tepees came to see what she cooked and to ask how
to make the new food. They were no longer rude. Rarely did they
laugh at her. Now they greeted her like they did each other. How
ironic, she thought, that cooking, the activity she once abhorred
but which her mother had insisted she learn, had become her
way of gaining acceptance into Cheyenne society. Georgia's
Cheyenne vocabulary expanded from words to phrases to simple
sentences. With all but Gray Wolf she spoke the Cheyenne
tongue.

Long before she began understanding the language, it was
clear to Georgia that Gray Wolf and Meadow Lark were highly

regarded by the others. Once Georgia understood more of the language, she knew the many visitors to Gray Wolf's tepee were asking his advice. Watching him, she could see that Gray Wolf's heart and soul were open to his fellow Cheyenne. He had been no different when he lived among the settlers. Everyone had accepted him, liked him—everyone except the residents of Denver. She shuddered remembering that trip that had changed everything between them.

Gray Wolf ate every meal with Meadow Lark and Georgia. His delight every time they served a new food made Georgia rack her brain for new things to try. Forgotten biscuit batter leftovers had fermented into a delightful sourdough starter, so they had sourdough pancakes and biscuits and passed starter on to their neighbors. She had climbed out of the black hole that engulfed her following the death of her pa and had learned to get along with the Cheyenne. Gray Wolf's good-natured laugh, never at someone's expense but in good humor with them, enthralled her. She did not want to ever leave him, but she had to have an answer to who had killed her father and where Gray Wolf had been when it happened.

"Come, walk with me," Gray Wolf invited her when she asked about it. They walked toward the horse herd and sat facing the horses, the village to their backs. "I have dreaded telling you about your father's death, because I had a part in it." He looked away from her. She found it difficult to believe he had done anything to harm her pa. But, if he had, it would change everything between them.

"Most of the Cheyenne are good people, but some are hot-headed about the whites and their broken treaties. They think that brutality toward the settlers will drive them out of Indian land." He picked a long stem of grass and rolled it between his thumb and finger. "I made sure to never mention your family and to intentionally lead them away from the Bijou Basin, but..." Gray Wolf covered his face with his hands. When he looked up, tears were pooling in his eyes. *What could he have done, surely not ...*

Gray Wolf continued. "It was a very evil man who killed your father, Georgia."

"Who was it?"

"It was a dog soldier who accompanied my uncle when he brought me to your house. I had a fight with him, and I think he attacked your father just to get back at me." Again, Gray Wolf buried his face in his hands. He spoke without looking at her. "It's my fault, Georgia. I angered him. Moonwalker and I tracked him, so he couldn't go there without us knowing, but he tricked us. I'm so sorry, Georgia. I know you loved him so much. I did too."

Georgia felt her father's agonizing death all over again, but she had to be strong for Gray Wolf. "It wasn't your fault." She grasped his shoulder as if to emphasize her words: "I don't blame you, Gray Wolf."

"I blame myself."

"Don't. I know how much you loved him. I know you would have done all you could to protect him. Please, don't blame yourself."

"Thomas was like a father to me. A better father than my own." They sat watching the horses graze.

There was one more question Georgia had to ask. "Who is this brave who killed my father? Please tell me."

"I cannot tell you, Georgia."

Georgia knew why Gray Wolf refused to tell her the name of her father's killer. He wanted to protect her. She understood. But, already, she was piecing it together.

Chapter 24

Cheyenne Campsite, Eastern Colorado,
August 29, 1864

All Cheyenne braves found it difficult to keep their
family's pots full of meat. Gray Wolf's tepee still had
beans he had brought from the MacBayes, but it
wouldn't be enough to last them through the winter, especially if
they continued to share the beans with those who were hungry.

There had been no significant rain for almost two moons
now. The prairie grasses turned brown and the pools of water
that had lined the creek beds disappeared. The horses, just a
moon ago fat from spring grasses, were beginning to show ribs
beneath their dulling coats. Game was hard to find. Gray Wolf
had managed to find a deer here and there, which along with
rabbits and prairie grouse had filled their stomachs and the
stomachs of widows from a half a dozen tepees. Some of the
Cheyenne had resorted to eating their dogs and even older or
lame horses. That was not the kind of meat Gray Wolf could
bring himself to eat, not until he had no other choice. He hoped

that day would never come.

There had been no sightings of buffalo. As recently as six summers ago, immense buffalo herds roamed the prairie. When Gray Wolf was a boy, the braves brought down enough animals this time of year to feed themselves and their families until the next spring and beyond. He remembered buffalo robes piled higher than his head at every tepee. The women would work for many days scraping and tanning the hides. In those days, they had so much meat they fed the less desirable pieces of meat to the dogs.

Lean Bear had been right. The days of living off the buffalo were drawing to a close. The Cheyenne would have to raise cattle or puts seeds in the ground to feed themselves. Gray Wolf could see the time had come, but he felt powerless to move his people toward the new way of life. He didn't know where they would get the seed or where they would plant seed if they had it. They moved often now in search of game and to elude the soldiers.

Gray Wolf pondered their plight. Was he the only one who saw the bleak future, the need for change? It seemed so. The Cheyenne went about their work as always. He could see them from the hill above the village, the hill where the horses tried to find bits of grass to fill their bellies.

When he looked down on the village again, he saw Georgia. She was surrounded by village children. He could tell from the way she grabbed the hands of one child and spun her around in a circle that she was entertaining them as she was wont to do. When Georgia first came to the camp, she was a curiosity to all the Cheyenne, but her bravery and vitality had soon won them over. Even the craggiest old squaw begrudgingly admitted Georgia had the heart of a Cheyenne.

"I don't know what it is about her, but everyone loves her," Meadow Lark, herself loved by her people, had gushed to Gray Wolf.

Georgia cooked more with Meadow Lark than he remembered her ever doing at the ranch. Maybe she understood that she would have to win over the people, first as a woman before they would accept her as a horse trainer or hunter or healer.

"Take me hunting with you, Gray Wolf," Georgia had implored him at dawn one morning about a moon after her arrival at the camp.

To the amusement of Moonwalker and the other braves in the small hunting party, Gray Wolf had relented and allowed her to accompany them that morning. Gray Wolf had instructed Georgia how to use his bow. Few of the men had hides to trade for ammunition, and most had gone back to using the traditional weapons. Her strength was impressive. He was certain that with practice, she would be as good with a bow as she was with a rifle, but the sparse selection of game made practice impossible. The party returned with three rabbits between eight men.

Georgia continued to walk up the hill toward him. The children ran back to the tepees. She had a lariat over her right shoulder and a bridle in her left hand.

"I've come to help you work horses." She dropped the lariat from her shoulder and swung it overhead before casting it at an imaginary target in front of her.

Gray Wolf had not planned to work horses, but why not? It might distract him from his dismal thoughts about the future of the Cheyenne, and hunting would be a vain pursuit this late in the morning. "You wanna start a colt or work on some better manners—that's what Georgia called it—on one that's already broke?" he called after her.

"Up to you." She continued to practice her roping.

Half an hour later, they had caught Moonwalker's horse and were getting it used to ropes being thrown over its back, behind the haunches and under the belly. A crowd was gathering to watch the white squaw train a horse. Georgia appeared oblivious to the onlookers. Word must have gotten back to Moonwalker that Georgia was working with his horse. He came marching out to see Georgia training his powerful black-and-white paint war horse to drag a rope, and then a buffalo robe, without spooking.

Gray Wolf spotted his miffed friend. "Remember when we went hunting and you asked me how I got Wise Heart to stand while I loaded the deer carcass on his back? Well, this is how I got him to do it. You get a horse used to the rope, then a hide. Pretty soon, it'll let you put anything you want on its back."

Moonwalker snorted but continued to watch. The training session ended with Georgia throwing a string of rattles on the horse's back. The horse looked nervous, but it didn't spook or pull back. Georgia walked to Moonwalker, and the horse followed as if he were one of the village puppy dogs. She handed Moonwalker the reins of his horse and returned Gray Wolf's string of rattles to him.

※

It was one of those hot days that refused to cool down, even as evening arrived. The hot, windless air kept Gray Wolf, Georgia and Meadow Lark from going into their tepees to sleep. They sat outside waiting for the night to cool when a young boy ran toward them.

"Come quickly to Bull Bear's tepee, Gray Wolf!" the boy shouted, catching his breath.

"Now? Why now?" Gray Wolf asked.

"Bull Bear sent me to get you. He said it's urgent. Black Kettle is here. He wants to meet with our clan leaders." The boy lowered his voice and with pride said, "I wasn't supposed to hear them, but I think the meeting is about the white captives that the Dog Soldiers and Arapaho warriors brought in when they raided the settlers to the east of us."

"What white captives?"

"One of them, a squaw of about sixteen summers, was with Arapaho Chief Left Hand yesterday. Didn't you see her?"

A captive with Left Hand? Couldn't be. He was one of the chiefs speaking for peace with the settlers.

The boy must have read Gray Wolf's confusion. "Left Hand didn't capture the white squaw. He or his brother Neva bought her from the Dog Soldiers that took her."

Gray Wolf entered Bull Bear's tepee and sat. In addition to

Black Kettle, Cheyenne Chiefs War Bonnet, White Antelope and One Eye sat smoking the pipe. He also saw Arapaho Chief Little Raven and some other Arapaho he did not recognize. It was too hot for a fire, but they sat in a circle, facing each other. Kerosene lamps, bought from traders, provided just enough light. As Gray Wolf's eyes adjusted to the light, he saw that his friend Beaver, Dog Soldier Chief Tall Bull and several braves he didn't know sat in the tepee. He gestured to Beaver, who gestured back, tension showing in his movement.

"We will write a letter to the white leaders and ask them to meet with us. We must make peace with these settlers now, before winter. We also will ask them to return our prisoners that they hold in Denver." The intensity shone in Black Kettle's eyes. "The whites have pledged to make peace with peaceful Indians."

"Why go crawling to the white man like a snake on its belly when they have broken every treaty they've ever made with us?" Tall Bull stood and paced before the chiefs. "The latest treaty signed by our chiefs and the Arapaho chiefs gave us a tenth of the hunting ground we were granted in the previous treaty. Years later, they haven't given the promised land, seed and tools promised in their treaty for our people who want to eat from the seed they put in the ground." His face reddened.

Black Kettle wasn't used to such outward defiance. "Were it not for the killing and stealing of settler's goods by the Dog Soldiers, we could go to the whites and demand they fulfill their treaty with us. Many want to annihilate all Indians. I tell you, we'll be lucky to escape with our lives and enough food to get us through the winter."

"I'll not make peace with the white man. He is a foul stench to the Cheyenne. The thought of it makes me sick. Makes me want to vomit." Tall Bull spewed. He stood, gesturing to the scars on his legs and arms. "I cut once for each Cheyenne killed by a white, and I have no more places to cut my skin." His lip curled in disgust. "Do you ask me to make new cuts on top of the scars?"

Gray Wolf had been in council meetings with contention. He'd even accompanied the chiefs on their unsuccessful trip to meet with Indian Agent Samuel Colley, but he had never felt such tension.

Black Kettle stood and moved to face Tall Bull. "Do you think we don't know of your killing and carrying off captives from the white man's settlements? Surely, you don't mean to hide the things you have stolen from them or you wouldn't parade them before the Cheyenne to show your bravery!" Black Kettle was shouting. His lips quivered. "No Cheyenne likes the invasion of our hunting grounds or that the white man has decimated the buffalo, but continuing to fight an enemy that is larger, so much larger than us, is foolishness!"

Tall Bull moved toward Black Kettle. Gray Wolf thought he would strike him, but the old chief, once a formidable war chief, held his ground. "We will write a letter to ask for a meeting and send it with haste to Fort Lyon." Black Kettle sat and motioned for Beaver to sit in front of him.

Tall Bull twisted his face into an ugly sneer, as if to speak, but Black Kettle had dismissed him and paid him no mind. Uttering curses, Tall Bull rose and gestured for his Dog Soldiers to follow him out of the council. Most did.

Black Kettle continued conversing with the other chiefs and instructed Beaver what to write, as if the confrontation with Tall Bull had never happened. The letter was simple. It stated that the majority of the Cheyenne and Arapaho were friendly to the whites and not involved in the depredations over the summer.

"I fear the anger of the whites may be so great that they will not believe we want peace. They will refuse to return our captured braves." Black Kettle looked up from the parchment. He could stand up to an angry dog soldier but advocating for his people before angry whites was not a war he knew how to win. "How do we convince them?"

"Offer to return the white captives," Gray Wolf blurted out. "Our prisoners for theirs."

"Does that include your white squaw?" one of the remaining Dog Soldiers taunted.

Gray Wolf was surprised at the question. *Do the Cheyenne*

think I hold Georgia against her will? Does she want to leave?
"She's not a captive. She is free to leave or stay. When her father lay dying from a dog soldier arrow, he made me promise to take care of her." What had he done? Why hadn't he thought before he talked about Georgia, about his relationship to Thomas, about why she lived with the Cheyenne?

"We all thought you enjoyed sharing your bed with her. She's quite a lively and entertaining squaw." The same man laughed, bitterly. "Now that you tell us that is not the case, maybe I can take her as my wife. I'll take care of her, just like I do my other four wives." He laughed again. His words were not what one brave said to another. He rose to leave, rather than being expelled from the council.

Gray Wolf had trouble concentrating on the rest of the council. He thought about how the Cheyenne viewed Georgia. Had he sullied her reputation? Would she prefer to return to live with the whites? His whole world was again turning upside down.

"Left Hand, I thank you for pledging to return your white captive and for asking the other Arapaho to do the same." Gray Wolf snapped back to the council and Black Kettle's words. They were doing as he suggested. "Delivering the letter will not be easy. We understand that soldiers have been told to shoot all Indians they see."

"I will take the letter to Fort Lyon. I will take my wife with me, so they can see we mean them no harm. If I am wrong, we will die trying," said One Eye, an old chief, known for his wisdom and sacrifice for his people.

"And I will go with One Eye and his wife," said Eagle Head, a chief Gray Wolf knew only by name.

The council ended as bright orange peeked over the eastern horizon.

※

Still tired from the all-night council the night before last, Gray Wolf lay down to sleep just as the sun set. When he heard

Georgia's voice outside his tent, he woke with a start. She must have come to fetch him for breakfast. He rushed to open the tent flap, but the moon was just beginning to rise in the east. Then he saw Georgia. She looked like the Indian maiden every young brave saw in his visions. She wore a soft antelope hide dress embroidered with traditional decorations of porcupine quills and elk teeth, no doubt the project he'd seen her and Meadow Lark working on for the last month. The moonlight shone from the other side of the tepee, highlighting the red in her hair, which was neatly braided and then wound in a circle on the back of her head. She had secured the braid with a comb she had brought from home. Georgia's freckles, which Gray Wolf had grown fond of, were covered with red face paint. In her hand she held a basket filled with the traditional wedding night meal.

He held back the tent flap so she could enter, and he lit a kerosene lamp. He wanted to see her, Georgia, presenting herself to him as a traditional Cheyenne bride. She had come alone, not delivered to his tepee by her father, as the Cheyenne once practiced when a girl accepted a man's marriage proposal. Gray Wolf already had her father's blessing. No, more than that, he had pledged to take care of her. Now she was telling him that she wanted him. They stood in silence. No awkwardness, only deep desire between them. He ached to pull her into his arms, but he would wait for her. He could hear, no feel, her heart beating fast and hard as she reached out a hand and placed it on his shoulder. With his other hand, he touched her cheek. Was that her trembling he felt? He kissed her cheek where he had touched it. Yes, she was trembling. He pulled her close to him.

Abruptly, Georgia pulled back from Gray Wolf's embrace. "I brought you some food." Gray Wolf was sure she was blushing, but the face paint hid the evidence. "Well, not me, it was Meadow Lark. She said to bring you this basket of food."

Reality dawned. "And the braided hair, the dress and the face paint—were they Meadow Lark's idea also?"

"Meadow Lark showed me how to decorate with the quills and teeth, but I didn't know we were making the dress for me.

Meadow Lark fixed my hair and face. I think she tried to tell me something when she did, but I have not learned the words." Georgia sat and opened the basket. "Do you want to eat?"

Gray Wolf felt like he'd had the wind knocked out of him. Georgia wasn't pledging herself to him. It was all his sister's doing. How dare she! But there was no denying the moment of passion that had passed between them. She *did* love him, even if she didn't know it yet.

Now that Georgia had come to his tepee attired as a bride, he only had two choices. He could reject her and send her away free to marry another or keep her in his tepee. The thought of some vile brave claiming her as his wife unnerved him. The thought of *any* brave claiming her unnerved him.

"Georgia, will you stay in my tepee, as my wife?" There he'd said it. They both knew Indian braves didn't marry white women unless the women were slaves, captives. The last thing Gray Wolf wanted was for Georgia to feel cornered, like she had no choice but to marry him.

The silence stretched on. "Do you love me, Gray Wolf?" She looked at him through moist eyes.

"Yes, I love you, Georgia." His smile showed love, joy, even relief. He did love her. He had loved her ever since she'd tricked him into eating that chili sauce and he returned the favor by making her think she had stumbled into a rattlesnake den by the creek. Suddenly, she was in his arms again. He kissed her cheek, her head, but the embrace was one of joy, more than the passion that had rocked them earlier.

"I cannot stay in your tepee until we are married." Gray Wolf looked perplexed. "Married by a preacher."

She marched out into the darkness, leaving the basket of food behind.

Married by a preacher, Gray Wolf thought. Now that the Indians and whites were at war, the preachers no longer came to the Cheyenne camp. He wasn't sure how to accomplish being married by a preacher. *But if that is what Georgia wants, that is what I will give her.*

Chapter 25

Smoky Hill River, Western Kansas,
September 9, 1864

An older man they called Eagle Head rode into the camp, his pony's coat frothy with sweat. "The white soldiers and their leader are coming. He says to tell you they come in peace!" Eagle Head shouted as he rode through the camp to Black Kettle's tepee. Georgia could now understand basic Cheyenne words.

The news from Eagle Head spread through the Cheyenne camp like wildfire. Men adorned their fighting weapons and regalia. They caught and painted their horses with haste. Georgia wondered if she misunderstood the "come in peace" part of Eagle Head's proclamation. At Gray Wolf's request, she caught and bridled Wise Heart and brought him into the camp for Gray Wolf to mount.

"Be careful," Georgia shouted out to Gray Wolf in English as he rode Wise Heart to join the others. Soon hundreds of braves were moving southwest toward the soldiers. Rain had not fallen for weeks, and the dust of the soldiers could be seen for twenty, maybe thirty miles.

She feared for Gray Wolf, for all of them, for the soldiers. She struggled every day to live in joy, as her father and mother would have wanted. Life with the Cheyenne was not easy. Food was scarce, communication was improving but still difficult, and some of their customs were beyond comprehension. They cut themselves deeply to show they were in mourning; she had treated many mourners whose cuts had become infected. Then there was eating dogs and old horses.

Riding into the camp on the Smoky Hill a week earlier reminded Georgia of the first time she saw the Cheyenne village just after her father died, except that this one was much larger. There were tepees in every direction as far as the eye could see. The golden, sun-bleached color of the buffalo hides made the tepees look like appendages of the huge cottonwood trees, which were just beginning to turn gold and orange. The tepees were split in two by a winding riverbed. Unlike creeks farther west, water still flowed in the Smoky Hill River. Because of the water, the grazing looked a mite better as well. After dark, the women snuck down to the riverbed and rinsed off. Not a bath, exactly, but it felt good to banish three days of travel dust and sweat. Later, when Georgia looked in her hand mirror, one of the few luxuries she had brought with her from the ranch, she thought she might pass for an Indian. Her hair was only a couple of shades lighter than black. She had seen Indians with brown and reddish hair. Her skin was tanned from hours in the sun. The only traits that screamed she was a white woman were her greenish eyes and freckles, and no one could see those from a distance.

Unlike other times when reports of buffalo herds came to the camp and the braves rushed to hunt them, only to find the report false, there were buffalo, lots of buffalo, here. For six days in a row, the braves brought skinned, quartered buffalo back to camp for the women to finish cutting and smoking. The women tanned the hides to use for clothing, tepees or trade. Most of the women in Gray Wolf and Meadow Lark's clan worked together to prepare the meat before it spoiled.

Gray Wolf and Moonwalker brought back more than their share of buffalo hides and quarters, but they shared it in proportion to the meat needed by each family in the clan. Georgia pondered this one day, as she and Meadow Lark walked to the river for water. They carried buffalo bones they would clean for use as work tools, hunting implements or eating utensils. When they returned, the men had brought in more buffalo. The work was welcome. It assured their pots would be full.

Gray Wolf's clan worked hard during the day, and at night, there were campfires, dancing and feasting. The weather had cooled enough that a fire after dark felt good.

Georgia and Gray Wolf sat before an outdoor fire, eating roast buffalo with nuts and berries from the trees and bushes along the river. It tasted good to have fresh meat and to eat as much as they wanted. Georgia thought Gray Wolf had been preoccupied throughout the hunt. Earlier, he told her that One Eye, One Eye's wife and Eagle Head had taken a letter to Fort Lyon to ask for peace and to request a captive swap.

"Do you feel you are a captive, Georgia?" he asked.

The question surprised her. "No, I came here by choice." She assumed she would return to the ranch someday. It had never occurred to her that she couldn't. "Am I a captive?"

"Certainly not."

"What troubles you, Gray Wolf? You are always worried lately." Georgia looked into his eyes for answers, for it seemed he didn't hear her.

"The days of hunting buffalo are soon over." Was it sadness, perhaps despair, that caused the skin around his eyes and mouth to wrinkle?

"It has been a good hunt. We'll have enough for all winter, no?"

"We'll have enough for now." He turned toward her, taking her hands in his. "What I mean is that the days of hunting buffalo on the prairies and camping where we wish will soon be over for the Cheyenne."

"Why do you say this?"

"My Uncle Lean Bear is right. The Cheyenne must learn to put seed in the ground and raise cattle or they will be no more."

"But even now One Eye and Eagle Head have delivered Black Kettle's letter to Fort Lyon, no?"

"Yes, but it is only a short—what do you call it? A short-time solution." Gray Wolf returned to gazing over the encampment. "We may continue this way of life a little longer, but it is not one our children will know."

"What will happen?"

"I don't know." When Georgia looked alarmed, he added, "Don't worry, I will take care of you—of you and our children." His smile always unnerved her. He would do as he said.

※

Now she waited, nervous for Gray Wolf and the other braves to return from their meeting with the soldiers. *Had the soldiers really come in peace as Eagle Head announced?* She worried that the meeting was not a meeting at all but a battle. By midday, the braves began to filter back into camp. Georgia and Meadow Lark waited, anxious to see Gray Wolf return. Georgia swallowed hard when she remembered Gray Wolf telling of his Uncle Lean Bear who was gunned down by soldiers. Sweat beaded on the palms of her hands and her brow. She looked toward the horizon. Gray Wolf did not come, but Moonwalker rode into camp, coming directly to her and Meadow Lark's tepee.

"Gray Wolf wants you to come!" Moonwalker shouted to Georgia as he pulled hard to stop his horse in front of her. The other braves had returned at an easy gait, but not Moonwalker.

"Is Gray Wolf hurt? Was there fighting?" Georgia asked in the simple Cheyenne words she could muster.

"He is good. No battle," Moonwalker responded. "I get horse for you." He turned his pony and rode toward the grazing horses.

Moonwalker returned with Cheyenne. Georgia quickly bridled and saddled her. Who knew how long she would be gone or where she would go. She had to be prepared. Meadow Lark handed her a skin of water and a bag of food. She tied them to Cheyenne's saddle.

The two rode at a lope for a half-hour when she saw Moonwalker pull back his horse to a trot. He waved a greeting to a Cheyenne warrior who was standing as sentinel. Topping a small ridge, Georgia saw the camp in the ravine. Gray Wolf ran out to greet her.

"I thought something bad had happened to you!" she shouted, nearly collapsing in relief to see him well.

"I'm fine. I have a surprise for you." Merriment danced in Gray Wolf's eyes. Georgia thought he looked happier than he had in a very long time. "Moonwalker will take Cheyenne to graze and drink at the creek. Come with me."

Georgia dismounted and handed her reins to Moonwalker. Gray Wolf extended his hand to her, and she grasped it. He led her toward a small grove of oak trees on the opposite side of the camp. As they neared the trees, a man in a U.S. Army officer's uniform stepped toward them, giving her a fright. His hat was pulled down over his face. Gray Wolf smiled and pushed her ahead of him toward the officer. The officer looked up at Georgia. "James!"

Georgia ran to him. He picked her up by the waist and swung her in a full circle. He seemed stronger, bigger than before.

"I had no idea ... were you with the soldiers that ... how did you get here?" Georgia felt like she had forgotten how to speak English. Of course, she had not. She spoke it every day with Gray Wolf.

"Yes, little sis, I rode out with Major Wynkoop to parlay with Black Kettle and his chiefs at their request. When we arrived over yonder, earlier this morning, we were met by a line of maybe eight hundred warriors. We were outnumbered five to one." James whistled. "We sure were relieved to find Black Kettle wanted to meet with Major Wynkoop. The major says he has no authority to make an official peace agreement with them, and he has told them as much. Chief One Eye, his wife and Eagle Head arrived at Fort Lyon with the letter from Black Kettle and the other chiefs several days ago. The major was so impressed with their loyalty and bravery that he felt he had to do something. I talked to him following his conversation with them, and I think his exact words describing One Eye and Eagle Head were 'I was bewildered with an exhibition of such patriotism on the part of the two savages and felt myself in the presence of superior beings.' "

"And have Major Wynkoop and Black Kettle met?" Georgia was anxious to know the outcome. It had been the talk of the Cheyenne for several days now.

"Black Kettle promised to come tomorrow and to bring some captives that the Cheyenne and Arapaho are holding. Have you seen them? A girl a little younger than you named Laura Roper was taken from the Blue River area in Kansas. There are some other women and children, as well. Their families were brutally murdered."

Gray Wolf cut in. "We've not seen them, but I heard they are somewhere with the Cheyenne or Arapaho. You have to know, James, we warned these braves not to take captives, not to raid, kill and steal, but they are so angry with the whites, and the buffalo herds are disappearing now." He twisted his mouth in the way he did when he was angry with someone or something. "And some of the braves who go on these raids are just foolish. They want to prove themselves and win a young girl as a wife. That's the Cheyenne way, you know—a man must prove his bravery before he can convince a girl's father to give her to him in marriage. In the past, a man could show his bravery in battle or by bringing down buffalo, but now these childish boys think killing unarmed men and women proves them brave." He snorted in disgust.

James sighed. "Their actions will cause all the Cheyenne

problems. Governor Evans, the chief in Denver, is under tremendous pressure from the settlers, Denver residents and even Washington to put an end to the killing. Can't Black Kettle and the other chiefs control these braves?"

"It is not as easy as you think. In the Army, all soldiers do as their chiefs tell them, and the chiefs do what the big chiefs tell them, and the big chiefs do what the Great Father Lincoln tells them. The Cheyenne are different. We live in clans. Our chiefs are advisors. They don't always decide if we go to war or not." Gray Wolf paused, as if wondering what to say next. "And this invasion of the land. Few buffalo. Almost no deer. The people are hungry. Braves don't know how to fill their family's cooking pots. Soldiers have killed many Cheyenne too, you know, not always the guilty ones." Gray Wolf rubbed the back of his neck and sighed.

"There are few men in the Army who try to understand Indians. Major Wynkoop is one who does. My commander, Captain Silas Soule, is another." James shook his head. "I try to make my fellow soldiers understand, but I can't be too hard on 'em. I wasn't much different in my attitude toward Indians." James swallowed hard and looked down at his hands. "Truth is, I have to beg your forgiveness for being so hateful when ya lived with us." His voice cracked.

James wiped his eye with his left hand and then extended his right one to Gray Wolf. Gray Wolf grasped his hand and the two men embraced. It was awkward but heartfelt.

"I don't know why I figured I was better than anyone else," James said as the men stepped back from their embrace. "I guess it took the nasty attitudes of my fellow soldiers 'fore I realized my hypocrisy. Took me livin' in barracks to accept and give grace."

Georgia figured it was as good a time as any to bring up their father's death. "James, I have something to tell you ... it's about Pa." She choked back a sob.

"I know he's dead." James clasped her hand.

"You do? How do you know?"

"I got a letter from him written a few weeks after you returned to the ranch. He was, well, really depressed. He made it sound like his death was imminent. He told me he purchased the Johnson place when they went back east and where to find the deed. He said you and I should have the land and that we could send money to Henry in good years." James removed his Army cap and ran his hands through his hair. "I was so worried that I asked for leave and rode back to the Bijou Basin. I found his grave and saw some evidence of Indians. Never really knew what happened. One thing I do know from talking to him after Ma died and then reading his letter is that his will to live had left 'im."

Gray Wolf cut in, recounting Thomas's death from an Indian arrow. He didn't mention the killer by name, but Georgia could tell he knew who it was. She already suspected the man who killed her father was the brave they called Soaring Falcon. When Gray Wolf described the killer as a hateful brave who resented the MacBayes, she was almost certain it was the young dog soldier that had knocked her off her horse and taunted her. He had also been responsible for the killing of the stagecoach passengers. Georgia had been courageous, even foolish in her bravado then. Now she knew that she would have perished or been taken into cruel captivity were it not for Gray Wolf's intervention.

"We came to Colorado Territory as five, now that Henry is at university back East, we are just two," Georgia said with a faraway look in her eyes.

"Can't say as to if I'll go back to ranchin' or not, so maybe the ranch is down to one." James looked at Georgia. "I'm happy soldierin', at least for the time being. I hope I can do some good with my little bit of understanding of Indians. Guess the Good Lord wud have me here extendin' his grace to the soldiers and Indians alike."

That night Georgia slept between Gray Wolf and James. Deep, restful sleep engulfed her.

Chapter 26

Smoky Hill River, Western Kansas,
September 10, 1864

Gray Wolf, Georgia, James and Moonwalker rose with the sun and shared the rest of the pemmican, plums and dried buffalo that Meadow Lark had packed for them. James gnawed at his hardtack and was delighted when Georgia offered him a handful of juicy plums.

"Sure does hit the spot. Just as sweet as can be!" James licked his lips. "Don't think I've had one since I left for the Army. When I was home, they were outta season."

James got his Army-issue tin pot and headed to the stream. When he returned, he put the pot on the fire to boil. "It ain't much, but I'd be obliged if you all would share a cup of coffee with me." He poured the weak coffee in his two tin cups and handed them to Gray Wolf and Moonwalker. Georgia pulled two wooden cups from her pack and handed them to James. "Whewee, now that's a fine job of carving, Gray Wolf." James traced his finger over the intricate designs on the wooden cups.

"Thank you. I try to spend the winter doing productive things."

James filled the wooden cups and handed one to Georgia.

Moonwalker nodded his thanks to James's offer of sugar and spooned so much sugar in his coffee that Gray Wolf thought the sugar might absorb all the coffee. Gray Wolf drank his coffee black, a habit he acquired from the MacBayes. He wasn't above adding cream when it was available, which was pretty much never since returning to village life.

Gray Wolf waited for an opportunity to speak with James in private, so when he saw Georgia gathering the morning dishes, her hair brush and the soda powder she used to clean her teeth, he knew she would be at the stream for a while. In all practicality they were alone, since Moonwalker spoke no English.

"James, I must ask you something." He fidgeted with his knife, his nervousness growing.

"Yeah, sure, what is it?" James stopped what he was doing and looked up.

"I don't know the white man's customs ..." How could he ask a man if he could marry his sister? Especially a white man. What was he thinking?

"Customs?" James was sitting back now, looking squarely at him.

"When a Cheyenne brave wants to marry a girl, he must prove himself ... I want your permission to marry Georgia." There, he'd said it. James stared at him. "If you're wondering, I've killed plenty of buffalo and taken some scalps, but not white scalps—Pawnee warriors attacking our camp."

Before James could answer or Gray Wolf could do anymore bumbling, Moonwalker shouted to alert them to an approaching rider. It was a Cheyenne from Black Kettle's clan.

The rider stopped nearly on top of their campfire. He glanced at James and then spoke to Gray Wolf: "Black Kettle asks you to come to the council with the white chief. Beaver is sick, and he wants you to come because you know the white tongue and the white ways."

If Black Kettle requested he be at the council meeting, he would go. He turned to James and translated the rider's words.

"I promised Captain Soule I'd be back this morning. I'll ride along with you," James said. "You get our horses while I tell Georgia goodbye. Will she be safe? Alone?"

"Moonwalker will take her back to camp. We're on Cheyenne ground." Gray Wolf winked at James as if he had to remind him.

They mounted their horses and headed due west, toward the Army camp. Gray Wolf was glad for the interruption, but now he would have to start all over asking James for her hand in marriage. He couldn't think about it now. He had to focus on the council meeting. Black Kettle wasn't likely to ask him to speak, but he would want Gray Wolf at his side to translate.

Gray Wolf saw Black Kettle and greeted him, telling the chief he was honored to be of service to him, to the Cheyenne. Together they entered the white man's large square tent. The other chiefs and subchiefs followed them into the tent. They sat on one side of the tent, the white chiefs on the other side. The tall chief, the one the whites called Major Wynkoop, called in men to serve them sugared coffee. Major Wynkoop spoke through an interpreter, a white man named William Bent, who spoke almost perfect Cheyenne. The man looked like a white version of Beaver. It was Beaver's father. Gray Wolf was sure of it. Major Wynkoop invited all the chiefs to smoke the pipe. Either Major Wynkoop knew Indian ways or he listened to advice from Beaver's father. It was a good start to a peace council.

Gray Wolf was surprised that his Uncle Bull Bear spoke first. Gray Wolf listened intently to Bull Bear's words and then to the English translation. He wanted to make sure Beaver's father told the white chiefs exactly what was said.

"The soldiers killed Lean Bear before he could speak. Just a few moons before they killed him, my brother had visited the Great White Father Lincoln in Washington." Bull Bear paced, fists clenched. "Whites can't be trusted to make peace. The Cheyenne have no choice but to fight back."

Bull Bear's angry words incited angry murmuring among

the Indians.

Next, Arapaho Chief Left Hand rose. "I was fired on when I approached Fort Larned in peace." He sat.

Others rose and spoke, most expressing distrust in the whites.

Finally Black Kettle stood and turned toward the Tall Chief. "I believe you are sincere and that your words are honest. We thank you for welcoming us here." He continued in English, "I want to deliver the white prisoners to you, Tall Chief, and we hope you will return our prisoners to us. However, many of our chiefs do not want to return prisoners until we are guaranteed peace. Some of the prisoners you seek are with the Sioux."

The Tall Chief followed the Indians, standing to speak. "As I told you yesterday, I am too small a chief to make a peace treaty with you, but I will do all I can to bring you into council with a chief who has this authority." He waited for his words to be translated. "I urge you to release all white prisoners now, and I will implore Governor Evans to release any Cheyenne or Arapaho prisoners held in Denver."

The council ended with the Tall Chief telling Black Kettle that he would wait at Fort Lyon for him to deliver the white prisoners.

✳

The following day, Gray Wolf rode with Black Kettle and his braves from their camp on the Smoky Hill to the Tall Chief's camp, Laura Roper with them. Black Kettle was angry that they were unable to locate the other prisoners. "We will have to ride a second time to the Tall Chief's camp with the other prisoners."

Laura seemed anxious to be back among her people, although cheerful toward her captors. Another woman, one the Tall Chief had called Mrs. Snyder, had hung herself the day before. Had she given up? Was life among the Cheyenne so bad that she took her own life? For the Cheyenne, it was a senseless death. They understood sacrifice in battle but not killing oneself without cause.

The soldiers' new campsite was nearly a day's ride from the Cheyenne camp. They arrived late in the afternoon. After coffee, the Cheyenne prepared to leave. As they rode out, a soldier followed them. Gray Wolf looked back and saw it was James. He was yelling something. Gray Wolf pulled his pony back to join him.

"Yes," James shouted as he came up alongside Gray Wolf. "Yes, you have my permission to marry Georgia if you think you can live in her world or if she can live in yours. You will have to choose, you know." They both slowed their horses to a trot. "The thought of an Indian marrying my sister would really have bothered the old me, and I do worry about you, about your children. But I know you are a good man, Gray Wolf. You will take care of her. I know my father would have wanted it too." He smiled. "Now, go. Catch up with Black Kettle."

James turned and rode back toward the soldiers' camp.

Gray Wolf was elated that James had given him permission to marry Georgia, but he had not considered where they would live. James spoke truth. They would have to choose. Gray Wolf had experienced the restlessness of living with one foot in the Indian world and the other in the white world. He loved Georgia, and he would marry her, but it would change both their lives forever. It was something they would decide together, but first, he would have to talk with Beaver. He would know where to find a preacher.

※

Black Kettle did his best to fulfill his promise of returning the remaining white prisoners. He asked all the braves and chiefs who rode with him to meet with the Tall Chief to search the Cheyenne encampment. Gray Wolf found three white children playing in the river with the Indian children. He spoke to them in English, asking if they would like to go back with their people. They nodded they would, one of them crying, "Mommy?!

Mommy?!" His heart went out to the child. The white children had been content playing with the Indian children, but when Gray Wolf lifted them onto the horses' backs the next day to ride to the soldiers' camp, fear and desperation sprung to their faces. It must have reminded them of the violence and loss that brought them to the Cheyenne camp as captives. He wondered if they would ever be united with their mommies, or if their mommies and daddies were alive. Gray Wolf's best effort at reassuring them they would be fine was well-received. They left the camp cautious but confident.

Gray Wolf had returned to camp from the council meeting to find Georgia in her element, treating ailments.

"Gray Wolf, I've met a Cheyenne healer. Her name is Howling Coyote Woman. She uses many of the same herbs I use, plus she showed me some new ones to numb the skin. We've used them already for a child with a terrible toothache." She spoke fast. "I always thought the medicine men tried to trick people and use magic to make patients feel better, when they really didn't help them. That isn't the case with this woman. And my Cheyenne is good enough that I can talk with her, well, at least a little." Georgia finally stopped to breathe.

"Cheyenne has good medicine too." Gray Wolf thought the Georgia he fell in love with at the ranch was returning.

"Have you heard about Meadow Lark?"

"Heard what?"

"You're her brother." Georgia snorted in frustration. "All men are alike. Oblivious to the obvious!"

"Ob-lee-be-us, what's this?"

Another snort from Georgia. "She's met a young man. She's in love." Georgia slowed down, emphasizing each word.

"I didn't know this."

"That's what I'm saying. Men are oblivious."

"How do you know this?"

"Since we came to the Smoky Hill to hunt buffalo, she has been happy. She sings when she works." Georgia looked pleased with herself. "So I asked her why she was happy. I didn't quite understand what she said, but yesterday I saw her talking to a young man. She was smiling at him in that way a woman smiles at the man she loves."

Gray Wolf thought about it. Yes, Georgia smiled at him, laughed at his jokes in a way she didn't do with others. "Who is this man?"

"I think he is Arapaho. Maybe the son or nephew of Left Hand."

Gray Wolf would ask her. He was surprised Meadow Lark had not chosen a Cheyenne, but the Arapaho were brothers. He had no doubt she had chosen well.

That evening, Gray Wolf confirmed Georgia's observations. The young brave was Meadow Lark's age. He was pleased to find a traditional woman, not a young girl. Meadow Lark and Left Hand's son planned to celebrate their marriage before the buffalo hunt ended. Since Meadow Lark had no mother near which she would lodge with her husband—the Cheyenne custom—she had agreed to live with her husband's band. Gray Wolf was happy for her, but he would miss her.

※

Gray Wolf would speak with Georgia about her request to have a preacher to marry them. Beaver told him that a preacher might not marry a white woman and an Indian brave, especially not now when the whites and Indians were at war. "But a Franciscan monk might marry you. He married a white friend of mine to an Arapaho squaw a few months ago." Gray Wolf had asked where to find this Franciscan. "Follow the Purgatory River south and west until you are near Ute Mountain country. Ask for the father at Parras Plaza."

The Purgatory River was south of Bent's Fort, the trading post, on the Arkansas River. Gray Wolf had been to Bent's Fort once with his Uncle Lean Bear. He knew how to find it. When he was a boy, the Cheyenne traded buffalo robes at the fort for fair prices and their choice of goods, not like now when the whites refused to trade for ammunition and rifles. Whiskey. Now there was plenty of that for trade.

He would talk to Georgia about it. They were enjoying a buffalo stew made with bone broth, tougher cuts of buffalo and wild turnips and onions when Howling Coyote Woman hobbled into Gray Wolf's circle of tepees, hollering urgently for Georgia.

"A brave has fallen from his horse into a ravine. His bones are mangled," the healer said. Gray Wolf translated for Georgia when he realized she did not understand what Howling Coyote Woman had said.

If he's a dog soldier, he probably deserved it, Gray Wolf thought with disdain. His thoughts were interrupted by half a dozen Dog Soldiers who rode toward them, the patient on a travois pulled behind one of the horses. *He must be near death if he allowed his comrades to bring him to camp in a travois*, Gray Wolf thought ruefully.

The braves deposited the injured man on the ground in front of their tepees. The man writhed, crying out in pain. He grabbed at his lower right arm. Gray Wolf saw bones protruding from the skin just below the elbow. Georgia instructed the men to put the patient on a buffalo robe.

"It's a really bad break," Georgia said more to herself than anyone else. "We'll have to align the bones before they begin to grow together. Otherwise, he will never use his right arm." She spoke English, tending to fall back to her native tongue when tension elevated.

The brave heard her words and turned sharply to look at her face. Gray Wolf winced and pulled back when he saw the patient's face. *Soaring Falcon!* Georgia stepped back from him and looked at Gray Wolf. He saw a look of horror in her face. She knew.

Georgia walked backward, turned and ran. Gray Wolf did not blame her. Howling Coyote Woman hovered about Soaring

Falcon. She did not know how to handle the compound fracture. She looked in desperation at the tepee into which Georgia had fled. Howling Coyote Woman reprimanded Soaring Falcon for his cowardice and the patient quit screaming, but it was clear his distress was genuine. Gray Wolf hated Soaring Falcon. He had taken Thomas from them, and in so doing, he had taken Georgia, at least the courageous, always smiling Georgia that Gray Wolf first knew. He glared at the man, feeling no sympathy for him.

Gray Wolf was ready to send Soaring Falcon away when he saw Georgia emerge from the tepee, her medical bag in tow. Her eyes were red, but her face was without emotion. Gray Wolf wondered, not entirely in jest, if she had decided which scalpel she would use to kill him. The wide, short one or the long, jagged knife used for amputations? *Either will do.* He smirked.

Soaring Falcon saw her and tried to flee. She yelled at Howling Coyote Woman and his fellow braves to hold him down. She was pouring the sleeping water onto a cloth. *So that is how she will kill him*, Gray Wolf thought. *A pity*, he thought sarcastically, *to let the murderer slip into oblivion without suffering.*

Soon Soaring Falcon was unconscious. Georgia moved in to better examine the protruding bones.

"Not as bad as it looks," Georgia said as she instructed Gray Wolf to hold Soaring Falcon's upper arm just above the elbow. "Hold it real tight." She pulled her unconscious patient's wrist and twisted it. One more little jerk and the bones from the lower arm lined up with the fragmented ones from the elbow. "I think that should do," Georgia said as Soaring Falcon groaned, consciousness returning.

Georgia instructed Howling Coyote Woman to clean the fracture and wrap it. Gray Wolf could see that Georgia was struggling to keep her composure. He admired her. He also worried about her, watching as she fled to her tepee, her medical bag tucked under her arm.

Then Georgia stormed out of her tepee, Cheyenne's bridle over her right shoulder. "I need to get away from him." She gestured at Soaring Falcon, now conscious but still on the ground where she had left him.

"I'll ride with you," Gray Wolf said, running to catch up with her.

Chapter 27

Parras Plaza, Purgatory River Settlement,
Colorado Territory, late September 1864

Look!" Georgia pointed toward a stone and adobe church, clearly defined by the cross that rose thirty feet above the second story. A massive brass bell hung below the cross. "Do you think the priest will marry us, Gray Wolf?" She doubted there was a priest at the little church at all, and if there was, would he marry a Cheyenne brave and a white woman? A Protestant woman, at that.

"Yes, Georgia. He will." Rather than return to Sand Creek from the Smoky Hill buffalo hunting grounds, Gray Wolf had led Georgia on a quest to find a priest to marry them. The Purgatory River Valley was dotted with sagebrush and tufts of buffalo grass. Hilly mounds and mesa tops flanked the river. Scrub oak and scraggly piñon pine trees jutted out in no particular pattern. Red rock outcroppings provided shade from the sun and shelter at night. The Purgatory had carried them from the plains to the base of the Sangre de Cristo Mountains.

Purgatory River was the shortened, Anglicized name for El Rio de Las Animas Perdidas en Purgatório or the River of Lost Souls in Purgatory. Her father had recounted the legend that gave the river its name. A Spanish military detachment, including the priest who always accompanied Spanish explorations, had been killed by Indians along the river, making it impossible for the dying to receive their last rites. The Spaniards believed all who were killed were trapped in Purgatory. It was a haunting story, Georgia thought as they rode past two headstones inscribed in Spanish. Behind the graves were the roofless remains of two adobe structures: a two-room house and outbuilding. The unattended graves and crumbling adobe bowed in surrender to the harsh land amid desolate beauty. It made her think about her ranch home. How long before the adobe would start to crumble? Were weeds and thistle even now overtaking her parents' graves?

She willed herself not to think about it. Today could be her wedding day. The afternoon sun warmed them and the horses as they crossed the plaza to reach the front of the church. The church and its enclosed garden occupied most of the northern side of the plaza. The settlement's social center was a large, flat grassy area with trees, flowers and seating, not at all like the frontier towns Georgia knew. On the other three sides of the plaza were a schoolhouse, a lumberyard, a blacksmith, livery, bakery, mercantile, cafe and jail. Passersby paid scant attention to them as they passed. Georgia assumed they were accustomed to people coming and going to and from their town.

They were in front of the church now. They dismounted at the hitching post anchored to the right of the wooden double doors. Georgia had taken extra care that morning to bathe and dress for the occasion. She wore the brown calico splashed with yellow and blue flowers. It was the dress her mother made for her sixteenth birthday. She plaited her wavy auburn hair in the French style, a single braid down the back of her head. She could have been mistaken for a Cheyenne squaw had she not changed out of her doeskin dress. Only her green eyes and freckles might have given her away, but it was not her intention to fool anyone. Gray Wolf wore his best beaded buckskin shirt. Georgia had made it with Meadow Lark's help. Buckskin trousers and moccasins completed his wedding attire. His shoulder length hair was not unlike that of the white settlers or freighters, but his broad face and distinct cheekbones set him apart from them. A summer of hard work in the sun had turned his skin several shades darker than its coffee-with-cream color. The Franciscan would know exactly who stood before him.

Even with the buckskin shirt covering his chest and arms, she could see his muscles flexing and relaxing as he secured the horses to the hitching post and retrieved the gifts from the packs. He moved toward her, smiling. He laid his right arm parallel to the ground, just above his waist, tipping his elbow like any proper gentleman escorting a lady.

He opened the door to the church for her. It was dark inside. And cool. "Hello, is anyone here?" he called out.

As her eyes adjusted to the dark, Georgia saw heavy, rough-hewn benches on either side of an aisle that led to an altar. Behind it, up on the wall, was a life-size carving depicting Christ suffering crucifixion.

Georgia first smelled the beef-tallow candles that flickered from wall sconces and benches throughout the adobe and stone sanctuary. She was so engrossed in the sights and smells that she started when she saw a figure shuffle across the packed earth floor toward them. *This must be the Franciscan.* He was a small man with graying, disheveled hair and a white beard. "*Buenas tardes,*" he greeted them.

"*Buenas tardes,*" she returned the greeting. Gray Wolf looked confused. She had learned some Spanish phrases from the Mexicans who built the MacBaye ranch house, but it had been many years. "Do you speak English?"

"A little," the Franciscan responded. "How can I be of service, *señorita*?"

Georgia turned to Gray Wolf. "We want to be married," he said to the Franciscan. "We believe in Jesus." He gestured to the statue.

"But you are not Catholic," the Franciscan said. It was a statement, not a question.

Georgia felt her shoulders slump. Gray Wolf continued. "What is Cath-lic?"

"No, father, we are not Catholic," Georgia said. "We're also of different races." She wanted to run out of the church, but she wouldn't be rude. She chided herself for the giddiness she felt, for believing today would be her wedding day.

"Do you love each other?"

"I love this woman with all my heart," she heard Gray Wolf say. She felt heat rising in her cheeks as she swallowed hard to hold back the tears.

"Then I will marry you. I will do my best to marry you ... in English." He motioned for them to follow him into a small room at the back of the church. The only furnishings were a rough-hewn chair and table.

"Please, you write your names here." He handed Georgia a piece of parchment and a pen dipped in ink. He assumed Gray Wolf illiterate. Georgia carefully wrote *Georgia Ariana MacBaye*. She handed the pen to Gray Wolf, who wrote *Gray Wolf*. His penmanship was perfect.

"Gray Wolf, do you have a family name? I need to write a family name in my book and on your marriage certificate. The church is very fussy about its priests keeping precise records." He smiled. "If you don't have a family name, maybe you can use your father's name?"

Gray Wolf leaned over the parchment, pen in hand, and without hesitation, he added *Thomas* behind *Gray Wolf*.

"Very well. We can begin." The Franciscan led them outside to a small, enclosed garden. "I cannot marry you in the sanctuary. Church has rules, you see, but you will be just as married if we do it out here." He chuckled. "And the light is better."

It was true—the early afternoon sun lit the garden terrace with a golden hue. Indian paintbrush in deep reds and golds and delicate bluebells provided color and fragrance. Georgia blinked, her eyes adjusting to the light. She felt a huge lump in her throat.

"Will you, Gray Wolf Thomas, take this woman, Georgia Ariana ...."

When the Franciscan pronounced them "man and wife," Georgia cupped Gray Wolf's face and kissed him. He was taken aback by her uncharacteristic forwardness. "That's right, young man, you may kiss your bride," the priest cooed as he turned to leave the terrace. "I'll have your marriage certificate in the office *hace un minuto*."

Gray Wolf pulled her into his arms. He kissed her head then pushed her away from him and kissed her forehead, sliding down to encircle her mouth with his. Georgia's knees felt unsteady. She was sure she would have fallen had Gray Wolf not held her in a rock-solid embrace. They were drawn together by an unseen bond. It was like the night in Gray Wolf's tepee when she told him she would not share a tepee with him until they were married. She had willed herself to leave. She would never have to do that again.

"Your marriage certificate is complete." The Franciscan's voice broke the reverie.

"Thank you for marrying us even if we aren't Cath-lic." Gray Wolf extended his right hand to the old priest. "We wish to give you these to thank you for your kindness." Gray Wolf presented the buffalo hide boots and deerskin gloves.

The Franciscan's eyes lit up in delight. He ran his hand over the smooth fur and soft leather. "Winters can get really cold. My old bones will be much comforted by these. *Gracias*." He started to turn back to his office but stopped. "You two, always trust Jesus. Love Him. Love each other. That is all that really matters now, isn't it?" Not waiting for an answer, he left the terrace, clutching the boots and gloves.

Back out on the plaza, Gray Wolf pressed a gold coin into Georgia's palm. "Buy us some food for the journey home and anything else you need. I'll wait outside with the horses."

Georgia was surprised he had a gold coin. "You saved the

coins my father gave you." It had been more than a year ago
when her father gave them each ten dollar coins to spend as
they wished. "My hunting knife cost only a dollar and a half."
She wondered if he was thinking about the hostility of the
shopkeepers in Denver.

She was surprised to see that the tiny, windowless mercantile
was well-stocked. The shopkeeper's wife piled Georgia's
purchases of dried fruit and roasted grain on the counter.
She was ready to pay when her eye caught a clump covered in
muslin. *Surely not.* Her mouth watered in anticipation. How
long had it been since she'd eaten cheese? "*¿Queso, sí, señora?*"
The woman pulled back the muslin to reveal a creamy, white
half circle of cheese. The pungent smell wafted toward her. She
asked the woman to cut her a wedge. With the gold coin not
even half-spent, she scanned the shelves. Her eyes landed on a
pair of candles in carved wood holders. *Perfect. A wedding gift
for Meadow Lark.* She paid the woman who had been so kind
and left the shop to find Gray Wolf where he said he would be.
He smiled at her, taking her purchases to secure in their packs.

They left the plaza and headed back the way they had come.
As the sun set behind them, Gray Wolf led her to one of the
red sandstone rock formations. Gray Wolf took her hand as
they watched a blazing orange sphere sink below the horizon.
Brilliant pinks, oranges and purples splashed the sky beyond
the winding river.

By October, Bull Bear's clan had joined several of the other
clans camped in the Sand Creek, a day's ride from Fort Lyon.
The chiefs said the area was designated safe for peaceful Indians.
Safe it might be, but pleasant it was not. The creek was dry, so
the women had to dig deep into the creek bed for the water they
needed to drink, cook and clean. And it had been unusually cold,
with the north wind bringing two blizzards in as many weeks.
The banks of the creek provided little shelter from the wind. All

the dead wood had been collected and burned for cooking and warming tepees. Without water or trees, the game had moved out. The braves traveled farther from the camp on each hunting expedition.

As the skies cleared from the second blizzard, Georgia was surprised to learn that James had ridden into the camp to see her and Gray Wolf. She worried what James would say when he learned they had married the previous month.

"Now that is the best news I've heard in a while." James hugged Georgia and pumped Gray Wolf's hand in congratulations.

"Come inside. Warm yourself by our fire." Gray Wolf pulled back the tepee flap for James. "Georgia's got some rabbit and turnip stew in the pot. Please, sit."

James sat on the tepee floor spread with buffalo robes. "I'm afraid I don't have good news." He cleared his throat, looking up at the smoke rising to the vent at the top of the tepee. "I fear for your safety."

"Was not Governor Evans pleased that the white captives were released?" Gray Wolf raised his eyebrows in bafflement.

"According to Captain Soule, Governor Evans was not happy that Wynkoop had arranged the peace talks. The governor said it was too late." James removed his hat and wiped the sweat from his forehead, even though Georgia thought it felt cold in the tepee. "When they returned to Fort Lyon, Major Wynkoop found he was relieved of his command. The new chief, Major Scott Anthony, the one the Cheyenne and Arapaho call the red-eyed chief, is the new commander."

Georgia knew this change in command was an incomprehensible concept. Cheyenne chiefs remained in their positions for life. "What do you think of this Major Anthony, James?"

"I think he is no good. My men see that he drinks too much. Worse, he talks out of both sides of his mouth." James leaned back, propping himself up with his hands. "He told Major Wynkoop that he would continue his policies toward friendly Indians, but one of the men I know is his secretary. This man knows Anthony's real intentions and they are not good. I think you should leave Sand Creek."

"And go where?" Georgia asked.

"These are my people. I cannot leave Bull Bear's camp." Gray Wolf rubbed the sides of his jaw with his hand as he did when contemplating a decision.

"I don't know where to tell you to go, back to the ranch or further east maybe. I have this really bad feeling." He gazed into the fire in the middle of the tepee.

James left at midday to return to Fort Lyon by nightfall. He would have to sneak back into the fort under the cover of darkness.

James's pronouncement left a chilly disquiet. Georgia understood Gray Wolf's reluctance to leave the Cheyenne at Sand Creek, but the winter cold and food shortage in the camp weighed on her.

❋

Most every day, and sometimes in the middle of the night, Georgia was called to attend to a patient. Her medical supplies were nearly gone. She consulted with Howling Coyote Woman about herbal options, but October, especially this October, was not the time to hunt for herbs. She had not seen scurvy or rickets among the Cheyenne. The berries and roots they collected and dried prevented scurvy. Though they had no source of dairy products, their exposure to the sun, even during winter, along with consumption of buffalo meat, marrow and offal gave the Cheyenne strong bones and teeth. Tooth decay was uncommon. The only explanation for the rise in sickness was malnutrition. Hungry bodies could not ward off disease. Howling Coyote Woman was beside herself with worry, but there was little Georgia could do to help.

Gray Wolf kept their cooking pots full of fresh game. He got up earlier and traveled farther than the others. They shared extra game and dried buffalo, berries and vegetables with the squaws whose husbands had died and had no one else to provide for them. Georgia felt the despair of the women and children who had no one to bring them game. At first she attributed her lack of energy, lessened appetite and moodiness to the cares and heavy workload, until the obvious stared her in the face. Meadow Lark noticed too. Gray Wolf did not. She would tell him when she knew for sure that she carried his child.

In an uncharacteristically melancholy mood as she returned home from delivering a baby early that morning, Georgia saw Blue Bell tied by the horns to one of the few large trees along the creek. Three braves, none of them she knew, were preparing to kill her. The gentle brown cow pulled her head from side to side, jerking at the rope, but was too docile to put up much of a fight.

A rage ignited in Georgia. She flew toward the cow, screaming in English, "That's my cow, you idiots." Startled, the men stopped, dropping their knives to their sides. "It's a milk cow. Can't you see that we can feed our children for years with her milk?" She was at the cow's side now, fury driving her as she shoved the leader backward onto the snow-covered ground.

"Crazy squaw," he said, scrambling to his feet, his knife pointed at her.

Inches from her face, the knife brought Georgia to her senses. The cow wasn't Blue Bell. Its face looked different, and there was no MacBaye brand on its hip. Gray Wolf in the lead, Meadow Lark behind him, raced toward her. Gray Wolf pulled an unresponsive Georgia away from the brave she had attacked. He held her until they were inside their tepee. Anger still coursed through her. She knew it was irrational.

"I thought it was Blue Bell," was all she could say, her eyes begging him to understand.

Her anger took over. "They butcher milk cows and put dogs that lay at their feet in their cooking pots." She was shaking as she spewed venom. "The children are malnourished but they won't make peace with the white man. They maim their bodies to honor the dead." She talked to no one in particular. "I can't live here anymore. I'll not have my—" She couldn't tell Gray

Wolf her secret. He would never let her leave, but she wouldn't raise her child here and watch it die of malnutrition. What if something happened to Gray Wolf and she was forced to be a third or fourth wife of another brave? No, she would leave while she still could, before he knew.

Gray Wolf tried to comfort her. He pulled her into his arms and kissed her on her head and cheeks. She felt nothing but anger and panic.

"I'm going back to the ranch ... as soon as the sky is clear." She scurried about, gathering her belongings at random, stuffing them into her saddlebags.

"Georgia, you cannot leave!" Gray Wolf took the saddlebags away from her.

"Why? You said I am not a captive, didn't you?" She lunged at the saddlebags. He pulled them out of her reach. "You cannot hold me here against my will."

"You are crazy to think you can leave here by yourself and travel back to the Bijou Basin."

Calling her crazy and telling her she couldn't do something—didn't he know it was a challenge she could not back away from? She felt the blood coursing through her veins. Her temples throbbed.

"Gray Wolf, you are wrong." She was resolute, and his look told her he knew it. "I can and I will."

"You can't leave now, Georgia. I promised your father."

"Promised my father? Promised him what?"

Gray Wolf sighed. He sat down and motioned for her to do the same. She stood, not facing him, her chin jutted forward in defiance.

"When he was dying, he made me promise," he spoke as though it pained him. "I promised Thomas I would take care of you, Georgia."

Bitter realization flooded over her. Gray Wolf didn't love her. He married her because he promised her father he would care for her. Devastation crushed every bit of defiance that had bolstered her a moment earlier, but she would not let him see the gaping wound in her heart. She would leave but not to defy him. She would leave because Gray Wolf didn't love her. He married her out of duty.

She would leave in the morning, as soon as Gray Wolf left to hunt. She fell to the floor of the tepee, trembling. Pulling the heavy buffalo robe over her body, she willed herself not to cry, not now. Gray Wolf still sat, gazing into the fire. Had he tried to comfort her, she would have crumbled, but her anger kept her from going to him.

Chapter 28

Sand Creek, Colorado Territory,
mid-November 1864

Gray Wolf woke long before dawn. There was little point staying nestled in the buffalo robes when the slumber he sought eluded him. The little sleep he managed was interrupted by nightmares of soldiers overrunning the camp or Georgia running into danger while he watched, helpless to save her. Throughout the restless night, he had hoped Georgia would turn to him, would speak to him, but she had not. Now he listened for her slow, deep breathing, but it never came. He was startled to see that she was gone. He forced reason to calm him, to keep his imagination from stirring his unexplained disquiet into outright panic. He convinced himself she was collecting twigs to refuel the fire or visiting a patient on the opposite side of the camp.

Gray Wolf found Wise Heart in the dark and slipped the bridle over his ears. He swung onto the horse's back, feeling ribs as he hugged the stallion's midsection. The horses weren't the only ones losing their protective coverings of fat. He was desperate to find meat, but not even a rabbit ran across his path this morning. The ice from the snow that had melted during the day and refroze when the sun dropped below the horizon, now sparkled in the morning light, crunching and breaking as Wise Heart moved through the expanse of white. Gray Wolf needed to focus on finding breakfast, but his mind kept returning to Georgia. He understood her dismay with finding braves slaughtering a milk cow, and, having lived with the settlers, he understood why she found other Cheyenne habits and customs revolting. Trudging on, he looked beyond the naked tree branches on the creek. It was Moonwalker. Gray Wolf had been so engrossed with thoughts of Georgia that he had forgotten to rouse his friend.

"What, you got yourself half a dozen young bucks cornered and don't want to share with me?" Moonwalker's sense of humor always put Gray Wolf at ease.

Even Moonwalker's lighthearted conversation could not put Gray Wolf at ease. "Since yesterday, I've been … preoccupied."

"All is not well on the home front?"

Gray Wolf figured the whole camp had heard of Georgia's tirade. "She has been very amenable, but Cheyenne life is very different from life as a settler. I think it got to her." Gray Wolf swallowed and looked away. "It will be better when winter passes and game returns." He said this with more conviction than he felt.

"I fear the game will never be like it was when we were children." Moonwalker reined his horse to move beside Wise Heart as the two continued walking up the dry creek bed. "You've heard what the people are saying now, haven't you?"

"What do you mean?"

"Many, even the Dog Soldiers, are saying Lean Bear was right. The Cheyenne must return to a life of putting seed in the ground, maybe raising cattle."

"It's not a bad life, you know. When you stay in one place, you can build strong houses and barns. When there was game, we hunted, but if not, there were cattle, chickens, pigs and beans to fill our bellies." Gray Wolf realized he was reminiscing about his year living with the MacBayes.

"Sounds nice. Sounds like you've already made your decision."

"What decision?"

"To live in one place and put seed in the ground. Seems you're already there."

Moonwalker was right. Gray Wolf had thought often about ranching.

"What about you, Moonwalker? Would you ever live by putting seed in the ground?"

"I haven't thought much about it, but I know that we won't stay here on Sand Creek much longer. The game is gone, and there is no protection here from the blizzards." Moonwalker looked straight at Gray Wolf. "My wife is pregnant. That changes everything."

Gray Wolf's stern face transformed into a broad smile. "Congratulations, my friend. That's great news. Where will you go and when?"

"Smoky Hill River, farther east of where we hunted buffalo two moons ago. Many of the widows whose cooking pots you and I fill will go with us. We leave in a day or two when the snow from this storm melts."

"Georgia and Meadow Lark will pack you some food for the journey."

"Didn't Meadow Lark tell you? She and her new husband will go with us." Moonwalker must have read Gray Wolf's look of confusion—even hurt—that he had not been told. "We talked with her husband before, but just yesterday they told us they would come." He lifted the reins of his horse, signaling it to stop. "I would ask you to join us my friend, but I think your mind—and your heart—are going in another direction. No?"

Moonwalker was right.

The men hunted until almost midday but without success. It was the first time in many moons they returned home with not even a rabbit or prairie chicken for their cooking pots. They would have to dig into their stores of dried buffalo and squash. Gray Wolf couldn't remember using dried food until the deep of winter in past years. The dried food was enough to last them two, maybe three moons.

Gray Wolf returned to his tepee to see what Georgia had waiting for him to eat, but she wasn't there. A scan of the tepee told him one buffalo robe and all her clothes were gone. Her pack was not in its usual place either. Panic began to rise in Gray Wolf. He sprinted to the horse herd. Wise Heart was scavenging for food, pawing through the snow to eat, but Georgia's red filly was gone.

Meadow Lark. She would know. Georgia would not have left without talking to his sister. It was an unseasonably warm day, but it was not the reason Gray Wolf perspired.

He burst into Meadow Lark's tepee without the customary polite call signaling his desire to enter. "Where's Georgia? Her things are gone and her filly isn't with the herd." He paced, balling his hands into fists.

"Why would she leave?" Meadow Lark averted her brother's gaze.

"Do you know where she is? Is she in danger?" He thought it strange she would answer a direct and urgent question this way.

"She woke me early this morning, even before you left to hunt." Meadow Lark hesitated, blinking back tears. "She has left us."

"To go where?" Gray Wolf's fear came out as impatience, anger. "Where is she, Meadow Lark? Where did she go?"

"The Bijou Basin. Everything has changed. I tried to persuade her to stay, but she was determined to return to her home."

Gray Wolf was in turmoil. He strode back and forth, thinking, *Should I go after her? Would she want me to follow her?* She had made it clear to Meadow Lark she would not return to the Cheyenne camp.

Meadow Lark placed her hands on his shoulders. She looked into his face, her eyes boring into his soul. "My brother, this white woman of yours is good. She is kind and hardworking. Her love for you is as passionate as the fire that devours the kindling in our tepee fires. You must stay with her, even if it means living among the white man, putting seed in the ground to feed yourselves." She took a very deep breath. "Even if it means your children will not know the Cheyenne ways. I will help you prepare for the journey."

Meadow Lark packed buffalo robes, weapons and food while Gray Wolf went for the horses. He bridled Wise Heart and haltered a black-and-white two-year-old paint filly Georgia had started to train before the snows began. He secured the buffalo robes and packs of supplies on the back of Wise Heart, his trusted mount. He would ride the greener paint horse.

He pulled his sister into a tight embrace, uncharacteristic of Cheyenne formality. "The rest of Lean Bear's horses, they are yours."

She looked up at him, smiling amid her tears. "Go to her now!"

Adrenaline surged through Gray Wolf. He vaulted onto the back of the paint, spooking the unseasoned horse. Both horses proved full of energy. *We think horses are so big and strong that they would not notice our emotions, but that is not correct. A horse senses everything a rider is feeling, even if the rider doesn't know he's feeling it.* Gray Wolf smiled, remembering Georgia's words.

Panic returned as he thought of Georgia out on the plains, alone. He wondered if Soaring Falcon still carried his grudge against her. Pawnee, Comanche, even Apache had been known to roam the plains between Sand Creek and the Bijou Basin. If she was dressed as an Indian squaw—likely he thought— patrolling soldiers might even fire on her. *Oh, Georgia! What was my sweet, spunky girl thinking when she rode out alone?* He was wrong. *Not a girl, a woman.*

Wise Heart and the paint filly were breathing harder now, but he allowed them no relief from the pace. He guided them to dry ground, away from where snow drifts melted, keeping

Georgia's tracks in sight. The snow made it easy to track her. It would take her two days, maybe more if she had to walk through mud, to reach the MacBaye Ranch, but she had a full day on him. When he felt panic rising, he reminded himself that she was an expert horsewoman and a good marksman. In surveying the tepee before he left, he was relieved that the rifle was gone.

He was entering the pine forest now. Reluctantly, he sought shelter for himself and grass for the horses. It was the same campsite Georgia had used the previous night. No denying that, he surmised, flicking Cheyenne's red hair from a tree. The horse must have had an itch.

He would have continued all night, but the horses were spent. They needed to eat and rest. He gnawed on buffalo jerky and dried fruit. He had insisted that Meadow Lark keep their dwindling supply of dried food, coffee, flour and sugar to take with her to the Smoky Hill.

He slept in fits and starts, giving up altogether as the sun peeked over the bluffs, casting its golden light between the pine trunks. He packed and readied to go. He hated pushing the horses, but he had to do it.

They were all faint—the horses from exertion, Gray Wolf from worry—when they crested the hill that brought them into the Bijou Basin. He had forgotten how beautiful it was. Pines dotted the landscape. Bur oak and cottonwood trees would add to the greenery when spring came. The Bijou Creek ran north to south, along the west edge of the basin. As they descended, Gray Wolf noticed the creek still flowed. He could make out the barn and adobe ranch house. He willed himself not to kick the paint horse into an all-out run.

He trotted the horses through the pasture where the MacBayes' cattle and horses had grazed. Then he crossed the barren fields. The memory of working with Thomas, James and Henry to harvest hay, corn and wheat overwhelmed him. The barbed-wire fence between the house and the creek was still there, except for where Soaring Falcon had cut it to herd off the cattle on that hot July day that now seemed a lifetime ago. He had spent less than a year here, but it felt like home. If only Georgia wanted him to stay ... if only she wanted *him*.

Then came the most glorious of sights. It was Georgia, coming toward him. The beading on her buckskin dress flapped as she ran. He dismounted and dropped the reins of the paint, running to scoop her up into his arms. Her hazel eyes shone. The tough, mischievous young woman was back.

"I didn't think you'd come." Her lips quivered. "I didn't want you to come. Then I did." She wasn't making sense, but he didn't care. He understood what she meant.

He held her so tight he thought he might squeeze the air from her lungs, but she clung to him, her head burrowed into his neck.

"I never want you to leave me again. I ... I was so scared something would happen to you," he said.

"I left because, I ... I thought you didn't want me," she said, pulling back to look up at him, the wind whipping her hair into his face.

"How can you say that?" He ran his fingers through her soft auburn waves. He missed this.

"Your promise to my father—was it why you married me?"

"No, I could have taken care of you without marrying you."

"I wanted it to be your choice."

He pulled her close again, his lips on her head. "I loved you from the moment you fed me that green chili sauce, but I couldn't marry you until I knew you loved me."

"Really? The green chili sauce didn't make you angry with me?"

He laughed. "No, it didn't make me angry. It made me laugh. You hooked me like a fish." His smiled faded. "I shouldn't have told you about my promise to your father. Not then, but I was afraid you would leave. I wanted you to know that he would have approved of us."

She smiled, looking away as she swiped at the moisture brimming in her eyes. "Let's get the horses and ourselves something to eat. Sound good?"

It felt right to be seated at the table in the ranch house. The fire in the hearth warmed them as they ate pancakes, eggs and canned apples.

"Everything was pretty much as we left it." Georgia got up to collect their dishes and began washing them in the basin. "I was surprised to find the laying hens still around. Guess they found enough to eat and were able to outsmart the foxes and coyotes."

"The barn and fence out back need repairs." Gray Wolf rose to help her with the dishes. "I'll start tomorrow."

Gray Wolf piled the dishes by the basin and brought in water from the back porch while Georgia poured the boiling water from the stovetop into the basin. She added the cold water and began washing their supper dishes. He could see she was contemplating something. He was about to ask her what was on her mind when she blurted out, "I'm sorry I embarrassed you. I promised you I wouldn't. Then I went kinda crazy when I saw them trying to butcher that Jersey cow." She paused, grabbing a dish towel. "You don't have to worry. I won't do it again."

"I don't blame you, Georgia. There was a lot of truth in what you said, about the Cheyenne's customs, I mean." He chuckled, thinking about the shocked look of the braves she yelled at. "It was so unlike you."

"Sometimes things happen that change everything." She smoothed her palm over her stomach like she protected a treasure.

Things happen that change everything. It was the third time in two days someone had said this. First Moonwalker, then Meadow Lark spoke something similar in Cheyenne. Now Georgia said it in English. It was not the first time he had seen her touch her stomach with tenderness. It could only mean one thing. Georgia carried his child! She wasn't thinking of herself when she left. She was thinking of the baby.

"I was afraid ... for the baby." She nodded, confirming his conclusion.

Chapter 29

MacBaye Ranch, Bijou Basin, Colorado Territory,
November 25, 1864

Make sure the rifles are loaded. I'll lock the horses in the barn!" Gray Wolf shouted as he bolted to the corral where the horses ate.

Georgia's hand trembled as she pulled their two best rifles down from the fireplace mantel. She ensured both were loaded and laid them at the ready near the front door.

It had been an unseasonably warm day, and she had dug the last of the root vegetables from the garden and stashed them in the cellar. After pouring herself a cup of coffee, she had moved to the front porch to enjoy the warmth of the afternoon. Several sips into her coffee, she noticed the dust cloud on the eastern horizon. As it grew, so did her concern.

She rang the dinner bell to bring Gray Wolf to the house. "Could be Cheyenne, could be Cavalry, could be buffalo. Whatever it is, we must get ready."

Georgia opened the door to let Gray Wolf back into the

house. It reminded her of the first time she saw him run. She thought he ran like a pronghorn antelope. His eyes went to the waiting rifles. Then he disappeared into the main floor bedroom, returning with his bow and a quiver full of arrows. He was a reasonably accurate shot with a rifle but always dead-on with his bow. Like him, Georgia favored the weapon she learned to use as a child. Gray Wolf had tried to teach her to shoot his bow, but when she was under pressure, she always opted for a rifle.

Door bolted, Georgia and Gray Wolf watched through the front windows as the cloud dust came closer. Maybe buffalo stampeded toward them. They would be safe in the two-story adobe house and might be able to pick off a couple of the beasts. Since her pa was killed and the cattle stolen, they had eaten only wild game and chicken. The reliable laying hens were all that was left, and game was holing up for winter. She smiled at the prospect of buffalo meat in their bellies and buffalo robes on their bed.

"Cows! It's a herd of stampeding cows!" Georgia exclaimed.

"No, not stampeding. They're being driven by Cheyenne braves." Gray Wolf had jerked back the lace curtains and was straining to see who drove the cattle.

Georgia could see that Gray Wolf was perplexed, but there was more. His grip on the bow tightened. He pulled an arrow from the quiver. She saw the muscle under his cheekbone twitch, then tighten, as the braves pulled into view.

"It's him." Georgia drew in a deep breath and held it. Now it was her turn to tighten her hands around her weapon.

Soaring Falcon pulled his horse to a stop outside the front door while the other braves whooped and hollered as they drove the cattle into the corral. Georgia could see the MacBayes' rocking "M" on the hips of the cattle.

"Blue Bell. It's Blue Bell. She's still alive." Georgia let out the breath she hadn't realized she was holding. "What on earth is he doing with our cattle?"

"Soaring Falcon is never up to any good." Gray Wolf kept his eyes on Soaring Falcon, and his bow poised for action. "I aim to find out what he's up to."

"Be careful!" Georgia shrieked as he bounded out of the house.

Moving back to her place at the front window, Georgia saw Soaring Falcon raise his hands, palms outward to signal he was unarmed. Gray Wolf lowered the bow but kept the arrow at the ready. Georgia moved to the door, opening it a crack to listen to the Cheyenne words.

Soaring Falcon lowered his right arm, swinging it from side to side. "White woman is a good healer. She is very brave to use her medicine on the man who killed her father." His arms fell to his sides. He slumped forward in contrition. "She shows me not all white men are bad. I can't bring back her father, but tell her to please accept these gifts." He threw a buffalo robe bundle on the ground at Gray Wolf's feet. "We go back now."

Georgia nearly collapsed. *Grace—that is the only thing that could change this evil-minded man's heart.*

She would assess the cattle in the morning when they moved them out to pasture, but it looked as if all were accounted for, Blue Bell and her calf included. She saw Gray Wolf drop his bow to his side. His stance appeared relaxed, but she knew he could have an arrow in his bow and be ready to shoot in less than a second.

"Ask the Wise One Above to send His spirit to guide you, Soaring Falcon," Georgia heard Gray Wolf say.

Then Soaring Falcon and the other braves turned their horses and sped east. Georgia and Gray Wolf watched as they disappeared over the horizon.

"The evil in his heart is gone, Georgia. I believe him, but just in case I am wrong or there are other less honorable braves, I think we should lock the cows in the corral tonight."

Georgia nodded. She noticed that after supper, Gray Wolf checked to make sure the bars on the inside of both doors were lodged tightly in their metal housings.

A week later, the fences had been repaired and the cattle grazed the crop stubble and pastureland. Emerging from the henhouse late that afternoon with ten brown eggs in a bucket, Georgia again saw a cloud of dust, this time to the northeast. She ran to the ranch house and rang the dinner bell to bring Gray Wolf in from hide-tanning in the barn. He had told her he preferred to work outside as long as the weather allowed.

"There, to the north," Georgia pointed at the growing dust cloud. "Do you think Soaring Falcon is bringing us more cattle?" She chuckled.

They performed their now practiced security routines. Gray Wolf locked the horses in the barn. They came easily when they heard him rattle corn in a leather pouch. There was no time to gather the cattle. Georgia gathered Gray Wolf's bow and arrow and the rifles and ammunition. This time, as the riders came into view, it was U.S. Cavalry uniforms they saw.

"James!" Georgia erupted, putting down her rifle.

James and a man with stripes indicating his rank as captain on his coat pulled their horses to a halt in the ranch yard. They dismounted and led their horses to the adobe ranch house's front door. They both looked stiff as if they carried a burden.

"You're awful early for Christmas, brother," Georgia said, flinging herself into James's open arms. He pulled her in, as if hugging a long-lost friend. The burden, whatever it was, sucked the joy from her once lighthearted brother.

He swung her around. "Whoa, whoa, little sister." He set her down and stepped back to look at her. Georgia noticed that his gaze rested on her thickening middle. "Am I gonna be an uncle?"

Georgia rested her hand on her middle. " I just wish Ma and Pa coulda been here to meet their grandchild."

"I think about 'em all the time too." James removed his Cavalry-issue cap with one hand and wiped his forehead with the other. The air was cool now. He couldn't be sweating. *What is bothering him?* Georgia wondered.

"Gray Wolf," James said, extending his hand in greeting.

Gray Wolf also must have noticed James's discomfort.

"What brings you here?" Then Gray Wolf said with haste, "Of course, you are welcome anytime. We did not expect to see you until Christmas, maybe later."

Both of James's hands were on his Cavalry cap now. He squeezed and released it as he rotated the cap brim back and forth, back and forth. "I brought my captain with me." James gestured toward his companion, who held both horses where they had dismounted. "Captain Silas Soule, this is my sister, Georgia, and her husband, Gray Wolf. My brother-in-law is the man I told you about. He's Cheyenne, the nephew of Lean Bear and Bull Bear."

"Silas Soule at your service, ma'am, sir." The captain tipped his cap at Georgia and hesitated for just a moment before extending his hand to greet Gray Wolf.

"Welcome to our home," Georgia said, gesturing for him to enter the ranch house.

The men sat in the parlor while Georgia fired up the stove to heat water for coffee. While she waited for the water to boil, she lit the beef-tallow candles. She heard the men making small talk, mostly about the ranch, the cattle and preparations for winter. As soon as the water boiled, she poured it through the cheesecloth suspended over her ma's coffee server. Placing the coffee and four cups on a tray, she headed for the parlor.

"I'm afraid we come with some bad news—really bad news." The captain's voice quavered. "Two days ago, Colonel John Chivington ordered several companies of the Colorado First Cavalry and his blasted Third Regiment of one-hundred-day volunteers to attack an encampment of Cheyenne on Sand Creek."

Georgia put the tray down on the table. Gray Wolf turned toward Captain Soule. "That's impossible. Major Wynkoop himself told Black Kettle and White Antelope that they had been recognized by the Army as friendly Indians because they camped at Sand Creek."

"You're right. They had no reason to fear the Army, which is why they didn't defend themselves."

Captain Soule poured himself a cup of coffee. Georgia had completely forgotten her mother's rules for being a good hostess. As he poured, his hands shook. "I'm still trying to comprehend it myself."

No one else poured coffee into his cup. The captain added sugar and stirred. Instead of drinking, he pushed the cup aside. "That dammed Chivington snuck to the fort, then he ran a picket around it and said he would shoot anyone who dared leave the fort for any reason. We believe he woulda."

"Didn't they know Black Kettle's band was friendly?" Georgia couldn't believe what she was hearing.

"They arrested William Bent, the great trader and Indian negotiator, and put guards around his house. When they announced their intention to attack the Indians at Sand Creek, we couldn't believe it. We thought it was some sort of a practical joke, but Major Anthony, who had just replaced Major Wynkoop seemed eager to join Chivington in the attack."

He paused, steeling himself to continue. "Lieutenant Joseph Cramer and I told the men they were fools to continue in this campaign. Later, I went to Lieutenant James Cannon's quarters, where a number of officers from both the Cavalry and the volunteers congregated and told them that any man who would take part in the murders, knowing the circumstances as we did, was a low-life coward and some other names I can't repeat in front of female company. If Chivington would have gotten wind of my comments, as sure as I'm sitting here, he'd have hanged me before we moved out that night. I told them my company would only fight warring Indians. They let us think we would have this opportunity." He buried his face in his open hands.

James picked up where Soule left off and continued the horrible tale: "We rode all night, arriving at Sand Creek early the next morning. I'll never forget November 29, 1864, as long as I live. As we approached the camp, we saw an American flag flying above one of the tepees. Below it was the white surrender flag. Colonel Chivington ignored it all and ordered us to cut the Indians off from their horse herd and attack head on. Thankfully, Captain Soule ordered us not to fire a shot." He looked at Soule and nodded. "Otherwise, I would have had to disobey a commanding officer."

The captain had managed to take several sips of coffee. It must have bolstered him to continue with the most grisly part of the massacre. "The Indians put up little defense because they didn't expect to be attacked and also because few braves were at the camp," Soule said. "The camp was mostly inhabited by women, children and old people. What kind of fight is that?" He slammed his fist onto the table. The coffee server and cups jumped with the impact, but he didn't indicate he noticed. "It was a slaughter. I saw—" again his voice quavered, "little children begging for their lives as supposedly civilized men beat their brains out. I saw a squaw cut the throats of her two children and then herself, rather than wait for the soldiers to humiliate them. The dead were scalped and mutilated, soldiers taking ears, genitals and other body parts as souvenirs. If I live to be a hundred, the horrible acts will never be erased from my memory."

As if reading Georgia's mind, James said, "There was nothing we could do to stop them. We couldn't fire on our own men, and even if we had, they were in such a frenzy they would have butchered us like they did the Indians. The captain was able to snatch Charlie Bent, but they refrained from butchering him only because he is William Bent's son, a half-breed." As he said this, he looked at Georgia and Gray Wolf. She could see in his eyes the dawning that their child would be just that, a half-breed. Then he said, "We saw a pregnant woman cut open and her unborn child jerked from her. I retched. It was more than I could stand, and the worst was the helplessness." James convulsed and great sobs sprang forth. It was a reaction Georgia had never seen from James or any other man.

Gray Wolf sat through the telling of the slaughter at Sand Creek without uttering a word. She saw his biceps and the muscles in his forearms tighten. His hands clenched into fists. She thought he would explode like the black powder rifle when she pulled the trigger. Instead, he bolted out of his seat and into the kitchen. She heard him moving around. Then, silence.

She rose to follow him, but James grabbed her shoulders from behind and pulled her back. "Give him some time. It's a hard thing to hear. I doubt he wants to talk to any white man 'bout now ... not even his wife, Georgia."

James was right. She was thankful for his insight and for his compassion for Gray Wolf, a man he had despised a few years ago. She would wait until Gray Wolf was ready to talk, to be in her presence.

James and Silas Soule stayed the night and left early the next morning. They would travel to Denver, vowing to tell the truth about Sand Creek.

Chapter 30

Fingers trembling, Gray Wolf stuffed dried venison and vegetables into his buckskin travel pack. He plucked a cook pot and one set of eating utensils from Georgia's dish rack. He grabbed his heavy deerskin coat and boots off the rack on the back porch and left the house through the back, closing the door without a sound. He didn't want to talk to any of them, not even Georgia, while the images of disemboweled children churned through his mind.

He fetched Wise Heart's bridle from the tack area of the barn and slipped it over the ears of the gentle, strong stallion and led him into the barn, where he threw Thomas's saddle on his back. When the cinch was snug, Gray Wolf rolled two cattle hides together into a long log shape. He had finished tanning the hides just before James and his captain rode into the ranch with news of the massacre. He hoisted the rolled hides behind the saddle and secured them with the long, thick saddle strings. Packing Wise Heart in the traditional Indian manner with travois and carrying cinches would have taken much longer, and he didn't want to spend another minute at the ranch. Night had already fallen, but he had to get away. He had to think about what to do.

Instead of heading east toward the Cheyenne encampments, as he supposed he would, he found himself urging Wise Heart south, toward the pine forest. He camped in the exact same spot where he and Georgia had stayed the night that summer when she left the ranch to live with the Cheyenne. He remembered her stunned reaction to losing her father. He thought it strange at the time, but now he understood a bit better. His emotions ranged from rage to oblivion. He wanted revenge, and he wanted the men who did this to be punished. More so, he wanted to help his people.

He had arrived at the campsite just as dawn was breaking. He unrolled the hides and placed them under the outcropping, fur sides together. He crawled between the hides and slept, then woke and raged, then slept again, exhausted. In the middle of the night following the day he arrived at the campsite, he woke, unable to sleep. He cried out to the Wise One Above for answers. All that answered him was silence, silence and a deep yearning to return home. He was astonished to realize that he yearned to return to Georgia, to the ranch, to the child that would be born to them in early summer. They were his home.

Not waiting for daybreak, he saddled Wise Heart and turned north. The closer they got to the Bijou Basin, the quicker Wise Heart's pace. When the ranch was in site, Wise Heart broke into a lope. Georgia must have seen them coming. She was standing outside the front door, her hands on her hips, her hair and dress disheveled. Regret flooded Gray Wolf. He had left her alone with no word on when, or if, he might return.

Jumping down from Wise Heart, he ran toward her but stopped short. "I was wrong ... to run off like that without talking to you. Please forgive me."

"Don't you ever, ever leave like that again. I thought you'd gone off to find that snake Chivington and you'd been shot or that you were being transported to a jail cell in Denver." She looked away from him, at nothing in particular, and he saw her swallow hard and wipe her eyes. "It is one thing to leave me alone in a Cheyenne village, but it is quite another to leave me here alone with no one around for miles."

He closed the gap between them, and she melted into his arms. She was shaking. "I'm so sorry, Georgia, but I didn't truthfully know myself where I was going or what I would do."

"Where did ya go?" She stepped back and let her eyes bore into his. "Come, have some breakfast, and you can tell me."

As soon as he stepped into the kitchen, the smell of bacon reminded him that he hadn't eaten in almost two days. He had packed food and cooking utensils, but had not cooked or hunted. Georgia set a plate of hot bacon, eggs and fried potatoes before him, and he ate like the starving man he was. After a second plate of food, he could not escape her expectant stare.

"I wasn't thinking clearly when I left. I first thought to go to the Cheyenne but didn't make it past the pine forest. I couldn't dismiss those terrible images from the massacre."

"They are your people, Gray Wolf. How can you not be sickened by news of this massacre? I know you want to help them. I can't get them out of my mind either. Maybe we shouldn't get them out of our minds."

"What do you mean? It keeps me from sleeping. I can't do anything but think about all the Cheyenne who were massacred, especially the children. The children are the worst ..."

Georgia caressed her belly with tenderness. "I can't even imagine what it would be like to have your child ripped from your arms and killed before you. It is a horrible image but one that shouldn't be buried with the people who were killed at Sand Creek."

"But you said you feared I had gone after Chivington. I want more than anything to hunt him down, but I would die doing it. Then what would become of you and the baby?"

"The soldiers who committed these horrible acts under the guise of war would be only so glad to gun you down as another warring Indian out of the way. That is not how to fight this, Gray Wolf."

"Then how?"

"I don't know, but in the spring when we can travel, we must find Meadow Lark and Moonwalker and make sure they are well. We can load up the wagon with supplies and go to them, no?"

"That's good, but we need to do more or the truth about Sand Creek will be gone like those killed there."

※

A few days later, Gray Wolf woke early to howling wind. One glance out the window told him the anticipated blizzard had arrived. They were ready for the blizzard, both inside and out. Even now, coals left from last night's blazing fire warmed the parlor. Unable to sleep, he paced and thought until morning. He still marveled at the two windows in the front of the adobe house that let in light and let them look outside without going out. He saw snow swirling and drifting. He could see the outline of the barn when the wind let up for a moment, then it disappeared again.

He used the rope that he had strung between the house and the barn the previous week to guide him. He reached the barn door, tugged it with all his might and pushed through the opening as the howling wind slammed the door shut behind him. He checked the livestock and threw some hay down from the loft for them. Satisfied that the animals were well-fed and warm, he tossed two hides over his head and pushed the door open to begin his trek back to the house. The hides provided protection from the driving cold, and if the blizzard continued, he could work on tanning the hides to occupy his time. There was no cow to milk since Blue Bell had dried up, and Georgia didn't allow him to gather eggs, muttering something about him scaring the hens silly.

Georgia was clattering around in the kitchen when he returned from the barn. After breakfast he would work on the hides, maybe make some more boots.

When they were half-finished with their eggs and sausage,

Georgia fetched the coffeepot from the stove and filled both their cups. Her brow wrinkled, and her eyes had that faraway look that told Gray Wolf she was deep in thought.

"Do you remember, Gray Wolf, when Ma taught us about Frederick Douglass?" She chuckled, sounding just like Loraine. "I only half-listened, but you were really interested in a man who fought for his people with words."

"I remember. I thought Frederick Douglass was a brave and clever man." He turned to her, his lips pursed, one eyebrow raised.

"Maybe you, Gray Wolf, are that brave and clever man who fights for his people with words."

"How would I do that?"

"Well, maybe we can start by writing about what you learned about the white man—that like Indians, some are good, some are evil, some work hard, some are lazy. I can add my experience living among the Cheyenne and that I experienced similar things. Then we can write about the awful things we've heard about Sand Creek, how much pain it brings us and how Indians should not be treated like animals. You can say that there will be ongoing killing and destruction if we don't try better to understand each other and live together in peace."

Gray Wolf thought it ironic that he, who had once thought that fighting with a bow and arrow was the only way to defend his people with honor, now found himself in a position that fighting with words was the best form of warfare.

He nodded, a smile spreading across his face. "It's a good plan, Georgia. I will write. You will help me. We can send the words to James and Captain Soule."

Georgia got out parchment and ground coal for ink. The words seemed to roll off the quill pen like magic. Georgia said the words were good, strong and meaningful. It was noon, and still Gray Wolf wrote. As he did, a strange emotion surged through him—thankfulness. *Why thankfulness?* he wondered. Overwhelming thankfulness flooded his thoughts, so much so that he put down the quill pen.

"Are you finished?" Georgia asked, looking up from her final preparations for the noon meal.

"Maybe. It's the strangest thing. The more I write the more I feel thankful."

"Thankful?"

"I'm thankful that you and I, Meadow Lark, Moonwalker ... well, that none of us were at Sand Creek. I'm still angry about the massacre and to my dying day, I'll tell folks what really happened there, but you, I, Meadow Lark, Moonwalker, even Bull Bear, none of us were there. We all left for different reasons: Meadow Lark and Moonwalker for better hunting along the Smoky Hill River, you because, well, you—"

"I left because I didn't want my child—our child—brought up in the middle of uncertainty, not knowing where the next meal would come from. I thought you married me out of devotion, not love and that I was foolish for agreeing to it."

Georgia's cheeks reddened. Knowing her, Gray Wolf was sure she was remembering the ugly scene when the braves tried to kill the Jersey cow she thought was Blue Bell. She had gained her composure at the sink, and turned back toward him. "If not for God's grace, we could have been killed at Sand Creek."

Prairie Grace: Fact or Fiction?

Prairie Grace is a work of fiction, although it incorporates dozens of actual historical places, events and people. The Colorado Gold Rush; the Denver Flood of 1864; establishment of the *Rocky Mountain News* by use of a printing press transported to Denver from the east in an oxcart; the Hungate murders; the slaughter of innocent Indians in small villages; Indian depredations in the Bijou Basin; the historic meeting of President Abraham Lincoln with key Cheyenne and Arapaho chiefs; settlement on the Purgatory River in Southern Colorado; the murders of Lean Bear and Star by the U.S. Army; treaties of Fort Laramie and Fort Wise; the U.S. government's unwillingness to keep these treaties; and, of course, the Sand Creek Massacre on Nov. 29, 1864, are all actual events. The MacBaye family and Gray Wolf are fictional, however Lean Bear, Bull Bear, Roman Nose, One Eye, Beaver aka George Bent, William Bent, Black Kettle, Tall Bull, Cheyenne captive Laura Roper, Issac Van Wormer, Indian Agent Samuel Colley, Edward Wynkoop, Silas Soule, Joseph Cramer, Governor John Evans and Col. John Chivington are all historical figures. The author spent hundreds of hours reading history texts and talking with experts to ensure that daily tasks, medical practices, attitudes and dialogue accurately reflect historical fact or probability.

Acknowledgments

Many, many people contributed, some of them unknowingly, to this book. Thanks to my book review group, especially Tonya, Laura and Linda, for your suggestions to hone my manuscript. I appreciate the editorial suggestions of authors Kathleen and Michael Gear, Linda Evans Shepherd and Norma Thurston Holtman. Without the historical and other technical advice of teacher and history buff Cliff Smith, as well as Black Kettle Buffalo proprietor Dick Gehring, former Purgatory River resident Robert Fritch, and my father, Marvin Bay, *Prairie Grace* would lack technical precision. Also, thanks so much to the ladies of my Friday morning Bible study who encouraged and prayed for me as I wrote: Teresa, Mary Anne, Donna, Deb, Christina and Roberta. Thanks to my sister Shelly for her efforts to help me acquire a Native advisor and for all she has taught me over the years about working with horses. I so appreciate the thorough proofreading of Patty McNeff and Sue Carter, as well as the designers, editors and marketers at Koehler Books.

CPSIA information can be obtained at www.ICGtesting.com
Printed in the USA
BVOW02s0906151013

333784BV00001B/1/P